I am a god.

I, Tchazzar, crown myself War Hero of Chessenta.

As I always did and always will, I have returned when you need me most. War is coming. Enemies, hateful and envious, threaten Chessenta on every side. But don't be afraid. With me to lead you, you'll butcher them to the last man!

But vengeance and victory are tomorrow's business. We have other matters to address today.

I told you I come to my people when they need me. And how do I know you need me? Because I hear your prayers. Over the years, many have deemed me a god, and now it pleases me for everyone to know the truth.

And you will worship me as such.

FORGOTTEN REALMS

RICHARD LEE BYERS

BROTHERHOOD OF THE GRIFFON • BOOK II

WHISPER OF VENOM

Wizards
OF THE COAST

Brotherhood of the Griffon
Book II
WHISPER OF VENOM

Cover art by: Kekai Kotaki
First Printing: November 2010

9 8 7 6 5 4 3 2 1

ISBN: 978-0-7869-5561-9
ISBN: 978-0-7869-5808-5 (e-book)
620-21099000-001-EN

U.S., CANADA,
ASIA, PACIFIC, & LATIN AMERICA
Wizards of the Coast LLC
P.O. Box 707
Renton, WA 98057-0707
+1-800-324-6496

EUROPEAN HEADQUARTERS
Hasbro UK Ltd
Caswell Way
Newport, Gwent NP9 0YH
GREAT BRITAIN
Save this address for your records.

Visit our web site at www.wizards.com

FOR MEG

ACKNOWLEDGMENTS

Thanks to Susan Morris and Phil Athans
for all their help and support.

Welcome to Faerûn, a land of magic and intrigue, brutal violence and divine compassion, where gods have ascended and died, and mighty heroes have risen to fight terrifying monsters. Here, millennia of warfare and conquest have shaped dozens of unique cultures, raised and leveled shining kingdoms and tyrannical empires alike, and left long forgotten, horror-infested ruins in their wake.

A LAND OF MAGIC

When the goddess of magic was murdered, a magical plague of blue fire—the Spellplague—swept across the face of Faerûn, killing some, mutilating many, and imbuing a rare few with amazing supernatural abilities. The Spellplague forever changed the nature of magic itself, and seeded the land with hidden wonders and bloodcurdling monstrosities.

A LAND OF DARKNESS

The threats Faerûn faces are legion. Armies of undead mass in Thay under the brilliant but mad lich king Szass Tam. Treacherous dark elves plot in the Underdark in the service of their cruel and fickle goddess, Lolth. The Abolethic Sovereignty, a terrifying hive of inhuman slave masters, floats above the Sea of Fallen Stars, spreading chaos and destruction. And the Empire of Netheril, armed with magic of unimaginable power, prowls Faerûn in flying fortresses, sowing discord to their own incalculable ends.

A LAND OF HEROES

But Faerûn is not without hope. Heroes have emerged to fight the growing tide of darkness. Battle-scarred rangers bring their notched blades to bear against marauding hordes of orcs. Lowly street rats match wits with demons for the fate of cities. Inscrutable tiefling warlocks unite with fierce elf warriors to rain fire and steel upon monstrous enemies. And valiant servants of merciful gods forever struggle against the darkness.

A LAND OF
UNTOLD ADVENTURE

PROLOGUE

Is this wise?" Ananta asked.

Surprised, Brimstone turned, and his tail whispered across the cavern floor. Though the chamber was spacious, Ananta stood against the wall, her sturdy, scaly body wrapped in a gray cloak and her blackwood staff in her hand. In the course of her duties as guardian of Dracowyr, she'd no doubt learned to give wyrms room lest they accidentally step on her.

"Why, Ananta," Brimstone said, "I didn't know you cared."

The guardian responded with what Brimstone had come to recognize as a frown, a slight baring of the fangs coupled with a twitch of the frills on the sides of the saurian head. The facial expressions of the strange new creatures called dragonborn had much in common with those of true dragons.

"My lord Skalnaedyr commanded me to look after you," Ananta replied, "and so I do."

The explanation lacked a certain warmth. Still, it pleased Brimstone to think that Ananta was at least getting used to him. Given his vampirism, perhaps that was much as he could expect.

"Well," he said, "to answer your question, I survived the first time, and even if the magic misbehaves just as badly tonight, I daresay I can bear up again. And we needn't assume it will. I'm a highly competent scryer, even if you couldn't tell from my performance thus far."

"Yes, milord," Ananta said.

Brimstone turned back to the pool, if one cared to dignify it with that term. It was really more of a shallow puddle in a low place in the floor. A mirror or crystal orb might have suited him better, but it took time to import the amenities when one chose to lair in an earthmote, an island floating in the sky high above the wilderness known as the Great Wild Wood.

He stared into the water, focusing his will on it. He whispered incantations that both gathered mystical energy and helped put him in the proper receptive frame of mind.

In time, nothing remained but the pool and his desire to see what it could show him. Then the surface of the water turned gray with red sparks shining inside it. As it rippled, it looked like his own smoky breath weapon streaming forth from his jaws.

The water smoothed and cleared, becoming like a window opening on a deep, rocky bowl in the earth with crags and spires jutting from the top like the points of a broken crown. Their scales glinting in the starlight, dozens of dragons perched on ledges and outcroppings. Brimstone was peering out from the same high shelf he'd occupied when the convocation had happened in reality.

He stared at what appeared to be an empty balcony. He knew it wasn't really, and after a moment two shadows appeared there, framed in an arched opening to the warren of passages honeycombing the rock. It was impossible to tell if they were ghosts or the spirits of living folk who'd temporarily left their bodies. Impossible as well to make out their blurred, wavering features.

When the event had really happened, Brimstone had attacked the phantoms, and they'd escaped. In the recreation, he simply gazed, whispered words of command, and willed their features to come clear.

The bulkier of the two figures resolved itself somewhat into what was probably a powerfully built human male. The implement in his hand was a staff. No, a spear.

His companion—

The view exploded into blazing light and heat. Seared and dazzled, Brimstone recoiled, and then, mercifully, the puddle was just a puddle again.

"What was *that*?" a deep voice snarled.

Startled, Brimstone whirled and beheld the newcomer. Alasklerbanbastos filled the opening between that cavern and the next. Perhaps the Great Bone Wyrm didn't want to come all the way through because he feared his skeletal wings would snag and scrape on the rim.

Brimstone hated it when anyone sneaked up on him. He was supposed to do the sneaking. And it seemed especially unfair that anything as huge as Alasklerbanbastos could do it. Why didn't all those bare bones clink together?

Frustrated by the failure of the divination, pained by the burns on his face and neck, Brimstone had to strain to maintain civility and to remember that he had no particular reason to hate dracoliches anymore. He could lay that quarrel to rest along with Sammaster, who'd created the undead wyrms.

"Greetings, Lord of Threskel," Brimstone said.

Alasklerbanbastos came a stride deeper into the chamber. Sparks jumped and popped on his bones, and the air started to smell like the advent of a storm. Ananta backed away to give him extra space.

"I asked what that was," the undead blue dragon said.

"Well," Brimstone said, "you remember our convocation, when I laid out the precepts, and everyone agreed to them."

"Of course," Alasklerbanbastos said.

"I'm trying to use divination to discover the identity of the phantoms who came to spy on us. Unfortunately, some Power is opposing me."

Alasklerbanbastos gave a disgusted-sounding grunt. "That was true daylight bursting forth from the pool."

"I know," Brimstone said. "Given my nature, the burns it inflicted are something of a giveaway." He felt a tickle partway down his snout as one of the chars started to heal.

"I meant," the dracolich rasped, "that the specific nature of the Power may provide a clue to the trespassers' identities."

"In theory, I agree. Unfortunately, Faerûn abounds in spellcasters who can evoke sunlight. Now, my lord, what brings you here? Surely you didn't travel so far just to assist my inquiry, especially since you didn't know I'd undertaken it."

"I came about Tchazzar." Alasklerbanbastos hesitated. "You know he's reappeared?"

"Yes," Brimstone said.

"I want your assurance that he isn't a part of this. That you won't allow him to take part."

"Thus condemning him to eventual servitude, exile, or worse."

Logic indicated that it was impossible for Alasklerbanbastos's flesh-less, wedge-shaped skull of a head to smile, but Brimstone could have sworn that it did so anyway. "If you want to put it like that."

"I regret," Brimstone said, "that I can't oblige you."

The smile, if it had ever been there, vanished. A blue glow flared in the dracolich's eye sockets, and more sparks leaped and crackled on his bones.

Ananta unobtrusively hefted her staff. It was her responsibility as guardian to enforce the truce that was supposed to prevail on Dracowyr. And though her weapon had formidable powers, her tense features made it plain that she didn't relish the prospect of trying to subdue the colossal undead blue.

Brimstone didn't feel especially enthusiastic about it either.

"Tchazzar didn't attend the first assembly," Alasklerbanbastos said.

"That doesn't preclude his participation," Brimstone said, meanwhile trying to decide which spells to cast, and in what order, if it came to a fight. "Not according to the rules."

"Rules you cite without warning, as it suits you."

"*Complicated* rules. Would you like me to teach you the entire codex? Do you have a few years?"

"*Don't mock me.*"

Brimstone's breath weapon burned painlessly in his chest and throat. He struggled with a spasm of anger, with the urge to forget prudence, strike first, and take his chances against the arrogant, petulant spawn of Sammaster's madness.

When he had himself under control, he said, "I beg you to pardon my flippancy. It was inappropriate. But surely you can see it would be even more inappropriate to forbid Tchazzar to join in what amounts to the adoration of our Dark Lady. He was her anointed champion."

"That was another time. Another world."

Brimstone privately conceded the point. It was the time and world before the cataclysm called the Spellplague, when all the dragonborn lived somewhere unimaginably far away, and no islands floated the sky.

But there was no point in agreeing out loud. "Surely it was only a moment ago in the life of a dragon. An instant in the span of an undead."

"But I didn't agree to Tchazzar!"

"But surely you recognized that the world is a chaotic, ever-changing place and that unforeseen challenges would arise. That's all part of the fun. Honestly, I don't even know why it matters to you whether Tchazzar's in or out. You'd have to deal with him either way."

"Of course you know! The difference lies in whether the others will treat him as a peer."

Brimstone sighed, and stray wisps of sulfurous smoke blew from his nostrils. "I suppose that's true. Still, the situation is what it is, and I don't see that it's so terrible for you. You control a kingdom and an army. Most of the others are making do with less."

"Always," Alasklerbanbastos growled, "it was three against one. Tchazzar, Gestaniius, and Skuthosiin all conspiring to bring me down. And now it's the same again!"

Actually, Brimstone thought, it's worse than that. And you're so obsessed with Tchazzar that you'll never see the new threat coming. He could almost have felt pity for the dracolich. If Alasklerbanbastos hadn't so thoroughly annoyed him, and if pity were anything more than a vestigial part of his nature.

"You have your own dragon vassals," he said.

Alasklerbanbastos spat a small, crackling arc of lightning. "Young ones. It's not the same." His fleshless limbs bent as he gathered himself to lunge. "I *insist* that you ban Tchazzar."

"No," Brimstone said, "and I suggest you pause to reflect before you do anything rash. If you destroy me, it all comes to an end. And it's already fascinating, isn't it? As lovely and intricate as any treasure in your hoard. It will only become more so as events unfold."

The dracolich glared, blue-white radiance seething in the pits where his eyes had once resided. Then he shivered, and at last Brimstone heard bone clink against bone.

"If I ever decide," said Alasklerbanbastos, "that you're not impartial, we'll continue this conversation." He backed out of the opening in one sudden surge, and exited the caverns a moment later. Brimstone could neither see nor hear his departure, but an oppressive feeling of power and menace abated.

Ananta lowered her staff and let out a long exhalation. "That was . . . stimulating," she said.

Brimstone smiled. "I knew he'd stop short of an actual fight," he lied.

"It's like a drug, isn't it? Like dreammist or bloodfast. Once your people have tasted it, they need more."

"It's one of the Dark Lady's great gifts to her children, and like most of them, it comes with some barbs and sharp edges."

Ananta's eyes narrowed. "*Are* you impartial? Or do you have an agenda of your own?"

"Because if I do, you have a responsibility to report it to your master."

"Yes."

"Then it's just as well my probity is intact." Brimstone felt a cool tingle on his neck as new scales grew over another burn. A dryness in his mouth and an ache in his fangs told him the rapid healing was rousing his thirst. "I'm going down to the forest for a while." It might be a wilderness, but there were wild men and goblins to hunt and drink.

ONE

It started out the way it was supposed to. The two teams of dragonborn approached one another in formation, each warrior in the front lines covering himself with his shield. They jabbed at the fighters on the other side with the padded lengths of wood that represented spears. When a fellow was hit, he kneeled down to indicate he was a casualty, and the soldier waiting behind him shifted forward to take his place.

But then everyone got excited. If a warrior pushed a foeman back, he lunged forward to chase him. The dragonborn waiting in the rear grew impatient and either tried to shove forward prematurely or swarmed out of the formation to engage an opponent. What had been a clash between two organized squads dissolved into an amorphous brawl.

"No!" bellowed Khouryn Skulldark. "No, no, no! Break it up!"

Some of the combatants heard and obeyed. Some kept fighting.

Khouryn understood that. Dragonborn and dwarves possessed a similar fighting spirit. It was one reason he felt at home among the manlike saurians.

But the vanquisher's troops weren't in the muddy field to entertain themselves. They were there to train. Khouryn strode in among those who were still fighting and rapped knees with his cudgel. His smaller stature allowed him to do so without too much concern that a stray thrust or cut from a practice weapon would score on him.

Finally, everyone calmed down. Then he took up a position in front of them, and they all stared down at him expectantly, some no doubt with veiled resentment or apprehension, as so many trainees had before them.

"That was pitiful," he said. "My blind, one-legged granny fights better than that. Why is it so difficult to stay in the damn formation? Stand where you're supposed to stand and hold your shield where it's supposed to be, so it protects your neighbor and yourself. Stay alert for chances to stick the enemy who's in front of your comrade. A lot of the time he's not looking at you, and that makes it easy to hit him."

"In other words, fight like a coward," muttered a yellow-eyed, bronze-scaled warrior standing behind two others. He had two copper owl-shaped piercings—the emblem of Clan Linxakasendalor—gleaming in the left side of his blunt snout.

Khouryn smiled at him. "What was that?"

The Linxakasendalor looked momentarily taken aback. For some reason, such grumblers never expected the instructor to catch what they said.

But then he glowered. Since Khouryn had found him out, he figured he might as well stand up for his opinions.

"I meant, sir," he said, "with all respect, that this isn't how dragon-born fight. It isn't how our ancestors fought when they won their freedom."

Others muttered in support of his opinion.

Khouryn raised his voice to cut through the drone. "Then it's a wonder they prevailed. You'll notice *you're* not prevailing. The giants are kicking your soldiers from one end of Black Ash Plain to the other."

"We'll beat them in the end," said the Linxakasendalor. "We always have."

"Maybe," Khouryn said. "But not by doing the same things you've always done. The giants are fighting differently, and you have to fight differently too. Now, I could go on trying to pound that simple truth into your thick skulls. Or I could remind you that Tarhun hired me to train you, so you have to do as I say whatever you think. But I'm not going to do either of those things. Do you know why? Because I heard the word *coward*."

The Linxakasendalor blinked. "Sir, I didn't mean that personally."

"I don't care a rat's whisker what you meant. Come here. And you, and you." He pointed to two other dragonborn, and the trio emerged from the crowd. "The three of you are going to try to stun, cripple, or otherwise incapacitate me, and I'll do the same to you. At the end of it all, everyone can judge for himself whether I know enough about fighting to teach you anything."

The three exchanged glances. Perhaps it was their sense of honor that balked them. The average dragonborn possessed that in abundance— another characteristic they shared with dwarves—and three against one must have seemed like long odds, especially when each of the three towered over the one.

"Do it!" Khouryn roared.

The three fanned out, plainly intending to surround him. As Khouryn had learned fighting among them on the journey from Chessenta and on Black Ash Plain, dragonborn were capable of using teamwork when a situation called for it. But only the teamwork that came naturally. It hadn't traditionally been a part of their martial training.

Khouryn feinted a step to the right, then whirled and raced left, straight at a warrior with silvery scales. The reptile thrust with his practice spear. Khouryn dodged and then he was inside the reach of the weapon, where it was more or less useless.

The dragonborn tried to clout him with his oval shield. He had good technique, but Khouryn was expecting the attack and evaded it as well. He stepped up beside the warrior and clubbed him in the knee, using almost enough strength to break it.

The silver-scaled saurian fell onto both knees. By then his comrades were rushing in, but his body shielded Khouryn for a heartbeat. Long enough to bash him in the head, make his steel and leather helmet—fashioned with holes so his crest of thick, scaly tendrils like braided hair could flop out the back—clank, and lay him out in the trodden muck and the new spring grass.

Khouryn scuttled backward. His foot slipped, and a spear thrust nearly cost him some teeth. He whirled his baton in a circular parry and slapped the attack out of line less than a finger-length from his mouth.

By the time he felt sure of his balance, he had his opponents' patterns and rhythms too. When they both jabbed, missed, and pulled their spears back at the same moment, he charged between them. When they tried to follow the motion and keep their long weapons pointed at him, they more or less tangled together.

Dragonborn were big, but they weren't ogres. Khouryn had no trouble stabbing the one with the dark green scales in the throat with the end of his club. Once again he was careful not to kill. The warrior just reeled, dropped his spear, and clutched his neck while making choking sounds.

Hoping to end the fight, Khouryn rounded on his remaining opponent, only to find that the Linxakasendalor had been too quick. He'd retreated, taking himself beyond Khouryn's reach and reestablishing the proper distance to use his spear.

He wasn't attacking though. Maybe Khouryn had thrown a scare into him—although given that he was a dragonborn, it was more likely he was simply taking his time.

Hoping to goad him into doing something reckless, Khouryn grinned and said, "Now in East Rift, where I come from, we say a fellow fights like a coward if he hangs back while his friends take all the chances."

It worked a little too well. The Linxakasendalor's face twisted, and he sucked in a breath. He meant to spit frost, fire, or something equally unpleasant, a trick the dragonborn shared with actual wyrms.

And here was Khouryn without a shield to block the spew. He hadn't appropriated one because he wanted to impress, and fighting with only the baton was impressive. Right up until the moment he got frozen solid or burned to cinders.

The Linxakasendalor's head jerked forward, and his jaws opened. Pearly frost streamed out.

Khouryn dodged left. The edge of the jet still gave him a chill, but nothing worse. He rushed the Linxakasendalor, knocked his spear out of line, and rammed the end of the baton into his gut. The dragonborn grunted and doubled over. The involuntary movement brought his head within easy reach. Khouryn hit him in the temple, and that was that.

Controlling his breathing—the win was supposed to look easy, after all—Khouryn turned, surveyed the rest of the troops, and judged that he had indeed impressed them.

"You see?" he asked. "That's how a small fighter—and we're all of us small compared to ash giants—turns his size to his advantage. That's part of what I'm trying to teach you. Now, somebody clear these fools out of the way until they're ready to resume the training. I want to see the rest of you fight the Beast. Move!"

The Beast was a big, drum-shaped, timber shell that one of the vanquisher's wizards had enchanted to Khouryn's specifications. When someone touched one of the small runes carved on the sides, it floated up and flew around three feet off the ground. The object then was to jab a rune with a spear point and render the contraption inanimate again.

The game was difficult because the Beast spun and changed direction unpredictably. And if a person didn't fall back smartly when it lurched in his direction, it gave him an unpleasant bump. The point was to teach warriors how to assail a large adversary when its back was turned, then scramble out of reach when it turned in their direction.

Khouryn watched for a while and was pleased to see that at least some of the trainees were getting the hang of it. Then hoof beats thumped the earth. He turned to see Daardendrien Medrash trotting toward him astride a big, black mare.

Big and powerfully built even by dragonborn standards, Medrash had russet scales and bore the six white studs of Clan Daardendrien pierced into his left profile. He was an oddity among his people, a worshiper of one of Faerûn's gods. In fact, he was a paladin of Torm—a champion whose rapport with the Loyal Fury granted him certain mystical abilities.

Behind him, Djerad Thymar rose from the grasslands against a blue sky striped with wisps of white cloud. It was the strangest and most impressive city Khouryn had ever seen in a life of wandering, because it was all one colossal structure. The base was an immense block of granite. On top of that sat hundreds of pillars supporting a truncated pyramid.

Specks soared and swooped around the apex. The aerial cavalry called the Lance Defenders were coming and going on various errands. Their mounts were enormous bats, nocturnal by nature but capable of daytime service, and, seeing them, Khouryn felt a pang of sadness. He still missed Vigilant, his own winged steed, killed by a topaz dragon on the trek south from Luthcheq.

Medrash swung himself off the mare. "How is it going?" he asked.

Khouryn waved a hand at the training exercise. "See for yourself. I had to thump a couple of them to get this batch to take me seriously."

Medrash smiled. "I know how you fight well, but eventually that ploy is going to turn around and bite you."

"We'll see."

"I'm just saying they know how to fight too. All dragonborn do. Some of them have already served a year or two with the Lance Defenders."

"I know. That's why I only called out three of them. Ordinarily it's four. Now tell me about the horses."

"We've selected the most spirited and the steadiest. The riding masters tell me there's no way to train them naturally in the time we have. But after conferring with the mages, they grudgingly agreed that if an animal carries the proper talismans of courage and obedience, it might do what you want it to."

"'Grudgingly'?"

"They love horses. They don't want to see them get anywhere near the giants or those lizard things they conjure out of the ash."

"I don't blame them. But we need lancers on horseback as well as batback."

That too would be an innovation. Khouryn suspected that back in wherever-it-was, when Medrash's people had rebelled against their dragon overlords, war-horses had been in short supply.

"We'll have a few," Medrash said. "Let's hope they're enough to make our troops look as impressive as the Platinum Cadre's."

"And that Balasar learns something that will discredit the Cadre in any case."

Across the field, the trainees raised a cheer as someone finally managed to thump a rune and make the Beast drift back down to the ground.

* * * * *

Jhesrhi Coldcreek loved flying, and never more than today. It was exhilarating to see the buildings and tangled streets of Luthcheq laid out before her and hear the cheers and hymns of thanksgiving rising from the folk crowding the streets, hanging out the windows, and gathered on the rooftops.

Not, of course, that the cheers were for her. They were for Tchazzar. His scaly crimson wings shining in the sunlight, the red dragon was returning to the city he'd ruled a century before. His long-tailed shadow swept along beneath him, and the griffon riders with whom he shared the sky looked tiny by comparison, like hummingbirds escorting an eagle.

Still, until recently Jhesrhi had feared and loathed the city of her childhood as it had feared and loathed her. Its prejudices were to blame for the nightmarish captivity that had scarred her spirit for all time. But recent events had given her the chance to heal at least one of her psychic wounds, and like it or not, Luthcheq was going to change for the better as well. Tchazzar had promised that it would.

Luthcheq sat at the foot of a towering cliff, and the citadel called the War College actually protruded from the rock face. Tchazzar landed in the plaza in front of it, which the city guard had kept clear for him. On the other side of the peace officers and the barricades, a collective moan rose from the crowd, many of whom carried the scarlet banners or wore the trappings of the Church of Tchazzar. For a moment Jhesrhi thought they'd rush in and mob the dragon, but somehow they managed to control themselves.

She set Scar down in the fenced-off corner reserved for griffons, and her fellow mercenaries did the same with their mounts. Stocky, bald, and covered in runic tattoos, his blue eyes glowing noticeably even in the daylight, Aoth Fezim had flown down from Soolabax with plump, pretty Cera Eurthos riding behind him. The sunlady, a high priestess of Amaunator, wanted to observe the ceremonies and had prevailed on her new lover to bring her.

Jhesrhi could tell that the captain of the Brotherhood of the Griffon was somewhat more ambivalent about attending, and she reckoned she knew why. Aoth needed to be there to make sure the company received the credit it deserved for Tchazzar's deliverance and any rewards that came with it. But on the other hand, war was brewing in the north, and he resented the time filched from his preparations.

Meanwhile, Gaedynn Ulraes smiled as if all the drama and pomp was an entertainment staged for his personal amusement. Elegantly clad in a purple, red-slashed doublet, not a shining coppery hair out of place despite the fact that he'd just flown for miles, the lanky archer gave Jhesrhi a wink as he swung himself out of the saddle.

Tchazzar twisted his long neck to survey the waiting throng, then spat an arc of flame high enough to avoid incinerating anyone or setting a building on fire. The onlookers screamed in excitement.

Then the red dragon shrank, dwindling into a tall, broad-shouldered warrior with golden armor and a flame red cloak and plume. Though seemingly human, and despite his massive frame, he had a long, tapered face and slightly pointed ears subtly suggestive of his wyrm form. His slanted eyes were as tawny as Jhesrhi's. She, Gaedynn, Aoth, and Cera hurried to attend him.

Tchazzar offered Jhesrhi his arm, and despite the extraordinary honor the gesture represented, she froze. If he scowled in response, it was only for an instant, and then the expression became a look of rueful comprehension.

"Forgive me," he murmured. "But since you have no difficulty touching me when I'm a dragon, it makes it hard to remember you flinch from the man."

"I'm sorry, Majesty," Jhesrhi said.

"Don't be." He glanced around, evidently making sure everyone had taken up his or her proper ceremonial position. "Shall we?"

They climbed the stone staircase that led up to the terrace where Chessenta's foremost dignitaries waited. The butt of the staff Jhesrhi had carried away from Mount Thulbane clicked on the steps. Behind them the city guards admitted the crowd to the plaza. As they streamed in, they made a noise like the rush of water when something breached a dike.

Tchazzar walked to the edge of the platform and gazed out at his people. As one, the folk in the crowd fell to their knees. So did everyone on the platform.

Then, as had been arranged, Shala Karanok paced out onto the terrace. A strongly built woman in her middle years, the war hero carried a steel and diamond circlet in her hands. Her face with its scarred, square jaw was without expression, and it was impossible to guess how she felt about what was happening.

She kneeled before Tchazzar and proffered the diadem. "I acknowledge your sovereignty and surrender my office," she said.

Tchazzar took the circlet, raised it high to gleam in the sunlight, and set it on his own brow. "I crown myself War Hero of Chessenta," he said. "And you may all rise."

As soon as they did, the cheers began. The noise rose and fell, surging up at the platform like waves battering a rocky headland.

Tchazzar let his subjects vent their jubilation for a while. Then he raised a hand, and over the course of several heartbeats they fell silent.

"I thank you for your welcome," the transformed dragon said. "It's good to be back in the land and the city I love."

That set off more cheering. After a few moments, he quelled it as he had before.

"As I always did and always will," Tchazzar continued, "I have returned when you need me most. War is coming. Enemies, hateful and envious, threaten Chessenta on every side. But don't be afraid. With me to lead you, you'll butcher them to the last man!"

Again he had to pause and let the crowd roar.

"But vengeance and victory are tomorrow's business. We have other matters to address today.

"I told you I come to my people when they need me. And how do I know you need me? Because I hear your prayers. Over the years, many have deemed me a god, and now it pleases me for everyone to know the truth. I am a god. A god in every sense, a being as exalted as Amaunator or Waukeen, and you will worship me as such."

At that, no one cheered. Even if a person believed in Tchazzar's divinity—and many Chessentans did—there was something disconcerting about hearing him proclaim it outright.

Jhesrhi peered surreptitiously at Cera, stout Daelric Apathos—her superior in the Church of Amaunator—and the other high priests assembled on the terrace. Presumably they all had their professional opinions concerning Tchazzar's claim, but she couldn't tell what those were from scrutinizing their solemn expressions.

"Some of you already worship me," Tchazzar continued. He looked down at the front of the throng, where a profusion of scarlet standards and red cloaks cut to resemble scalloped dragon wings revealed the presence of many adherents of the Church of Tchazzar. "Who is your prophet?"

For a moment it looked like whoever it was, he or she was too shy to say so. Then a skinny adolescent girl stepped forward. She had crimson symbols painted on her starveling, acne-pitted face and wore a fine vermilion cloak—a gift from a follower, perhaps—over the grimy rags underneath.

"I am, Majesty," she quavered. "My name is Halonya."

"From this day forward," Tchazzar said; "you're a lady of the realm. Your rank is the same as that of any of the patriarchs who stand behind me, and the church you lead is equal in dignity and importance to any of theirs. Others will heed my call and offer themselves to serve as priests and priestesses under your direction. Together, you will build the grandest temple in Luthcheq. My deputy"—he gestured in Shala's direction—"will assist you with everything you need."

Halonya started weeping and dropped back onto her knees. "Thank you, Majesty! I love you! I won't let you down!"

"I know," Tchazzar said. "Now, I wish to acknowledge someone else who has done me great service. Jhesrhi Coldcreek, come forward."

Tchazzar hadn't warned Jhesrhi he meant to do that. She suddenly felt intensely awkward, and Gaedynn's sardonic smile made the sensation worse. Somehow she managed to walk the several paces to the war hero's side without tripping or otherwise disgracing herself.

"As some of you know," Tchazzar said, "this woman is a wizard. And after she . . . used her magic to my benefit, I offered her a boon. She could have asked for a title, wealth, and land, but she didn't. She asked me to correct a long-standing injustice, and so I shall.

"I hereby rescind all laws that apply only to folk possessed of arcane abilities. Henceforth, sorcerers need not have their palms tattooed. They can live where they like, assemble as they like, and practice their arts as they like, provided they do no harm. Priests and scholars are forbidden to teach the false and pernicious belief that all arcane magic derives from the lower worlds, and those who seek to persecute warlocks and wizards will face severe reprisals."

No one cheered for that declaration either. Jhesrhi supposed that in its way it had shocked the assembly as much as Tchazzar's unequivocal claim to godhood, and was surely less popular. Luthcheq had always loved to hate her kind. Well, choke on it, you ignorant bastards, she thought.

"There will be more new edicts in the days to come," Tchazzar said. "Bold new ideas and ventures to make Chessenta into the great land it was always meant to be. But for now, celebrate my ascension! Your lord has provided for your needs. You'll find food and drink on every corner, and musicians, jugglers, and players performing for your amusement in every street!"

That got them clapping and shouting again. Tchazzar turned in a swirl of scarlet cloak and headed into the War College.

* * * * *

As Aoth followed Tchazzar into the fortress, he made psychic contact with Jet. *Everything all right?* he asked.

If that strutting jackanapes is a god, the black griffon replied, *the world is even worse off than I thought.*

Aoth snorted. *I have a more specific criticism of his performance. But I'll be sure to give him your opinion.*

Once through the doorway, he found that Tchazzar had stopped on the other side to accept congratulations. Trampling the rules of protocol, Zan-akar Zeraez, the Akanûlan ambassador, had somehow managed to make himself first in line. Maybe everyone else had hesitated to crowd the genasi for fear of the sparks that crawled and popped on his deep purple, silver-etched skin.

While Aoth waited his turn, Nicos Corynian approached him. Trimly built, with a broken nose and a cauliflower ear that bespoke the Chessentan enthusiasm for the more violent forms of athletic competition, Nicos was in theory the Brotherhood's patron, although the relationship was slightly muddled. The nobleman had hired the sellswords to serve the crown, and Shala had in fact accepted their service in due course.

And now she wasn't the monarch anymore. Aoth sighed and wondered why nothing was ever simple.

"I'm sorry the war hero didn't mention you during his address," he murmured. "I trust he'll prove more appreciative in private."

Nicos shrugged. "He didn't mention you either," he replied just as softly, "or your man Ulraes, although I gather he had as much to do with the rescue as the wizard. I assume it's because we're not supposed to talk about the fact that His Majesty needed to *be* rescued."

"That's fine by me," said Aoth. "We want the troops to think he's invincible. They'll fight better."

Smiling, Tchazzar turned in their direction. "What did you think of my little oration?"

"It was inspirational," Nicos said.

For a heartbeat Aoth wondered if it wouldn't be better to say something just as empty and let it go at that. Then he decided, to the Hells with it. He was a soldier, not a courtier, and he'd talk like what he was, especially with Chessenta facing war.

"You said some things I didn't expect," he said, "and left out one thing I did."

Tchazzar smiled. His teeth were white and even, as flawlessly handsome as the rest of him. "I was addressing my children for the first time in a hundred years. I had to speak my heart, even if it meant deviating from the script."

"I understand that, Majesty. But I thought you were going to tell everyone that the creatures behind the Green Hand murders weren't really dragonborn at all, but rather fiends conjured from the netherworld." By the Black Flame, he and Cera had damn near died penetrating that particular secret!

"Unfortunately," Tchazzar said, "it isn't always possible to address every topic of interest in a single speech."

"I understand that too. But this particular topic is important. At a time when Chessenta needs friends, you could have reestablished the alliance with Tymanther."

"Tymanther has its own problems," Tchazzar said. "They won't be lending us troops anytime soon."

"Still, it might hearten the people to know they don't truly have enemies lurking across *every* border."

"Perhaps at the cost of rekindling their suspicions of those they were originally inclined to blame—the mages. Which would violate the spirit of my pledge to Lady Jhesrhi."

A pledge she exacted without consulting me, Aoth thought bitterly.

Not that he didn't agree with it in principle. How could he not, considering that he was a war-mage himself? But the Brotherhood hadn't come to Chessenta to spread justice and enlightenment. After two brutal campaigns that had diminished their ranks, produced little profit, and tarnished their name, they'd come to fill their coffers and rebuild their reputation fighting the country's wars. And it wouldn't help to have the people at large blame them for an unpopular edict.

"And now, if you'll excuse me . . ." Tchazzar said. He was already turning and smiling at Luthen, Nicos's chief political rival.

* * * * *

Gaedynn was the son of minor nobility and knew how to behave like a gentleman when it suited him. In some parts of Faerûn that meant gorging on whatever viands the host provided, to show appreciation for his largess. In Chessenta, with its mania for physical fitness, a fellow made a good impression by merely picking at the refreshments or ignoring them entirely.

But that night, he didn't care. He and Jhesrhi had spent a hard, hungry time of it trapped in the Shadowfell. He'd be in the field soon, where the timing and quality of meals were always uncertain. Accordingly he meant to eat as lustily as Khouryn would in his place. And if his voracity repulsed any ladies worth charming, then he'd just have to try a little harder.

He had the lackeys behind the serving tables heap his plate with suckling pig, chicken breast with blueberry glaze, peas, buttered dark rolls, and slices of candied peach. His mouth watering, he turned away from the buffet, then froze.

Jhesrhi had come up behind him, but not a Jhesrhi he'd ever seen before. Some maid—or more likely a whole squad of them—had arranged her golden hair in an intricate coiffure and dressed her in a scarlet brocade gown. Rubies glittered on her earlobes and around her neck. Her attendants had even managed to pry the staff out of her hand.

"Good evening, milady," he said. "You bear an uncanny resemblance to a wizard of my acquaintance. But she shuns occasions such as this."

Jhesrhi scowled. "I couldn't shun this one. The war hero told me to come and gave me this . . . outfit to wear. He wanted me to have myself announced too, but that was too much. I came in one of the side doors."

Gaedynn grinned. "Well, you arrived before the dragon, so he'll never know about your breach of protocol."

Jhesrhi hesitated. "I've never worn anything like this. Does it look all right?"

She looked ravishing, but he realized he didn't want to say so. Maybe it was because they'd already gone down the road of compliments and fond blandishments and found out that for them, it led nowhere at all.

"The important thing," he said, "is that after tonight, you'll be able to sell it all for a tidy sum."

Something moved behind her amber eyes, and he wished he could take his answer back. Then the trumpeters blew a brassy fanfare, and, attired in crimson velvet and cloth of gold, Tchazzar came through the high arched doorway at the end of the room. The open leaves framing the entrance sported carvings of high points from the dragon's previous reigns.

The men bowed and the women curtsied. Tchazzar beamed and gestured, signaling everyone to straighten up. Then he turned and nodded to the musicians, who struck up the first dance, a galliard.

Standing near the buffet, Gaedynn and Jhesrhi were already removed from the dance floor. But she took a reflexive step backward anyway.

Then Tchazzar shouted, "Stop!" His voice shouldn't have cut through the galliard. But it did easily, as though he still carried a dragon's roar within his seemingly human throat to use when necessary. The orchestra stumbled to a halt. The couples who were waiting for the war hero to choose a partner and start dancing so they could do the same peered at him in surprise.

"When last I walked these halls," said the dragon to the conductor, "the dance in fashion was the longing. Or as some called it, the tease. Do you know it?"

The orchestra leader was a stooped little man with a pinched face. Gaedynn might have thought he looked more like a miserly shopkeeper than an artist, except for the zest that lived in his bright gray eyes. "No one has asked for that one in a long while, Majesty. But yes, we do know it. Or at least the older players do, and the rest can join in as they catch the sense of it."

"Then let's have it," Tchazzar said, "and I'll teach the steps to those who care to learn."

The conductor smiled and switched the index finger of his off hand back and forth, telling his associates how quick he intended the beat to be. Then he raised his baton and swept it down. As promised, about half the musicians immediately began a lively tune in three-quarter time. The harper joined in a couple of measures later.

Meanwhile, Tchazzar walked straight toward Jhesrhi. When she saw him coming, she blanched.

"My lady," he said. "Will you do me the honor?"

"I'm sorry, Majesty," Jhesrhi said. "I can't. I never have. Never in my life."

"Neither has anyone else," the dragon said. "Not this dance. You're all starting even. What's more, it's a dance where the lady and gentleman don't touch. Not even a brush of their fingertips, not even once. So please, won't you give it a try?"

And to Gaedynn's astonishment, she did. After a while she even smiled.

Something was weighing in his hand. He looked down at his heavily laden plate and realized he didn't want it anymore.

* * * * *

Balasar woke suddenly from a sound sleep to the darkness of his bedchamber. At first he had no idea why. Then he heard, or perhaps merely sensed, a voice calling his name. It was less like speech than the whisper of a breeze, but somehow he understood it anyway.

It was undoubtedly the summons that Nala had promised would come. Plainly magical, it likely had something to do with the fuming, sour potion she'd given him to drink.

He threw off his blankets, dressed quickly, strapped on his broadsword, and slipped a dagger into his boot. He was supposedly going to the Platinum Cadre as a supplicant. But he'd feel like a jackass if they figured out he was actually a spy and managed to kill him because he hadn't hidden a weapon on his person.

The common areas of Clan Daardendrien's suite were deserted. Even the doorman was snoring. Balasar slipped out without waking him. The phantom voice whispered again, urging him toward the stairs that led downward.

As it turned out, he had to tramp all the way down to the floor of the City-Bastion's central atrium, where fountains gurgled and shrubs and verdure grew in planters and flowerbeds. Striped and studded with balconies, the walls soared to the loft that served as the barracks of the Lance Defenders and the roost for their giant bats. The ambient magical glow was almost nonexistent at that hour, as conducive to sleep as the natural darkness outside.

The voice led Balasar down again, out into the cold night air. Onto the Market Floor, the pillared open space between the half pyramid above and the granite block below. Points of yellow light shined in the gloom, and somewhere to the north a longhorn whined. Clearly some of the taverns were still open, and for a moment Balasar dared to hope that Nala had summoned him to a meeting in such convivial surroundings.

Alas, no. The whisper—he still couldn't judge if it existed only in his head—led him to another staircase, one descending into the bowels of the stone cube that formed the foundation of Djerad Thymar. Into the Catacombs.

The warren of tunnels and chambers contained storerooms, foundries, and other well-traveled areas with mundane and legitimate functions. They also held burial crypts and, according to rumor, desolate sections where outlaws conducted illicit business, fugitives went to ground, and specters walked.

Balasar sighed because he suspected he knew in which sort of precinct the priestess of the dragon god had set up shop. Sure enough, the voice called him into a narrow, snaking side passage and then down a steep and treacherous ramp. Most of the globular magical sconces had gone out, either because of time and neglect or because someone had taken the trouble to extinguish them.

Eventually he came to a point where the darkness was all but absolute. There *might* be a faint glimmer somewhere up ahead, but it could just as easily be a trick his light-starved eyes were playing on him.

Running the claws of his right hand along the wall, he pushed on. After what seemed a long time, he traversed an oblique bend in the passage, and then the light finally brightened. It led him into a bare pentagonal chamber where four dragonborn waited. Hoods of silvery cloth concealed their heads.

But not quite well enough. A big male with red scales had three chains dangling visibly from the underside of his jaw. They were the piercings of Clan Shestendeliath—and enabled Balasar to identify Patrin.

He almost grinned. The clandestine meeting with masked, silent cultists was clearly supposed to seem ominous, and it did. But he found it difficult to believe that the paladin of Bahamut intended any treachery or harm. Though misguided, Patrin was honorable, and he and Balasar had battled the ash giants side by side.

Still, his voice was steel and ice as he asked, "Who comes?"

Balasar gave the ritual response Nala had taught him. "A seeker of truth." *Just not the truth you think.*

"What will you give to learn it?"

"All that I have and am."

"Then strip him," Patrin said. The other worshipers moved forward.

Balasar had to force himself to stand still and submit to the subsequent rough handling. No one had warned him about that part of it.

* * * * *

For a time Aoth savored the glow of contentment, the feeling of utter, spent relaxation. Then, without him willing it, his mind resumed gnawing at all the matters that troubled him.

Her sweaty body snuggled up against his own, Cera seized his nose between thumb and forefinger and gave it a twist.

"Ouch!" he said, though it hadn't really hurt. "What was that for?"

"It's all right if you fall sleep after," Cera said. "A woman learns to expect that sort of swinish male behavior. But if you're going to stay awake, I want your attention."

"Sorry," he said. "It's just . . ." He gestured with the arm that wasn't wrapped around her.

"Tchazzar's not what you expected."

Aoth snorted. "Starting out, I didn't expect anything. What were the odds that Jhesrhi and Gaedynn would even find a trace of him, let alone fetch him home? But yes. What do *you* think of him? I remember the first conversation we ever had. You made it clear you don't believe he's a god."

She hesitated and brushed one of her curls away from her snub-nosed pretty face. He liked it that his spellscarred eyes could see the bright yellow color of her hair, and everything else about her, as clearly in the dark bedchamber as under the sun she worshiped.

"People use the term 'god' in more than one way," she said at length. "I think Daelric and the other patriarchs won't make an issue of it, as long as he keeps his pretensions within bounds. And obviously I, dutiful daughter of the faith that I am, will follow my wise superior's lead."

Aoth grinned. "In other words, in your opinion he's just a big, strong dragon. But Chessenta needs him, so it makes sense to humor him."

"Pretty much. At this point, I'm actually more vexed by the same thing that irked you. Why didn't he tell everyone about the abishais? At first he seemed so interested, and now it's like he doesn't care at all."

"I can't explain it," he said. "He gave me a couple of reasons, but none that made a lot of sense."

"Do you think he'll investigate? We still don't understand the reason for it all."

He shrugged. It made her breast bounce ever so slightly where it rested against his chest. "He said yes, but I wouldn't count on it."

Cera glowered. "That's . . . unacceptable! Somebody has to find out what's really going on!"

"If there's one thing I learned growing up in Thay, and during my time as a sellsword, it's that someone always has some sort of secret agenda or scheme. You could go mad trying to unravel it all."

"But *Amaunator* wants it unraveled. Or else he wouldn't have showed us the assembly of dragons."

"With all respect, my sweet sunlady, you don't *know* that's why your ritual went awry, or that the gathering had anything to do with the abishais."

"I don't understand. One moment you're upset that Tchazzar isn't going to do anything. The next it's like you agree with him that what we discovered isn't even important."

"It's not that exactly. But I have a war to fight. It won't matter who wanted to blacken the name of the dragonborn, or why, if the Great Bone Wyrm and his troops slaughter us all."

Frowning, she studied him for a time. Then she said, "I think you're perverse. Your truesight gave you at least one vision to warn you that something mysterious and dangerous is happening."

"I don't know that that's what it meant," he interjected.

She continued on as if he hadn't spoken. "Then the Keeper gave us both a sign indicating the same thing. That would make many another man *more* eager to search for the truth. But I have the feeling it made you more reluctant. Why?"

He sighed. "You mean above and beyond the intelligent, practical reasons I've already given you?"

"Yes. So tell me."

He hesitated, as he supposed most men would hesitate to admit any sort of fear or weakness to a woman. But his instincts told him it wouldn't make her think any less of him. Mustering his thoughts, he ran his palm over the top of his head. His calluses scratched his hairless scalp.

"I told you where my visions led me before," he said. "To that mountaintop in Szass Tam's artificial world. Where, until my comrades showed up, it was just me against Malark Springhill and all the undead horrors under his control."

"Where you saved thousands of lives," she said. "Perhaps even all the lives there are."

"Yes! That's exactly the point! I didn't really feel the weight of the responsibility at the time. You can't allow yourself to feel things like that in the midst of battle or they'll slow you down. But I've felt it over and over in the months since. I feel it in my nightmares."

"I don't understand. By your own choice, you've always carried a lot of responsibility. You're responsible for the welfare of your company. For the fate of the lords and realms that hire you to fight."

"That's different. Battle sorcery and leading the Brotherhood suit me. I understand them. I'm big enough to handle them. But what happened on the mountaintop . . ." He shook his head. "It was too strange, and too much."

"Throughout the centuries," she said, "Amaunator, either as himself or in the guise of Lathander, called many champions to serve the cause of righteousness. Some of them protested that the burden was too heavy for them to bear. Yet they acquitted themselves nobly in the end."

"That's one reason I like worshiping Kossuth. He doesn't have stories like that."

She scowled. "You're impossible."

"Just let me work on driving Alasklerbanbastos back into his hole. I promise we'll all be better off."

"All right. If that's what you think is best."

They lay in silence for a while.

Then, when he'd begun to wonder if she'd drifted off to sleep, and if she'd start snoring the gurgling little snore he liked, she said, "I can't go back to Soolabax with you tomorrow."

"No?"

"No. Daelric wants me to report what I know about the raids out of and into Threskel, Tchazzar's return, and all the rest of it. I'll come home as soon as I can."

Aoth scrutinized her. But if there was more she wasn't telling him, his fire-kissed eyes failed even to hint at what it might be.

* * * * *

To Balasar's relief, no one remarked on the knife hidden in his boot. Many warriors carried an extra weapon in a similar fashion, particularly if, like him, they made a habit of patronizing Djerad Thymar's seamier taverns and entertainments.

When he was naked, Patrin picked up a steel helmet. For a moment, Balasar couldn't see what distinguished it from an ordinary one. Then he noticed the lack of eyeholes, and the **U**-shaped piece intended to fit under the wearer's snout.

Patrin put it over his head and so deprived him of sight. The locking mechanism clicked shut. The chin piece was snug enough to dig uncomfortably into the spot where a dragonborn's lower jaw joined his neck, but not quite tight enough to choke him.

"Now," Patrin said, "your pilgrimage begins." A hand, perhaps the paladin's, perhaps another initiate's, shoved Balasar stumbling forward.

He groped to keep from running into whatever was in front of him. He found an empty space that was presumably the mouth of another passage leading away from the pentagonal room. He headed down it, once again running his hand along the wall to steady and orient himself.

The voice whispered. Eerie though it was, he supposed he ought to be glad. It should keep him creeping in the right direction.

He tried to slow his breathing and so quell the fear nibbling at his mind. He'd heard of secret societies initiating their recruits via nerve-racking ordeals. His current state of extreme vulnerability didn't mean anything was going to happen to him. To the contrary. The members of the Platinum Cadre wouldn't bother with this game if they realized he was here to spy.

Somewhere in the blackness, the voice breathed his name.

Then somehow he lost contact with the cool, granite surface he'd been touching, and instinct told him he'd entered a much broader space. Still, he judged that the most sensible way to traverse it was to work his way along the wall. But when he groped, first to the sides and then behind him, he couldn't find anything solid.

All he could do was walk toward the whisper.

It grew colder with every step. Something crunched beneath his naked feet, chilling them. He realized it was snow. A frigid wind rose and, howling, tried to shove him back the way he'd come. He leaned into it.

This can't be here, he thought. It's some kind of trick. But it felt real. It felt like he was outdoors traversing some bitter winter landscape.

Then he heard something else moving through the snow. But the sound was a continuous slithering drag, not the rhythmic crunch of footsteps. He felt a malicious scrutiny, and then the wind roared.

No, not the wind, not this time. A blast that stabbed cold into his very core. He reeled off balance, and something swept his feet out from under him. He crashed down on the ground.

He scrambled to his knees, then lashed out with his claws. They didn't connect with anything.

Shuddering with the cold, he tried to stand and was grateful to find that the blow that had knocked him down hadn't broken his ankles. The voice whispered, and he turned toward it.

His unseen tormentor knocked him sprawling in the snow with a hard thump to the chest. He clawed and missed again.

Whatever was abusing him, he couldn't fight it weaponless and blind. The cultists surely didn't expect him to. He was just supposed to persevere and get past it.

He crawled toward the whisper, enduring the freezing discomfort of wallowing in the snow. Because if he wasn't standing up, his adversary couldn't knock him down.

But it could shove him down onto his belly. Suddenly something big and heavy pressed on his back and smashed him into the snow, like a foot squashing an insect.

It was crushing him. And there was no air to breathe, just snow filling his mouth and nostrils.

He struggled, but couldn't break free of whatever was holding him down. Terror screamed through his mind.

You're fighting the dragon in your own soul, whispered the voice, finally saying something besides his name. *The dragon nature you have always scorned. Claim it and all will be well.*

With the words came a sense of something stealthily prying at his mind, trying to open it up like an oyster. Apparently the idea was that if raw fear alone didn't convince a fellow to yield to the voice's demand, a touch of enchantment might tip him over the edge.

Yes! Balasar thought, *I accept the dragon!* Meanwhile, he tried to hold his deeper self clenched tight against the Power seeking to penetrate it.

He could only hope it would work. He was no mystic, and no one had ever taught him how to feint or parry on a psychic battlefield. But he'd always been a good liar, and he was stubborn by nature.

Both forms of pressure abated. The dragon's foot, if that was what it was, lifted off his back. The sense of influence faded from inside his head. As he floundered back onto his knees, spat out snow, and gasped in breaths of frigid air, the phantom voice called his name. But it was only a whisper, no longer a force trying to breach his soul.

Hoping the harassment was over, he rose and stumbled onward. After a few steps, the snow under his feet disappeared and the wind stopped screaming and shoving him around. He groped and found walls to either side. He was back in the corridor.

I was right, he told himself, *it was all an illusion.* The thought was reassuring, but not enough so to quell every trace of his anxiety. For all he knew, a person could die in a dream if it was a magical one.

Suddenly the air was humid and smelled of rotting vegetation. His lead foot plunged deep into muck. He waded onward. The slippery, sucking ooze was even harder to traverse than the snow had been.

A prodigious roar jolted him. Then liquid sprayed him from head to toe. It clung to him and burned.

He dropped to his knees and ripped up handfuls of mud and weeds. Using them, he tried to scour the corrosive slime off his body. Gradually, the worst of the searing pain subsided.

But by that time, he could hear the pad of the new dragon's stride. It was coming at him.

Something pierced his shoulder from both front and back. Fangs? No, claws. They lifted him into the air and tossed him. He crashed into what might have been a tree. As he slammed down on the ground, something—broken twigs dislodged by the impact?—pattered down around him. The wyrm advanced on him.

The punishment continued in the same vein for a while. Balasar endured it as best he could, holding panic at bay by insisting to himself that none of it was real, nor was it meant to harm him.

Finally, the voice spoke. *You despised the dragon inside you, and so you are afraid. Accept its gift of courage and all will be well.*

He responded much as he had before. Then the second dragon allowed him to pass.

Next came a sandy place and a hammering storm that erupted in an instant. The wyrm in residence blasted him with a crackling something that made him dance an excruciating, spastic dance in place. He had to accept his inner dragon's gift of strength to pass through.

After that was a place where the rocky, uneven earth groaned and rumbled, and the hot air stank of smoke and sulfur. Its drake seared him with what he took to be flame, and he promised to accept the gift of rage.

Then he entered a place where the air was cool. Something that might have been fallen leaves rustled beneath his soles. Unlike the other environments along the way, this one wasn't immediately unpleasant. Was the nasty part of the initiation over?

Something hissed, and agony seared his nose, mouth, throat, and the inside of his chest. He collapsed, coughing and retching, trying to expel the vileness. But the vileness was in the air. It was all he had to breathe, and with every inhalation he sucked in more of it.

The dragon in your soul and the dragon deity are one and the same, whispered the voice. *Embrace the deity as your own and all will be well.*

I do! Balasar replied. *I embrace him!* Meanwhile, on a deeper level, he thought, never. Never in this life or any other.

The burning air didn't clear. Perhaps it started to, but then the hiss sounded again, and afterward the floating, burning poison was thicker than before.

The sensation of psychic pressure intensified. The voice whispered its requirement once again. Evidently, this time it wasn't satisfied with Balasar's response.

Fearing that he was on the brink of passing out, Balasar repeated his assurance with all the vehemence he could muster. He did his best to mean and not mean it, believe and disbelieve it, at the same time—in much the same way a fellow pledged undying love to a female he wanted to seduce.

Enormous talons gripped him, but without piercing his hide. The dragon dragged him out of what must be a localized cloud of poison. Once he was clear, it permitted him to lie there, cough, and clear his lungs in peace.

The voice whispered, *Balasar.* When he felt able, he stumbled after it. He stretched out his hands so he wouldn't bump into a tree.

Other hands took hold of him. They weren't rough, but, his nerves frayed to tatters, he strained to break free anyway.

"Easy!" Patrin said. "It's over. Let me take the helmet off."

Balasar did. After being deprived of sight, even the soft amber glow of the magical sconce made him squint and blink.

He was back in the pentagonal chamber, and he wondered if he'd ever left it at all, even to the extent of fumbling his way down a passage. He seemed to be free of frostbite, blisters, bruises, scrapes, and all the other injuries that his ordeal, had it been entirely real, would likely have produced.

The cultists had removed their silvery masks, and Nala had at some point arrived to preside over whatever festivities remained. She had brown hide speckled with gold, and a pale puckered scar on the left side of her brow ridge. It was where she'd carried her piercing before her clan cast her out for the sin of adoring wyrms. She wore a vestment made of platinum scales. As she swayed rhythmically and ever so slightly from side to side, traces of other colors rippled through the folds of the garment. A glint of blue, a shimmer of red.

"Welcome, brother," she said. "You're one of us now."

"Thank you," Balasar said. His response felt too brief and matter-of-fact for the occasion, but he was too spent to come up with anything better.

"Let us pray," Nala said. She raised her hands and recited in a language Balasar didn't recognize. He caught the name Bahamut but nothing more.

Whatever she was babbling, there was magic in it. He felt a hot sting of Power in the air. As it in some measure possessed them, the other cultists—all but Patrin—started to writhe from side to side like she was.

Balasar did his best to imitate the motion. He supposed he was going to have to practice.

TWO

In a different year, the fields around Soolabax would have been busy with peasants attending to the spring planting. Instead, they were empty.

Well, empty of anyone who belonged there. As they winged their way north, the griffon riders periodically saw some of Alasklerbanbastos's men, orcs, or kobolds scouting, foraging, and—for no apparent reason beyond pure malice—setting farmhouses and barns on fire. Columns of dirty smoke striped the blue sky.

Aoth surveyed it all with a certain sense of contentment. He wasn't oblivious to the fact that innocent people were having their property destroyed, and that was, well, sad. But he didn't know those people, and war was his trade. Certainly he felt more at home there than mired in the intrigues and rivalries of Tchazzar's court.

Thanks to their psychic link, he knew Jet felt much the same, only without the occasional mild twinge of empathy for the victims. And with the hope that soon he'd have a chance to kill and eat some horses.

But Oraxes might feel very differently. Though the adolescent had an insolent tongue, he'd gotten quieter when he mounted up behind Aoth and Jet lashed his wings and carried them both up into the sky. And he'd been completely silent for some time.

"Does seeing this bother you?" Aoth asked.

"No!" Oraxes replied, a little too quickly and vehemently.

"That's good. Because you're likely to see worse before you and your friends are done."

On Tchazzar's authority, he'd ordered four of Luthcheq's sorcerers, ones who looked fit and claimed some knowledge of combat magic, to travel north with him. As far as he was concerned, it was fair recompense for saving their skins during the riot and ending the ongoing persecution. Besides, some of them might even discover they liked the soldier's life. Certainly, his wizardry notwithstanding, Oraxes hadn't seemed to be doing much with his days beyond slouching around and acting like a street tough.

Or maybe he and his fellows would hate war and prove utterly useless to boot. Only one thing was certain—Aoth would have traded them all to have Jhesrhi back. But she was stuck in Luthcheq for the moment. Tchazzar wanted her to help him draft new laws on magic, or some such nonsense.

Soolabax appeared on the plain ahead. "Curse it," said Aoth.

"What?" Oraxes asked.

"You'll see in a heartbeat or two if your eyes are good."

During Aoth's absence, the enemy had arrived to lay siege to the town. Since Soolabax controlled one of the primary routes south, it was only what he'd expected. But he wished the enemy had allowed him a little more time to prepare.

You always think that, said Jet.

The Threskelans were still in the first stage of the seige, pitching tents, digging trenches and latrines, and throwing up earthworks. Looking for ways to disrupt their activities, Aoth studied the vista below. Then on the far side of the town, a blue dragon spread its wings, lashed them, and soared upward. Its scales glinted in the late afternoon sunlight.

Aoth was no authority on wyrms, but he judged that the specimen wasn't as big, old, and accordingly powerful as some. So that much was good. What was bad was that none of his companions seemed aware of the foe soaring up into the air to attack them. Thanks to some spell or talisman, the creature was currently invisible. Not to Aoth's spellscarred eyes—or to Jet, who could look through them at will—but to everybody else's.

Aoth pointed his spear and rattled off a charm. A spark leaped from the point and streaked over Soolabax. When it came close to the blue, it exploded with a boom, engulfing the reptile in a burst of yellow flame. The dragon screeched.

It kept coming though, and as soon as it hurtled beyond the point of detonation, everyone but Aoth and Jet lost track of its exact location. But at least the other griffon riders understood they were facing some sort of threat. They veered off and unlimbered their bows.

Meanwhile, the blue opened its jaws wide and spat a dazzling bolt of lightning. Jet swooped lower, and the thunderbolt burned over Aoth's head.

Aoth struck back by hurling darts of green light. Jet's wings pounded as he sought to maneuver and climb. They were rapidly approaching the dragon, only at a lower altitude, and neither of those things boded well for their survival.

Talons outstretched, the blue plummeted at them. Jet raised one wing, lowered the other, and flung himself and his riders to the left. The gigantic reptile plunged by. It leveled off fifty feet above the ground and then, wings beating, began to rise again.

An arrow appeared in the dragon's back. Aoth hadn't seen who loosed it, but he was sure it was Gaedynn. Master bowman that he was, he'd hit a rapidly moving target he couldn't even see. Unfortunately, the reptile didn't even appear to notice.

Aoth abruptly became aware of a band of pressure around his torso. Even though he was securely strapped to Jet's saddle, Oraxes was hanging on to him. The youth was panting too, a ragged, rasping sound.

Positioned as he was, Aoth couldn't grab the lad and shake him, so he elbowed him in the stomach. "Calm down!" he snapped. "Make yourself useful! The thing we're fighting is a dragon. Do you know a spell to turn it visible?"

"Yes."

"Then cast it. My attacks will show you where to aim."

He conjured localized rains of pounding hailstones and silvery flares of frost. The blue still wasn't slowing down. Jet zigzagged and wheeled, swooped and climbed madly, fighting to stay out of reach of the dragon's fangs and claws and dodge its bright, crackling breath. Oraxes chanted an incantation. After a pause he repeated it, once again to no avail.

"If he botches it a third time," Jet growled, "cut him loose and shove him off. I could do without the extra weight."

Oraxes drew a long breath, then started again.

Then somehow, despite the griffon's cunning maneuvers, the blue was above them and the rooftops of Soolabax below. Lightning blazed down, and Jet just managed to dodge it. The thunderbolt blasted shingles tumbling loose from the roof of a house and set the structure on fire.

Even spellscarred eyes weren't immune to glare. Squinting against the flash of the attack, it took Aoth a precious moment to perceive that the blue had spat its lightning, then immediately dived after it. "Dodge!" he screamed.

Jet threw himself to the right. One of the dragon's claws grazed him anyway, tearing feathers from his wing in a shower of blood. Aoth felt the slash of pain through their psychic bond.

Can you still fly? he asked.

You'd better hope so, the griffon replied.

Raising his voice, Oraxes snarled the last line of his incantation. Neither Aoth's frightened outcry, Jet's last frantic evasion, nor the sudden appearance of the bloody wound had shaken his concentration.

A greenish shimmer danced across the dragon's body. Afterward, the creature didn't look any different to Aoth. But he could tell from the way the other griffon riders oriented on it that they could finally see it too.

Arrows flew at the wyrm from all directions. Some glanced off its scales, but others stabbed deep into its flesh. Two of the other mages riding behind sellswords threw magic. One conjured a flying sword made of golden light. The blade slashed rents in the dragon's leathery wing. In his excitement, the other resorted to a thunderbolt of his own. It was likely his favorite attack, but essentially useless against a creature with a natural affinity for the powers of the storm.

Realizing it was in trouble, the dragon wheeled and climbed. Its head swiveled at it looked for the easiest way through the foes who surrounded it.

Aoth snarled words of power. A line of floating, whirling blades abruptly materialized in front of the wyrm. The reptile's own momentum carried it into the magical weapons, and they sheared gory wounds into various portions of its body.

Oraxes crooned a rhyme in a demonic tongue. Some of the flesh on the dragon's shoulder melted and flowed like wax.

An arrow, one of the poisonous black ones Gaedynn had brought back from the Shadowfell, punctured the reptile's left eye.

And then at last it fell, crashing down on a house that partially collapsed beneath the impact. Aoth studied it until he was sure it wasn't going to get up again.

Oraxes let out a whoop.

Aoth grinned. "I take it you enjoyed that."

The adolescent hesitated, and when he spoke again, it was in his customary sullen tone. "It was all right."

* * * * *

Today, Tchazzar seemed content for Jhesrhi to wear her usual functional, comfortable clothing, and thank the gods for that. She told herself that if she never had to wear ridiculous court attire again, she'd count herself blessed.

But if she didn't relish fancy dress, Halonya plainly did. The prophetess still didn't look especially clean, but she'd donned layer upon floppy, trailing layer of bejeweled and embroidered garments, all in various shades of red. Apparently the ensemble represented her notion of the regalia appropriate to a high priestess.

At the moment, a parade of architects was regaling her and the rest of those assembled in the audience chamber with concepts for the new temple. Halonya listened with rapt attention, although Jhesrhi suspected the girl didn't understand more than half.

Tchazzar looked just as interested, but as time passed, his frown made it clear that he was dissatisfied as well. Finally he turned to Jhesrhi and said, "What do you think, my friend?"

Caught off guard, she fumbled for an answer. "Uh, the second one? With the fountain of flame?"

"The design has possibilities," the transformed dragon said. "But it isn't grand enough. None of them are." He gave the architects an indulgent smile. "How could they be, when Halonya herded you into my presence when you'd scarcely had time to think? Return in a tenday, and we'll see who deserves the commission."

As one, the builders bobbed their hands and professed their eagerness to obey.

"One thing to bear in mind," Tchazzar continued, "is that we're going to build on the opposite side of the city from the War College. We'll have all Luthcheq cradled between the two poles of power, the temporal and the divine. A neat conception, don't you think?"

Shala Karanok cleared her throat.

The former war hero had relinquished her crown, but she still wore mannish garments trimmed with bits of steel that suggested armor. Apparently they weren't part of the monarch's formal regalia. She stood before a marble statue of a crouching, snarling warrior with a broken sword in his right hand and an axe in his left, one of the many martial decorations scattered throughout the chamber.

"Majesty," she said, "may I speak?"

Tchazzar turned his grin on her. "Of course, High Lady, of course."

"I can find room for your temple on the mall in the religious quarter," she said.

"I'm glad you're thinking," Tchazzar replied, "but I like my notion better. It wouldn't be very friendly of me to crowd my brother and sister deities."

"I wouldn't know about that, Majesty. But if I understand you correctly, the spot where you intend to build is quite built up already. That will add considerably to the expense."

"Oh, I know you'll find the coin somewhere. The important thing is that we finish the temple before the end of the year."

Shala hesitated, and Jhesrhi had the feeling she was choosing her next words carefully. "Majesty, with all respect, that too will add to the expense if it can even be done at all. Chessenta has a war to fight and pay for."

"You see, there's your answer," Tchazzar said. "The plunder we seize will subsidize the temple."

"All the more reason then to take to the field as quickly as possible."

"Soon," Tchazzar said. "As soon as I set the government to rights."

"Then may I have your permission to head north immediately? One of us should be there."

Tchazzar's smile disappeared. He studied Shala for several heartbeats, then said, "No. I need you here. Don't worry, we have plenty of brave soldiers and shrewd captains to hold the line for now."

Shala gave a stiff half bow of acquiescence. "As Your Majesty commands."

"Now, everyone leave me," the dragon said. "I need a time of contemplation."

Jhesrhi bowed with the rest.

"Oh, not you," Tchazzar said, "nor you either, Halonya. The two of you must help me ponder."

So Jhesrhi and the newly minted high priestess remained.

"That woman," Tchazzar said, once everyone else was gone. "That Shala. Do you think she resents me?"

"Well, *I* wouldn't trust her," Halonya said.

"I would," said Jhesrhi. "I do. She's just giving you the best advice she knows how to give."

"Hm," said Tchazzar, gazing at the doorway through which Shala had exited. "We'll see."

* * * * *

Aoth hastily unbuckled himself from Jet's saddle. Leaving Oraxes to fumble with his own straps, he moved to inspect the end of Jet's wounded wing. The griffon still held the member partly extended, and through their psychic link Aoth could tell that it would ache worse if he folded it up against his back as usual. Blood pattered steadily onto the ground.

"I told you," said Jet, "it's all right."

"Not if I want to ride you tomorrow, it isn't." Aoth turned to survey the courtyard of Hasos Thora's smallish castle in the center of Soolabax. Various retainers stood gaping at the griffon riders still setting down in the space.

"Get me a healer!" Aoth shouted. "Fast!"

In time, a plump, gray-bearded fellow scurried from the keep with a satchel tucked under his arm. Aoth was glad to see he wore the yellow robe of a priest of Amaunator. As far as he was concerned, a cleric of Kossuth would have been better still, but at least he was one of Cera's subordinates. Maybe, knowing she was fond of him, he was willing to believe Aoth might be a decent fellow even if he was a mage, a sellsword, and a Thayan.

Although the sunlord balked when he saw the blood and realized whom he was supposed to treat. But that was probably because—huge, crimson-eyed, and otherwise deepnight-black from his beak to the lashing tip of his leonine tail—Jet looked every bit as dangerous as he was, and a lot less tractable.

"Come on!" Aoth called. "He won't hurt you."

"Not unless you hurt me," said the familiar.

Aoth shot him an annoyed look. "You're not helping."

The sun priest approached rather gingerly, inspected the wing, stanched the flow of blood with a healing prayer, rubbed a pungent amber salve into the wound, and finally stitched it shut. Jet stiffened once or twice, and Aoth felt the jabs of pain that made him do it. But the griffon resisted the temptation to spin around and rend the healer limb from limb.

When it was done, Aoth scratched Jet's neck, ruffling the feathers, stooped to uncinch his saddle, and then saw Hasos glowering at him. The tall, long-nosed baron looked petulant, but there was nothing new about that.

"I should go talk to him," said Aoth.

"Yes, go," said Jet, a trace of humor in his rasp of a voice. "I know you've been looking forward to it."

As Aoth crossed the muddy courtyard, Hasos said, "I would have appreciated it if you'd come and conferred with me right away. Someone else could have seen to your steed."

My "steed," thought Aoth, is a lot more useful and important to me than you'll ever be.

"Please excuse me, milord," he said aloud. "But I thought the situation deserved my personal attention. Now, I have something for you." He opened the pouch on his belt, brought out a rolled parchment, and held it out to the nobleman.

Hasos accepted it with a certain air of wariness. "What's this?"

"Tchazzar's writ giving me ultimate authority over all of Soolabax's troops and military resources for the duration of the war."

Hasos's eyes shifted back and forth as he skimmed the first few lines. His aristocratic features turned a gratifying mottled red. "This is outrageous! Preposterous!"

"If you read the whole document, you'll come to the part where His Majesty says it's no reflection on you. It's just that the previous arrangement, where you and I each led our own troops, was keeping us from getting things done."

Hasos took a long breath. "If your scouts hadn't stumbled across Tchazzar in the wild, if they hadn't done him some sort of service—"

"Then maybe I couldn't have persuaded him that a clear chain of command is better," said Aoth. "But it is what it is. If you want to argue about the wisdom of His Majesty's decisions, you know the road to Luthcheq. If not, I expect your full support."

Hasos took another breath, and some of the red faded from his cheeks and brow. "I know how to obey a royal decree. I just don't know why you felt you had to bother. What decisions are left to make? The enemy's outside the walls, and we're in. Now it's just a matter of waiting them out."

Hasos relished the trappings of war. He often wore a breastplate and lugged a shield around even when there was no reason for it. But Aoth wondered if the nobleman had ever actually experienced a siege. If he had, he might not have been so blithe about subjecting his own town to the protracted misery such an action often entailed. For certainly Soolabax, its streets jammed with fugitives and livestock from the surrounding farmlands, was a prime candidate for starvation and disease.

"That's not how we're going to play it," said Aoth. "We griffon riders can pass in and out of the city as we please." Well, give or take arrows flying up from below, but there were ways of contending with that. "I have troops camped outside the city, and Tchazzar himself is bringing more up from the south. Put it all together, and it means we can smash these fools who think they have us trapped. Our men outside the walls will be the hammer, and the town and its garrison will be the anvil."

Hasos shook his head. "The risk is too great. We'll lose too many."

"Not if we do it right. Besides, Tchazzar doesn't want to stay on the defensive. He doesn't want to fend off the Great Bone Wyrm now, let it go at that, and have to do it all over again in a couple of years. The plan is to push north and make Threskel a part of Chessenta again. If I were you, I'd pack my kit."

* * * * *

The giants had killed or driven back the dragonborn who'd dared to confront them on Black Ash Plain. The fighting had all moved inside Tymanther, in the fertile fields and patches of woodland south of Djerad Thymar.

A bat rider had spotted one of the raiding parties slaughtering people, pigs, and cattle. By good luck or ill, the scout had then found Medrash's patrol within easy reach of the foe. As the paladin studied the terrain ahead for some sign of the enemy, he ran over Khouryn's training in his mind. Even though his people considered him an expert warrior, he'd had to go through the exercises with everyone else because he'd never fought with a lance on horseback either. In fact, he still hadn't—not in a real combat, not with his life on the line.

He wished Khouryn were there, but the dwarf was busy schooling other fighters. He tried to comfort himself with the thought that Torm the True was always with him.

But that reflection came with a measure of shame. Because he knew he'd failed the god of heroes repeatedly, even if others didn't see it that way. His efforts to catch the Green Hand murderers had destroyed the alliance between Chessenta and Tymanther. And, commanding the first company that Clan Daardendrien fielded against the giants, he'd led his kinsfolk to disaster.

He had to do better this time. Had to. Even if the giants were not capable of actually conquering Tymanther—and that no longer seemed like such a preposterous possibility—somebody had to prove that it wasn't only adherents of the Platinum Cadre who could defeat them. Otherwise, in their desperation, more and more of his people would embrace the cult's vile, dragon-loving creed, corrupting themselves in the process.

"Look!" a rider said, pointing.

Medrash turned his head. A white dog lay half hidden in the grass with the rear part of its body more or less smashed flat. Somehow it was still alive, whimpering, its chest expanding and contracting rapidly.

"Put the poor beast out of its misery," Medrash said. A rider dismounted, kneeled beside the dog, stroked its head and murmured to it for a moment, then slipped a knife between its ribs.

Medrash surveyed his comrades and saw the same mixture of determination and doubt he felt within himself. As leader, it was his responsibility to do something about the latter.

"All right," he said, infusing his voice with the power to encourage and persuade that was one of the Loyal Fury's gifts to his champions, "we're obviously close, so let's get ready. Let's go give the brutes a surprise. Keep your heads, remember your lessons, and we'll crush them."

Some of the riders nodded or growled their agreement. Then they all pulled their lances from the tubular sheaths the saddlers had added to their tack. They placed the weapons on the rests, angling them upward for the time being. Inwardly, Medrash winced to see how clumsily some warriors still handled the long spears. But he didn't let it show in his outward demeanor.

They walked their horses to the top of a rise. The gentle slope on the other side led down to a cluster of low huts adjacent to a cherry orchard. The trees were just beginning to flower.

The bodies of dragonborn lay scattered and in some cases dismembered on the ground. One corpse dangled from a wall, pinned there by an enormous flint axe. Each twice as tall as the average Tymantheran, hairless, gray-skinned ash giants were roasting an ox on a spit. Evidently too hungry to wait till their supper cooked, others yanked and gobbled handfuls of raw meat from a fallen plow horse.

Even before the current highly successful invasion, they'd always possessed their share of cunning. So it didn't surprise Medrash that they had a sentry posted. The huge barbarian bellowed something in his own guttural language. His fellows oriented on the patrol, then moved to take up their weapons.

They were doing so reasonably quickly too, but not with frantic haste. Probably because they knew how dragonborn cavalry customarily fought. They dismounted, made sure their mounts would be there when they needed them again, then advanced on foot.

Medrash grinned and shouted, "Walk!" The patrol started their horses forward, slowly for the first few paces.

Some of the giants faltered and stared.

"Trot!" Medrash called. The riders in turn spoke to their steeds, or touched them with their spurs, and the animals accelerated.

A couple of giants were still frozen in surprise. Others were scrambling to get ready. One bawled, "Shangbok!"

Medrash wondered if that was somebody's name. "Canter!" he yelled. Once again the riders urged their horses to go faster. "Lances!" Two and three at a time, the weapons swung down to parallel the ground.

By then the enemy was close enough for Medrash to clearly discern the sunken, pitch-black eyes in their long, gaunt faces. Then suddenly one horse, evidently realizing its rider had no intention of veering off, panicked. It turned of its own volition, and in so doing, plunged toward the steed and rider on its right.

Medrash flinched in anticipation of the impending collision. But somehow the rider who still had control swung around the other and drove on.

Medrash looked right and left and saw that only the one horse had balked. The mages' charms were working on the rest.

Which didn't mean everything was perfect. The line had gotten ragged. It wasn't the moving wall Khouryn recommended. Nor did the riders have the open ground that would best have served their purposes. The huts and various pens broke up the space.

Still, he felt a sudden surge of confidence that the tactic would actually work. "Gallop!" he roared. "Kill the brutes!"

The giant directly in front of him whirled a sling. Sensing more than truly seeing the fist-sized stone hurtling at his head, Medrash raised his shield. The missile hit it with a crack, hard enough to jolt and sting his arm.

He hastily lowered his shield again so he could see. The lance still didn't hit the spot he was aiming at, but at least it punched into his huge foe's shoulder. In so doing, it nearly heaved Medrash out of the saddle. But he was bracing himself in the posture Khouryn had taught him, and that, combined with the high cantle of his newly altered saddle, held him in place.

The lance tore free in a shower of blood. The giant staggered, and Medrash plunged onward. At that moment, it would have been impossible for a human knight to make a follow-up attack. He was too close to his foe for a jab with the lance and had no time to drop it and ready a shorter weapon.

But Medrash had a weapon he didn't need to ready, and so he used the tactic Khouryn had recommended for when a lance thrust failed to neutralize its target. He sucked in a deep breath, then spat bright, crackling lightning at the giant's head.

His horse carried him by before he could see how much damage he'd done. As soon as he could arrest the animal's forward momentum, he wheeled it around. Carnage spun past his eyes.

A giant with jagged black streaks of war paint supported himself on one hand and both knees. There was a broken lance stuck all the way into his belly and several inches out his back. Despite his size, his screams were shrill.

Another hulking barbarian swatted a lance out of line, then plucked the lancer out of the saddle. He gripped the dragonborn's shoulder with one massive hand, seized his head with the other, and wrenched it off. Blood sprayed from the stump.

A horse repeatedly reared and hammered its front hooves down on a fallen giant, who writhed beneath the punishment but seemed capable of nothing more. The dragonborn on the animal's back had lost his lance and uselessly brandished a war hammer. He wasn't sufficiently adept at mounted combat to lean out of the saddle and land a blow. Fortunately, it didn't look like the horse needed the help.

Another lancer missed. As he passed by his foe, the giant lunged after him, stone club raised for a blow that would at the very least dash him from the saddle. But another dragonborn rode at the barbarian's back and speared him between the shoulders. Like Medrash, the rider had plainly finished his initial pass and turned his mount, because the animal wasn't moving very fast. Still, the stab staggered the giant, and his intended victim galloped beyond his reach.

As near as Medrash could tell from such brief, chaotic glimpses, his side was winning. He oriented on the giant he'd injured. His breath had charred the brute's face black, and he was unsteady on his feet. Medrash was still trying to judge whether the barbarian remained a threat, whether he should finish him off or go after one of his fellows, when another giant appeared in the doorway of one of the huts.

The new one barely fit there, and would have to crawl to squeeze through—the Loyal Fury only knew why he'd bothered to go inside in the first place. But from the runic scars carved into his long, bony face and the necklace of raw crystals and bones dangling around his neck, Medrash took him for a shaman and wondered if he was Shangbok.

Whoever he was, it would be wise to kill him before he started casting spells. Medrash rattled off an invocation and jabbed at the air with his lance. White light flared from the point. It slammed the giant with the burned face and wounded shoulder back against the front of the hut, which swayed beneath his weight. But it only rocked Shangbok back a little, like a startling but harmless slap in the face.

The shaman thrust his hand into the sack tied around his waist and brought out a green crystal egg, polished and perfectly formed. Staring at it, he rattled off a rhyme.

The burning wood and coals beneath the roasting ox heaved upward, and then—as if springing up from a hitherto hidden pit—a creature exploded out from underneath them, knocking over the spit in the process. It was about the size of an ash giant, but covered in green scales and possessed of a saurian head. It walked on its hind limbs, which were short and thick. The front ones were ungainly looking batlike wings.

Medrash cursed. He'd seen giant shamans create comparable creatures before. But on those occasions they'd conjured them from the endless drifts of ash in their own desolate country, where their magic was strongest. He hadn't known they could play the same trick with just the ash in a cookfire less than a day's ride from Djerad Thymar.

The scaly green head of a second beast popped up into view. Medrash wondered if killing the shaman, or simply disrupting his concentration, would stop that one from manifesting completely. But before he could try, the first conjured reptile gave a rasping screech. It bent its legs, leaped into the air, and spread its wings to glide, though it seemed to hurtle at him fast as an arrow.

Medrash turned his horse—biddable even in the face of this horror, thank Torm and the vanquisher's wizards—and aimed his lance. With luck, the gliding creature would impale itself.

Its jaws opened, and it spewed slime at him. He raised his shield, and most of the spray splashed against the barrier. But stray droplets spattered his skin and seared him and his mount. His mount screamed. Noxious fumes from the slime choked him and flooded his eyes with tears.

Suddenly half blind, he barely saw the glider lash its wings and bob harmlessly above the head of the lance. It then whirled one of the limbs like it was striking a blow with a flail.

Once again Medrash lifted his smoking, sizzling shield. The claw-like extrusions at the ends of the bony fingers inside the wing slashed, clattering across the armor. Already crumbling under the corrosive onslaught of the spew still clinging to it, the heater couldn't withstand the added punishment. It shattered, leaving Medrash with only the leather straps that had held it to his arm.

But at least the arm was still attached.

Having altered the attitude of its wing to strike a blow, the glider couldn't stay in the air. It thumped down behind Medrash's horse, then whirled, yellow eyes blazing.

Twisted at the waist to keep track of it, he saw he'd never turn his horse around as fast as his foe was spinning. Which meant only a mystical weapon could serve him. He glared at his foe and willed the creature to perceive him as the agent of divine majesty he truly was.

Crouched, the ends of its wings dragging on the ground, the creature snarled and recoiled. Hauling on the reins, Medrash brought his horse around. He aimed his lance and urged the animal forward.

The conjured reptile flexed its legs to spring back into the air. Once again Medrash reached out to Torm. A torrent of Power poured through the core of him, and he shaped it according to his purpose. His lance glowed, and his horse streaked across the intervening distance, less running than flying.

As a result, he reached his adversary before the beast could get into the air. The shining lance stabbed through its torso, and it collapsed in a heap.

But then, to Medrash's astonishment, it rose on its stumpy legs once more. Snarling and screeching, it started to shove itself up the length of the lance. Its neck repeatedly swelled and contracted, perhaps working up another discharge of burning sludge. Its wings whipped out and back, out and back, straining to reach the foe at the other end of the long weapon.

Regretting the loss of his heater, Medrash kept hold of the lance with one hand and drew his sword with the other. Maybe he could land a killing stroke before his foe maimed either him or his steed, although it didn't seem likely.

Then a second lance punched into the creature's body from the flank. The brute threw back its head, screamed, thrashed madly for one more moment, then collapsed, pulling the ends of the two embedded weapons down with it.

The rider who'd finished off the winged beast gave Medrash a wild, fang-baring grin. "I like fighting on horseback!" he said.

"Good," replied Medrash, meanwhile thinking that it had taken a lot of magic just to kill the one creature. Torm's might was limitless, but his servants' capacity to channel the Power wasn't. If he had to use his gifts against every one of the conjured beasts—

But when he glanced around, that didn't appear to be the case. He didn't know how many creatures Shangbok had initially conjured, nor—amid the frenzied confusion of battle, with huts blocking some of his view—could he be sure how many still posed a threat. But he only saw two.

One dived at a rider. A second warrior urged his horse up beside the dragonborn the glider threatened, and then there were two lances poised to catch the creature. Medrash judged that it would have a difficult time evading both.

The other reptilian beast was stuck on the ground, a bloody, broken wing furled awkwardly against its torso. Lunging and spinning, it used the undamaged wing to lash at the five dismounted dragonborn surrounding it. Whatever had become of their steeds, they didn't seem to need them at the moment. They harried the creature from behind, then leaped back to safety when it wheeled to face them, just as Khouryn had taught them.

Still other dragonborn appeared to be holding their own against the surviving ash giants.

Suddenly a cloud of embers appeared around a rider. No doubt startled and stung by the sparks, the dragonborn faltered and his horse reared. Taking advantage of their distraction, their ash giant foe shifted into striking distance, swung his axe, and nearly beheaded the steed.

The magical attack meant Shangbok was still alive and might still be capable of winning the fight for the raiders. As he tugged in a futile effort to free his lance from the glider's carcass, Medrash glanced around for the adept.

For an instant he couldn't find him amid all the snarling, shrieking, pounding confusion, because Shangbok wasn't peering out of the doorway anymore. At some point and for some reason—better visibility, perhaps—he must have crawled out into the open. But where had—

Medrash abruptly perceived that Shangbok was still right in front of him. The giant was crouching behind the hut, using it for cover in the same way a dragonborn might use a low wall or a boulder.

Medrash dropped the useless lance, drew his sword, bellowed a war cry, and rode at Shangbok. He veered right to circle the rustic home widdershins. The shaman scuttled in the same direction, staying ahead of him while growling words that alternately sounded like rocks grinding together and ash whispering on the wind.

A huge spear appeared floating above the thatched roof of the hut. It glowed red and looked like somebody had made it by fusing hot coals together. It stabbed down at the head of Medrash's horse. Medrash swung his sword and parried with all his strength. The impact stung his arm and just barely sufficed to knock the enormous weapon out of line.

The spear leaped back up into the air and thrust at Medrash. He ducked, and then, to his momentary relief, the conjured implement faded away. But, glaring across the roof with his dead black eyes, Shangbok was already reciting another charm.

Medrash suspected it would be unwise to stay where he was and trade ranged mystical attacks. Shangbok might well be his master in that regard. But he couldn't close with the shaman by chasing him around and around the hut. The giant's legs were too long, and a horse couldn't negotiate the corners quickly enough.

Medrash reached out and seized all the divine Power he could hold. He sent it surging down his sword arm into his blade, then cut down at the barrier in front of him. For an instant he seemed to glimpse a much larger sword, forged of light and too big for even an ash giant to wield, surrounding his own weapon and making the identical attack.

When his blade sheared into the wattle, the hut flew apart in a flash of light, one half of it tumbling and crashing to the right and the other to the left. Suddenly deprived of his cover, Shangbok gaped in surprise.

For his part, Medrash felt a kind of hollow ache inside. It meant that for the time being he'd exhausted the ability to channel the might of Torm and henceforth would have to engage Shangbok using only mundane tactics. Well, so be it. He urged his horse forward over the rush-covered earthen floor the destruction of the hut had left behind.

Shangbok retreated and resumed chanting. Medrash had hoped that, startled, the adept had hesitated long enough to lose the cadence of his incantation. But manifestly not, because the giant thrust out his big gray hand, and embers blasted from his fingertips.

Medrash lowered his head and squinched his eyes shut. He couldn't do anything to protect his poor horse, but the animal endured the blistering barrage and kept surging forward.

Shangbok reached for the axe hanging at his hip but failed to unlimber it in time to contend with Medrash's first attack. The dragon-born slashed the shaman's neck and rode on by.

When Medrash wheeled his mount around, Shangbok was on his knees. He was clutching his neck, but blood still spurted between his fingers. He groped in his sack and brought out the green egg. His mouth moved, and shadow squirmed inside the crystal.

No, thought Medrash. We've seen enough of your lizard friends. He rode at the giant and drove his point into the shaman's chest.

Shangbok collapsed, and the egg rolled from his hand. Then, all at once, it shattered into glittering dust. Medrash realized the giant hadn't been trying to create more minions after all. He'd used the last of his strength to destroy the talisman.

Off to the right, people started to cheer. Medrash looked around and saw that he and his comrades had eradicated their foes.

He tried to share in the other riders' jubilation. It seemed reasonable that he should, for after all they'd won a victory. In so doing, they'd validated Khouryn's training and proved that a warrior didn't have to be a wyrm-lover to stand a chance against the giants.

But his instincts told him the egg had been important. What might they have learned from it if they'd captured it intact?

THREE

Wings beating, Eider climbed into the cool night air, attaining the altitude necessary to protect her from bowshots from the ground. She couldn't find an updraft to carry her, and gave a querulous little rasp at the effort involved.

"Lazy beast," Gaedynn said. "Do as you're told, or it's off to the knackers with you." He gave the griffon an affectionate, rustling scratch amid the feathers on her neck.

When he judged they were high enough, he flew her over the city walls and the enemy camp beyond. The Threskelans' yellow fires flickered, just barely revealing the nearest soldiers and tents. No one called the alarm as Gaedynn soared overhead, and he inwardly conceded that Eider might have had a point. Maybe it hadn't been necessary to rise so high. Maybe the night was shield enough. But also maybe not. Kobolds, orcs, and some of the other beings in the Great Bone Wyrm's employ saw pretty well in the dark.

Gaedynn flew some distance beyond the force encircling Soolabax, then set down behind a stand of oaks. If he'd been in command of Alasklerbanbastos's army, he would have stationed a picket or two among the trees. But he hadn't spotted any when he'd flown over in the daylight.

He scrutinized the shadows under the branches and decided no one was there now either. Something made a tiny rustling sound in the underbrush, but his hunter's instincts told him it was a small animal, a vole or stoat perhaps, not a threat.

He unbuckled his safety straps, swung himself out of the saddle, and led Eider into the cover the coppice afforded. "Wait for me here," he said. "Keep out of sight."

Eider grunted. No wizard had altered her in the womb, and she didn't possess a quasi-human intelligence like Jet. Still, Gaedynn was confident she understood.

He patted her head, then headed for the far side of the oaks. By the time he reached it, he was crouching low and creeping.

He was reasonably sure the enemy force was directing most of its vigilance inward, toward the town that was their objective. But they surely had at least a few sentries looking out at the countryside too. So he all but crawled across the open ground between the coppice and the tents and fires on the near side of the half-erected earthworks and half-assembled siege towers and trebuchets. He paused often to study the ground ahead.

He supposed a charm of invisibility could have made the little excursion easier. But relying on such an enchantment could also mean disaster. There were wards that could strip away invisibility. Bareris Anskuld had run into one at the Dread Ring in Lapendrar. And since Gaedynn was no spellcaster, he doubted his ability to detect and avoid them. Better then to rely on the woodcraft he'd learned during his captivity in the Yuirwood.

Of course, were Jhesrhi with him, the task might be easier too. They might not need to sneak into the enemy camp at all, because she could command the wind to carry the sounds of voices to her from far away. He wondered what she was doing back at Tchazzar's court. Dancing? He grinned and tried to find the thought ridiculous.

An owl hooted, and Selûne's silvery light glinted on the iron blade of a plow. The implement looked undamaged and accordingly valuable by peasant standards. Perhaps some unlucky farmer had dropped it as he fled the advance of Threskel's army.

Five paces beyond the plow blade, Gaedynn spotted a small, round shape in the gloom ahead. At first glimpse he took it for a stone or shrub, but he froze and peered at it anyway. There was a triangular bump like a snake's head sticking up from the rounded part. He decided the form was really a kobold sentry sitting on the ground with most of his body hidden behind a shield.

Could Gaedynn swing right or left and avoid the kobold's notice? Possibly, but what if that meant moving straight toward another? He suspected there was more than one sentry, and he had no way of knowing how far apart they were.

He eased an arrow from his quiver, laid it on his bow, then stood, drew, loosed, and dropped back down all in a heartbeat.

The shaft punched into the kobold's crown. The reptile flopped onto his back without making a sound.

So far, so good. Gaedynn just had to enter the camp, accomplish his objective, and sneak away again before anybody found the corpse.

As he passed the body, he looked for a badge he could appropriate. He didn't see anything, and didn't want to linger by the body to search. But fortunately, even though Threskel was a poor realm—or a poor province in rebellion, if you took the traditional Chessentan point of view—Alasklerbanbastos had somehow found the coin to hire a fair number of mercenaries from overseas. As a result, his army consisted of a diverse lot of warriors who were mostly strangers to one another. If Tymora smiled, Gaedynn could blend in for at least a little while.

He kept low until he was near the perimeter of the camp, near enough that a fellow might have wandered that far out simply to piss in peace. He peered, searching for anyone who might be looking right in his direction, then straightened up. Pretending to close the fastenings of his breeches, he sauntered on toward the tents and crackling fires.

As he'd hoped, he didn't attract any special notice even though most of the human soldiers lay snoring, either in their tents or wrapped in blankets under the open sky. It was mainly nocturnal creatures, swaggering pig-faced orcs and other goblinkin, who were awake.

He glanced around and spotted eight orcs sitting around one of the smaller fires. They all wore tabards marked with the eye and crossbones emblem of the Red Spears, a mercenary company made up exclusively of their kind. More to the point, they were passing a jug around, with another, still corked, waiting for when the first one ran dry. Gaedynn judged that it gave him a plausible pretext to approach them.

"Well met," he said. "What would a fellow sellsword have to do to get a pull from that jug?"

The orcs all turned to look at him. The biggest, who wore a necklace of severed ears and had apparently gouged out one of his own eyes in devotion to the war god Gruumsh, sneered. "Grow tusks," he said.

His companions laughed.

"And the stones to go with them," said another orc.

The Red Spears laughed again.

"Too bad," said Gaedynn. "I was hoping the answer was contribute some kammarth to the party." He made a show of peering about, making sure no officers were looking, then removed a little cloth bag from the pouch on his belt.

Kammarth was a drug compounded of a rare woodland root and subterranean fungi. It quickened the reflexes and imparted a feeling of boundless energy. Combined with alcohol and natural orc belligerence, it all but guaranteed a brawl, but Gaedynn hoped to be gone before the hostilities erupted.

"Let's see," said the one-eyed orc.

Gaedynn tossed him the bag.

The Red Spear caught it, untied the thong securing the mouth, stuck in a finger, and brought it out with sand-colored powder on the tip. He sucked it clean, then shuddered.

"Not bad," he said thickly. "All right, human, sit down if you've a mind to."

Two of the other orcs shifted apart. As Gaedynn claimed the space they'd made, One-Eye uncorked the fresh jug, poured the kammarth into it, then gave the vessel a shake.

When it came around the circle, Gaedynn considered only pretending to drink. But he didn't want to risk the orcs noticing. The jug turned out to contain hard cider likely pilfered from some farmhouse. It might have been all right if the kammarth hadn't turned it bitter.

As it was, he didn't like the taste or the jolt that started his heart pounding and sweat seeping from his brow. But he tried to look as if he did.

"So," he said, "another stinking siege."

One of the orcs grunted.

"I like the loot when you finally get inside," Gaedynn continued. "But I hate the waiting."

One-Eye grinned. "I guess you haven't heard."

*   *   *   *   *

Oraxes crouched in the turret peeking out at the sentry prowling up and down the wall walk. He and his companions had crowded into their hiding place before sunset, and he was hungry, cold, and generally uncomfortable. But mostly, though he was doing his best to conceal it, he was nervous.

The Threskelans were sending something in the dark. Something that could make its way to the top of Soolabax's walls, find lone guards, and rip them apart.

It was only a minor problem in the overall context of the siege. But, in what Oraxes believed to be a rare instance of accord, Aoth and Lord Hasos both wanted it stopped. To that end, they'd decided to set a trap. The bait was one of the ablest combatants in the Brotherhood of the Griffon, who was nonetheless counting on Oraxes and the other men in the turret to rush to his aid.

Oraxes suspected killing the killer, who- or whatever it was, was likely to prove considerably more difficult than using his magic for petty theft to survive in Luthcheq. But it was apt to be more interesting too.

Suddenly the sentry cried out and hefted his spear. A bare instant later, something big, dark, and eight-legged swarmed over the parapet. It moved fast, in a swirl of shadows blacker than the night.

The sentry jabbed with the spear, but it glanced off his attacker's shoulder. The spider thing—which, Oraxes observed, had a horned head and clawed feet more closely resembling a lizard's—spewed something that instantly congealed into strands, which wrapped around the warrior, sizzled, and smoked. He cried out and strained to break the bonds. The spider thing opened its slavering, steaming jaws to bite.

Oraxes rattled off words of power, jerked his right hand through a jagged pass, then pointed. A serpent made of bright, crackling lightning leaped from his fingertip and flew. It plunged its fangs into the spider thing's flank and vanished in a flash.

For a moment, the creature convulsed. It gave the sentry time to struggle free of his gluey, blistering restraints.

Meanwhile, the men-at-arms in the turret scrambled out onto the wall walk and discharged their crossbows. Then they drew their swords and advanced on the beast.

Which didn't seem to mind that it was facing half a dozen foes instead of one. In fact, it sprang to meet them. A toss of its head and horns hurled the first mercenary crashing back against the next in line.

Oraxes looked through the turret window for a clear line to the spider thing. He couldn't see one. The mercenaries were in the way.

He scurried out onto the walkway. It didn't help.

He told himself that the soldiers might not need any more magical aid, but saw immediately that it wasn't so. The same problem that was hindering him could easily prove to be their downfall. The wall walk was just too narrow for them all to assail the spider thing at once, and they were no match for it two and three at a time. It tore away mail and flesh with a snap of its jaws, spun to spit more acidic strands at the warrior it had first entangled, then whirled again to rip away another piece of the man it had just bitten, before the poor bastard had even finished falling down.

Oraxes climbed up onto a merlon. It was a step in the right direction, but not good enough. He swallowed and moved to the outer edge of the stone block.

He felt the possibility of losing his balance and falling like a dizzying thinness in the air. He also felt the ghostly stab of the arrows the enemy might loose at a man standing in such an exposed position. But he finally had a clear shot, so he stayed where he was and recited an incantation.

Force flared from his outstretched hand. It whipped the spider thing's head all the way down to crack against the wall walk like a blow from an invisible hammer. Before the creature could raise it and resume an aggressive posture, two warriors landed sword cuts.

Unfortunately, that wasn't enough to finish the spider thing. It lunged again, horns stabbing, jaws snapping. So Oraxes raked it with a flare of yellow fire.

It snarled and sprang back over the parapet. For an instant, Oraxes assumed it had decided to flee. Then he saw that it was actually scuttling horizontally along the wall faster than a man could sprint. Coming for the foe who was hurting it the worst.

Fear turned Oraxes's bowels to water, but he knew that if he froze or flinched, he'd die. He shouted words of power, and, as the thing turned to charge straight up at him, he thrust both arms down at it with all the strength in his body.

Fist-sized hailstones materialized in midfall, clattered and thudded against the spider thing, and knocked it off the wall. It fell and smashed against the ground.

Oraxes felt relief until he realized that his last, excessively forceful mystic gesture had shifted his center of gravity. He was toppling outward and about to plunge down right on top of the foe.

A hand grabbed him by the belt and hauled him backward. Trembling, he climbed back down onto the wall walk.

Once there, he and the sellsword who'd pulled him to safety looked down at the creature. It wasn't moving, and the seething gloom that had shrouded it was gone. Which paradoxically meant that despite the distance, Oraxes could see it about as well as before.

The sellsword panted. "That was good work."

The remark made Oraxes feel awkward, which was something he generally hated. But it wasn't so bad this time. "We were all beating on it, I guess. We should get the men who are hurt to the healers."

* * * * *

"I know we're intent on winning the war against Threskel," the burly, white-haired merchant said, his breath scented with brandy. He'd evidently served in the navy when he was younger and, as was the Chessentan fashion, still wore his collection of gleaming medals stamped with anchors, sea serpents, and other nautical emblems looped around his neck. "But I ask you, have we forgotten all about the filthy pirates?"

"I'm sure His Majesty hasn't," said Jhesrhi, marveling that the rich, self-important old man, who'd probably spent his whole long life despising arcanists, had sought her out for a conversation. "But it won't do much good to protect our shipping and harbors if we lose the rest of the realm while we're accomplishing it."

"That's sound thinking as far as it goes," the merchant said. "But still, if the most important trading vessels could travel in convoy with a proper escort, it would benefit Chessenta immensely."

Jhesrhi assumed that by "the most important trading vessels," he meant the fleet he owned himself. Amused, she said, "If you care to request an audience, I imagine His Majesty will at least listen to your proposal."

The shipping magnate beamed as though her response all but guaranteed success. Who knew? In the oblique parlance favored by courtiers, maybe it did. "Thank you, lady. Rest assured I won't forget."

Jhesrhi glanced out the casement at the western sky, gauging the position of Selûne and the glittering haze of tears that forever trailed the goddess across the firmament. With a twinge of reluctance that surprised her, she decided it was time to leave the party.

She took a final look around. Tchazzar had commanded that mementoes of his past campaigns be placed on display in a hall in the War College to inspire martial ardor in his subjects, and the court was attending a private viewing. Some of the trophies were functional arms and armor, others a pavilion, captured banners, and obsolete maps.

For the most part the lords and merchants paid little attention to them. They were too busy talking. To Tchazzar, resplendent in crimson and gold, if he chose to favor them with his attention. Or to Halonya, more gaudily robed than ever, her entourage of newly anointed priests hovering in attendance, as a second choice.

Or, Jhesrhi suddenly wondered, to herself? Now that she thought about it, she hadn't lacked for companionship over the course of the evening. Other courtiers loitered nearby, waiting to take the place of the elderly sea trader, and they looked rueful now that something in her demeanor told them she meant to go.

For some reason that made her blush, which in turn annoyed her. "I may be back," she said. "If I can." She turned and strode away.

She had to climb stairs to reach her apartments—which, despite the exertion involved, was a mark of Tchazzar's favor. The finest and most coveted suites in the citadel were near the top, where the view looking out over Luthcheq was at its most spectacular. She nodded to the sentry the monarch had insisted on posting at her door, then went inside.

A servant had already lit a fire in the hearth. She kneeled down and traced a star-shaped but asymmetrical figure on the floor. Her fingertip left lines of yellow phosphorescence.

When the sigil was done, she rose and took her staff in both hands. The rod wasn't alive, but it possessed a sort of quasi consciousness, and it always yearned to create and manipulate fire. She could feel its eagerness when it sensed that was her intent.

She recited words of power while shifting the staff around. First she held it vertically to her right, then in the same attitude on her left, then horizontally over her head. Together with the floor, the three positions defined a rectangle. Or, as she imagined it, a window.

She wasn't adept at long-distance magical communication. Her talents lay elsewhere, and the same was true of Aoth. But they both possessed some mastery of fire. And since all fires were in a mystical sense the same fire—manifestations of the same cosmic principle and essential force—if they prearranged a time, they could sometimes use flame to talk to each other.

A tapestry started to smoke, and she silently commanded it not to ignite. Then the blaze in the hearth leaped higher. Dimly at first, then more clearly, she spied Aoth and Gaedynn—or shrunken images of them—standing on the far side of the flames. Spear in hand, Aoth was standing and making magic in much the same fashion as herself. Looking relaxed and self-possessed as a cat, Gaedynn sprawled in a chair with a cup in his hand and one long leg thrown over the armrest.

The archer leaned forward and peered. "Is that sweet Lady Firehair herself descended from the heavens to speak to us? Or have you acquired even more new finery?"

Jhesrhi scowled. "These are wizard's robes, not some useless gown."

"But not especially practical for the field either," Gaedynn said. "Are those garnets or rubies in the flame pattern?"

"Enough," said Aoth, scowling. "I'm not holding this conduit open so you two can bicker. Jhes, I assume that if you haven't left Luthcheq, neither has Tchazzar."

"No," she said. It felt like an admission, which annoyed her because it was unfair. She couldn't order the monarch around, nor could she leave until he gave permission.

"What about the legions"—the Chessentan forces weren't actually called that, but the Thayan way of speaking still occasionally colored Aoth's speech—"in and around the city?"

"They haven't moved either."

"Curse it!" said Aoth. "Soolabax is already under siege. There's fighting all along the border. I need reinforcements, or a dragon of my own to counter the wyrms flying out of the north. Preferably both. What's Tchazzar waiting on?"

Jhesrhi knew Aoth's frustration was justified. So perhaps it was her suspicion that he blamed her for the problem that made her want to defend the war hero. "He was gone a hundred years. He has a lot to sort out."

"None of which will matter a lump of dung if Threskel overruns us," Gaedynn drawled. "Do you think the old snake's afraid to fight?"

She hesitated, then remembered how Tchazzar had destroyed the blight wyrm Sseelrigoth. "He's a dragon," she said.

"Fine," said Aoth, a trace of the blue light in his eyes gleaming through the wavering yellow haze of the fire. "He isn't scared, just unwise. The point is this: Gaedynn did some spying and learned that more dragons are on their way here. Fortunately not too quickly. They're herding some other creatures along, and not all of those can fly.

"I don't want them joining the siege," the war-mage continued. "I want to break out, then ambush the procession before it gets here. I've picked out a good spot."

"That's a bold plan," she said. The notion of attacking flying creatures by surprise was always problematic, and if said creatures also possessed the cunning of dragons, it compounded the difficulties. But if anyone could do it, the Brotherhood could.

"At this point," said Aoth, "Luthcheq's soldiers can't get here in time to help. But Tchazzar can."

"I'll talk to him," she promised, "and tell you tomorrow night what he said."

"Good." Aoth hesitated. "How's Cera?" he asked gruffly. Behind him, Gaedynn grinned.

"I haven't seen her for a couple of days," Jhesrhi said.

Aoth's eyes narrowed. "What? Everyone knows Soolabax is surrounded, don't they? She wouldn't try to return here without a flying steed to carry her."

"Everyone knows," Jhesrhi said. "Your messenger arrived. Now that you mention it, it's strange, because I've seen plenty of Daelric." Mostly trying fruitlessly to arrange to talk to Tchazzar without Halonya in attendance. "You'd think Cera would have accompanied him at least part of the time."

"I'm coming down there."

* * * * *

At the end of the palaver, Aoth waved his hand. Jhesrhi's image vanished, and the leaping flames subsided to mere flickering wisps among the coals. They'd devoured most of the wood while the magic was active.

"You realize," Gaedynn said, "this is stupid. Maybe not let's-go-to-Thay-and-fight-Szass-Tam stupid, but stupid nonetheless."

"Somebody has to prod Tchazzar into motion."

"And that somebody is Jhesrhi. The drake picks his favorites, and for the moment at least she's one of them. So if she can't do it, you can't either. You'll just make yourself look bad by showing up at court when you're supposed to be here attending to business."

"I'll be there attending to business."

"It's Cera, isn't it? You only just met the wench. How can she mean so much to you?"

"You're one to talk."

One corner of Gaedynn's mouth quirked upward. "I have no idea what you mean by that. But if I did . . . Never mind. Just because Jhesrhi hasn't seen her for a day or two, why do you leap to the conclusion she's in trouble? A vision?"

"I wish. It's because she believes Amaunator wants her to find out what's really behind the Green Hand murders and all the other mysteries. She urged me to help, and I refused. I told her fighting the war was my proper concern."

"Which was sensible. But you're afraid she took advantage of being in Luthcheq to snoop around by herself and has come to grief because of it."

"Pretty much."

"Then let me go look for her."

"It may take truesight to pick up her trail. Now, I give you my word. Whether I find her or not, I won't stay gone for long. While I'm away, you're in command. Don't make any big moves unless you have to. But use scouts to track those wyrms and other creatures coming down from the north. If you decide you need to go ahead and break the siege to spring the trap as planned, do it."

It had been a long time since Aoth had seen Gaedynn succumb to consternation. "I know how to lead my bowmen and skirmishers," the lanky redhead said. "But the whole Brotherhood?"

"You can handle it."

"Khouryn's still in Tymanther doing Keen-Eye only knows what."

"That's why you have to handle it."

"With both you and Jhesrhi absent, there'll be scarcely any sorcery to speak of."

"Despite being a surly young snot, Oraxes has some power, and some sense and grit to go with it. He can help you use what magic you do have to best effect."

"You realize Hasos won't be happy taking orders from your lieutenant."

"I'll order him to obey you as he would me." Aoth snorted. "For whatever that's worth."

* * * * *

Clad in her favorite purple robe with the silvery sigils sewn on, Nala spun her shadow-wood staff through complex figures and chanted in the secret, sibilant language the dragon god evidently preferred. As usual, her body writhed from side to side like she was a snake trying to crawl straight up into the air.

As the chant progressed, that sinuous motion became contagious. The half dozen true neophytes started doing it too.

Balasar knew why. He could feel Power buzzing around his head like a swarm of flies. But because he'd resisted the temptation to yield to his dragon nature during his initiation, it couldn't get inside.

He just had to hope Nala couldn't tell. He shifted back and forth like his fellows in an effort to keep her from taking a closer look at him. Which made him feel like a jackass with spectators watching.

Up until then, the Platinum Cadre had conducted nearly all its rituals and other activities removed from the hostile public eye. But since the cult had gained a measure of acceptance, Nala and Patrin had decided to conduct the trial of faith in a corner of the shaded, breezy Market Floor—with thick columns along the edge of the platform, the prodigious bulk of the City-Bastion suspended overhead, and the cries of vendors sounding not far away.

Nala twirled the staff faster and faster. Her voice rose until she was all but screaming. Then, on the final word of her chant, she whipped down the rod to rest in front of her with the butt exactly equidistant between her feet. Except for the constant boneless shifting, she stood motionless. Even to Balasar, who'd learned sword forms from some of the most exacting masters-at-arms in Tymanther, the instantaneous transition from frenzy to stillness was impressive.

Nala scrutinized the recent converts. Perhaps her gaze lingered on Balasar for an extra moment. More likely it was just his imagination.

"You're ready," she declared. "Arm them, Sir Patrin."

The paladin with his deep blue surcoat and clinking beard of silver chains opened a wooden box and started handing out knives. Balasar felt a pang of dismay.

Which, he supposed, had its comical side. He'd fought a topaz dragon and its strange, formidable minions on the journey down from Chessenta. And he was worried about a pen full of pigs?

Well, yes. Because they were the enormous, savage variety sometimes called dire boars, and an unarmored knife fighter—no matter how skilled—would be at a substantial disadvantage. Especially in the somewhat cramped confines of the pen, where an animal could pin him against the fence.

Yet it was obvious the other neophytes didn't share his trepidation. Shifting, they stared at the pen like they could hardly wait to start the slaughter.

Nala didn't keep them waiting any longer than it took to distribute the dirks. "Begin!" she cried, and Balasar's fellows rushed the pen. He saw little choice but to rush right along with them.

The rules said an initiate couldn't attack until he was inside the pen. Balasar arguably cheated just a little by breathing frost at the nearest boar while still vaulting over the top of the fence.

Rime painted the pig's snout white and, as he'd intended, encrusted its eyes. Too ferocious to balk or even flinch, the hump on its back as high as he was tall, the black beast charged him anyway. He sidestepped its slashing tusks and stabbed at its neck.

The knife penetrated, but failed to draw the arterial spurt he wanted. The accursed animal was moving too fast. Its bristle-covered hide was too thick, and there was too much fat and muscle underneath.

Elsewhere in the pen, gouts of fire leaped and lightning crackled. Carried on the breeze, a stray trace of poisonous vapor stung Balasar's nose and filled his mouth with an acrid taste. His companions were using their breath weapons repeatedly, because unlike him, they could. After a dragonborn truly gave himself to Nala's deity, the ability renewed itself more quickly.

The boar slammed into the fence. The heavy rails lurched and banged, and the spectators gasped and recoiled. But the barrier held. The pig spun, faster than such a massive, short-legged beast had any right to, and Balasar had to give ground before it. To scurry back toward the center of the pen.

He was horribly conscious of squeals and grunts, the thump and scrape of trotters on stone, and the smells of blood and burned flesh right behind him. But he couldn't even glance around to see if a second boar was about to gore him. He didn't dare take his eyes off the one that he knew for certain meant to kill him.

The frost had largely fallen away from its little red eyes. Which, evidently not frozen and blind, were glaring straight at him.

The boar surged forward. He dodged, and it compensated. He sidestepped again, and his foot slipped. Because, while the Market Floor was made of granite, the pigs had been in the pen long enough to start fouling it with muck.

Balasar floundered for balance and saw that he couldn't avoid the hog. At best he might be able to avoid being sliced open by one of its tusks. As it charged into range, he planted his hand on top of its head and jumped.

It was nothing like the agile spring that had carried him over the fence. It heaved him above the tusks, but the boar's bulk still slammed into him and bounced him off to the side.

He landed hard, and for a moment the world was just a jumble of lunging shapes and noises that didn't mean anything. Then he remembered what had happened to him and knew the pig was already turning to attack him again.

It lunged, dipping its head to slice a target so low to the ground. Balasar twisted, somehow avoided the stroke, then snatched with his off hand. His fingers closed on one of the lower tusks. As long as he maintained his grip, the pig wouldn't be able to gore him.

Unfortunately, it could wrench its head back and forth and up and down, trying to break his hold. The motion pounded him against the granite. Meanwhile, he repeatedly plunged his dirk into its throat and the underside of its jaw.

He felt his fingers slipping. Then, finally, blood spattered him and the stone in rhythmic gushes. The boar thrashed in a convulsion that flung him loose, charged, but collapsed a pace or two short of its target.

Balasar just wanted to lie still and gasp for breath. But with a fight raging all around him, that was a good way to get killed. He lifted his head and looked around.

Some of the other pigs were dead, and by and large those that were still active looked in worse shape than the cultists who seared them with repeated blasts of flame and vitriol. Balasar had just about decided he could sit out the rest of the fight when, from the corner of his eye, he saw a hog toss its head and slice a green-scaled dragonborn from thigh to shoulder.

Even as Balasar scrambled to his feet, it occurred to him that the injured fighter was a wyrm-worshiper and thus, in the truest sense, an enemy. Someone he himself might want to kill someday. But his instincts were stronger than that consideration. He charged the boar, meanwhile yelling as best he could in the hope that he could distract it from the foe sprawled helplessly before it.

The huge pig started to turn. Hoping the blade would pass unimpeded under bone and find some vital spot, Balasar thrust his point at the base of its jawline.

The boar exploded into a great thrashing spasm, and it was luck as much as Balasar's nimbleness or battle sense that kept it from slashing him in the process. But it didn't, and then it flopped over onto its side.

Still keeping an eye on it, he moved to check the wounded cultist. The son of a toad lay in a sizeable pool of his own blood, but at least he was breathing.

Balasar looked around. All the pigs had fallen and lay inert, mere ugly mounds of bristles and charred, bloody flesh, while Patrin was already trotting in his direction. The paladin evidently realized that if he used his healing powers quickly enough, he could save the maimed cultist.

Patrin kneeled down in the gore, murmured a prayer, summoned silvery light into his hands, and then applied them to the long gash in his fellow worshiper's body. The magic worked exceptionally well. The wound closed completely, and the fellow dazedly raised his head.

When Patrin helped him to his feet, the cheers erupted, with only a scattering of holdouts among the crowd looking disgusted at everyone else's reaction.

Balasar registered the acclaim with mixed emotions. He really didn't want anyone applauding the Cadre for anything. But curse it, he'd fought well, and there was a part of him—no doubt the part the elders of Clan Daardendrien had always decried as frivolous, immature, and irresponsible—that simply wanted to wave and bow.

Then Nala came to the side of the pen, and her cool, appraising gaze reminded him he was playing a deadly serious game—and nowhere near winning it yet.

"You only used your breath once," she said.

Balasar smiled. "My way was more sporting, and more fun."

"He fought well," Patrin said.

"Yes," Nala said. "But I'm not sure I saw the god's gift of fury augmenting his strength."

"My teachers trained me to fight with a cool head," Balasar said. "Sun and sky, when we faced the giants, Patrin didn't constantly spit fire, and he didn't go berserk either."

"It's because I'm a paladin," Patrin said. "Bahamut blessed me with a different set of gifts."

"Well," said Balasar, "maybe he'll end up making me a paladin too."

Nala snorted. "I doubt it. Still, it's true that the god doesn't bless everyone in precisely the same way, and occasionally it can take a while for his blessings to manifest. Even so, the next time—"

The war drums started thumping. They'd sounded often across the Market Floor, and through all Djerad Thymar, ever since the giant tribes had set aside their feuds and joined forces to assail Tymanther. Sometimes the drummers had pounded out the steady cadence of an alert and sometimes the slow, hollow beats that announced defeat. Only rarely had they hammered out the fast, intricate, largely improvisational rhythms used to celebrate a victory, but they were doing so now.

The spectators headed toward the center of the marketplace, where many folk were starting to cheer. Nala, Patrin, Balasar, and the rest of the neophytes followed.

On horseback, the lancers loomed above the heads of the crowd. Despite all the excited people crowded together in front of him, Balasar could more or less see Medrash and the rest of the procession riding past. Unlike the Platinum Cadre, the patrol hadn't mutilated the bodies of fallen giants for trophies. But they had appropriated the barbarians' huge stone weapons to show what they'd accomplished.

"This is glorious!" Patrin said.

He didn't see the scowl Nala gave him, but Balasar did. At that moment, it was difficult to believe the two were lovers.

* * * * *

As the servant ushered Gaedynn into Hasos's study, he reflected that he and the baron had a good deal in common. They were both gently born and followed the profession of arms. They were still young and good-looking, and in their disparate styles took pains with their appearances. Still, he could tell from Hasos's frown that it wasn't likely to be a particularly cordial meeting.

I don't like it either, Gaedynn thought. But if I have to swallow the stone, then so do you.

Hasos stood up from behind his desk, although not with any great alacrity. "Sir Gaedynn," he said. "What can I do for you?"

"My scouts report that the dragons and their creatures are closer than we'd hoped." Gaedynn noticed a map on the desk and pointed to a spot in Threskel. "As of this morning, they were here. Which means that to carry out Captain Fezim's strategy, we need to break the siege now."

Hasos's frown turned into an outright glare. "That's impossible."

"To the contrary. It's entirely feasible, especially since we have powerful wizards on our side." At least they might be powerful. Gaedynn hadn't seen any irrefutable evidence to the contrary.

Hasos made a spitting sound. "Wizards. Devil-worshiping degenerates."

Gaedynn grinned. "Not anymore. Not since Tchazzar proclaimed them to be fine fellows, one and all. More to the point, whatever you think of them, we can put them to good use."

"Still—"

Gaedynn decided it was time to move on from unfounded optimism to outright lies. "It's also my pleasure to inform you that the war hero and the army under his personal command are now on their way to Soolabax. They'll advance onto the battlefield when their sudden appearance will do the most damage."

"Where's the messenger who carried this news? Why didn't you bring him to me right away?"

"Because it was the mage Jhesrhi Coldcreek, speaking to me from far away. The spell didn't last long enough for me to send someone to fetch you."

"Then have one of the 'powerful' wizards who are still in the city communicate with her. Or Captain Fezim. Or the war hero himself."

Gaedynn smiled and spread his hands. "I wish that were possible. But as you may know, every sorcerer has his own secrets and specialties. Oraxes and his fellows truly are formidable, but alas, none of them is a master of the particular art in question."

Hasos sneered. "You have an answer for everything."

"I like to think so. Unfortunately, it's clear you don't find any of them especially convincing. But you can believe this: We're going ahead with Aoth's plan, and Tchazzar will receive a report of the outcome. It's up to you whether he hears that you gave your wholehearted support or balked at every turn."

His voice tight with resentment, Hasos said, "When exactly are we planning to launch the attack?"

FOUR

Nicos Corynian loved his family and made a point of taking his evening meal with them whenever practical. That night, however, the bright, trivial chatter of his wife and nieces grated on his already jangled nerves. As soon as he could make his escape, he headed for the private study that served him as a kind of refuge.

His hand with its scarred knuckles trembling ever so slightly, he opened the door, set the single white wax candle he'd brought along on the dice table, and headed for the walnut cabinet in which he kept strong drink. The taper was sufficient illumination for the moment. He'd worry about lighting the lamps when he had some brandy inside him.

A deep voice sounded from the shadows. "Good evening, milord."

Startled, Nicos lurched around. A robed and hooded figure rose from one of the chairs between the dice table and the wall. The apparition stepped forward and Nicos saw the eerie blue glow of its eyes.

Aoth pushed the cowl back, and the yellow candlelight gilded his tattooed face. "Please excuse the clothes. I realize they're filthy and smell like garbage. But it's not easy to

77

wander around without being recognized when you look like I do."

"How did you get in here?" As soon as the question left Nicos's mouth, he realized the answer wasn't important. But he was still too rattled to think straight.

"You have a kindly cook. She was willing to feed a beggar. Then I slipped out of the kitchen when her back was turned. I stole a bottle of cooking wine and left the door ajar so she'd assume I'd departed the house."

"All right, but why are you in Luthcheq at all?"

"Partly to prod Tchazzar into heading north." The mercenary hesitated. "What?"

Nicos realized that his expression must have changed when Aoth spoke the dragon's name. "It's nothing."

"Plainly it isn't, and since I'm planning to talk to him, I need to know about it."

Nicos sighed. "Have it your way. At court today, a minstrel sang a song he'd written about Tchazzar's past triumphs. In it he made mention of one of the wyrm's old lieutenants. Someone Tchazzar evidently remembers fondly."

"Go on."

"Tchazzar flew into a rage. He said the bard had insulted his friend and ordered him whipped."

"That's harsh, but I've known other princes who might have done the same."

"So have I," said Nicos, "but here's the difference. No one else could perceive the insult. I still can't. Every word the singer used was complimentary."

"Maybe if you'd actually known the fellow, you'd see that the words conveyed some hidden irony?"

"I doubt it, and anyway there's more. A guard started the whipping, but Tchazzar wasn't satisfied with the results. He insisted on taking over, and I think he must have some portion of a dragon's strength even when he's a man. He went on and on, tirelessly, until he'd all but cut the minstrel to pieces."

Aoth frowned. "And we brought him back to Chessenta. Well, Jhesrhi and Gaedynn did, but I sent them on your orders."

"Yes."

"Well, we'll just have to hope that Tchazzar's good qualities offset his quirks. Meanwhile, I've delayed presenting myself at the War College because Cera Eurthos has disappeared, and I wanted a free hand to poke around. What do you know about it?"

Nicos blinked. "Me? Nothing! Why would I?"

"She was staying in Amaunator's temple, but no one's seen her for a while. I gather Daelric's not especially concerned. He assumes she headed back north. Which she shouldn't and wouldn't have done without asking permission. But he's apparently too jealous of Halonya's sudden rise to think the matter through."

"Perhaps she left the Keeper's house to visit family or friends in the city."

Aoth shook his head. "She doesn't have any living family. She probably does have old friends hereabouts, but I'm certain she had something else in mind. As I'm sure you realize, no one ever figured out the whole truth about the Green Hand murders. She believed her god had given her the task."

"That sounds potentially dangerous."

Aoth smiled a crooked smile. "I agree. Yet I left her here to snoop around alone. I was preoccupied. I thought my responsibility was to lead the Brotherhood and defeat Threskel."

"You were right. It is."

"I know. Still, I mean to find her."

"And you think that somehow, I can help you."

"Yes, milord, I do. I don't spread this around, but the Blue Fire did more than extend my life. It changed the way I see. Once in a while I have visions that point to hidden truths. The first time we met, I saw a green dragon looking over your shoulder."

Making sure his voice would remain steady, Nicos took a breath. "What in the name of the Yellow Sun did that signify?"

"At the time, I had no idea. I'm still not sure. But ever since the

Brotherhood came to these lands, there have been dragons, dragon-worshipers, and creatures with draconic traits popping up everywhere."

Nicos forced a smile. "Well, obviously Chessenta is fighting a war against a dracolich and his circle of dragon followers—"

"I mean above and beyond that, as you understand perfectly well. I hadn't gotten around to mentioning that I once smelled the lingering odor of a certain gum you'd burned in your study. A gum used in mystical rituals."

"And that concerned you? All right, I confess I have a small talent for sorcery, which I've always concealed to avoid the stigma. But now that Tchazzar's changed the law, what does it matter?"

"It matters because, together with my vision, it indicates there's more to you than most people realize. Now, I'm not your enemy. By the Black Flame, I work for you, give or take. But I demand to know what you know. To find Cera, and to help me look out for the Brotherhood's interests."

"And if I refuse to surrender all my secrets?"

"Then I'll tell Tchazzar what I know. Maybe you'll be lucky and he won't think anything of it. But I'm pretty sure Lord Luthen will talk until his teeth fall out trying to make it seem damning. You never know—tomorrow, or the next day, it could be you tied to the whipping post."

Trying to look defeated, Nicos sighed and slumped his shoulders. "All right. I'm not some sort of scoundrel, but there are . . . things you probably should know. I'm afraid it will take a while." He waved toward the pair of brown leather chairs in front of the hearth. "Sit. I'll get us something to drink."

"Fine." Aoth flopped down in one of the chairs.

Nicos headed for the cabinet containing the bottles and goblets. Which put him behind the war-mage.

I can do this, he told himself. I'm a pugilist. I know how and where to hit. And the man said himself, no one knows he came here. I can dispose of the body somehow.

He looked at the nape of Aoth's neck and clenched his fist.

Aoth sprang up out of the seat and whirled. He kicked the chair into Nicos's legs

It stung and made Nicos stagger back a step, but that was all. He started to rush Aoth, but by that time the Thayan was rattling off a charm. On the final syllable he snapped his fingers, and a pearly glow, dazzling in the gloomy chamber, appeared in the air between him and his attacker.

Squinting, Nicos instinctively balked, then realized the light was harmless. At the same instant vicious blows hammered him in the kidney and the jaw in quick succession. A foot sweep jerked one leg out from under him. Aoth slammed him down hard on the floor, then drew a dagger from one of his voluminous sleeves.

"Are you going to be sensible?" the sellsword asked. "Or do I have to hold the blade to your throat and go through the rest of the routine?"

Aching and breathless, half stunned, Nicos managed, "I'll be sensible."

"Good." Aoth offered a hand and pulled him to his feet. "This time, you sit and I'll fetch a bottle."

Nicos collapsed into a chair. "How did you know? Another vision?"

"No. It's just that I've spent the better part of a hundred years reading the faces and stances of men who were about to try to kill me."

"It was an impulse. I didn't mean—"

"Don't apologize. I'm glad you panicked. I didn't really have enough to go running to Tchazzar. I was bluffing. But I have it now."

"Yes. I suppose you do."

Aoth pulled the stopper from a decanter of brandy. The liquor gurgled into goblets, its scent filled the air, and, craving it, Nicos shivered.

Aoth gave him one of the cups, set the bottle on the low table between the chairs, then sat down opposite him. "Now," he said, "talk."

Nicos took a long drink first, and felt the brandy warm his belly. "I guess there's no way to say this except straight out. For a number of years, I've secretly provided certain services to a green wyrm named Skuthosiin."

Aoth's lambent blue eyes bored into him. "You're telling me," he said, his voice flat, "that the man who brought the Brotherhood to Chessenta, the man to whom our fortunes are still tied, is a spy and a traitor?"

"No! It's not like that. Skuthosiin never asked me to do anything that was clearly a disservice to the realm. And I wouldn't have. It's just that he was willing to reward me for . . . information and various favors."

"Wait. Is this the same Skuthosiin who used to live in Unther?" Aoth asked.

"So he says," Nicos said.

"How did he survive the Spellplague, and Tymanther more or less falling out of the sky on top of his country?" Aoth asked.

"I don't know," Nicos said. "He boasts that the Dark Lady favors him. Maybe she protected him."

"Where is he now?" Aoth asked. "Chessenta, Tymanther, or some-place else?"

"I don't know where he spends his time," Nicos said. "He taught me a spell to talk to him from far away. That's why I burn the gum."

Aoth grunted. "I've done a little studying since Tchazzar returned. Supposedly he and Skuthosiin were allies in the old days. So I take it you ordered me to look for him because your secret master wanted him found."

"Yes, but there's more to it. From the start he wanted you and your sellswords in Chessenta, and he somehow knew in advance that your company would meet with defeat and disgrace in Impiltur and need a new employer. That's how my messenger reached you at just the right time."

Aoth's eyes seemed to burn brighter. " 'Somehow knew in advance' is the mush-mouthed way of saying, 'Made it happen.' That's why that whoreson Kremphras and his company didn't show up to support us, and why there were dragonlike creatures helping the demon-worshipers. They were all working for Skuthosiin, just like you."

"I don't know that for a fact," said Nicos, "but I think it's likely."

"How many agents does he have, anyway?" Aoth asked. "Over how wide an area?"

"I don't know," said Nicos.

Aoth drew breath to make a reply—an angry one, to judge from his scowl—then caught himself and paused to take a drink. "Well, what else do you know? There had better be something."

"Looking back, I can at least speculate," Nicos said. "Skuthosiin somehow knows about your eyes. He initially wanted you here because he thought they might enable you to unmask the Green Hand killer."

"Which arguably hurt Chessenta more than it helped. So, if Skuthosiin knew what we'd find, maybe he's no friend to your country," Aoth said.

"If he knew," Nicos said, "there were easier ways to steer the city guards in the right direction."

"Well, possibly," Aoth said. "You truly have no idea why he wants what he wants? What his ultimate purpose is?"

"No."

"Or if he's even let Tchazzar know he's still alive?"

"No. Are you going to denounce me?"

Aoth scratched his chin, and his fingertips rasped in the beard stubble. Nicos had the wholly irrelevant thought that he would have heard the exact same little sound if the Thayan had scratched his shaved scalp.

"I don't especially want to," Aoth said after a moment. "You didn't cause the debacle in Impiltur, and I haven't known many lords who weren't involved in secret dirty dealings of one kind or another. I'd rather stay your friend and do what you and the Crown are paying me to do. But it's not going to be that easy unless I find Cera. And nothing you've said so far points me in the right direction."

"I told you, I don't know what happened to her!"

"But you're the damned spy and the damned courtier too. You keep track of everything that happens in the War College and the city at large. Think of something."

Nicos did. He thought that if he called for help, the servants might respond quickly. And if they all attacked Aoth together, they might conceivably overwhelm him.

But when he took another look at the man on the other side of the low little table, the hopeful fantasy withered. At the moment the Thayan might not have his enchanted spear or his griffon either, but even so it was impossible to doubt that he could handle anything his unwilling host could throw at him.

Then a more useful thought occurred to Nicos. He sat up straighter, and Aoth said, "What?"

"The Church of Tchazzar," Nicos said.

"What about it?"

"Tchazzar promised Halonya that a priesthood would form around her, and it did with remarkable speed. You'd think it would be mostly the same commoners who marched with her in the streets, seeking to rise along with her. But quite a few of them aren't. Before the coronation she'd never even seen them before, and they seem at home in their new roles. Like educated men accustomed to ritual and protocol."

"And Halonya doesn't think it odd that these strangers came out of nowhere to attend her?"

"Halonya is a half-mad pauper moving through a dream of pomp and glory. Everything that's happening seems miraculous, and so nothing seems peculiar. But here's my point. At one time Tchazzar was widely regarded as Tiamat's champion or even her avatar. So, if trained priests have come to officiate at his altar, who do you think they might be?"

"Wyrmkeepers," said Aoth. "And there are wyrmkeepers all through this tangle. Gaedynn and Jhesrhi ran into them in Mourktar, and another tried to murder me in Soolabax."

"If Cera Eurthos knew that, and if she made the same guess we just made, then that's where she might have gone for answers."

*   *   *   *   *

Oraxes had the urge to pace. Instead he and his fellow mages were expected to stand still and at least pretend to listen while Gaedynn Ulraes ran over their instructions—Oraxes refused to think of them as orders—another time.

The archer's coppery hair was gray under the night sky, and he'd traded his usual bright, foppish attire for a black brigandine and clothes to match. "I know it will be difficult to cast a veil over so many," he said. "But you only have to hide the skirmishers. We're moving up in advance of the rest. And the dark should help."

Meralaine—a diminutive, snub-nosed girl whose pixielike appearance belied a considerable talent for the sinister art of necromancy—nodded and said, "It will. And we're good at concealment spells. The way Luthcheq treated us, we had to be."

"When I give the word," Gaedynn continued, "you'll light up the enemy and keep them lit. The rest of us can kill them if we can see them."

"Right," said Meralaine. It seemed like she was trying to impress Gaedynn, maybe because she hoped to replace Oraxes as interim leader of the mages. Not, of course, that he cared one way or the other.

"As soon as you can," Gaedynn said, "get behind men with shields and stay there. There's no target so important that it's worth one of our only four wizards taking unnecessary chances to strike at it."

"We understand!" Oraxes snapped. "We understood the first time. You'd do better giving us a moment of peace to clear our heads."

Gaedynn studied him for a moment, then grinned. "Don't go out of your way to remind anybody, but I've never done this before either. Led a whole army, I mean."

Oraxes sneered. "Then maybe Hasos should be in charge."

"Maybe," Gaedynn said, "but then the garrison would still be bottled up inside Soolabax when Alasklerbanbastos himself shows up to perch his bony arse atop the baron's keep."

"We trust you," said Meralaine, sycophantic bitch that she was.

"Why wouldn't you?" Gaedynn replied. "My talents are plain for all to see. As are yours. I realize that none of you has been in a full-scale battle before, and night fighting's not the most comfortable way to begin. But keep your heads and you'll do fine. Now go take your positions."

Said positions were at intervals among the vanguard of bowmen, all members of Aoth and Gaedynn's Brotherhood. Oraxes recited a rhyme, and for a moment the cool night air grew positively frigid. A blur rippled across his portion of the loose formation, and the darkness thickened around it.

He surveyed his work and felt a twinge of pride. He'd like to see Meralaine's necromancy do better than that.

He somehow missed the signal that started his neighbors moving, and had to trot a couple of paces to catch up. As the archers advanced, he wished he could skulk as quietly as they did. He was an accomplished sneak thief, but that was on floors and cobbles. He couldn't match the sellswords on grass and mud.

Gaedynn abruptly drew and released. Oraxes hadn't realized there was anything to shoot at, nor did he see where the arrow flew. He supposed the lanky redhead had shot at a picket and killed him too, because they all kept slinking forward and nobody sounded an alarm.

The vague black mass that was the enemy camp and the east wall of Soolabax rising behind it swam out of the murk. Gaedynn raised his hand, and, up and down the formation, sergeants did the same. Everybody stopped advancing.

Gaedynn turned to Oraxes, smiled, and waved his hand at the foe like an elegant host inviting his guests into a feast.

Oraxes swallowed away a sudden dryness in his mouth. He tried to call the words of a spell to mind. For one horrible moment they wouldn't come, but then he had them. He whispered the rhyme, building to a crescendo even so, and thrust out his left hand. A spark leaped from his fingertips and streaked over the ground.

Gaedynn had made it clear that above all, he wanted light. But the trouble with a simple enchantment of illumination was that a sorcerer on the other side could rather easily dispel it. It might be more difficult to extinguish the glow of a burning tent.

Besides, Oraxes had a yen to show those hardened professional warriors, those Brothers of the Griffon, that he was as dangerous as any of them. And certainly the most dangerous of the spellcasters they'd recruited in Luthcheq. Even if it was the first time he'd ever used magic in such a blatant, savage way.

The spark exploded into a blast that engulfed and ignited two tents. Silhouetted against the yellow blaze, bodies tumbled and flew to pieces. For a heartbeat the destruction amazed Oraxes, like he hadn't had anything to do with it. Then he felt sick to his stomach.

But excited too.

Off to the right, another blast set fire to a different part of the camp. Less bloodthirsty, creative, or ambitious, the remaining mages contented themselves with conjuring pools of phosphorescence, one amber and one a sickly green.

"Shoot!" Gaedynn called, drawing and loosing. The skirmishers followed his example.

The arrows arced high and plummeted down. Men, orcs, and kobolds reeled and collapsed beneath the barrage.

Aoth Fezim had put together the force from a portion of his own company and various native Chessentan troops stationed along the border. By itself it was still smaller than the army besieging Soolabax. But the hope was that a surprise attack would more than compensate for the numerical disadvantage.

And it might. But it looked to Oraxes like the Great Bone Wyrm's warriors wouldn't remain stunned and disorganized for long. Already there were officers bellowing orders and goblins scrambling to grab their weapons and form up into squads.

Oraxes abruptly remembered that his part of the fight wasn't over. In fact, it had scarcely begun. He threw darts of crimson light at something big. An ogre maybe, or some sort of tame troll. The creature staggered but didn't fall down.

"What are you still doing here?" Gaedynn barked. Startled, Oraxes jerked around to find the archer right beside him. "I told you to get behind the shields!"

Oraxes scowled. At himself, because he'd forgotten all about that part of the plan, or even that there were any shields. He turned and saw that the spearmen had moved up unnoticed behind him. As he ran in their direction, an arrow or crossbow bolt whistled past his head.

* * * * *

Someone—Shala Karanok, most likely—had found a mansion on the edge of the religious quarter to serve as Tchazzar's interim temple. As he surveyed the place from the air, Aoth wondered what the former war hero had needed to do to persuade the householder to vacate.

If I were you, said Jet, speaking mind to mind, *I'd worry about what moved in after he did vacate. The last time you broke into a wyrmkeeper's lair, you nearly got killed. And then it was just one wyrmkeeper.*

Maybe you should be the captain, answered Aoth. *You always know just what to say to inspire confidence.*

The griffon gave a rasp of annoyance. *My point is that Jhesrhi and Scar are at the War College.*

Where I can't go unless I want to waste a day explaining why we're in Luthcheq, and alert the wyrmkeepers to our presence while I'm at it. This way is better.

Suit yourself. Maybe my next rider will be lighter.

Jet set down in an alley near the mansion. Aoth reluctantly left his spear secured to the familiar's saddle. It was too recognizable, too threatening, and impossible to conceal. He'd make do with the short sword hidden under his shabby beggar's robe. At least it had a little magic stored inside it.

He scratched Jet's head, then, shaking a wooden bowl to rattle the coppers inside it, shuffled in the direction of the temple. Behind him, wings rustled and cracked as the griffon took to the air again.

He was careful to keep his head bowed. The cowl did a good job of shadowing his face, but he couldn't depend on it alone to mask the light in his eyes. Fortunately, a servile posture jibed well with the other features of his disguise.

Seen from ground level, the mansion was even more impressive. Reflecting the Chessentan fascination with martial endeavor, it had turrets and battlements like a fortress, and friezes carved with men-at-arms slaughtering one another. It also had rosebushes at the foot of the facade, and even in the dark Aoth's fire-touched eyes could see that the new buds were crimson, like drops of blood fallen from the carnage overhead.

A priest with a shaggy black beard sat on a stool beside the door. From his casual air, his mismatched and no doubt improvised red and pink vestments, and the jug sitting beside him, Aoth took him for one of Halonya's longtime followers, not a priest of Tiamat. The newly minted cleric tossed a coin in the begging bowl.

"Thank you, holy sir," Aoth mumbled, bobbing his head. "But I want to go inside too. To pray."

The bearded man grinned. "And sleep indoors? I know how it is. Go on, then. But if you snore, we'll have to toss you out."

Beyond the door was a hall of considerable size. It smelled of sawdust as well as incense, and it was plain that carpenters had been working hard to turn it into a proper sanctum complete with benches where the rich and nobly born could sit and worship in comfort.

The chamber was already full of works of art, painted and sculpted depictions of Tchazzar as both dragon and man. Aoth assumed they were left over from the living god's previous reigns.

A second priest stood behind the elevated bloodstone altar. Tall, with a long, ascetic face and mottled, sun-damaged skin, he stared intently into the chalice cradled in his hands. The fire flickering up above the rim burned blue, then green, then black. The shifts reminded Aoth of the variously colored candle flames he'd seen in the wyrmkeeper's lair in Soolabax.

The priest glanced up when Aoth entered. Then, perhaps deciding that a grubby mendicant wouldn't comprehend the significance of what he was seeing, he sniffed and returned to his meditations.

Aoth glanced around, taking note of the other doorways leading out of the room. He didn't see how he could slip through either of them without the wyrmkeeper spotting him. But maybe he could wait the fellow out. He positioned himself in front of a painting of Tchazzar in wyrm form rearing bloody-jawed over the corpses of a green drake and a blue one. He folded his hands and watched the cleric from the corner of his eye.

And watched. And watched. While the flames in the cup danced from one color to the next.

He doesn't show any signs of leaving, said Jet. Thanks to their psychic link, he could see what Aoth was seeing.

No, Aoth replied. *Maybe someone is always supposed to tend the altar. Or he's not inclined to leave a beggar alone with valuable carvings and the like. Whatever the problem is, I can't just stand here until someone gets suspicious of me. So . . .* He whispered an incantation.

Smoke streamed up from the cup of fire into the wyrmkeeper's face. He started coughing.

Aoth charged the altar, counting on the thick smoke to hide his approach. Unfortunately, it hid the wyrmkeeper too. Though spell-scarred eyes ignored darkness and pierced illusion, they couldn't see through something that was real. But he'd taken careful note of the priest's position, so maybe it wouldn't be a problem.

He at least managed to scramble up onto the dais and into the heart of the smoke without hurting himself. At the same time, the coughing stopped. That was bad. If the wyrmkeeper had caught his breath, he could either cry for help or cast a spell.

Aoth glimpsed a shape in the smoke, plowed into it, and carried it down to the dais beneath him. In the process he inhaled smoke, and he too started to cough. Still, groping, he managed to grab the cleric's neck and squeeze.

After a while, the priest stopped flailing and scratching at him. Despite the burning in his chest, Aoth made himself stop coughing long enough to wheeze a counterspell. The magic cleaned the smoke from the air.

He lifted his head and peered over the altar. No one seemed to be rushing to the wyrmkeeper's aid.

He looked back down at the priest. The fellow was breathing.

You can fix that, Jet observed.

I could. But in theory, this whoreson is Tchazzar's holy servant. If I can, I want to find Cera and get out of here without killing anybody, and without anyone recognizing me.

He pulled off the filthy robe, stripped the priest of his outer vestments, and put them on. They were a poor fit, but might do at a distance. Since they too possessed a cowl, they were definitely more likely than his beggar's robe to pass inspection in the private precincts of the house.

He made sure the unconscious wyrmkeeper was well hidden behind the altar, then arbitrarily chose the door on the right. So far, no one had started modifying the rooms on the other side. *They just look like parts of an opulent private home, some in disarray from the celebrations and slovenly habits of the new residents.*

But Cera had to be there somewhere.

No, said Jet, *she doesn't. You only went in there on a guess. If there's nothing, get out before they catch you.*

I'll be all right, Aoth answered. *Most of the candles and lamps are out, and nearly everyone's asleep. . . .* Then, suddenly, peering through yet another doorway, he saw it.

Many aristocrats and wealthy merchants built homes that had secret areas, and the interim temple appeared to be one of them. A section of oak paneling was set a hair deeper than the pieces to either side. The button concealed in the trim was similarly recessed, and the grain in the darker wood didn't line up precisely.

No one else would have noticed it, certainly not across the length of an unlit room. But just as Aoth could see in the absence of light, so too did he view the world in minute detail.

He stalked across the nondescript, mostly unfurnished chamber and pushed the button. The catch clicked. He cracked the door open. On the other side, a spiral staircase twisted down to some portion of the cellars.

Aoth made sure he could easily reach the hilt of the sword beneath his stolen vestments. Then he started down.

* * * * *

The orcs howled as they charged. It was the fourth time they'd rushed their foes, but Oraxes still flinched. He couldn't help it.

The enemy crashed against the shields and the warriors who carried them like a great wave battering a rock. And after a time of frenzied stabbing, slashing, and shoving on both sides, like a wave they receded.

Or reeled back, or stumbled away, where they didn't lie dead or maimed on the ground. One of the things Oraxes had learned early on in this terrifying, fascinating night was that he mostly couldn't watch a battle and truly grasp the import of what he saw. But still he had a sense the orcs had had enough, and when his companions relaxed, he knew he was right.

A spearman spat. At some point, something had chopped or broken off the point of his weapon, but he'd continued fighting with the shaft in preference to the mace on his hip. Oraxes suspected it had something to do with reach.

"The mighty Red Spears," the sellsword sneered, and the warriors around him laughed.

A pillar of flame leaped up in the midst of the enemy formation.

For a heartbeat, Oraxes assumed that one of his fellows from Luthcheq had hurled an incendiary attack. Then he glimpsed a horned, skeletal head and clawed hands inside the blaze. Tall as a hill giant, the burning figure stalked forward while its allies scurried out of the way.

Oraxes and his comrades knew the enemy had spellcasters too, mostly conjuring from behind cover, just like their counterparts. The griffon riders in the air had loosed a lot of arrows at them. Seemingly to no avail, because periodically the bastards materialized some new entity to fight on their behalf.

Humor and scorn wiped from his face, the man with the broken spear looked around at Oraxes. "What is that thing?" he asked.

"I don't know," Oraxes admitted. But his instincts told him it was deadlier than any of the creatures that had preceded it.

He reflected with a pang of fear that he'd largely depleted his magic. Still, maybe he could destroy the thing before it came any closer. He spoke words of power and brandished his hand before him. Frost flowed over it from his fingertips to his wrist. He could feel that it was cold, but the chill wasn't painful.

Mimicking the attitude of his extremity, a huge, disembodied hand made of ice appeared in front of the oncoming fire creature. Oraxes reached and clenched his fingers shut, and the hand of ice did the same, gripping the entity around the torso and pinning its arms to its sides.

The demon, if that was what it was, snarled and heaved, and the hand of ice shattered. Oraxes gasped at a sudden hot pain. When he inspected his own hand, there were blisters spotting the palm.

He told himself it could have been worse. At least the entity hadn't broken his fingers.

Its aura of flame illuminating mangled corpses, as well as wounded men and goblinkin who struggled to crawl aside, the spirit advanced on Gaedynn and his archers. The bowmen stood in a somewhat protected position, with Oraxes's formation of spearmen on their right and a company of native Chessentans to the left.

The archers shot at the advancing fire thing for several moments. Some of them hit it too, but the arrows burned away instantly, and it was impossible to tell if they were doing any real damage.

Then, still steadily drawing and releasing, Gaedynn shouted, "Bows, fall back! Spears, engage!"

Oraxes's companions scrambled to plant themselves squarely in the fiery giant's path. He scurried after them.

As they reformed their shield wall and extended their spears, the demon was still a stone's throw away. But it swept one hand in an arc, and a tongue of flame leaped from its fingers to slash across several sellswords. They staggered and screamed, their garments burning.

The demon charged the point where it had weakened the formation. It snatched, snagged a sellsword on its talons, and heaved him into the air, letting him char in its fiery grasp for a moment before dashing him to the ground. It lashed out again, and a warrior's head tumbled off his shoulders.

Even several paces back Oraxes felt like he was standing next to a bonfire, and he soon saw that often, the creature didn't even have to attack a man to take him out of the fight. When their spears and clothing caught fire, or every breath seared their lungs, the mercenaries had no choice but to fall back.

More quickly than Oraxes would have imagined possible, given its steadfast performance against the orcs, the formation started to fall apart. The warriors weren't routed yet, but he could feel their fear just as he'd felt it when the orcs lost heart.

Griffon riders wheeled overhead, shooting, but their shafts didn't seem to trouble the demon any more than the ones Gaedynn and the skirmishers had loosed from the ground. The Chessentans kept their distance, unwilling to engage the thing that was ripping and burning its way through the sellswords. One spearman yelled, "Jhesrhi! Jhesrhi!" In his terror, he'd forgotten the Brotherhood's chief wizard wasn't there.

But Oraxes was, and he had to do something. He rattled off a spell, meanwhile making stabbing and slashing motions with both hands.

A dozen floating daggers materialized in the air around the demon. They too stabbed and sliced.

The demon snarled and sprang forward, smashing spearmen out of the way, extricating itself from the midst of the flying blades. Suddenly there was no one between it and Oraxes.

It slashed down at him. He jumped back and thought he'd avoided the attack. Then he felt fierce heat on his chest. He looked down.

He had two bloody grazes across his torso. But the truly alarming thing was that his tattered shirt and jerkin were on fire.

He dropped and rolled. But he couldn't put out the fire and defend himself against the demon too. It reached for him—

And kobolds rushed it from the left and slashed at its legs with short, heavy, cleaverlike blades. Some even climbed its legs to strike at higher portions of its body. Its corona of flame didn't deter them, and as he clambered back to his feet, Oraxes saw the reason why. They were already dead, and so incapable of pain, fear, or concern for their own survival. They didn't stop trying to carry out their reanimator's commands until they burned away to nothing.

Meanwhile, Meralaine chanted. The words sounded soft and dull, like shoveled earth dropping on top of a coffin, yet paradoxically they carried despite the din of battle. On the final syllable, she snapped a piece of bone in two.

The giant's halo of flame shrank in on itself, and for the first time Oraxes got a clear look at the inhuman skeleton at the heart of the blaze. Then the creature collapsed in a heap, with just a few small blue and yellow flames flickering among the bones.

Meralaine gave Oraxes a grin. "It was an immolith," she said. "An *undead* demon. So I knew how—"

Behind her, the immolith's fire leaped up again. Heaving itself to its knees, it reached for her. She pivoted, saw the huge, burning hand right in front of her face, and froze.

Oraxes cried a word of power and squeezed his hands together like he was making a snowball. Then he hurled the imaginary missile. It became real in midflight and struck the immolith's skeletal head in a burst of frost and steam.

An instant later, a black arrow punched into the side of the demon's skull.

The immolith collapsed as it had before. Panting, heart thumping and scratches and blisters smarting, Oraxes watched it for a while. It showed no signs of rearing up again.

"That was the last of those," said Gaedynn, striding nearer. Oraxes inferred that the sellsword meant the arrows he'd brought out of the Shadowfell. "Unfortunately." He peered at Oraxes's chest. "That doesn't look so bad."

Back home that dismissive comment might have incensed Oraxes. Here . . . well, he had to admit others had suffered worse. Much worse. "It's not. Are we winning?"

"Not yet," the archer said. "Maybe not . . . Never mind that." He turned to the spearmen who'd engaged the immolith and who were currently milling around in disorder. "Spears! What in the name of the Black Bow is wrong with you? Form up!"

* * * * *

Once Aoth descended to the secret portion of the cellars, there was no doubt whatsoever that wyrmkeepers had laid claim to it. They hadn't brought in a veritable treasure trove of icons the way Halonya had upstairs. But there were pentagons, and wheel-like emblems depicting five dragon heads with curving necks radiating from a central point, drawn with care on every wall. A rack in a cramped little armory held military picks, and, clustered together, the baneful enchantments smoldering in the steel made his teeth ache. The five tapers in every candelabra shined red, green, blue, shadowy black, and ghostly white.

Fortunately, he had yet to run into any of the wyrmkeepers themselves. He supposed they needed sleep like everyone else and would rather get it in a warm, properly furnished bedroom than a bare, chilly cellar, no matter how holy the latter was.

There'll be someone, said Jet. *Keep your guard up.*

Aoth passed a strong room, its sturdy, ironbound door standing ajar, and wondered how much wealth it had contained before the former householder cleared it out. Next came a torture chamber, sparsely equipped by Thayan standards—with only a rack in the middle of the space and a few whips, pincers, thumbscrews, and pears hanging on hooks on the back wall—but capable of inflicting its share of agony nonetheless. There were dry brown stains here and there, but even fire-kissed eyes couldn't tell just how old they were. Aoth scowled and quickened his stride a little.

But he need scarcely have bothered, because the one cell was just a few paces farther on, conveniently close to the torments. Her hands and ankles bound with coarse rope woven of multicolored fibers, a woman with golden hair lay on her side on the stone floor behind the iron bars.

"Cera!" said Aoth, keeping his voice low. "Cera!"

She opened her eyes and peered back at him. "Aoth?" she croaked. She seemed more dazed than joyful, like her captors had given her drugs or tortured the sense right out of her.

"Yes. Hang on." He tried the door. It was locked, and the key was nowhere in sight.

He drew his short sword. Among other things, it had raw force sealed inside it to enable the wielder to thrust or cut with prodigious strength. He slipped the blade between the door and its frame, right above the lock, pried, and released a portion of the power. The grille snapped open.

He hurried into the cage and kneeled down beside her. Up close she stank of blood, sweat, and other filth. "How badly are you hurt?" he asked.

She shook her head. "The rope . . . I can't think. . . ."

He set down the sword, drew a dagger, and sawed at the bonds that held her hands behind her back. They were tough and tried to squirm away from the edge of the blade like snakes. But he kept at it. Eventually one parted, and then the next.

"I . . ." she said. "I saw . . . there's a beast down here! A drake! A priest walks it by every so often. It stares at me like it wants to eat me." The action of the knife tugged on her arms, and she gasped.

"Did they rack you?" asked Aoth.

"I think . . . pulling on me. Yes."

He felt his jaw clench.

The last loop of rope confining her wrists parted. He shifted around to work on her ankles. "Once you're free, can you heal yourself? Enough to walk, and run if you need to?"

"I think so."

The final loop parted, and he pulled the writhing pieces of cord away from her feet. She closed her eyes, drew a long breath, and murmured a prayer. A warm golden glow supplanted the chill and shadowy dimness of the cellar.

And, down the hallway, something snarled.

Maybe the drake was close enough to see the magical sunlight, or maybe it had caught Aoth's scent. It didn't much matter which. Either way, it and its master were coming.

* * * * *

Hasos walked the battlements, spoke a word of encouragement to an archer or crossbowman from time to time, and surveyed the battle below. Pools of light periodically bloomed or guttered to darkness as wizards tried to illuminate their enemies and keep their allies hidden. Their supply of arrows depleted, griffon riders swooped down at the enemy like owls attacking mice. Masses of infantry shoved and ground together. Horsemen circled wide, maneuvering to attack some group of foemen from the flank or rear. Animated by sorcery, a trebuchet took laborious little steps. The throwing arm whipped like a scorpion's tail to hammer orcs and kobolds on the ground.

Hasos turned to the aide trailing along behind him. "What do you think?"

The man shook his head. "I don't know, milord. It looks like it could go either way."

Useless! Hasos thought, even though he knew it wasn't fair. A subordinate wasn't supposed to have keener judgment than his commander, and Hasos couldn't make up his mind either.

But precisely because he was the commander, he had to.

He could think of solid reasons to hold back. The war hero had put Aoth Fezim in charge, not Gaedynn Ulraes. The archer arguably had no authority to order Hasos to do anything.

And if the effort to break the siege failed, as it surely must without his wholehearted support, the Brotherhood of the Griffon would suffer heavy casualties. Afterward Tchazzar would strip Aoth of his authority, because the war-mage had abandoned his command at a crucial moment. Besides, no one would allow the captain of only a defeated, shattered company to lead the defense of an entire realm under any circumstances.

Which ought to benefit Soolabax, for how could it be wise to entrust the town's defense to a devil-worshiping Thayan arcanist? By the Yellow Sun, with the griffon riders gone, at least the food would last longer. The beasts ate prodigious quantities of meat.

But unfortunately, it wasn't just wretched outlander mercenaries trading spear thrusts and sword strokes with the kobolds and orcs. Aoth had mustered good Chessentan troops from elsewhere along the border, and they too would die without Hasos's support.

How could he call himself a true Chessentan noble if he let that happen? How could he ever again sit in the seat of judgment that he still privately thought of as his father's chair without a withering sense of shame?

He scowled. "Come on. Let's get to the gate."

He arrived in the nick of time. Faces twisted with anger, more of the sellswords stood facing ranks of Hasos's men, who had positioned themselves to protect the windlass that raised the portcullis.

"It's all right!" Hasos shouted. "We're going now! Save your anger for the enemy!"

A groom brought his destrier, and he swung himself into the saddle. Men and riders jockeyed about, returning to the positions they'd abandoned when the quarrel broke out.

Hasos nodded to the pair of men charged with turning the windlass. They did their work, and the grille rattled upward on its chains. Other fellows scurried to slide the enormous bar, then swung the gates open.

Heart thumping, mouth dry, Hasos brandished the sword of his ancestors, spurred his steed, and rode forth to attack the besieging army from one side while Gaedynn's troops harried it from the other. Pounding along behind him, his men howled like some titanic beast.

*   *   *   *   *

Aoth looked at Cera. Some of her bruises had faded. "Can you run?" he asked.

She shook her head. "Not yet."

"Keep working on it." As she began another prayer, he rose and rushed back out into the hallway.

The drake looked like a wingless red wyrm charging on all fours. It nearly filled the passage, making it difficult to discern the dragon priest behind it.

Scarcely slowing, the drake spewed slime. Aoth wrenched himself out of the way. The muck spattered the floor, where it sizzled and gave off vile-smelling smoke.

Unfortunately, the evasion deprived Aoth of the time necessary to cast a spell. Nor was there any ranged magic stored in his sword potent enough to neutralize the drake and its master too. Regretting the absence of his spear, he poised himself to receive the reptile's attack.

The spitting drake sprang in an attempt to carry him to the floor. Somehow, though there was barely room for it, he sidestepped, released more of the power inside his blade to augment his strength, and stabbed downward.

He missed the drake's neck but pierced its shoulder. The sword drove in deep, then tore free in a shower of gore as the beast plunged onward. A pulse of Cera's yellow light gilding its crimson scales, the beast reared onto its hind legs to spin around in the narrow hall. When it lunged again it was on three legs, the maimed one curled against its chest, but that didn't slow it down.

Aoth freed the last of the raw might stored in the sword, then heard the wyrmkeeper chanting at his back. A howl of frigid wind slammed into his back, knocking him forward. Off balance and chilled to the bone, he still tried to stab the onrushing drake. But it snapped, caught his sword arm in its teeth, and whipped its head.

Only the truesilver mail shirt he wore beneath his outer garments kept the shearing action of the fangs and the whipping action from severing his hand. As it was, the drake threw him to the floor, and the pressure of its bite was as unrelenting as it was excruciating. The armor wouldn't protect him for long.

The drake lashed him back and forth. He tried to transfer his sword to his free hand but couldn't reach it. He called darts of blue light from the blade to stab into the reptile's body. It snarled with pain, but that was all.

Her voice a little stronger, Cera chanted. A shaft of dazzling light blazed out of her cell onto the side of the drake's head and neck, burning red scales black and melting a slit-pupiled yellow eye.

Finally, recoiling, the reptile let go of Aoth. Then it glared in Cera's direction, and he sensed it meant to spit more vitriol. He heaved himself to his feet, flung himself at the reptile, and stabbed. Sadly, the weapon no longer had extra force to lend, but, bellowing, he put every iota of his own strength and weight behind the stroke.

The sword punched in one side of the drake's neck and out the other. The beast thrashed, and a flailing leg or tail clipped Aoth and knocked him staggering. As he recovered his equilibrium, the drake collapsed to lie twitching and bleeding on the floor.

He spun toward the wyrmkeeper. The priest was running and had already reached a branching corridor. He vanished around the corner before Aoth could even cast more shining darts from the sword, let alone recite an incantation. He growled an obscenity.

Which failed to improve the situation. So he turned back to Cera just as she came limping out of the cell. "If the whoreson didn't recognize me—" he began.

Cera smiled wryly and ran a finger along his bare, sweaty temple. Which demonstrated that at some point during his struggles, his cowl had fallen back, giving the dragon priest a clear look at his head—shaved scalp, tattoos, glowing eyes, and all.

He grunted. "Right. He did recognize me. So, now can you run?"

"I think I can at least hobble quickly enough to reach the stairs before our friend assembles every wyrmkeeper on the premises at the top."

"Satisfying as it might be to kill our way through the whole pack of them, we're not going out that way. Or at least I hope not."

"How, then?"

"Often if a rich man thinks he needs a secret area in his home, he thinks he needs a secret way in and out of the house as well. If there's one down here, I shouldn't have much trouble spotting it. Let's look."

When he saw how much trouble she was having keeping up, he put his arm around her and half carried her along. Then echoing voices called back and forth. The wyrmkeepers were coming after them.

They seemed to be proceeding cautiously, but it was still just a matter of moments before one of them caught sight of their quarry. Aoth had just about decided it was time to turn around and make a stand when he and Cera came to the largest room they'd seen so far.

The wyrmkeepers had turned it into the holiest part of their secret temple, complete with a sizable lacquered statue of their dragon goddess—batlike wings half unfurled, wedge-shaped heads glaring in all directions—that they'd somehow smuggled in. But what instantly snagged Aoth's attention were the tiny cracks defining a rectangle on the back wall.

In his haste he all but dragged Cera across the room, and she gasped in pain. "Sorry," he said, examining the hidden door more closely.

He found the catch and pressed it, and the panel clicked open. It was actually wood, with a stone veneer to make it look like the rest of the wall. On the other side was a tunnel. He and Cera scurried inside, and he shut the door.

"You realize," she whispered, "I can't see a thing."

"I know," he said. "I'll guide you."

He only had to do it for a short distance. Then they reached the end and a ladder leading upward. When he cautiously cracked open the door at the top, he found himself peeking out into a cobbler's shop where the air was redolent of leather. The place was dark at that hour, the proprietor likely asleep upstairs.

He led Cera inside. A little light seeped through the oiled paper windows, enough for ordinary eyes to discern the essential nature of the place, and so she breathed, "We made it."

He snorted. "Not yet. My guess is that the wyrmkeepers will run to Halonya, and she'll run to Tchazzar. But maybe we can get to him first."

FIVE

Some of the horsemen and griffon riders still had work to do. They had to chase the enemy warriors who'd fled the battlefield. Oraxes couldn't imagine how they'd find the energy. He felt utterly exhausted, and while his own contribution to the victory had required intense concentration, at least he hadn't had armor weighing him down or needed to swing a mundane weapon over and over again.

He'd ridden out of Soolabax behind Gaedynn on griffonback. Since the archer was busy elsewhere, he had to find the stamina to trudge back into the town. He made it through the gate, then flopped down on the ground with his back against a wall. A steady stream of soldiers passed before him, their strange mix of satisfaction and weariness a match for his own. The scene stuttered as he repeatedly dozed, then jerked awake.

"The sellswords who looked after me said I should stay and loot the bodies with them," said a soprano voice.

Startled, Oraxes snapped his head around. Meralaine was standing in front of him.

"But I was too tired," she continued.

He dredged up a sneer. "Besides, it's wrong to rob your friends."

She stared at him for a moment. Then she said, "No zombie ever cheated me or threw stones at me just because I had green marks on my hands. There are worse friends than the dead."

"And I guess that if you can't find any living ones, that's good."

She sighed. "I thought that fighting the immolith together might help us be friends. But maybe not. Is it because you think I want to be the leader of the mages?"

He frowned. "Don't you? You were certainly kissing Gaedynn's boots."

"I was not!" She hesitated. "But if I seemed like it, it was probably just because he and the other Brothers act like they don't hate arcanists. Why would I care about being in charge of just three other people? Especially knowing how contrary the rest of you are. Especially since this Jhesrhi person will take over the job as soon as she comes back."

He surprised himself by chuckling. "When you put it like that, it does seem kind of stupid. I just . . ."

"Was never put in charge of anything or anybody before?"

"I don't know. Maybe."

She sat down beside him. "You should learn necromancy. Then you'd always have dead things to order around."

* * * * *

Tchazzar kissed his way down Lady Imestra's body. Like so many Chessentans, she had a taut, athletic frame, and her milky skin was smooth as silk. She was also the wife of one of the city's principal lords, and that made her even more desirable. It had always been thus, and evidently a century in exile hadn't changed his proclivities.

At first she squirmed and arched her back in delight. He didn't notice precisely when that changed. Eventually though, he realized she'd started screaming and struggling, tangling her fingers in his hair and straining in a vain attempt to pull his head up.

When he raised it, he saw reddened, blistered skin. A trace of a red dragon's fire must have warmed his lips and tongue.

In wyrm form, mating with one of his own kind, he would have deliberately caressed his lover with his flame. He wondered if, addled by passion, he'd made an embarrassing mistake.

But that possibility only troubled him for an instant, and then he perceived the truth. He was a god, and so his divine nature protected him. Imestra couldn't bear his touch because she was disloyal.

"Traitor," he said. "Traitorous bitch." He jumped up, grabbed her arm, and jerked her off the broad canopy bed onto the gleaming marble floor.

"Majesty!" she wailed.

"I know how to deal with traitors." He dragged her across the floor to the chair where he'd tossed his clothing and the dagger he'd worn along with it.

Then someone knocked on the chamber door. "Majesty!" called the sentry posted outside. "Is everything all right?"

"In a way!" Tchazzar snarled. "My guards are evidently too stupid to keep traitors away from me. But fortunately a deity can protect himself!"

The sentry hesitated, then said, "A lot of people are here waiting to see you, Majesty. Even though it's late, and we told them you gave orders not to be disturbed. There's Lady Halonya, Lords Daelric and Nicos, the sellsword captain—"

"You mean Fezim?"

"Yes."

Even with the insight of a divine being, Tchazzar couldn't imagine what was going on. But it seemed clear he needed to find out. He started to call the guard in, then hesitated.

He'd proved Imestra's guilt. But would mere mortals understand that? It might make life simpler if he provided more conventional evidence.

He left her sprawled and sobbing, picked up the dagger, unsheathed it, and tossed it to clank down beside her. Then he told the sentry to come in.

"Arrest her," Tchazzar said. "Watch out for the knife she smuggled in."

"Yes, Majesty," said the guard.

"Arrest her pimp of a husband too. Where did you put all these folk whose problem can't wait until morning?"

"In the Green Hall."

"That will do." Tchazzar momentarily considered dressing properly, then decided that given the hour and the impromptu nature of the assembly, a robe was good enough. He pulled on one sewn of crimson mocado and headed for the door. Behind him, Imestra blubbered.

An escort formed around him as he exited the royal apartments, and they all marched into the Green Hall together. Tapestries depicting Chessentan naval victories adorned the walls. The seas in the woven pictures were the color one would expect. So were the tiles on the floor, and the upholstery on the high-backed, ornately carved chair atop the dais.

As Tchazzar seated himself, he surveyed all the frowning folk awaiting his pleasure. They stood in three clumps.

On his right were Halonya—he really would have to tell the poor child to stop second-guessing her dressmakers, jewelers, and hairdressers—a couple of her subordinate priests, and plump Luthen with his balding head and goatee.

In the middle, as if to separate the other two groups, were sour-faced, mannish Shala Karanok and one of her clerks.

And on the left were Jhesrhi, Nicos, Daelric, Aoth, and the sunlady the war-mage had brought to the coronation—Cera, that was the name. The priestess had scratches and bruises all over her, and her yellow vestments were torn and stained.

That seemed a little ominous, but what bothered Tchazzar more was seeing the only two mortals he completely trusted on opposite sides of the hall. Halonya was the visionary who most clearly perceived his divinity, while Jhesrhi was his luck, the agent of destiny who'd helped him escape the endless torture of the Shadowfell. Even the hint that they might be at odds was . . . disquieting.

He let the men bow and the women curtsey, then told them when it was enough. As they straightened up, he said, "All right, what is it?"

Several people starting babbling at once.

"Stop!" Tchazzar glowered at Shala. "*Chamberlain*, what is it?"

"Captain Fezim and Cera Eurthos were the first to arrive," Shala said. "That was a while ago. They claim that after she sneaked into your interim temple to look for evidence of treason, the sunlady was held against her will in a secret dungeon. They further claim the priests tried to kill both of them when Fezim entered the building to set her free."

"That's nonsense!" Halonya shrilled. "I'm told Cera Eurthos was detained—briefly—after she broke in to snoop around. Then the Thayan broke in too. Together they assaulted two of Your Majesty's holy servants and killed a sacred beast."

"Several days isn't 'briefly,' " said Aoth. "And what gives your gang of ruffians the right to lock up anyone for any length of time, under any circumstances? If they thought Cera had committed a crime, why didn't they summon the city guards?"

"The Church of Tchazzar is the instrument of his sacred will," Halonya replied. "Whatever we do is lawful and proper by definition."

"Amen," Luthen said.

"If your fellowship was truly and only the Church of Tchazzar," said Aoth, "that *might* be a proper sentiment. But Cera and I found proof that some of the folk who pledged you their service are really priests of Tiamat."

Tchazzar snorted. "Is that was this is all about? I already knew that, of course."

Aoth stared at him. "You did?"

"Why wouldn't they serve me, when I'm the Dark Lady's champion, and she's my mother and my bride? When I am her and she is me?"

Aoth took a breath. "Majesty, as I'm sure you realize, you're talking about mysteries beyond a mortal's understanding. What I do understand is that wyrmkeepers sent abishais disguised as dragonborn to murder me in Soolabax. There's every reason to believe they used the same ploy to commit the Green Hand murders here in Luthcheq. They captured

Jhesrhi and Gaedynn when they were in Mourktar and delivered them to Jaxanaedegor. They're enemies of Chessenta, and that means they're your enemies too."

"It's the way of wyrmkeepers," Tchazzar said, "to attach themselves to one dragon or another. Those who committed offenses against Chessenta plainly serve Alasklerbanbastos or his lieutenants. The ones who pledged their devotion to me are just as obviously a different group."

"Then why did they keep me prisoner for days on end without telling anyone?" Cera asked. "Why did they torture me to find out what I knew about their schemes? Why, if they have nothing to hide?"

"Frankly, milady," Luthen said, "if they held you for a little while and twisted your arm a bit, that's regrettable. But no more than you deserve for your meddling. Undertaken, I would assume, without the knowledge of your patriarch." He turned an inquiring eye on Daelric.

Stout and ruddy-faced, his yellow vestments trimmed with amber and topaz, the sunlord took a long breath, then let it out again. "I knew nothing about it, and, rest assured, I will discipline her. But I must also say that the person of a priestess of Amaunator is sacred, and I'm outraged at the treatment she's received."

Halonya made a spitting sound. "No one cares a turd about your outrage."

"Did you even *understand* that many of your new clerics are actually wyrmkeepers?" Daelric replied. "Did you even know they were holding a sunlady prisoner? I think not, just as I'm reasonably certain you can't perform even the simplest feat of divine magic to support your pretensions to sanctity."

"*I* proclaimed her a prophet and a priestess!" Tchazzar snapped. "Do you question my 'pretensions' to divine Power as well?"

Daelric's pink block of a face turned white. "No, Majesty, of course not. It's just . . . Lady Halonya is a visionary, but likewise an innocent. That may be precisely the quality that enables her to see what others don't. Still, to appoint her leader of your church and thus, in effect, a part of the government, is perhaps no benefit to anyone, herself least of all."

"Apologize," said Tchazzar. "On your knees."

Daelric swallowed. "Yes, Majesty." He started to lower himself before the throne.

"No," said Tchazzar. "To her."

The high priest faltered.

"Do it," Tchazzar said. "Or I'll break you into something so wretched that even an illiterate pauper will look like a queen to you."

Daelric stiffly kneeled before Halonya. "I apologize," he said, "for doubting your fitness for your office."

Halonya lashed him across the face with the back of her hand. The big red stones she wore on every finger tore his skin, and Tchazzar smelled the coppery tang of the beads of blood. "Now I forgive you," she said in a tone as sweet as honey.

It was funny, and Tchazzar laughed until he realized that except for Halonya, no one else was laughing or even smirking along with him. These humans didn't enjoy the perspective of a god, so he supposed they might not see the joke. Still, their failure to join in irked him nonetheless.

Well, if they wanted their master serious, so be it. There were still judgments to hand down.

"Captain Fezim," he said, "we have yet to explore a fundamental point. What are you doing in Luthcheq at all?"

"I came back to urge you to come to the border as fast as possible," the war-mage said.

Tchazzar noticed that unlike many other people, Aoth had no difficulty looking him in the eye. There was a part of him that respected that, and also a part that wondered if such boldness was the outward manifestation of disrespect. "I already told you I'll come when it's necessary."

"Majesty, it's necessary now. The dracolich is bringing all his strength to bear, including his circle of dragons. We griffon riders managed to kill a wyrm at Soolabax, but we can't handle all of them. Not without your help and the support of the troops still hanging around this city."

"Majesty, this is misdirection," Luthen said. "Since the Thayan already had your assurances, it's obvious he ignored his responsibilities in the field to search for his missing accomplice."

Like Daelric before him, Nicos didn't look happy about needing to speak up on behalf of his protégé, but he evidently felt that he couldn't let his rival's remarks pass unchallenged. "Majesty, who is Lord Luthen to criticize any decision that a soldier as famous as Captain Fezim might make concerning the conduct of the war?"

Luthen sneered. "He does have a kind of fame, I'll grant you that. Or maybe notoriety is a better word. For breaking his contract with the Simbarch Council of Aglarond, taking the zulkirs of the Wizard's Reach on a foredoomed expedition that cost each and every one of them their lives, and losing to a rabble of crazed demon-worshipers in Impiltur. When Shala Karanok was war hero, I warned her about trusting such a man, or relying on the judgment of the counselor who sponsored him. Unfortunately she ignored me, but perhaps Your Majesty will find a measure of prudence in my words."

"Yes," Tchazzar said, "if only because I don't like people creeping around behind my back." He fixed his gaze on Cera. "I leave your punishment to Daelric. I'm confident it will be severe, because I'm going to require him to donate the tenth part of your church's revenue until such time as my new temple is complete."

"Yes, Majesty." Daelric dabbed at his face with a bloody handkerchief.

Tchazzar turned his gaze on Nicos. "Poor judgment is a lesser offense than sacrilege. Still, it carries a penalty. You'll donate the twentieth part of your income."

"Yes, Majesty," Nicos said.

Tchazzar glowered at Aoth. "Now, what to do with you?"

The war-mage still had no difficulty meeting his gaze. "Nothing. Not if you're wise. Cera poked into the wyrmkeepers' business because she thought Amaunator wanted her to, for the good of Chessenta. Maybe she was right, or maybe not, and I was just as misguided to try and pull her out of trouble. Either way, this little affair means nothing compared to the defense of the realm. And you need the Brotherhood to see to that."

"You forget I've been to war with sellswords many times. I know what drives you. Your men will happily fight under a new commander if the price is right."

"I'd make damn sure of that before you do anything you can't undo."

Tchazzar recognized that he almost certainly could make good use of Aoth Fezim. But it felt like the mortal was defying him, and suddenly that blasphemy seemed more important than any mundane consideration of military matters ever could. He drew breath to order the Thayan's arrest.

Then Jhesrhi cleared her throat. It surprised Tchazzar a little. So often uncomfortable in crowds, she'd been quiet and still up until then, so much so that despite her golden comeliness and the esteem in which he held her, he'd all but forgotten she was there.

His anger cooling slightly, he said, "My lady? Is there something you wish to say?"

"I want to plead for clemency." She waved her tawny-skinned hand in a gesture that indicated Aoth, Nicos, Cera, and Daelric too. "For all of them."

"Are you sure?" Tchazzar asked. "It occurs to me that with Captain Fezim locked away to contemplate the fruits of sacrilege and insolence, you could command the Brotherhood of the Griffon."

"That's kind," the wizard said. "But I don't want to be a war leader. Even if I did, I would never want to steal what rightfully belongs to Aoth. He once saved me in much the same way. . . . What I mean to say is, I know in my heart that he and Cera truly were trying their best to serve Chessenta and you."

"They desecrated your sanctuary!" Halonya snarled. "They have to pay!"

"Not if His Majesty shows them mercy," Jhesrhi said.

"Witch!" Halonya replied. "Witch whore to a Thayan wizard! Naturally *you* don't understand the importance of sacred things!"

Jhesrhi took a long breath as though quelling the impulse to answer Halonya's gibe in kind. Then she said, "Majesty, you've been more than generous to me, and I'm grateful. But unlike Lady Halonya, I've never asked you for anything—"

"Liar!" Halonya cried, drops of spittle flying from her lips. "You asked him to let the dirty green hands live like honest people!"

"I was going to say," Jhesrhi said, her teeth gritted, "I never asked for anything *for myself*. Now, I am. If what happened on that dark hill we both remember means anything to you, pardon these people. At worst Aoth and Cera are guilty of overzealousness in your service. What's the point of punishing devotion?"

Tchazzar looked at the determination in the set of Jhesrhi's jaw and the blaze of her golden eyes, then at the rage and disgust manifest in Halonya's scowl and rigid posture. He realized he simply wanted the unpleasantness to end. Jhesrhi had a point. What did any of it mean, anyway?

Then he smirked. Because actually, there was a point of sorts. A secret the sunlady might conceivably have uncovered, if she'd been clever or lucky enough. But it wasn't a secret intended for human beings.

"All right," Tchazzar said. "I pardon everyone." He looked at Jhesrhi. "Understand, I'm still your friend. But if I owed you any sort of debt, this pays it. So no more talk of dark hills."

"I understand," the wizard said.

Meanwhile, Halonya glared. Well, another present or two should mollify her. For all his deficiencies as a high priest and counselor, Daelric was right about one thing. She was endearingly childlike in some ways.

"That's that, then," Tchazzar said, gripping the arms of the throne as he prepared to rise. "We can still get a little sleep before my brother Amaunator summons us from our beds."

To his astonishment, Aoth took a step forward. "Actually, Majesty, I still need you to tell me when you're coming north."

In truth, Tchazzar knew he had to go. He reminded himself several times each day he needed to announce his departure. But it was hard to forsake the pleasures of Luthcheq after decades of pain and deprivation.

Nor was he eager to launch a campaign that would take him back to Threskel and conceivably even the Sky Riders.

He didn't fear Alasklerbanbastos or any other foe he could fight with sword or fang. But no one could fight bad luck, and who could doubt that the hills were unlucky for him? It was there that the Blue Fire had crippled him and hurled him into the Shadowfell for Sseelrigoth to find and imprison.

"If Aoth says the matter is urgent," said Jhesrhi, "then I promise you it is."

And she'd be there with him, good luck to counter bad. He sighed and said, "So be it. Those of us who can fly will leave tomorrow. The rest of the army will follow as soon as it can."

* * * * *

It was like the night of Balasar's initiation. As he stood in the shadow of a stall on the dark Market Floor, laughter and the music of a mandolin, longhorn, and hand drum trio drifted on the breeze. He wasn't close enough to hear the clatter of dice, but his imagination supplied it, just as it put the tart heat of spiceberry liqueur in his mouth.

Although he didn't actually have to depend on imagination for the latter. He opened the pouch on his belt, removed a silver flask, pulled the cork, and took a swig.

Medrash might not have approved of him drinking when he had important work to do. But as far as Balasar was concerned, he'd earned a nip. Because it turned out that he didn't care for spying. Not so much because of the ongoing strain of trying to pass himself off as a true worshiper of the dragon god, although that could be nerve-racking. Because it was so cursed hard to find out anything.

He'd infiltrated the Platinum Cadre on the assumption that there was something truly sinister about it, something that tied it to the wave of calamities that seemed to be afflicting countries all around the Alamber Sea. But he still had no idea what that might be. It didn't become obvious just because a fellow wormed his way inside.

That left Balasar to grope for clues. Things that made no sense or didn't fit, although he had little faith in his ability to recognize them. How was he supposed to know what was anomalous when none of this praying and groveling before altars made sense to a rational, properly raised dragonborn like himself?

But finally, he noticed *something*. It might not mean anything, but, bereft of more promising leads, he meant to find out for sure.

Raiann was one of Nala's most fervent converts, and one far advanced in the mysteries. She swayed constantly from side to side like her mentor, went berserk in every battle, and could spew lightning a dozen times before running dry. More to the point, she'd abandoned her trade as a glassblower to serve the cult full-time.

So why did she still periodically slip away to the fields surrounding Djerad Thymar and fill a cart with fine white sand?

It was possible she was merely stockpiling the stuff for when the war ended and she could resume her profession. But hoping, if only forlornly, for a more damning explanation, Balasar had shadowed her to her dark, shuttered shop.

Two figures stalked out of the murk. Balasar couldn't make out their faces, but they too displayed the subtle slithering-straight-up-into-the-air tic that afflicted Bahamut's most devoted worshipers. They glanced around, then knocked on the door to the shop. Raiann opened it immediately, and the others went inside.

It was probably just Balasar's impatience playing tricks on him, but it seemed to take a long while for anything else to happen. Then hooves clopped on the granite, and Raiann drove her donkey out from behind the building. A tarp covered the sand in the bed of the cart, and the other cultists walked to either side like they were guarding something precious.

Balasar waited for them to get a little way ahead, then followed.

He wasn't surprised when they descended into the Catacombs, or when the wyrm-lovers subsequently chose a path that led into a part of them that wasn't patrolled. He just hoped they wouldn't turn down one of the passages where the working sconces gave out altogether.

Although he supposed they couldn't do that without striking a light of their own.

The echoing click of the donkey's hooves was somehow sad and dreamlike in the gloom. A draft from somewhere blew cold in Balasar's face and moaned almost inaudibly in his ear. It was like he was rubbing shoulders with a ghost, and it whispered his name as it brushed by.

Axles creaking, the cart turned another corner. Raiann or one of her companions whistled three ascending notes.

A signal? Balasar skulked onward even more warily than before. He peeked down the branching passage.

He glimpsed a surge of forward motion and the flicker of wings just beneath the ceiling. He started to look up, and then everything went black. At the same instant the floor beneath his feet became uneven. He lost his balance and fell on the hard edges of something. Stone steps or risers?

Before he could feel around and find out, something slammed down on the back of his head and neck. It reached around to scrabble at his face, slashing him just above one eye and just below the other.

He threw himself backward in an effort to crush his attacker between his body and whatever he was lying on. He grabbed, caught handfuls of what might be leathery wing, and shredded them with his claws.

Something hissed right beside his ear. Then his hands were empty. His attacker was simply gone, and his back and shoulders dropped through the empty space it had just occupied, giving him another bump.

A hiss rasped, then another from a point farther to the right. Balasar's assailant was in motion. He scrambled up, snatched out his broadsword, and cut at a spot where, he judged, its trajectory might have taken it. The blade whizzed through empty air.

Then one cold, slimy hand seized the wrist of his sword arm and dug its claws into his skin. Another, just bare bones smeared with deliquescence, gripped his throat, and the rotten stink of it filled his nostrils and made his stomach turn over. He realized his original attacker had hissed repeatedly to cover the noise of its ally's approach.

* * * * *

In time, Tchazzar dismissed everyone but Halonya and Jhesrhi. Perhaps he hoped to mend the quarrel between them. In any case, Aoth would have to wait for a private consultation with his lieutenant.

But there was someone else to talk to. When they were clear of the Green Hall, Nicos murmured, "I stood by you in there, even when Tchazzar's pet priestess cried for your blood."

"I know," Aoth replied. "We're in this together, and I'll look after your interests as you looked after mine."

"See that you do. And see that you acquit yourself well in the field." Nicos gave him a brusque nod and took his leave. Glowering, Luthen and Halonya's subordinates departed in a different direction even though, like Aoth's patron, they were presumably bound for the War College's primary exit.

Still a resident of the fortress, albeit in less exalted circumstances than before, Shala Karanok strode off in yet another direction with purpose in her gaze and, despite the hour, a spring in her stride. Her clerk had to scurry to keep up. Aoth inferred that she'd been impatient to march to war and meant to begin her preparations immediately.

With everyone else departing, that left him to watch the end of Cera's palaver with Daelric. Finally, looking about as glum as Nicos had, the high priest bade her farewell and tramped off with his underlings.

Aoth gave Cera a crooked smile. "Have you been properly scolded?" he asked.

She gave him a wry smile of his own. "I suppose."

"Well, one down, one to go."

"Is that why you rescued me? Couldn't you spank me instead?"

Flirting and banter generally came naturally to her. But now he saw that she had to make an effort, and no wonder. The wyrmkeepers had terrorized and tortured her. She said Amaunator's healing light had eased her body and mind alike, but she still needed time to recover.

"I rescued you for as debauched a reward as you're capable of giving," he said. "But later, when I'm not too tired to enjoy it. I'll stay with you for what's left of tonight though, if you want. I imagine we can prevail on one of the servants to find us a spare bedroom."

In fact, it turned out to be a nice one placed near the top of the fortress, with casements overlooking the city. Fire-kissed eyes could even make out the glimmering black thread of the River Adder some distance beyond. In bed, they lay on their sides, her back nestled against his chest. She'd only had the chance to clean up a little before the audience with Tchazzar, and her hair and skin still smelled of sweat. But it didn't bother him. He actually found he rather liked it, as he liked everything about her physical presence.

"I'm grateful that you came for me," she murmured, "and sorry Tchazzar was angry with you because of it."

He grunted. "Thanks to Jhesrhi, it worked out all right. And I know you only did what you thought Amaunator wanted. Black Flame, you pretty much warned me you meant to do it. I just didn't want to hear. Or maybe I didn't realize you'd go about it so crazily."

"It wasn't that crazy. You would have done the same thing in my place."

"But I would have known how to do it without coming to grief."

"Like when you sneaked into the wyrmkeeper's lair in Soolabax, about a hundred abishais tried to eat you, and I had to exorcise them?"

He tried to hold in a chuckle and was only partly successful. When his chest swelled, it gave her a tiny bump. "That was different."

"You know," she said, "nothing's changed. I still have to do this. Even Daelric . . . It's easy to think of him as more of a courtier and minister than a holy man. But he has his own connection to the Keeper. He wouldn't be the supreme sunlord of Chessenta if he didn't. And, annoyed as he was at me for stirring up trouble, when I explained why, he didn't order me to stop."

"Because he liked seeing somebody stick a finger in Halonya's eye."

"No. Or at least there's more to it than that. He senses that I truly am doing the god's bidding."

"And I suppose you still want me to help."

She hesitated. "You explained why you don't want to."

"That hasn't changed either. But curse it, I keep getting dragged into the thick of mysteries no matter how hard I try to stay clear. And they just keep getting murkier. Maybe I do have to figure them out to fulfill my contract and look after my men."

She rolled over and smiled. "You are going to help."

"Mainly, I'm going to defeat Threskel. That's still what's most important. But if I have time, if a chance presents itself, and if you promise not to do any more poking around on your own without my approval, then yes. I'll help you."

As if that highly conditional pledge settled everything, she kissed him.

* * * * *

There was a technique to breaking a grip on one's wrist. Balasar had learned it early and used it countless times against those who rightly doubted their ability to best him in a contest of weapons, but wrongly imagined they could out-wrestle or out-brawl a dragonborn smaller than the average.

Though startled by his new foe's assault, he automatically made the move. He twisted against the weak point where thumb and fingers met. His sword snagged on something in the dark—his adversary's body, presumably. But only for an instant. Then the blade jerked free, and so did his arm.

That left the grip that was crushing his throat and denying him air. It was awkward to use his sword at such close quarters, particularly when he couldn't see. But he thrust repeatedly. The weapon plunged into something mushy, then rasped on what he assumed to be bone.

Still the stranglehold persisted, and then his foe's other hand—the one that had more oozing flesh still clinging to the bones—locked on his neck. Though somewhat encumbered by the sword, he tried to break the hold by swinging his arm up, down, and across. It didn't work.

Knowing he had only moments left before his strength failed, he stepped in close, into the worst of his unseen foe's stench, and hammered at its head with the pommel of his sword.

Bone crunched. The clawed, clutching fingers dropped away from his neck. As he sucked in air, his foe's body thumped on the floor.

The winged creature hissed, and Balasar somehow sensed it swooping at him. He spat frost into the blackness. The thing screeched. And veered off, seemingly, because no fangs or claws ripped at him.

Not then. But he imagined the creature would take another run at him soon enough. Or something would. And no one would give a scrap of molt for his chances as long as he kept fighting blind.

So it was just as well he wouldn't have to.

Anticipating that his investigations might take him back into the Catacombs, or into some dark place, he'd brought a source of light. Events just hadn't given him a chance to take it out. But now, he hoped, he had the moment he needed.

He ripped open his belt pouch, snatched out a piece of black velvet, and dumped the silver ring inside it into the palm of his hand. The silvery glow of the moonstone in the setting leaped forth to illuminate the interior of a tomb with carved stone sarcophagi on low, stepped pedestals. He'd plainly lost his balance and fallen on one set of risers when he arrived.

The decaying occupants of the sarcophagi had shoved the heavy lids of their coffins partway open when necromancy or some other dark power called them forth. The zombie he'd stabbed and battered sprawled on the floor, fully dead once more. The other three were advancing on him. The smallest—the corpse of a dragonborn child, its eye sockets and the lesions in its face squirming with worms—was already close enough to strike.

It swiped at his arm. He tried to jerk the limb out of the way but was a split second too slow. The blow landed, jolting his hand. The ring flew from his palm to bounce and roll clinking across the floor.

It still gave light. But the winged creature swooped down from the ceiling, straight at it. He had no doubt that it could whisk the ring out of the tomb as easily as it had whisked him into it.

Even without the walking corpses pressing in around him, he couldn't have reached the ring first. He tossed his sword into his off hand, snatched the knife from his boot, and threw.

The dagger pierced the hurtling creature, and it vanished at once, like a soap bubble popping. Balasar still hadn't had a good look at it, nor could he judge whether he'd hurt it badly enough to keep it from coming back immediately.

But there was no time to worry about it. Slashing at his belly, groin, and thighs, the dead child drove in. Its elders did too. Claws raked to tear away his face, and he hopped back to avoid them. That landed him back on the three shallow steps leading up to the sarcophagus—or maybe on the steps of a different pedestal—and he stumbled and almost lost his balance once again.

Snarling, he kicked the child zombie. It reeled back and fell on its rump. By then, the full-sized ones were reaching out to tear at him from either side. It would be hard to strike at one without turning his back on the other.

So he heaved himself backward and rolled over the top of the sarcophagus. And scraped and banged himself up in the process. But he landed on his feet, and now he had a makeshift rampart between the walking dead and himself. They could only claw at him with difficulty, but he had no trouble slashing at them with the sword.

He concentrated on the one on his right, cutting slimy chunks away from its head. Meanwhile, the zombies started around the two ends of the coffin to close with him once more.

He rushed the one he'd been attacking. He landed a cut that split what remained of its skull, and it collapsed. By a happy chance, the child corpse had shambled up right behind it, and the two ended up on the floor tangled together.

He thrust his point deep into the child thing's tattered, wormy face, and it stopped struggling to wriggle out from under its larger comrade. He whirled. As he'd expected, the remaining zombie was right behind him. He cut, sheared slimy fingers from the hand that was reaching for him, then noticed how the creature's head dangled and flopped on just a rotted vestige of neck. He struck hard and decapitated it.

He felt a stab of horror when he saw that hadn't finished it. But at least it spoiled its aim, and he had little trouble evading its pawing as he kept on hacking pieces away. Finally, it too toppled and lay inert.

Panting, heart hammering, abruptly conscious of the sting of his cuts, Balasar picked his way through the corpses and the stray lumps and spatters of putrescence littering the floor. He recovered the silver ring and jammed it on his finger. Now no one could deprive him of light. He turned and surveyed his situation.

There was still no sign of the winged creature. Good. He hoped the wretched thing was busy dying a long and agonizing death.

The problem was that he couldn't see an easy way out of the vault either, only the oval piece of wall someone had mortared in place after the most recent interment.

Without the proper tools, could he remove it? Would he run out of air while he was trying? The thought was enough to make the stale, fetid atmosphere feel thin.

He spat fear away and told himself he wasn't going to die there. It had always been obvious that his end would be either glorious or scandalous, and suffocating alone in a box was neither.

So naturally, he finally did chip and bull his way out, though he ruined a good sword in the process. Beyond the hole he'd opened was a corridor lined with the sealed entrances to other tombs. One of the Catacombs' distinctive sconces hung on the wall, its glow faded to a mere hint of phosphorescence.

He still didn't know exactly where he was, but that was all right. If he simply wandered, he was bound to find a way back up to the Market Floor eventually. As he returned his ring to his pouch, lest its light attract unwanted attention, two thoughts were foremost in its mind.

The first was that he actually was on the trail of something incriminating. No one set a trap along a path without a reason to keep the wrong person from reaching the other end. The second was that he'd have to avoid his fellow dragon-worshipers for a couple of days, until healing magic erased all trace of the claw marks from his face and throat.

SIX

Tchazzar, Jhesrhi, Aoth, Cera, and Shala approached Soolabax with caution. Which turned out to be unnecessary, because the orange light of the setting sun revealed that the besieging army was gone. Nothing remained but burned and toppled trebuchets, unburied bodies, and trampled earth.

Scar screeched like he was angry he'd missed the fight. Jhesrhi peered down into the city. She wanted to know how many casualties the Brotherhood had sustained, but found it impossible even to guess from so high up and far away.

Tchazzar blasted flame across the sky. "A victory!" he thundered. "The first of my new reign!"

The flash and bellow made the folk down in the streets look up at the sky. When they saw the red dragon, they started to cheer.

Soolabax wasn't Luthcheq. There was scarcely room for Tchazzar to land inside the walls. But that didn't deter him. He somehow managed to set down in the intersection of three streets in front of Hasos's keep. A flick of one wing scraped shutters and paint from the facade of a house.

123

His tail swished and smashed a wooden horse trough, splashing the contents onto the ground.

Then he shrank, becoming the handsome warrior in red and gold. His companions landed beside him. For all her manifest toughness, Shala looked glad to be back on solid ground.

The enormous hawk the former war hero had ridden gave Jhesrhi a fierce, inquiring stare. She nodded, and it dissolved into a gust of air that stirred everyone's hair and cloaks, becoming pure wind once again.

Looking more serious than was her wont, plump, pretty Cera said, "There must be wounded. If Your Majesty will excuse me, I'll go help tend them."

Tchazzar smiled and waved a hand in dismissal.

Cera and Aoth exchanged a quick, fond look. Then the sunlady hurried away while Gaedynn, Hasos, and others came striding out of the keep.

Seeing the archer made Jhesrhi feel relieved but guilty too. The relief made at least a little sense. Gaedynn could have conceivably have died in the fight to break the siege, as any warrior could perish in any battle. But the guilt was nonsensical, yet another instance of the exasperating way just being around him could tie her emotions into knots.

The newcomers bowed, and Tchazzar quickly gave them permission to rise. "Well done, gentlemen!" he boomed.

"Thank you, Majesty," Hasos said. "The knights of Soolabax fought superbly."

"We Brothers and the fellows Aoth mustered from along the border were there too," Gaedynn drawled. "We held the knights' horses and such."

"And are there prisoners?" Tchazzar asked.

Gaedynn nodded. "Some."

"That too was well done," the dragon said. "Sacrifice them. It will give me the strength I need to crush Alasklerbanbastos."

For a moment, no one spoke. Then Shala asked, "All of them?"

Tchazzar grinned. "Why not? Every drop of spilled blood will make me more powerful. And it's easier than guarding and feeding the bastards, isn't it?"

"Probably so," said Aoth. "But there surely hasn't been time to question them all. We might be able to extract some useful information. We can certainly ransom the ones whose families have coin. And the sellswords might switch sides with a little coaxing."

"Besides," Shala said, "I've studied Chessenta's history—your history—and I don't understand. You never required such . . . such a thing in the past."

"No," Tchazzar said, gritting his teeth, "I didn't, and then when the Blue Fire took . . . Never mind. You've heard your orders. Does anyone have a mind to disobey?"

Another silence. Then Jhesrhi said, "Of course not, Your Majesty. Everyone here wants to serve you. It's just that there's a problem with carrying out your will."

Tchazzar frowned. "What's that?"

"Lady Halonya and the rest of your priesthood are back in Luthcheq, seeing to the construction of your temple. There's no one here to perform the sacrifices."

"Then Cera Eurthos and her clerics can do it."

"With all respect, Majesty, I doubt that. The Keeper's priests don't even sacrifice animals. I suspect they'd botch it, and then all that power would go to waste. Whereas if you keep the captives for a tenday or a month . . ."

The war hero fingered the ruby in the pommel of his sword. "You may have a point. But curse it, I'll have something to slake my thirst. Every twentieth man. Or orc, or kobold, or whatever."

"I'll see to it," Hasos said.

Tchazzar's smile flowered bright as before. "Good man! I'm thinking of creating a new knightly order, open only to those who render heroic service to a living god. You just might be the first inductee." He switched his gaze to Gaedynn. "And you the second."

"So long as the medal's made of gold," the bowman said. "That's the kind of honor a mercenary appreciates."

The dragon's eyes narrowed.

*   *   *   *   *

For the most part, the stairs, ramps, and walkways connecting the various parts of the City-Bastion honeycombed the granite. That left the walls of the atrium free for the private balconies that dragonborn considered an essential amenity of urban life.

But occasionally one of the paths that ran up, down, or across emerged into the open air. Maybe it was to allay the strange fear of enclosed spaces that afflicted people who weren't dwarves. At any rate it was pleasant to interrupt the long climb to the apartments of Clan Daardendrien on the strip of walkway, more or less a balcony itself. Since Khouryn was alone, no one else would guess that he was feeling the weight of his mail, or that his arse and thighs ached. It seemed to him that if a fellow could ride a griffon all day without distress, then he ought to manage just as well on a horse, but it apparently didn't work that way.

The granite balustrade came up to his chin, but the view was pleasant nonetheless. The ambient light had dimmed to mimic the night outside. Even high up the air smelled pleasantly of greenery, perhaps because so many dragonborn grew potted plants on their terraces. Lamps and candles glowed, and he made out the silhouettes of a household sitting down to a late supper. His belly growled, reminding him that he was as hungry as he was tired.

He supposed that meant he should resume the tramp upward and find out what his hosts' cook had prepared for the evening meal. As he turned away from the balustrade, he caught a pattering sound nearly inaudible amid the constant echoing murmur of the indoor city. Something that he couldn't see was rushing him.

He leaped to the side. His phantom assailant slammed into the balustrade. A portion of the railing came away from the rest and toppled into space. If Khouryn hadn't dodged, he would have fallen right along with it.

He hoped that, carried along by its own momentum and neatly caught in its own snare, his attacker would plummet. But as it seethed into visibility, the dark, scaly thing flapped its batlike wings, and the action held it poised on the brink of the drop. Red eyes glaring from its horned head, serpentine tail lashing, it pivoted while the piece of detached balustrade crashed to the floor far below.

The thing looked like some sort of devil, which meant it might have all manner of strange abilities. Khouryn judged that the sensible thing to do was kill it before it could demonstrate any more of them. He snatched for the urgrosh strapped to his back.

He'd just gotten the spiked axe into his hands when, its upper body jerking forward, the devil spat at him. Black fumes streamed from the fanged mouth in its bearded, satyrlike face.

The way the murky cloud expanded made it impossible to dodge. Khouryn bowed his head and raised his arms to protect his face.

The fumes seared him wherever they touched his skin. But his steel and leather trappings took the worst of it. Though his eyes stung and filled with tears, he could still make out the creature when it sprang. And still swing the urgrosh despite the pain.

The axe bit into the devil's torso. The stroke would have killed a dwarf or human, but the creature grabbed Khouryn by the arms. Its tail whipped around both their bodies to lash him across the back. His mail clashed. The tail whirled back into view, presumably for another stroke, and he saw the jagged stinger at the end of it.

He heaved, broke the grips on his arms, and chopped at the tail. The urgrosh cut it in two, and the devil screeched. Dissolving like breath on a windowpane, it backpedaled toward the gap in the balustrade.

Khouryn raced after it and got back inside striking range before it could become entirely invisible or retreat where wingless opponents couldn't go. He swung. The axe cut deep, smashing through ribs to cleave the organs beneath. The devil's legs buckled, and it fell. Its shuddering form became opaque once more.

When the twitching subsided, and he was satisfied the creature wasn't going to get up again, Khouryn looked to his own hurts. They weren't too bad—just blisters, basically. The worst damage was to his beard, not that that was an insignificant matter to a dwarf. Still smoking and sizzling in spots, it looked like an army of moths had attacked it, and its nasty burnt stink wrinkled his nose.

Half humorously, for he'd lived long enough in exile to know which parts of his people's customs and preoccupations looked comical to outsiders, he told himself that the person who'd conjured the devil would have to pay.

Maybe that was one of the ash giant adepts. He'd seen them summon a variety of horrors from their round crystal talismans, and it was possible they'd figured out that Khouryn was the one teaching the dragonborn to fight them to better effect. And then they'd decided to sneak an invisible assassin into Djerad Thymar to eliminate him.

But could a giant, who'd never set foot in the City-Bastion himself, instruct the devil to lie in wait along the particular route that Khouryn most often took to and from the Daardendrien apartments?

Maybe. Mages found ways to do lots of things that defied common sense. Still, it seemed unlikely.

He moved to inspect the balustrade.

Like any dwarf and any siege engineer, he understood stonework, and he saw immediately how the barrier was made of cunningly fitted sections. He saw too how it had been possible to detach one and leave it simply sitting loose in its place.

But would the devil have known how to do it? And if it had, where had it stashed its tools?

He wished, as he so often had since offering his services to the vanquisher, that Aoth, Jhesrhi, and Gaedynn were there. They were better at ferreting out secrets. Although it was also a safe bet that the archer would have made merciless sport of his singed and diminished beard.

*   *   *   *   *

Though he found it difficult to like a man who so openly scorned him and all who practiced his trade, Gaedynn had to admit that Hasos had done his bit during the battle. And that, tonight, he'd ordered the captives slain in a relatively humane fashion, by the simple expedient of stabbing them in the heart. Which fortunately seemed to satisfy Tchazzar.

The dragon had merely instructed that the bodies be laid on a pyre afterward. He then stood on the battlements of the keep, breathing in smoke and the smell of charred flesh like that was the way a god consumed the energy of a sacrifice.

Eventually he went back inside the citadel with most of the others in his inner circle, and Gaedynn surprised himself by lingering there with only drifting sparks and stars for company. He wasn't sure why.

The wind moaned. The fire leaped high, drawing a startled exclamation or two from the folk on the ground who were standing around watching it. The blackened corpses burned to ash in just a few heartbeats, and then the flames subsided to their former level.

Gaedynn turned and smiled at the woman who'd come up behind him. "Buttercup. I take it that Tchazzar finally decided he could do without you by his side for a little while. Or did you use magic to give him the slip?"

"Obviously," Jhesrhi said, "you were able to handle the battle."

"I handled it brilliantly," he said. "So well, in fact, that I think it's safe to say Aoth has become superfluous. It's time for the company to chuck him out and follow me. What would you say to a little mutiny?"

She gave him the scowl that was her frequent response to his jokes.

"No?" he continued. "Ah well. At least remaining in my current lowly estate will spare me the tedium of keeping track of the supplies and accounts. With Khouryn gone, the chore must be thrice as dreary."

"I hope he's all right," Jhesrhi said. "I hope he made it home."

"The Brotherhood is his home," said Gaedynn, "and I hope he comes back in time to help us fight the cursed dragons. By the way, I like your new outfit. It's very Red Wizard."

That brought a twist of genuine anger to her expression. "It's not like . . . It's a completely practical robe and cloak for a mage to wear to war."

"Is it? Then I suppose I'm just not used to seeing you put on new clothes until the old ones are covered in patches and falling apart even so."

"And I'm not used to hearing you speak to me with genuine spite in your taunts. Since you plainly don't want my company, I'll bid you good night." She turned away.

Fine, he thought, go, but then something made him speak up after all. "Wait. Stay if you like. I'm not angry at you."

She turned back around and, the golden ferrule of her staff clicking on the timbers, walked to the parapet. "At what, then?"

He waved a hand at the pyre. It was quickly burning down to orange coals, and the folk who'd stood watching it were drifting away. "That, I suppose."

Jhesrhi sighed. "Well, they were just kobolds."

"I know. Give Hasos credit for choosing those nasty little brutes if he had to butcher someone. Still, you know me, Buttercup. I'm not chivalrous. I'll cheerfully slit the throat of every bound, helpless prisoner and his mother too if I see a need for it. But this . . ." He shook his head.

"Well," she said, "each of them had committed treason by taking up arms against his rightful sovereign. It's common for people to pay for that offense with their lives."

"That assumes Chessenta's claim to Threskel is legitimate. Neither you nor I know that it is."

"Or that it isn't."

"My point is that if we don't know, the Great Bone Wyrm's people certainly don't. When they marched to war, they were just obeying the only rulers they've ever known."

"Maybe when they hear what happened here, they'll reconsider whether they really want to do that."

Gaedynn frowned. "I concede that sending a message might be a sensible reason to slaughter some prisoners. But that's not why Tchazzar did it."

Jhesrhi hesitated. "Sometimes a king doesn't explain his true reason for doing a thing. Not if he thinks he can gain some advantage by giving a false one."

"Why in the name of the Black Bow are you defending him? You thought he was being crazy and cruel just like the rest of us did. That's why you tried to talk him out of it. And why, just now, you made the fire flare up to burn the bodies quickly. You're ashamed of what he did."

"All right. There may be moments when his mind isn't altogether clear. If something had tortured and fed on you for a hundred years, you might have the same problem. He'll mend with time."

"Have you seen any signs of it so far?"

She scowled. "You shouldn't talk about him this way."

"Why not? Are you going to tattle?"

"Of course not! But when we first arrived, you were impudent to his face. That's . . . unprofessional, and bad for the company as a whole."

He realized she was right, but he didn't want to admit it. "I thought working for the zulkirs was bad, but at least they were sane."

"You're only seeing one side of him. He ended the persecution of those with arcane gifts."

Which you hope will ensure that no more little girls suffer the way you did, Gaedynn thought. But what he said aloud was, "And, more importantly, gave you the chance to flounce around in silk and jewels and play the princess."

"Enough of this," Jhesrhi rapped. "Enough of you." She turned back toward the stairs that led down into the keep, and that time, he didn't try to stop her.

* * * * *

The battlefield lay in the borderland between the desolation of Black Ash Plain and the fertile fields of Tymanther. There were no columns of solidified ash sliding around—which was good, since the giant shamans used them as weapons. But the vegetation was sparse and twisted, and when the breeze gusted from the south, the air smelled faintly of burning.

After the dragonborn had destroyed several giant raiding parties, the rest joined together to make a stand. They waited like gaunt, crudely sculpted figures of stone. Medrash studied their ranks, looking for the leader strong enough to unite the once-contentious barbarian tribes. He couldn't identify him. So far, no one had.

The giants stood with little apparent organization. Facing them across the length of the field, the Tymantherans had more, although Khouryn had grumbled that they still looked like a motley assortment of little armies instead of one big one. Lance Defenders and anyone else who'd received the dwarf's training stood in what amounted to one coherent formation, and the warriors who marched under the banners of the Platinum Cadre in another. Small war bands organized by various clans had rather haphazardly taken up positions between and around the two larger ones.

Balasar naturally stood among the dragon-worshipers. Medrash fought the impulse to make eye contact or even glance in his clan brother's direction. Balasar had told Nala and Patrin that his newfound devotion to Bahamut had estranged him from his kin, and Medrash didn't want to do anything to jeopardize that impression. He contented himself with silently asking Torm to strengthen his comrade's arm in the fight to come.

Horns sounded overhead. Tarhun was in the air riding a bat, and so were the buglers the vanquisher used to relay his orders to his troops.

Dragonborn archers drew and loosed. Bat riders swooped toward the enemy, and they too shot arrows. Medrash knew that every bowman who'd spotted an adept was trying to eliminate that particular target.

Meanwhile, the clan wizards chanted in unison. Wind howled in the faces of the giants. The idea was to scour away every stray fleck of ash on the plain before the shamans could use it to conjure one of their reptilian servants.

The giants heaved enormous javelins and rocks, the raw strength of their towering frames a match for the mechanical power of a bow. Dragonborn reeled and fell. A horse screamed, collapsed, and—rolling and writhing—ground its rider beneath it. A bat plummeted.

Meanwhile, impervious to the arrows streaking at them—or so it seemed—the adepts brandished their colored globes. The polished curves gleamed in the sunlight, and hulking, scaly creatures sprang into view.

They didn't scramble from drifts of ash, because the dragonborn mages had blown those all away. They leaped out of nowhere. Medrash realized they always had. The giants, to confuse their enemies, had simply made it look like ash was necessary.

A couple of the beasts looked like stunted, misshapen red dragons. Flames leaping not just from their jaws but rippling across their entire bodies, they jumped into the air, lashed their leathery wings, and soared toward the bat riders.

Other shamans summoned the winged green creatures and gray lizard-bears Medrash had encountered previously. The former hopped and glided, and the latter ran—but snarling and screeching, each charged the dragonborn ranks in its own particular fashion.

Behind them, hunched, dwarf-sized creatures skulked from nothingness. Their hide hung in loose brown folds, and their long arms dragged on the ground. Evidently intending to harass the Tymantherans from the flanks, they headed for the edges of the field.

"Lances!" Medrash bellowed. A split second later, the brassy notes of a bugle cut through the air. The vanquisher was ordering him to take the same action he'd just begun on his own initiative.

He felt taut with eagerness, because he'd learned from experience that Khouryn's methods worked. And they now had a chance to demonstrate that to a great many dragonborn, the vanquisher included. Everyone would see that Tymantherans didn't have to betray their ancestors and grovel before those heroes' ancient enemies to defeat the giants. No matter how many new tricks the savages mastered.

More smoothly and uniformly than they had mere days before, all the lancers canted their lances at the proper angle. On Medrash's command, they walked their horses forward. Then trotted. Then cantered. Their weapons dropped to threaten the onrushing saurians, and then they broke into a gallop.

But Medrash's brown gelding only ran for a couple of strides. Then the animal balked, nearly pitching its startled rider out of the saddle. The horse tossed its head and whinnied.

* * * * *

Shields overlapping, all but marching in stride, the spearmen advanced in good order. Khouryn gave a slight nod of satisfaction, then saw disaster strike Medrash's charging lancers.

Almost every horse spooked at the same instant. Despite the long weapons in the lancers' hands, and the way they were riding nearly shoulder to shoulder, some of the steeds managed to halt, turn, and bolt toward the rest of the vanquisher's army. Their masters were the lucky ones. Other animals slammed into their fellow steeds and knocked them stumbling, or off their feet entirely. Dragonborn yelled, hauled on the reins, and dug in their spurs, fighting to regain control. Meanwhile the first wave of conjured creatures swept over them. A glider ripped a warrior from the saddle. A lizard-bear seized a horse in its fangs and wrenched it down onto the ground, breaking both its front legs in the process. The steed screamed and thrashed. Vapor billowed from around the reptile's jaws as its corrosive spittle ate its way into the animal's flesh.

"Rock of Battle!" Khouryn cursed. "Charge! *Charge!*"

"That will break the formation," said a sergeant who'd apparently learned the lessons of drill a little too well.

"To the Abyss with the formation!" Khouryn roared. "Run up there and kill something!" Before the enemy killed every one of the riders.

* * * * *

Medrash's horse bucked and reared. He decided he had to get off before the animal threw him. He dropped his lance and kicked his feet out of the stirrups, which made his bouncing perch even more precarious than before. Clinging to his saddle with his one free hand— his shield prevented the use of the other—he swung his leg over the gelding's back and jumped.

He landed with a jolt, staggered a step, then caught his balance. All around him, gray and green reptile things lunged and pounced, rending dragonborn who were virtually unable to defend themselves. Posing nearly as much of a danger as the saurians, horses with bloody wounds and fuming burns surged one way and another.

At least, since he was no longer fighting his own terrified mount, Medrash could more easily focus his will. He took a deep breath, let it out slowly, then reached out to Torm.

The god's Power rushed into him like a flash flood surging down a gorge. He shook his steel-gauntleted fist above his head.

The sun was shining. A lesser light should have gone unnoticed. But somehow brightness, or a sense of it, pulsed from his hand. With it came a suggestion of quiet that was just as paradoxical amid the roars, shrieks, and crashes of blows on armor. For some distance around him, saurians hesitated in midattack. Horses stopped resisting the dictates of spur and rein.

Unfortunately, the artificial tranquility would only last for a few heartbeats. "Dismount!" Medrash bellowed. "Fight on foot, but like Khouryn taught you!"

Riders swung themselves down from their mounts. Shaking off passivity, one of the gray saurians charged a dragonborn who had one foot still in the stirrup and one on the ground.

Medrash couldn't intercept the threat in time, but his breath could. As he snatched for the hilt of his sword, he spat lightning. The crackling flare seared the lizard thing's body, bursting some of the tumorlike growths bulging from its flank. It stumbled and jerked for the moment the punishment lasted, then whirled toward the one who'd hurt it.

Medrash let it come to him, then sidestepped just as it rushed into striking distance. Its snapping jaws still bashed his shield and jolted his arm, but at least its momentum didn't knock him off his feet. He cut into the creature's hide and shouted "Torm!" The god's Power manifested as a thunderclap. Though Medrash perceived just how supremely loud it was, he heard it without distress. But, unprotected by the Loyal Fury's grace, the lizard thing lurched and roared like it had suffered a second and even more damaging sword stroke.

But that didn't finish it either. It spun in Medrash's direction, tearing his blade from its body and splashing him with a droplet or two of blistering fluid. It struck at him, and he interposed his shield. The attack slammed into the obstruction, and then the saurian twisted its neck and caught the edge of the shield in its fangs. It gnawed as it lashed its head back and forth. Bits of smoking, dissolving oak and hide fell away from the shield. Medrash's arm throbbed like it was coming out of its socket. He staggered in a frantic effort to keep his foe from yanking him off his feet.

He cut at the lizard-bear, only to find that off balance as he was, he could do no more than scratch its hide. He tried to pull his arm free of the straps securing it to the crumbling shield but, perhaps because of the attitude into which his adversary had twisted it, he couldn't.

He pushed aside incipient panic and drew down Torm's glory once again. He willed the saurian to recognize the Power burning inside him, and to fear it.

Which, from a mundane perspective, was absurd. At that moment, the lizard thing was like some enormous hound at furious play, while he resembled its helpless bone. Yet the brute faltered, its eyes widening.

Medrash recovered his balance, stepped, and thrust with all his strength. His sword punched deep into the creature's skull, and its legs buckled beneath it. But even in death it clung to the shield, and so dragged him down to the ground along with it. Finally, on one knee, he managed to slip his aching arm from the loops.

A shadow fell over him.

Instinct made him raise his shield arm as he turned. The slashing wing claws that might otherwise have shattered his skull or broken his neck clattered against his armored limb instead. Still, the multiple impacts stabbed pain through the already-tortured arm and flung him backward, away from the dead lizard-bear and the sword still embedded in its head.

The glider landed on its short, thick legs, then pivoted. Medrash scrambled toward his weapon. The saurian's head snapped forward. Its jaws opened wide and spewed greenish vapor over him.

Medrash's skin burned, and his eyes filled with blinding tears. He started coughing and couldn't stop. He needed to use Torm's Power to cleanse him of poison, inside and out, but he knew his foe wasn't going to give him the chance.

Then a spear jabbed through one of the creature's batlike wings. It snarled, turned, and found itself facing three more such weapons, two aimed high, the other low. It whirled a wing back to slash with the bony fingertips protruding from the scalloped edge, and its foes backpedaled. More spears jabbed it from behind, as warriors assaulted it with the same tactics they'd employed against the hovering wooden Beast.

Despite the handicap posed by his burning nose, mouth, throat, and lungs, Medrash wheezed a prayer. All his pains eased, including the fierce one in his shield arm. He flexed it and found that even if had been broken a moment before, it wasn't anymore.

Tears still streaming from his eyes, he scrambled onward to the lizard thing's carcass and jerked his sword out of it. Then he drew himself to his feet and looked around.

On every side, dragonborn fought saurians and the ash giants who'd advanced behind the conjured horrors. Some of the warriors were the surviving members of Medrash's dismounted cavalry, often using lances as spears for the sake of the reach they provided. Others were actual spearmen, who must have rushed forward to support their embattled comrades. Medrash recognized the hammer and axe emblem of the company Khouryn was commanding personally, although amid all the howling, crashing frenzy, he failed to spot the dwarf himself.

He could see that in such chaotic circumstances, when a new enemy could come at a fighter at any instant and from any side, Khouryn's tactics were less effective than they might have been otherwise. Still, they were working to a degree, and as a result the fight wasn't over yet.

Medrash looked around for a fallen lance, spear, or an intact shield. He failed to find any of them in his immediate vicinity, but spotted a battered heater lying between a giant's bare, filthy feet. He shouted a battle cry and charged.

* * * * *

Balasar winced when the horses balked, turning what should have been a devastating attack into little more than a sacrificial offering to the ash giants and their reptilian pets.

To their credit, Patrin and some of the other cultists looked just as horrified as he felt. Nala, however, simply kept swaying back and forth and crooning a sibilant prayer or incantation.

Over the course of the next little while, Medrash managed to jump off his panicked steed and use his paladin gifts. Balasar couldn't tell precisely what his clan brother had done, but it seemed to affect everyone and every beast in his vicinity, and to create a pocket of savage resistance in what was otherwise a massacre.

Then Khouryn's spearmen charged up to engage the enemy. Other dragonborn might follow eventually, but—perhaps astonished by the bloody fiasco the lancers' charge had become—they were slow to act. Nor were the flying trumpeters sounding the signal. Maybe Tarhun was currently incapable of giving the order.

In any case, it seemed clear that without more support that even Khouryn could provide, the Tymantherans fighting in the center of the field couldn't hold. Balasar turned to Patrin. "We have to help them."

"I agree," Patrin said. But instead of ordering everyone forward, he wound his way through his swaying, twitching, shuddering troops toward Nala. Balasar followed.

When he came close enough, he felt the sting of the magic seething in the air around her. It muddled his senses—for an instant, he experienced the purple of her robe as a sweet stink like that of rotting flowers and the unevenness of the ground beneath his feet as a shrill glissando.

With one hand, Nala gripped her staff. The other was clenched too, and Balasar's intuition told him it was holding something, even though no trace of the object protruded beyond her fingers.

He suddenly suspected he knew exactly what sort of spell she was working. And if he'd been confident of his ability to prove it afterward, he would have run her through that instant.

"Sir Balasar recommends that we attack immediately," Patrin said. He'd stopped walking, but his beard of chains was still swinging and clinking a little. "I do too."

Nala looked annoyed at having to suspend her chant, then smoothed her features into a fonder though solemn expression. "Not yet," she said. "The god will tell me when the moment is right."

"Our comrades need us now," Balasar said.

"I promise you," the priestess said, "I'll give the word as soon as I can."

Right, thought Balasar. Just as soon as Medrash and Khouryn's warriors are dead, and the new tactics discredited. As soon as you can once again make the claim that only dragon-worshipers can defeat the giants.

"As soon as you can," said Patrin. He turned away.

As they strode back to their positions in the vanguard, Balasar said, "No one respects Nala more than I do. As our priestess. But you're the soldier. The war leader. If you think—"

"No," Patrin said. "It's as hard for me as it is for you, but no. Why did we march here under this banner"—he nodded to indicate the purple pennon with the platinum dragon coiling down its length—"if not to assert our faith?"

Actually, Balasar thought, I'm here to destroy your ridiculous creed. But not at the cost of Medrash's life. He would have forsaken the cultists and run forward to help his kinsman that instant, except that it would have been an empty gesture. A single warrior couldn't turn the tide, no matter how skillful he might be. He needed all the split-tailed sons of toads swaying and jerking around him.

Swaying and jerking . . . with the fury of the dragon god boiling up inside them, they were as frantic to attack as he was.

Balasar started writhing like the others. "Bahamut!" he howled. "Bahamut!" His companions echoed the cry. He clashed his sword against his targe, and the others did that too.

He gripped his weapon midway up the blade, then used the foible to slice the right side of his face, where the bone piercings of Clan Daardendrien wouldn't snag it. He swept the sword through the air, spattering his neighbors with drops of blood. "Bahamut!" he roared.

The wyrm-worshipers cut themselves too. It spread through their disorderly ranks like a ripple in a pond. Balasar then punched the olive-scaled fellow on his left.

The cultist rounded on him with rage in his eyes and tongues of yellow fire flickering between his fangs. Balasar screamed, "Bahamut!" And instead of spitting flame at him, the dragon-lover punched him back, then turned to give someone else a shove.

When they were all thumping one another, Balasar judged that they were about as crazy as he knew how to make them. He brandished his bloody sword at the melee up ahead, bellowed, "Kill!" and charged.

For a heartbeat or two, he had the horrible feeling that despite all he'd done to stir them up, no one was going to follow. Then the cultists too screamed, "Kill!"—or else the name of their god—and pounded after him.

He would have been happy to let them catch up. Unfortunately, a person couldn't pretend to be mad with bloodlust and behave cautiously at the same time. So he kept running as fast as he could, and met the enemy before any of his companions.

But not the enemy he wanted to engage, not the ash giants and green and gray reptiles locked in battle with Medrash and Khouryn's troops up ahead. Earlier he'd noticed the brown, hunched, long-armed creatures with dangling folds of skin maneuvering to the edges of the battlefield. Now they came scurrying forward to attack the charging cultists' flank.

They didn't look like much of a threat compared to either the ash giants themselves or the other minions the barbarian adepts had summoned. Balasar hoped the ones that managed to intercept him would only delay him a moment or two. Then a pair of them lashed their arms at him like they were throwing rocks.

Wind screamed. Either scooped from the ground or simply conjured out of nothing, sand battered Balasar. It stung his eyes, forced its way into his nostrils and mouth, and choked him.

Blinking and spitting, he covered up with his shield, then peeked over its rim as soon as the blast subsided. Through a stinging blur of tears, he saw the brown creatures rushing him, one a scuttling stride or two in advance of the other.

Turning back and forth, he pretended he couldn't see them at all. Then he lunged and cut at the head of the one in the lead the instant it came close enough.

The brown creature's body dissolved in a puff of sand, and the sword swept through the grit. The sand leaped several paces away, where, swirling, it congealed into solid flesh and bone once more.

The trick startled Balasar, but not enough to make him lose track of the second sand thing, which had scrambled around him to strike from behind while its comrade had him distracted. He whirled and shifted his shield, and claws rasped across its surface. He riposted with a chest cut, and the creature collapsed. It was reassuring to see that the things couldn't evade every attack by dissolving into dust.

He whirled back toward its partner. It cocked back its apelike arm to hurl more sand. Balasar spat frost at it.

Its staggered and pawed at the rime suddenly encrusting its blunt-snouted, lizardlike face. Balasar rushed it. It wiped the ice off its eyes just in time to see the slash that sheared through its throat.

Balasar looked around. The sand things had proved tougher than anticipated, but, frenzied, spewing their breath weapons repeatedly, the members of the Platinum Cadre were making short work of them. He judged that in a few moments, everyone should be ready to race on to the real fight up ahead.

Then a huge black bat slammed down on the ground—not plummeting, but almost. A split second later, the life went out of its eyes.

Mangled and burned, it had plainly given the last of its strength to save its rider from a fatal fall.

For a moment Balasar thought it a valiant effort wasted, because the big dragonborn slumped into the saddle looked as dead as his steed. But then the fellow groggily lifted his head, revealing the square gold studs pierced into the green hide under his eyes. The rider was the vanquisher himself.

His trappings and armor charred, as was, no doubt, some of the flesh beneath, he fumbled with the straps holding him in the saddle. Then something else, something bigger even than a Lance Defender's mount, thudded down on the ground.

Like Tarhun's bat, the crimson reptile had shredded wings, with arrows embedded in various places where its halo of fire had yet to burn them away. It might have trouble returning to the air. But judging from the way it immediately headed for the vanquisher, each step igniting grass and weeds, it still had plenty of fight left in it.

Alas, Tarhun didn't. He managed to unbuckle the last of his straps, dismount, and lift his greatsword as high as his chest. Then he collapsed.

* * * * *

Patrin had three brown opponents alternately trying to flense the flesh from his bones with their talons or scour it off with blasts of sand. Still, as he pivoted to and fro, he glimpsed the maimed bat's plunge to earth and all that followed. He saw Balasar sprint to interpose himself between the huge red beast and the sprawled, motionless Tarhun.

No lone swordsman, no matter how skilled, was a match for such a behemoth. Patrin decided he had to help, and quickly. He'd held off using Bahamut's gifts, saving them for foes more formidable than his current adversaries, but now he reached out to the Platinum Dragon for aid.

Power thrilled along his nerves. It simultaneously seemed to descend from above and to well up inside him, a sensation impossible to describe to anyone who hadn't experienced it for himself.

Patrin whirled his sword in a circle, and brightness—or the pure, rarefied idea of it—exploded from the blade. The light became a spinning horizontal wheel of glowing glyphs with himself at the hub. Assailed by their holy Power, the summoned creatures shrieked and floundered backward.

He didn't know how badly he'd hurt them, nor did he care. Someone else could finish them off if need be. The important thing was that they didn't have him tightly surrounded anymore. He ran toward Balasar and his enormous foe.

Flames leaping from its jaws, the crested, wedge-shaped head at the end of the long neck struck like a snake. Balasar managed to sidestep and land a cut three times. But on its fourth bite, the reptile caught the edge of his shield in its fangs. It used that hold to pick him up, whip its neck, and fling him to the side. He slammed down hard and slid, and the beast strode on toward Tarhun. Either it innately understood that the dragonborn monarch was the more important target, or its summoner had so instructed it.

Fortunately, Patrin judged that Balasar had delayed the beast just long enough for him to place himself between the reptile and Tarhun and play the same role his comrade had played. But as he put on a final burst of speed, as he neared the huge creature and saw it even more clearly, doubt suddenly assailed him.

It had nothing to do with fear for his own survival, although obviously that was uncertain in the extreme. Rather, it involved the essential nature of the creature he was about to challenge.

He'd noticed that all the beasts the giant shamans summoned with their crystal globes shared certain characteristics with dragons. All, even the brown, hunched sand things, appeared reptilian. Some possessed acidic spittle or poison breath.

Still, the fiery beast was different. Patrin didn't think it was a true wyrm, but it was so like one that he wondered if, despite all the manifest reasons to do so, it could be right for a champion of the dragon god to oppose it.

But his uncertainty only lasted a heartbeat. Then came a surge of supernal strength he hadn't even requested, and with it clarity. He often asked Bahamut for guidance. For once, the god had chosen to provide it, assuring him without the necessity of words that it was, in fact, his sacred duty to battle creatures like the one that loomed before him.

When the reptile struck, it was like a tree or tower falling at him. He leaped aside, which saved his life, but didn't spare him from the blistering heat the saurian radiated like an oven. Grateful that at least at the moment flame didn't shroud the thing's entire crested head, he stepped in, shouted the name of his god, and cut.

Guided by Bahamut's Power, Patrin's sword found a place where the creature's scales overlapped imperfectly. As a result, the stroke bit deeper than any of Balasar's efforts. The creature jerked its head high. Hot enough to scald, blood showered down. Patrin twisted away to protect his face.

Unfortunately that meant he'd looked away from his foe, and instinct immediately screamed that he'd made a mistake. He sprang from the shadow of the immense foot hurtling down to crush him. Something—the tip of a claw, he realized—snagged the back of his surcoat and started to yank him down onto his back. But then the purple garment ripped instead. He reeled, then caught his balance.

As he turned, the ruined surcoat slid down low enough to hinder the action of his arms or even trip him. It was on fire too. But he didn't have time to rid himself of it, because his foe was already striking at him again.

He leaped aside, then hurled more of Bahamut's Power. Silvery light flared from his sword to splash across the side of the reptile's head. Its neck twisted as it oriented on him once again, but it moved more slowly than before. The god's Power had robbed it of its quickness.

Patrin tore the tattered, burning surcoat off his body, then dashed past the creature's head to its body. He thrust, seeking the enormous heart that had to be beating somewhere behind its armor of scales.

The sword drove in deep. But it didn't stop the beast, which tried to stamp on him. He dodged out from under its foot, slashed the extremity, then glimpsed motion at the periphery of his vision. He turned his head. Blazing jaws open wide, the creature was twisting its neck around for another bite.

Good. Maybe this time, with Bahamut's Power hindering the saurian, he could put out one of its eyes or even reach the brain behind it.

But then, in midstrike, the creature broke free of the lethargy with which his magic had afflicted it. Suddenly its head was streaking at him twice as fast as before. Caught by surprise, he couldn't dodge, only attempt to interpose his shield.

It was enough to save his life. But the crashing impact flung him backward and slammed him down onto his back. Flame leaping and rippling across its entire body, his foe reared over him. He lifted his sword to impale whatever part of its body came hammering down to finish him.

Then a feeling of beneficent Power, not the glory of his own deity but surely something akin to it, wrapped around him. The world blinked. Afterward, he was still lying on the ground, but his foe wasn't right on top of him.

He sat up and looked around. The huge reptile was a little way off, and Medrash was in front of it. He'd used one of Torm's gifts to trade places with a comrade in distress.

The beast struck. But Medrash wasn't supine or dazed by the shock of a blow he'd just sustained. He dodged, and his blade sliced across one of the reptile's slit-pupiled yellow eyes. It shrieked and recoiled.

But then it struck again and would have snapped Medrash's head off if he hadn't dropped low at the last possible instant. Patrin scrambled to his feet and charged back into the fight.

Together, he and Medrash gashed their enormous foe with cut after cut and seared it with flare after flare of holy Power. Until Patrin felt himself slowing and his link to Bahamut attenuating to a useless, hollow ache. He insisted to himself that just one more cut or prayer might finish the beast. That it wasn't as unstoppable as it seemed.

Then sharp, sibilant words, spoken in an esoteric language that even Patrin couldn't understand, rasped through the air. Like himself, Nala had followed when the rest of the Cadre charged. Now she'd come to help protect the vanquisher.

Swaying back and forth, gripping her staff in both hands, she spun it through a complex series of loops and arcs. Then, on the final syllable of her chant, she thrust the tip at the saurian's head.

A blast of flame leaped from her weapon, engulfed the beast's upper body, and flickered out . . . leaving it unscathed. Head cocked, the reptile regarded Nala with its remaining good eye. Though Patrin had no real idea how intelligent it was, he had the feeling it was laughing at the fool who had attacked it with an element that constituted a part of its essential nature.

If so, then it was still laughing when bright, sizzling lightning leaped from the staff to complete the obliteration of its damaged eye. It convulsed, and Patrin and Medrash scrambled back from its stamping feet and lashing tail.

Next came a burst of fumes that set it retching, and then acid that dissolved scales and ate its way into the muscle beneath. Finally, frost extinguished the last of the flames dancing on its body, painted its head and neck white, and toppled it to the ground.

Patrin watched it, making sure it wasn't going to get up again, then turned to see if anything else was threatening Tarhun. Nothing was, and appearing essentially intact, Balasar was clambering to his feet.

Patrin realized it was a glorious moment. Torm and Bahamut sometimes battled side by side against evil gods and devils. Their earthly champions had just done the same and, by combining forces, had staved off a calamity. Then his beloved Nala had used her own divine gifts to administer the killing stroke to their foe. He gave Medrash a grin.

His fellow paladin smiled back, and Patrin judged that it was a genuine expression of good will. Medrash was incapable of withholding gratitude and camaraderie in such circumstances. But his feelings weren't wholehearted—there was ambivalence behind his eyes as well. Dismay that they'd needed Bahamut's Power to achieve their victory.

Curse it, why couldn't the Daardendrien just get over his prejudice? Why couldn't he accept that he and his fellow paladin were the same?

Maybe he just needs more time, Patrin thought. Then, as Nala stood panting and leaning on her staff, Balasar stumbled up behind her and planted a heavy hand on her shoulder.

* * * * *

Nala tried to slow her breathing. It wasn't easy; her masters would have scowled to see her struggle so simply to compose herself. But the assault on the redspawn had been as taxing a feat of magic as she'd ever attempted.

Suddenly something grabbed her shoulder, transferring a goodly portion of its weight to her slumping frame. Startled, sure an ash giant or one of their minions had crept up behind her, she let out a squawk and lurched around.

The hand maintained its grip. Still, her motion brought her face to face with Balasar. Both sides of his face were bloody. The right bore its self-inflicted cut, and the left was raw where being tossed had scraped it against the ground and torn out a couple of his white button piercings.

She could tell from the lopsided way he carried himself that other portions of his body were bruised and sore as well. Good. She prayed he was injured worse than he appeared. That he'd drop dead of it.

Because she didn't trust him. Perhaps that was unjust, for he'd passed his initiation. But there was a smug, impudent lightness to his character seldom seen in those who sought out her deity's altar. And earlier he'd fed the hysteria simmering inside her soldiers, prompting them to disobey her command. Maybe it had been true divine inspiration impelling him to act—and granted, since the charge had resulted in Tarhun's rescue, things had worked out fairly well. But she still didn't like it, and he'd just compounded his other offenses by compromising her dignity.

Which didn't change the fact that she needed Patrin, and Patrin liked him. Or the truth that she could scarcely rebuff one of the warriors who'd risked himself to save the vanquisher. Not with other people watching.

She arranged her face into a mask of concern, then asked, "Are you all right?"

"I hurt," Balasar croaked. "But if you can spare a healing spell, I think I can get back into it." He jerked his head at the combat raging on every side. Nala was no war leader, but it looked to her like the dragonborn and ash giants had at some point thrown just about everything they had at one another.

"Of course." Refusing to give in to her exhaustion, murmuring a prayer, Nala reached into the void and drew stinging, bracing Power into her core. Responsive to her true feelings, or her deity's, it tried to twist itself into poison. But she shaped it into vitality, then clasped the Daardendrien's shoulder as he was still clasping hers.

He shivered and squinched his eyes shut as the magic flowed into him. Then he straightened up and smiled. "Thank you, my lady. Thank you more than you know." He stooped, picked up the targe he'd evidently set on the ground, and turned to Medrash. "Kinsman, someone should get the vanquisher out of the middle of this. You could make sure he doesn't die on us, and then pull some of your followers out of the battle to help escort him. I think they might respond to orders faster than warriors of the Cadre. Will you help me?"

Medrash frowned like he no longer wanted Balasar claiming him as kin. But then he gave a nod and said, "Of course."

* * * * *

Standing guard, Balasar stayed on his feet while Medrash kneeled beside the unconscious Tarhun. On first inspection, it didn't look like the warlord was too badly burned inside his armor. At any rate he was still breathing, and that was the main thing.

Medrash reached out to Torm. The god's Power was as boundless as ever, but he'd virtually exhausted his capacity to channel it. He had to focus intently and strain to draw down even a trickle.

When he had it, he touched Tarhun's face where his helm didn't cover, resting his fingertips among the square golden studs. The point of contact glowed as the Power passed from his body into the vanquisher's. Without waking, Tarhun let out a sigh.

Medrash started to rise. "Wait," Balasar said, pitching his voice low enough that no one any farther away could have heard it over the crashing, howling din of battle. "Pretend you're still working on him."

Considering that they were supposed to have had a falling-out, Medrash had wondered why Balasar requested his help in particular. Now he realized that his clan brother had manufactured an opportunity to confer with him. "What's going on?" he murmured back.

"I don't know if you can tell it from here," Balasar said, "but I could, from the spot where the red thing tossed me. This fight could go either way, and we still have troops we haven't committed."

"Because Tarhun never had the chance to order them in."

"Partly, I suppose. But also because some of them are the other mounted squadrons Khouryn trained. They're scared to go in. But they don't have to be."

"What do you mean?"

"I'm pretty sure Nala used countermagic to interfere with the charms that made your horses brave and biddable. And that when the Cadre charged into battle, she stashed the talisman she used in here."

Balasar pivoted his shield outward like a door swinging on its hinges, revealing the beaded pigskin bag clutched in his off hand. Because he currently had his back to Patrin and Nala, neither of them would be able to see.

Medrash recognized the bag from his time traveling with the wyrm-worshipers on Black Ash Plain. Nala had worn it on her belt and used it to hold items employed in her spellcasting.

"I'm no cutpurse," Balasar said, "but she was spent and not especially observant when I was hanging on her. With luck, she'll think she dropped it when she was running around fighting."

"You say you're pretty sure."

"Have you ever known me to guess wrong when it truly counted?"

"Yes. But stay with Tarhun." Medrash rose to fetch some of his followers.

They fashioned a litter from lances and surcoats, then—keeping as far away from potential threats as possible—carried Tarhun from the field. Once they'd entrusted him to the healers, Balasar hurried back toward the heart of the battle. Medrash strode in the direction of the nearest company of horsemen.

By the time he reached them, they were dismounting, preparing to advance and fight on foot in the traditional dragonborn manner. "Wait!" he cried.

Prexijandilin Jhiri turned around. Crimson-eyed with umber hide, she had enameled primroses pierced into her cheeks and the tips of the long, ropy scales that made up her crest. Medrash had always considered the flower an incongruous emblem for such a warlike clan.

Jhiri looked momentarily surprised to see him away from his command, or maybe just to see him still alive. Then she said, "I know there haven't been any orders, but I don't care. We're needed, and we're going."

"Good," he replied. "But go on horseback, not on foot."

She shook her head. "We saw what happened to you."

"There was a reason for that." But as much as he wanted to share the details, it would be unwise to accuse Nala without proof. "A counterspell weakened the enchantment that makes the horses obey. But someone took care of it."

Jhiri eyed him dubiously. "Or maybe our charms just don't work as well as we hoped."

"Curse it, you and your followers have already fought giants from horseback. Successfully."

"When we skirmished with a raiding party. Maybe the mounts can handle that, but not a clash of armies."

He wished he could cloak himself in a bit of Torm's majesty to make his arguments more compelling. But for the moment that was impossible. All he had were his own wits and powers of persuasion.

Glad that it was easier to see what was happening from the fringes, he pointed at the battle raging in front of them. "Look there. See how the giants' flank is exposed. Imagine how badly we could hurt them if we circled around and charged."

Jhiri frowned, pondering, then shook her head. "No, I won't risk it."

"Then I will." Medrash turned and swung himself up onto a dismounted rider's roan gelding. The warrior gaped at him in surprise. "Since you're not planning to use it, or this either." He pulled the lance from the fellow's hand.

"What are you doing?" Jhiri asked.

"I hope that you at least aren't averse to using the horses to get close to the enemy. So here's the plan: I'll ride ahead of the rest of you. When we get close, I'll charge. If my horse does what he should, and yours don't show any signs of balking, you charge after me. Otherwise, abandon your mounts and engage the enemy on foot."

"Khouryn said that charging together is—"

"The moving wall. I remember. But it's my risk, not yours. So, are you game?"

Jhiri shrugged. "When you put it that way, why not?" She turned and shouted, "Mount up!"

As the riders maneuvered, some of the hunched brown creatures assailed them with blasts of sand. Medrash actually welcomed the harassment, because the horses bore it without panicking. He hoped it had a beneficial effect on the confidence of the warriors riding behind him. In truth, he himself was glad to see a bit of evidence that Balasar's hunch was correct.

Although the real test was yet to come. He turned the roan toward the massed giants. Patting the animal's neck, he said, "Do this, and I'll bring you apples for the rest of your days." Then he urged the steed into motion.

The roan moved forward, picking up speed until he was galloping, never wavering. The giants were busy watching or fighting other foes, and the horse covered a surprising amount of distance before anyone noticed him. Then one of the barbarians pivoted and hurled a big flint hatchet.

Medrash raised his shield, angled in such a way that the weapon ought to glance off. As it did, although the impact still jolted him back in the saddle.

Despite the bang, the horse still didn't balk. Medrash couched his lance.

The giant who'd thrown the hatchet tried to dodge. Medrash compensated by nudging the roan with his knee. The lance punched into the middle of the barbarian's chest, and his long gray legs with their knobby knees folded beneath him.

Medrash tried to jerk the lance free, but it was buried too deep, and that and his own momentum tore the shaft from his grip. As he hurtled onward, a lone rider with foes towering on every side, he snatched his sword from its scabbard.

A spear jabbed at the horse's flank, and he had to lean sideways to catch the thrust on his shield. As he heaved himself upright again, a sort of flail—rocks in a leather mesh bag—whirled at him. Somehow he shifted the battered heater quickly enough to catch that blow as well.

He slashed at the spine of a giant that still had its back to him. Unfortunately, that was the last one slow to react to his intrusion. Others moved in from every side. He wheeled his mount, looking for a way through. He couldn't find one.

Then, hooves pounding, lances making cracking sounds when they snapped, Jhiri's charge smashed into the giants. It really was like a racing wall with long spikes sticking out, and for an instant as it hurtled forward, Medrash felt a pang of fear that it would sweep him away along with the hulking foes surrounding him. It didn't, though. By dint of Khouryn's training or simple luck, the nearest riders galloped past without spearing or running into him.

When he looked at the slaughter they left in their wake, he suddenly felt certain that even without the vanquisher to lead them, the dragonborn were going to carry the day.

SEVEN

We've had griffon riders harassing them for days," said Aoth. "Loosing an arrow or two, then flying away. Presumably, they're sick of it and will jump at the chance to dish out some punishment in return. Especially when you consider that all those big beasts must eat a lot of meat, and men too stupid to run away will make a meal or two."

Shala Karanok frowned. "Maybe. If they don't realize that the small force they see before them is just the bait in a trap." She waved a gauntleted hand at the oaks and elms that surrounded them. "Are you sure you can hide so many men in these little patches of woods?"

His red hair gleaming in a shaft of sunlight that penetrated the interlaced branches overhead, Gaedynn said, "We're good at hiding, High Lady, especially my skirmishers."

Aoth noted that despite Shala's reduced status, the archer had still used a form of address indicative of great respect. He approved in principle, but wondered how Tchazzar felt about it.

But perhaps it would be more sensible to wonder if the living god even heard. Tchazzar stood gazing to the east. Toward the Sky Riders, although a person couldn't see the hills with all the trees in the way.

"Besides," Gaedynn continued, "we have wizards with a knack for veils. Isn't that right, Oraxes?"

The sharp-featured youth gave a brusque nod. Strands of his long, greasy black hair stuck out from under the steel and leather helmet he'd taken to wearing.

Hasos made a sour face. Tchazzar could decree that his subjects had to stop persecuting arcanists, but he couldn't make them stop fearing and mistrusting them in their hearts.

Well, choke on it, thought Aoth. Despite the trouble in Tchazzar's temple, he still outranked the baron in military matters, and as long as he did, they'd use every trick they had available.

He turned to Jhesrhi. She looked odd in her fine new cloak and robe, but the scowl marring her lovely face was much the same as ever. "And you can still play your games with the wind?" he asked.

"I think so," she said. As though simply turning her mind to the subject had roused it, a breeze gusted, toying with her yellow hair and wafting the scent of fresh spring verdure. "It would have helped if I'd reached this spot sooner—"

"But I suppose there were dances to dance," Gaedynn said.

Jhesrhi glowered. So did Aoth. He had some idea of what was rankling Gaedynn. He even sympathized. But it was not the time for the Aglarondan to vent his feelings.

Fortunately, Tchazzar still appeared distracted.

"If I'd had a few days," Jhesrhi said with an edge in her voice, "I could have done a thorough job of making friends with the winds. But they are restless on these plains. Angry from time to time. With the proper combination of insistence and propitiation, we mages should be able to induce them to do our bidding."

The petite, impish-looking Meralaine said, "Lady, forgive me if you already know this, but the spirits of the air aren't the only restless ones hereabouts."

"I have sensed something," Jhesrhi said, "but maybe not as much as you."

"People lived here a long time ago." Meralaine gestured toward a stone wrapped in helmthorn vine. It was hard to make out behind the long black thorns and green berries, and little more than a worn, rounded lump. Still, Aoth could tell that once it had possessed a sharp-edged regular shape that only tools could give. "Things didn't end well for them. I can't hear everything they're whispering— not in daylight, not without going into a trance—but I think a dragon came."

"That's good!" Oraxes said, surprising Aoth. He'd thought the lad disliked Meralaine, but evidently things had changed while he was away. "If they have a grudge against dragons, then they should want to help us fight the ones from Threskel."

"Wait," Hasos said. "Are you talking about summoning the undead?"

"It's her particular gift," Gaedynn said, "and she used it to good effect when we were saving your town."

"Well, she didn't use it with my permission," Hasos said.

"She didn't need it," said Aoth. "She doesn't now either."

Hasos sneered. "Of course a Thayan mage doesn't see the evil in necromancy."

"I see we're in for a tough fight," said Aoth. "I see we need every edge we can get."

Shala gave the baron a troubled gaze. "I don't like it either," she said. "Still, Captain Fezim has a point."

"Does he?" Tchazzar said.

Startled, Aoth pivoted. In human shape, Tchazzar was as imposing and magnetic a warlord as he'd ever met. But even so, he'd been so remote since the start of the discussion that one could forget he was even there.

Shala hesitated. "I think so, Majesty."

"Even though your god himself will lead you into battle."

"Majesty," said Aoth, "we all acknowledge your power. But surely there's a reason why you, in your wisdom, chose to fight at the head of an army instead of alone. And surely, for that army to serve its purpose, we need to be able to use our skills to best effect."

Tchazzar advanced on Meralaine. Who recoiled a step, though she'd supposedly fought bravely during the siege and confronted horrors on a regular basis practicing her art. Hasos looked eager for what was to come.

Tchazzar grabbed handfuls of Meralaine's mantle and jerked her off her feet, putting the two of them face to face. He looked like an enraged father shaking a naughty child. "Who freed you?" he shouted, spattering her with steaming drops of spittle.

Oraxes's eyes opened wide, and his upper body hitched forward like he could barely restrain the urge to intervene. Meanwhile Meralaine flinched again, either from the heat of the dragon's saliva, his vehemence, or a combination of the two. "You did, Majesty," she stammered.

"And is this how you repay me?"

Meralaine looked like she had no idea what Tchazzar wanted her to say. Aoth didn't either. He only knew that the young necromancer was currently dangling ashen-faced because he'd ordered her north. He had an obligation to protect her.

"Majesty," he said, "please. Obviously there's no need for any . . . debate. You rule here. If you don't want the girl to call the dead, she won't."

"Then why is she even here?" Tchazzar snapped. "Explain her presence!"

Aoth was still trying to frame an answer likely to mollify the dragon when, to his relief, Jhesrhi spoke. "Alasklerbanbastos is a dracolich. He's probably sent lesser undead south to fight us. We need a necromancer's special knowledge to help us destroy them."

Tchazzar frowned. "We have priests for that."

"Knowledge and faith working together often accomplish more than faith alone. I think even Sunlord Apathos would admit that. In any case, I command the wizards who fight for the Brotherhood. I promise you that Meralaine will only use her powers to banish ghosts, never to call them from their graves."

"So be it," Tchazzar said. He tossed Meralaine away like she was a bone he'd finished gnawing.

* * * * *

Gaedynn was well aware he had better things to do. Still, something made him watch from a distance while Oraxes hovered over Meralaine. Eventually she shooed him away. He sensed she was embarrassed that Tchazzar had frightened her and disliked attention that kept the memory fresh. Because she wanted to look and feel strong.

Gaedynn approved of that. If there was one thing he'd learned, it was never to expose a vulnerable spot to anyone.

Still not sure why he was bothering—the mages out of Luthcheq were Jhesrhi's and Aoth's problem, and thank the *true* gods for that—he ambled to intercept the skinny, slouching youth with his several daggers on ostentatious display.

Oraxes glared. "What? I didn't do anything."

Gaedynn grinned. "No, but you were thinking of it. Don't give in to the temptation. Tchazzar will swat you like a gnat."

"All my life, people have told me how he was everything great and good."

"The same people who said that every mage is evil at the core?"

Oraxes blinked. "I . . . Some of them, but it's not the same thing."

"It's time you recognized a sad truth. You Chessentans are brave, and good at athletics, but not very bright."

Oraxes bristled. "Tchazzar is good in his way. He truly did free us."

"And if you want to live to enjoy it when this is over, stay away from him. Don't accept an appointment at court, or any nonsense like that."

"How would you know what goes on at court? You've been up here in the north."

"I know a certain type of arrogance when I see it. I know how such lords behave." Even when it endangered the lives of their sons.

"You just don't like it that he likes Jhesrhi."

"Nonsense. Since I seem to be in an advice-giving mood, let me advise you that one woman is much like another, and none of them is worth so much as the loss of your composure, let alone a drop of your blood. In other words, don't go annoying the dragon—who also happens to be your sovereign—over a lass. By the Black Bow, you didn't even *like* the wench a tenday ago."

"I wasn't planning on it," Oraxes said.

"Good, because I have a job for you. I'm going out to scout, and with the enemy so near, I want a wizard with me. The outing can do double duty as your first flying lesson. We'll borrow Queen Umara. She's docile—well, for a griffon—and she'll follow Eider's lead."

Oraxes blinked. "I didn't ask to learn to ride a griffon."

"That's one of the advantages of military life. Your superiors provide you with interesting experiences you didn't even know you wanted."

Queen Umara was a trifle small for a griffon, with a hint of red in her plumage, a scarred, featherless spot on the side of her aquiline head, and a crooked hind leg. She'd sustained both injuries on the expedition into Thay, but fortunately neither rendered her unfit to fly or fight.

Oraxes seemed surprised and suspicious that Gaedynn gave him so few instructions. He thought there had to be more to riding a griffon than that. He was right, but he was also a child of Luthcheq's slums. Gaedynn had a hunch he'd never even ridden a donkey, and didn't want to confuse him with too much information. It was better to trust Queen Umara to handle what a novice rider couldn't.

"Ready?" Gaedynn asked.

"Let's go," the wizard replied. His voice cracked, and Gaedynn grinned.

He brushed a fingertip up Eider's neck. She trotted, lashed her wings, and rose into the air. Gaedynn glanced back and saw Queen Umara leave the ground with an awkward lurch. It might have tossed her rider out of the saddle if not for the straps and buckles holding him there. The problem wasn't a lack of agility. Oraxes had thrown the griffon off her rhythm by repeating a command, or giving it too forcefully.

Eider found a column of warm, rising air and used it to lift her and her master high above the plain. Gaedynn looked down at the copses and the high ground the decoy force would occupy. At soldiers busy digging earthworks or constructing archers' platforms in the trees, and others just arriving from the south and west, the unlucky fellows in the rear of a column eating the dust raised by their comrades in the front.

He wheeled Eider toward the north, and Oraxes and Queen Umara followed. After a while a griffon rider passed them heading the other way, for of course the Brotherhood had other scouts watching on the enemy. And Gaedynn trusted them—but, like Aoth, he still needed to see things for himself. That was how the elves had taught him to hunt.

He kept an eye on Oraxes. The mage's anxiety revealed itself in his hunched, rigid posture and in the grim intensity of his expression. But after a while, the ruffled feathers on Queen Umara's neck lay down, and she stopped screeching in annoyance. Because her rider wasn't directing her in the needlessly frantic manner he had before.

Some time after that, some of the stony grimness left Oraxes's face. He still didn't look like he was enjoying his situation, but he might have been feeling some satisfaction that he was able to cope.

Gaedynn nodded. Truculence and all, the lad would do. If—

Abruptly angry with himself, he cut off that line of thought. Plainly it would be worthwhile to recruit Oraxes, but it would have been a good idea at any time and under any circumstances. There was no *if* involved, because Jhesrhi wasn't leaving.

And if she did, to the Abyss with her.

Not long afterward, he spotted a blot on the green and brown earth ahead and felt glad of the need to focus on it. Attending to business would keep his mind from straying where he didn't want it to go.

But the relief, if that was the proper word for it, only lasted until he noticed there were *two* blots. It was barely conceivable the column had simply split lengthwise for some reason, but he wasn't optimistic enough to believe it.

At the moment just a crimson speck in the distance, one of the dragons was currently in the air. So were some smaller flying creatures, hanging over their comrades on the ground like a cloud of mosquitoes, perhaps to deter griffon-riding bowmen from getting too close. Still, Gaedynn would have to venture nearer to obtain a better look at the blots.

He needed to do it alone too. He didn't want a fledgling rider like Oraxes going any nearer. He waved for the wizard to stay back, then urged Eider forward. She grunted like she was questioning his judgment, but obeyed as willingly as ever.

Making sure he'd notice if his flying foes moved to attack him, he divided his attention between them and the ones on the ground. At first, squinting, he couldn't differentiate between the two columns. Points of yellow sunlight gleamed from each. But then he saw that in the larger one, it was reflecting from reptilian scales. In the smaller, it was glinting on steel.

A company of warriors—men, orcs, or goblinkin, he still couldn't tell—had reinforced the dragons and the beasts they controlled. Wary of the brutes, they were maintaining some distance until such time as they all needed to fight as one.

It was bad news, but, as he made a rough count of the soldiers, worse arrived. Leathery wings beating, a second red dragon flew out of the north to join the one in the air.

Praying that he'd somehow lost track of a wyrm, that it had gotten up into the sky without him realizing it, Gaedynn peered back down at the ground. No, curse it, the dragon he'd seen there was still striding among the lesser reptiles. It was green too, a fact he'd apparently repressed to give himself an instant of false hope.

He peered at the second red, trying to decide how old, large, and accordingly formidable it might be, and then it snarled. Though he couldn't speak the language of dragons, he could tell the sound was complex and patterned enough to have words inside it. Three of the lesser specks abruptly hurtled forward.

Gaedynn turned Eider as fast as he could, which was pretty fast. Yet in those few heartbeats the enemy flyers streaked close enough for him to make out the pale green of their hides, the long horns sweeping back from their almost birdlike heads, and their serpentine tails. They were the sort of reptile called spiretop drakes, and they shouldn't have been able to close the distance as fast as they were. The red had apparently cast an enchantment to make their wings beat as quick as a hummingbird's.

Hoping the magic would run out of power soon, Gaedynn kept glancing back as he fled, and each time the spiretop drakes were closer. But raw speed didn't equate to skill and maneuverability. If he turned again and fought, he might be able to kill the wretched things. But what if other flying foes, maybe even the dragons themselves, caught up to him before he finished?

A red spark streaked past him and then, with a boom, exploded into fire. The mote of light hadn't flown quite far enough for the blast to engulf any of the drakes, but they screeched and veered off. And as they aimed themselves at Gaedynn once again, their pounding wings finally slowed down.

Oraxes wheeled Queen Umara close enough to call across the intervening distance. Which was closer than Gaedynn would have preferred, given the wizard's lack of experience in the saddle. "That showed them!" Oraxes yelled.

"Shut up!" Gaedynn snapped. "Head for camp as fast as you can."

They didn't actually need to run all the way. The drakes gave up the pursuit before they'd flown much farther. But Aoth would want to hear their report as soon as possible.

* * * * *

Jhesrhi seldom minded killing people. She wouldn't have lasted long as a sellsword if she did. But helpless animals were a different matter, and as she approached the metal and wooden cages the army had brought from Soolabax, she felt a pang of reluctance.

She quelled it as every mage learned to silence distracting thoughts. She had to keep her mind focused on her purpose, or the power she'd raised with her purifications and invocations would slip from her control.

She opened the first cage, a dainty brass miniature palace. The canary inside was wise enough to mistrust her and, wings fluttering, tried to evade her grasp. But wizards have nimble hands, and she seized it anyway, although not before it gave her a stinging peck on the thumb.

She looked skyward, recited a final incantation, and drew the blade of a small silver knife across the canary's throat. Wind swirled around her, and the bird's blood spiraled upward, dispersing into mist and then disappearing entirely. A drop or two of her own blood went with it, but that was all right. It might make the binding stronger.

As she killed each bird in its turn, her inner eye gradually started to perceive entities who were vast, formless, and invisible to ordinary sight. Still for the moment, or nearly so, the winds of the plain hovered above her, greedy for a sip of life and magic. Willing to indenture themselves for the taste.

The final offering was a dove. She could feel its heartbeat through her wet, red fingers. She started to make the cut, and then Tchazzar said, "My lady!"

She hadn't realized he'd come up behind her. His voice startled her, and she didn't slice as deeply as she'd intended. Wounded but not slain, the dove shuddered.

She felt a shift in the attitude of the hovering spirits, a sudden doubt that she was strong and clever enough to command them. She rattled off words of power and made a second cut. The dove stopped struggling. For a moment it looked like the blood was going to drip to the ground, but then it whirled upward like that of the previous sacrifices.

Jhesrhi sighed and closed her eyes for a moment. Then she recited the closing incantation and made a chopping motion with her staff to end the ritual safely. She felt the residual power drain into the ground, and the winds departed with a *whoosh* that set her clothing flapping and branches lashing.

Tchazzar was a dragon, a monarch, and the Brotherhood's employer. All good reasons not to let on that she was annoyed with him. Still, as she turned around, she had to struggle to keep it from showing in her expression. She had yet to learn if he was a wizard or if all his legendary powers were innate. But either way, he surely knew enough about magic to understand that it was stupid to disturb a conjuror in the middle of a ritual.

But when she saw the contrition and anxiety in his handsome face, it took the edge off her irritation. "I'm sorry," he said. "I didn't realize you were still working. Did I spoil it?"

"No, Majesty," she said. Although the binding likely wasn't as strong as it could have been.

"Good. Come walk with me."

Her throat was raw from reciting so many incantations, and her body sore from standing in one spot for too long. Still, even at a moment when she would have preferred to flop down on the ground and drink a jack of ale, it was flattering that he desired her company. She found a smile for him and used the butt of her staff to open the circle she'd earlier drawn on the ground.

Then they strolled through the darkened camp with its paucity of crackling, smoky fires. (Aoth didn't want enemy scouts to count the points of light and arrive at an accurate estimate of the size of their army.) Chessentan soldiers and sellswords alike saluted as the war hero passed. Tchazzar acknowledged them, but in a perfunctory fashion.

For a while Jhesrhi wondered if they were simply going to wander around in silence. Then he said, "The enemy force is stronger than expected."

"I know," she said. By then everyone knew what Gaedynn and Oraxes had seen.

"Hasos recommends that we fall back to Soolabax."

She said what she knew Aoth must have said if he'd heard that particular proposal. "Your troops didn't break one siege of the town just to run back inside the walls and wait for another. We need to take the fight to the enemy to solve the problem of Threskel for good and all. That's what you want, isn't it?"

Tchazzar smiled a tight-lipped, troubled smile. "Of course. What king, what god, could tolerate a part of his dominions defying his authority? It's just . . . Do you understand why I didn't want that wretched little witch to call the dead?"

Jhesrhi hesitated. "Not entirely, Majesty."

"The dead are dark things. And it was here, in this very place, that dark things held and tortured me until I nearly lost my mind."

"It wasn't really here, Majesty. It was in the Sky Riders. It was also in the Shadowfell, a whole different world than the one we're walking and talking in now."

"Can I trust a necromancer, who draws her strength from darkness? Or a Thayan mage? They're all necromancers, aren't they? And when you consider that the man profaned my temple—"

"Majesty, I beg you to remember that like the rest of Chessenta's arcanists, Meralaine owes everything to you. And Aoth is as honorable a mercenary as you could hope to hire, and outcast from his own people for *fighting* necromancers. There's no question that either of them is loyal."

"I suppose." Some of the tension went out of his face. "I'm fortunate to have you for my *lovac*."

She could tell he meant it as a compliment, and that pleased her. Still, she had to admit, "I don't know that word, Majesty."

He hesitated, then said, "It's an old Draconic word. It means the faithful friend and lieutenant of a king."

* * * * *

The enemy had seen a few griffon riders. So Tchazzar's army wasn't giving away any secrets by having a few in the air as the foe approached. Aoth had chosen to be among them to obtain the best possible view of all that was happening.

The decoy force stood at the top of a rise behind earthen ramparts. He wished Khouryn were there to command it. He tried to draw some comfort from everyone's assurances that while it was always Hasos's instinct to avoid battle if possible, he fought well if you managed to push him into one.

Aoth had had a century to grow accustomed to his fire-kissed eyes. Still, it was momentarily disconcerting to look down at the various stands of oaks and elms and plainly see the rest of the illusion-veiled army. He had to remind himself that the Threskelans couldn't.

Or at least that was the idea. Unfortunately, dragons had keen senses. But if Tymora smiled, the wyrms would have other things to occupy their attention.

All three enemy dragons, the two reds and the green, were in the air along with other flying creatures. They were heading for the top of the rise. Aoth assumed the wyrms intended to start the battle by raking the position with flame and poisonous fumes.

My feelings are hurt, said Jet.

Don't worry, Aoth replied. *We'll give them a reason to pay attention to us in a moment.*

Though he lacked Jhesrhi's enhanced rapport with the winds, he was wizard enough to feel it when she started to command them. The enemy dragons and flying drakes floundered and plunged as gusts of wind shoved them one way and another, and the air beneath their wings thinned.

Aoth lifted his ram's horn bugle and blew three notes. No doubt the battlefield was already noisy with the thumping, clanking sound of Threskelan saurians, horsemen, and infantry—a mix of men, orcs, and kobolds—hurrying along beneath their flying allies. But his men were listening for the call, and he was confident they'd hear it even so.

They did. More griffon riders bounded from the copses, then—clear of the branches that would otherwise have hindered their ascent—beat their way up into the sky. Meanwhile, arrows flew from the trees and over the earthworks. Threskelan warriors and creatures began to drop.

Aoth grinned. Discerning what he wanted through their psychic link, Jet raced toward the nearer of the red dragons. Since the elementals weren't playing pranks on him, the familiar could fly as nimbly as ever.

Which was a good thing. Aoth judged that like its companions, the red was relatively young. But it was still capable of burning Jet and him out of the sky or biting and clawing them to shreds.

He chanted words of power and aimed his spear, releasing some of the energy bound inside it to augment the innate force of the spell. A silvery blast of cold erupted from the weapon's point and splashed across the dragon's crested back.

It roared, twisted its neck, and spat fire in return. But perhaps the turbulence around it threw off its aim, because Jet didn't even have to dodge.

Once they'd flown on by, Aoth conjured fire of his own and blasted two spiretop drakes out of the air. As Jet wheeled for another pass at the red dragon, there was a moment to take a look at how everyone else was faring.

Aoth's fellow griffon riders loosed arrow after arrow at the winged reptiles. Often, for all their skill, they missed, since few things were more difficult than hitting a moving target from the back of a flying griffon. Sometimes the unquiet air around their targets sent the shafts glancing and tumbling awry. But Aoth estimated that one arrow in five hit and penetrated its mark. With luck, that would be good enough.

On the ground, archery was exacting a heavier toll. Caught in a three-sided box, the Threskelan warriors and their saurian allies scrambled to break out. But whenever they reached the earthworks or the stands of trees, they ran into shield walls bristling with spears.

In short, everything looked like it was going well. Then the blue sky darkened.

Aoth snarled an obscenity. His old enemy Ysval had been capable of blotting out the sunlight. As had Xingax, after he grafted the nighthaunt's hand onto his own arm. Both were long dead, but someone or something on the Threskelan side knew how to create the same effect.

One of the dragons? asked Jet.

I doubt it, Aoth replied. *With the wind bashing them around and arrows sticking into them, it's unlikely they could exert the necessary concentration. Fly over the ground troops. Maybe we'll spot a wizard.*

They did catch sight of spellcasters of one sort or another—human sorcerers chanting and sweeping staves, wands, or orbs through intricate passes; wyrmkeepers doing much the same with their picks; and orc and kobold shamans brandishing fetishes made of bone, mummified hands, and shrunken heads. At another time Aoth would have seized the opportunity to hurl flame or hail at any one of them. But none looked capable of leeching the sunlight out of the sky.

Then he noticed a pocket of murk under a stand of oaks at the back of what passed for the enemy formation. No eyes but his could have made out the huge green form hidden in the darkness, or, quite possibly, even noticed the blotch of shadow itself amid the general gloom.

The dragon was staring into a night black orb supported by an iron tripod. So was a circle of his attendants—men, or things that had once been men, with gaunt frames and ashen skin. Judging from the way their mouths were moving, they were chanting in unison as well. The trees around them dropped their leaves as though spring had turned to fall.

The wyrm was almost certainly Jaxanaedegor, the vampiric dragon who was Alasklerbanbastos's chief lieutenant. Aoth recognized him from Gaedynn and Jhesrhi's description, and he knew it would be worse than reckless for Jet and him to attack the creature and his followers alone.

But somebody needed to disrupt their conjuring before it produced something worse than darkness. Aoth looked around to see how many griffon riders he could gather. Then he felt a chill and smelled decay. A sense of virulent wrongness knotted his guts.

EIGHT

Scar gave a querulous rasp. He wanted to fly and fight with his brothers and sisters, not hide behind the earthworks at the top of the hill.

But for the moment at least, Jhesrhi could direct the winds from where she was, so it would be foolish to take to the air and make herself a target. Entranced, perceiving what the winds perceived and in the same manner—by a sort of remote touching—she was nonetheless aware of the griffon's displeasure just as she heard the clash of metal on metal, snarls, and screams sounding along the ramparts. She stroked the feathers on his head.

Then the bright day dimmed to filthy twilight. Without leaving the battle line, Hasos bellowed for the sunlords the army had brought along to do something about it.

Jhesrhi could only wish them luck. She couldn't abandon her own task to help.

The priests chanted prayers and swept their golden maces over their heads in arcs that suggested the sun's daily passage from east to west. Power warmed the air. But the unnatural gloom persisted.

Until the dead began to rise from their forgotten graves, or perhaps the places where they lay unburied after Meralaine's ancient dragon had massacred them. For the most part they were invisible. But warriors on both sides felt their nearness, gasped, and cringed.

The ghosts ignored the combatants on the ground and soared up into the air. Where, insubstantial as the spirits of the wind, they assailed them as even dragons couldn't, snatching with hands that ripped away vitality.

Variously enraged, terrified, or shocked at feeling pain and weakness for the first time in their immortal existences, the winds struck back, faltered, or sought to flee. Few of them kept trying to hinder the dragons and other flying reptiles. The creatures roared and snarled in joy at the cessation of the harassment.

Concentrating, whispering words of command, Jhesrhi strained to reassert her control over the winds. To direct them so they could both defend themselves and continue hampering the winged saurians. Then warriors in front of her cried out and shrank back from the ramparts.

She looked up at the green dragon swooping at the top of the rise. Hating the necessity, she gave up on the spirits of the air, gripped her staff, and called for fire.

* * * * *

Shala's guts turned to water when she saw the wyrm diving out of the gloom. Still, it wasn't panic that sent her scrambling back from the earthworks. She did it to salvage the situation.

Meanwhile, Jhesrhi swung her staff over her head like the arm of a trebuchet. A point of light hurtled from the tip, hit the dragon in the head, and exploded into roaring, crackling fire. The wyrm screamed and veered off.

It occurred to Shala that they were lucky, if that was the right word for it, that the green had been the first to reach the hilltop. Fire likely wouldn't have harmed either of the reds.

Not that the spell had hurt the green enough to deter it for long. It was wheeling to come at them again. Jhesrhi leaped onto the back of her griffon. And Shala reached Tchazzar.

The living god was still in human guise. The plan had called for him to remain so until the enemy army had fully committed itself to battle. Only then would he transform and attack with all the allegedly awesome power at his command.

But at this point, the Threskelans *had* committed themselves—and anyway, the plan had turned to dung. Yet Tchazzar still stood passively, as far back from the melee as the sunlords and the reserves. His eyes were wide and darted back and forth.

Shala pointed at the oncoming dragon with her bloody sword. "It's there!" she gasped. "Right there!"

Jhesrhi hurled more fire as her winged steed sprang into the air. This time the wyrm bore the punishment without flinching and spewed vapor in return. Shala winced, but the griffon somehow wrenched himself and his rider out of the way.

Tchazzar still wasn't moving. "Change!" Shala said. "Kill the thing!"

"It's what they want," Tchazzar said.

"What? Who?"

"The things that come in the dark. They want me to transform so they can find me."

Shala didn't understand and had no idea what to say to him. She only knew that if the god wasn't going to fight, then it was all up to the mortals. Despising him, she sucked in a deep, steadying breath, then strode back to the ramparts.

* * * * *

Jet lashed his wings, bobbed above the drake that had apparently believed he didn't notice it driving in on his flank, and tore its head apart with his talons. *Where's Tchazzar?* he asked. *If he's anything like what he's supposed to be, he can still turn this thing around.*

I don't know, Aoth replied. Nor did he have time to try to spot the war hero. Without the help of the air elementals, the fight in the sky had become far more difficult. And after he won that—if he and his fellow griffon riders could win it—there were half a dozen other situations that needed their immediate attention.

He chanted and aimed his spear. A bolt of dazzling, crackling lightning leaped from the point and struck one of the red dragons. The creature convulsed and plummeted halfway to the ground before it regained control of its wings.

But while Aoth was busy with that one, the other red dived toward the archers and spearmen in one of the copses.

* * * * *

Relatively safe behind the sellswords and their shields, Oraxes hurled darts of force at the Threskelans who kept rushing the formation. Despite the ominous and unnatural darkness, it seemed to him that things were going reasonably well. Then their living enemies—scaly kobolds and pig-faced orcs—fell back and let the dead assault them.

Oraxes had felt though not seen the initial arrival of the phantoms, but then they'd simply gone away again. Now they were back and advancing in the form of skull-faced shadows. It was like they'd fed on something that made them more real.

Sellswords who'd faced the previous foes stolidly or even with sneering bravado quailed. But only for an instant, and then they braced themselves for what was to come. Oraxes remembered that they were men who'd followed Aoth into Thay and fought the undead horrors there.

But courage and experience didn't always save them. Sometimes their jabbing spears and slashing swords bit, but just as often passed harmlessly through their insubstantial targets. When that happened, the ghosts reached right through shields and mail to plunge their fingers into living bodies. Then men screamed, withered, and collapsed.

One phantom felled a mercenary, then glided through his body before he could flop all the way to the ground. Oraxes conjured a burst of vitriol, which flew right through the ghost to splash and sizzle on its previous foe.

Stupid! Oraxes should have thrown darts of light. Resolved to do so, he started to backpedal and chanced to look squarely into the vacant orbits of the murky, wavering skull face. Suddenly he couldn't look away, move, or even draw a breath. The ghost reached for him—

Behind him, Meralaine chanted rhyming words in a language that even he, a fellow mage, didn't recognize. Her voice was soft, but something about it made certain syllables seem to ring like hammer strokes on an anvil.

It was the ghost's turn to falter. Its form rippled in place like it was straining to break free of the power constraining it. Then, with a howl, it turned and launched itself at one of its fellow spirits. Two other phantoms did the same.

Oraxes sucked in a breath. He wanted to attack the enemy ghosts, not the ones serving Meralaine, but it was hard to tell which shadow was which. He was still trying to choose a target when he glimpsed motion overhead.

A dragon swooped at the coppice. It opened its jaws and spewed bright yellow flame. The lance of fire ignited or simply obliterated everything in its path—branches, archers on their elevated platforms, and living warriors and ghosts battling on the ground. And, like an artist's brush painting a line of ruin on the earth, it was heading straight at Oraxes.

He started to scramble out of the way, then noticed that if Meralaine didn't move, the wyrm's breath would sweep right over her as well. And, evidently startled, she wasn't moving.

He grabbed her and dragged her with him. His foot caught on a corpse's outstretched arm. He fell, carrying Meralaine down with him. The jet of flame slashed by just a couple of finger-lengths from their feet, close enough to make him gasp at the searing heat.

Close enough too for the grass and fallen twigs and leaves the flare set on fire to pose an immediate threat. He scrambled to his feet, dragged Meralaine up beside him, looked around, and felt a stab of terror.

At first glance it seemed that everything was burning, in all directions, with no path through the flames. The heat hammered at him. Smoke set him coughing. A burning platform, the charred corpses of the bowmen who'd perched there, and the boughs that had supported it crashed down in front of him. Meralaine yelped.

"It's all right," he said. "I can handle this." Fighting the need to cough again, for that would spoil the cadence, he rasped an incantation.

A corona of flame sprang up around him, staining the world blue— but it didn't burn him. Instead, it replaced the heat of the dragon's conflagration with a pleasant coolness.

He pulled Meralaine into the blue fire, and she cried out at what felt painfully cold to her. But once he put his arm around her and drew her close, she was completely inside the effect and experienced it as he did.

"Now we run," he said. Before the protective enchantment faded.

He tried to flee in the opposite direction from the enemy— although with his surroundings transformed, suffused with the glare of flame and the blur of smoke, he wasn't sure of his bearings. He also tried to lead Meralaine around the worst of the fires. But sometimes, if they didn't want to retrace their steps, they had no choice but to plunge right through. At those moments their shield couldn't keep out all the heat, and it was speed as much as magic that protected them.

They stumbled clear of the blaze an instant before their own halo of fire guttered out. Oraxes drew Meralaine onward for several more paces, turned, then cursed in surprise. Because, as he could see from the outside, the dragon's breath had only set a relatively small area alight. The blaze had seemed as big as all of Luthcheq while they were struggling to escape it.

Meralaine coughed so hard that it nearly jerked her free of his encircling arm. Once she stopped, he realized there was no longer any particular reason to hold on to her. Still, he let her go with some reluctance.

She rubbed tears from her reddened eyes. "What now?"

A part of him answered, Run! Before the ghosts and dragons find us again! But what he said aloud was, "Look. Some of the sellswords are right over there. We'll join up with them."

* * * * *

Gaedynn picked a target and drew the fletching back to his ear, and then Eider veered—probably to avoid a threat her master hadn't even noticed.

He automatically compensated for the shift and, leading the drake he wanted to shoot, loosed his arrow. The shaft drove into the reptile's flank, and the creature plummeted.

Gaedynn smiled and glanced around for another foe. A blast of fire, hurled by something else in the air, silhouetted a dragon flying near the top of the rise. Presumably it was the green, since most spellcasters would know better than to hurl flame at a red.

Though he couldn't make them out in the gloom, Gaedynn suspected it was Jhesrhi, riding on Scar, who'd thrown the attack. She was adept at fire magic, and the staff they'd looted from Jaxanaedegor's caverns had augmented her abilities.

Which didn't mean she could kill even a young dragon all by herself. He sent Eider winging in her direction.

Meanwhile, the green gained the high air. It shouldn't have been able to outmaneuver a trained griffon, but maybe Scar was injured. Why not? Everything else was going wrong.

Gaedynn reached to draw an arrow from one of his quivers, then left it where it was. If he didn't call attention to himself, maybe he could gain the high air relative to the wyrm and hit it with something likely to do more harm to a dragon than even a shaft sped by his own unerring hand.

The dragon's neck whipped, and its jaws opened. Barely visible in the dimness, vapor streamed out.

Scar lashed his wings and dodged. Instantly, the green dived. Somehow, it had predicted in which direction Scar would move and had poised itself to plunge and intercept him and the woman on his back.

Gaedynn sent Eider hurtling down at the wyrm. Jhesrhi blasted the ventral side of the reptile's body with a final flash of fire. Then Eider slammed into the base of its neck with a jolt that Gaedynn, standing up in the stirrups, felt through every portion of his body.

The griffon's talons stabbed deep. Her beak snapped, tearing away chunks of scaly hide and flesh.

The dragon convulsed and rolled over and over as it dropped. Gaedynn wondered if Eider could spring clear without a flailing wing or foreleg swatting her. But she timed the leap properly, and then they were gliding safely with the creature's body tumbling away beneath them.

As it smashed into the ground, he stroked Eider's neck and looked down at Jhesrhi. I did that, he thought. Not your stinking Tchazzar.

Then, impossibly, the green's broken body rolled over and heaved itself to its feet. After all the punishment it had taken, Gaedynn couldn't believe it was still alive.

Then he realized it wasn't. Filthy, stinking necromancy, the same vile art that had nearly destroyed the Brotherhood in Thay, had revived it. But either way, he and Jhesrhi would have to fight it all over again.

* * * * *

The drakes were no bigger than cats. Compared to the enormous horrors on the battlefield, they should have seemed like little more a joke. But, hellishly agile and quick, they swarmed over the rampart and attacked en masse. There were three or four of them for each of the several warriors in their path, and they struck with fangs like needles.

By the time Shala killed two, another was perched atop her shield, its hind legs bent to launch it at her face. Unable to bring the blade of her broadsword to bear, she struck a backhand blow with the pommel. The heavy brass knob caught the drake in midleap and knocked it onto the ground. Instantly, it sprang up and ran at her. She raised her foot and stamped. Bone cracked. She ground the thing beneath her boot until it stopped squirming.

She glanced around. The other small drakes were dead as well. The carcass of the big reptile she'd killed a while before sometimes impeded the rush of other foes to the rampart, and this was one of those moments. As a result, she had a chance to catch her breath and take stock of the situation as a whole.

It wasn't good. She and her comrades had killed plenty of the enemy, but there were plenty more left, and she thought she glimpsed a new problem—some sort of shadows or phantoms—stalking up the slope. How in the name of the Sunlord were they supposed to contend with those on top of everything else?

Had she allowed it, she could have succumbed to hopelessness or resentment at the sheer unfairness of it all. But she knew she couldn't afford to feel anything but the will to prevail, or think of anything but strategy and tactics.

She tucked her sword into the crook of her shield arm and reached for the leather water bottle hanging on her belt. Then, a little way down the rampart, Hasos staggered back. His helmet flew off, and the face and crown beneath were dark with blood. A horned, thick-bodied reptile the size of a draft horse clambered over the earthwork after him. Other warriors recoiled from it, opening a wider gap in the line of shields and weapons. Unless somebody did something about it, dozens of saurians would pour through.

Shala grabbed the hilt of her sword and ran toward the trouble. A warrior backpedaled toward her, and she rammed him out of the way with her shield.

As she closed with the reptile, she saw that Hasos had slashed its head and shoulders before it scored on him. That was something, anyway. She cut and added a gash of her own, slicing across one of the wounds the baron had inflicted to make an X under the creature's right eye.

It roared and pivoted toward her. But the back half of its body was still on the far side of the rampart, and maybe that made it clumsy.

When it bit, it wasn't too difficult to hop back out of range, then slash it across the snout.

Then it spewed fire.

Shala wasn't out of range of that. Reflex snapped her shield into position to protect her face and torso. But the defense effectively blinded her, and pain still seared her lower body.

Then fangs searing as red-hot iron caught her leg and wrenched it out from underneath her. Her dwarf-forged greave kept the bite from nipping it off immediately. But even enchanted armor wasn't likely to hold for more than a heartbeat or two. And even if it did, the heat would cook the limb inside.

Bending and twisting at the waist, straining to bring her blade into striking position, she wrenched herself around. Praying the awkward attack would penetrate, she thrust at the creature's scaly throat.

The sword stabbed deep, and when she withdrew it, steaming blood spurted. The reptile roared, releasing her, then fell over sideways.

But more reptiles were climbing over the rampart after it. She rolled to her feet and caught one squarely between the eyes with another lucky thrust. The beast collapsed. "Chessenta!" she bellowed. "Chessenta!"

And warriors who'd followed her on many a campaign scrambled back to the battle line. Together, they hurled the wave of saurians back.

Next came the shadows, ghastly things that could shrivel a young man into an old one just by touching him. "Sunlords!" Shala shouted. "Kill these ghosts!"

And the priests too heeded her call. They abandoned their fruitless effort to restore daylight to the field as a whole and conjured localized flashes. Those repelled the ghosts or burned them away to nothing.

The next time the combat gave her a momentary respite, she realized that some of her comrades had taken up her battle cry. "Chessenta!" they howled. "Chessenta."

While others chanted, "Shala! Shala! Shala!"

* * * * *

Aoth surveyed the battle. Neither darkness nor distance impeded his fire-touched vision. But the situation was so chaotic that even he, with all his experience with war, had difficulty making sense of it.

For the moment, the Chessentans were holding, although at a heavy cost and surely not for much longer. Not with all three enemy dragons still in the air, even if the one Gaedynn and Jhesrhi were fighting was just a mangled undead travesty of its former self.

On the positive side, even deprived of assistance from the winds, he and his fellow griffon riders had killed a substantial portion of the lesser winged reptiles. And some power—Meralaine's perhaps—was hindering the ghosts, turning some against their fellows or melting them back into the ground. It wasn't enough, but it was something.

Aoth tried to decide where he and Jet were needed most. The answer was everywhere. Which might mean that the only way for the Chessentans to survive the fiasco was to strike at the enemy commander, or at least his position. He blew the ram's horn, signaling every griffon rider who could to follow his lead.

Jet wheeled, aiming himself at the pocket of deeper darkness. *You don't have many spells left. And Jaxanaedegor hasn't even done any fighting yet.*

But he's been working powerful magic through that black orb, Aoth replied. *He drowned the field in shadow, summoned a company of ghosts, and turned a dead dragon into a zombie. It's possible he's just as tired as we are.*

That's fine, then, the familiar said. *By all means, risk our lives, just as long as "it's possible."*

Aoth looked around. Other griffon riders had maneuvered into position to accompany him. Perceiving what his master saw through their psychic link, Jet screeched, lashed his wings, and hurtled forward.

Jaxanaedegor and his assistants were slow to react to the aerial charge. Perhaps they didn't think that any of their foes could actually see them. Aoth disabused them of that notion by pointing his spear and hurling a thunderbolt from the tip. Unfortunately, though the lightning hit the black globe on its tripod, it didn't do any damage. Well, he'd just have to keep trying.

Exploding into motion, Jaxanaedegor sprinted clear of the trees, lashed his wings, and rose from the blot of darkness. His companions, however, stayed on the ground. Aoth had hoped they were lesser vampires, the kind that didn't turn into bats, and that appeared to be the case.

Don't get too excited, said Jet. *Jax doesn't look like he needs the help.*

Unfortunately, that was true. The wyrm was huge enough to dwarf the other three rampaging across the battlefield, and his pale yellow eyes blazed. Griffons wheeled and beat their wings, trying to stay away from him and above him while their riders shot their few remaining shafts as fast as they could draw and release.

Many of the arrows glanced off Jaxanaedegor's scales. Others stuck—but only in his hide, without piercing what lay beneath. One, however, drove deep into his brow. In response, he spat a stream of vapor that engulfed the marksman and his mount. The two plummeted together.

Aoth hammered the dark orb with blasts of fire, six detonating in succession quick as the beats of his racing heart. The blasts flung vampires through the air and even tore a couple apart. But the talisman remained intact.

He decided he needed to get close to the thing. He hated to abandon his men to fight Jaxanaedegor by themselves, but if they could distract the wyrm and survive for just a few moments, maybe they'd be all right.

Jet wheeled. When he was behind Jaxanaedegor, he swooped.

For a moment Aoth thought the undead green truly had lost track of them. Then he felt Jet's jolt of alarm and looked up. Growing larger by the moment, Jaxanaedegor seemed to fill the sunless sky. His claws were poised to catch and tear.

Jet lashed his wings to change course. Then he furled them and dropped like a stone into the leafless upper limbs inside the bubble of darkness.

Branches cracked beneath the griffon and his rider, and bashed and raked them as they fell through. The punishment was like enduring a beating and a tumble down a staircase at the same time. But at least a creature as huge as Jaxanaedegor couldn't pursue them down into the treetops.

At least not in solid form. Aoth had hoped the dragon would veer off, set down outside the copse, then reenter at ground level. Instead, he dissolved into mist. Aoth caught a whiff of the putrid-smelling fumes. It nauseated him and made him feel dizzy and weak.

Aoth judged—or perhaps merely hoped—that he'd have a few moments to act before Jaxanaedegor floated to the ground and turned solid again. Then Jet slammed down hard. Aoth felt the flash of pain as an aquiline front leg snapped.

I'm all right! the griffon snapped. *Go!*

Gaunt, pale figures rushed them. Jet gave Aoth just enough time to swing himself out of the saddle, then sprang to meet the vampires. His beak slashed and bit, and his good foreleg clawed to devastating effect. Yet even so, creatures pounced on him and clung, gnawing and tearing with their fangs.

As before, Aoth couldn't linger to help. He dashed toward the tripod. Another vampire ran in on his flank. It had a poleaxe with what appeared to be grimacing faces mirrored in the blade, although there was nothing outside the steel to cast the reflections.

The creature struck. Grunting with effort, Aoth parried with his spear, then thrust it into his opponent's heart. Since he couldn't leave it there, he used a bit more of his rapidly dwindling power to draw flame from the point, sear the organ, and so keep the vampire from getting right back up again.

That cleared the way to the black globe. He rattled off a spell to ensure he struck hard and true. Meanwhile, wisps of mist coiled together and congealed into a wedge-shaped head. Jaxanaedegor leaped forward, clearing Jet and his frenzied foes in the process.

Releasing every bit of force still bound in the spear, Aoth drove the weapon into the talisman. The orb shattered, and sunlight stabbed through the naked branches overhead.

Jaxanaedegor was lifting a foreleg to strike when the radiance caught him. At once his immense scaly body charred and smoked, and he jerked in agony. Backpedaling, Aoth thought, Burn, you whoreson! Die!

But the latter was too much to hope for. Mastering his pain, Jaxanaedegor snarled words of power and vanished. Magic had translated him through space, no doubt to somewhere dark and safe.

Aoth pivoted toward Jet. The lesser vampires actually had burned to death, and—still alive despite a dozen gory bite wounds—the griffon stood on three legs amid smoldering drifts of ash.

"Can you get me back up into the sky?" asked Aoth.

"Oh, why not?" Jet replied. "What's one more painful test of strength at this point?"

Feeling guilty—but only slightly, because he knew how hardy the griffon actually was—Aoth climbed back into the saddle. Jet limped out of the trees, accelerated, lashed his wings, and flew. The sellswords above them cheered, and their mounts screeched. Aoth acknowledged it by brandishing his spear.

Until a prodigious roar drowned out the acclaim. At the other end of the battlefield, from behind the earthwork at the top of the rise, Tchazzar soared upward in dragon form.

Bigger even than Jaxanaedegor, he annihilated the zombie dragon with a flare of fiery breath that nearly engulfed Gaedynn and Eider as well. Then, wings beating, he climbed.

One of the enemy reds tried to do the same. But Tchazzar gained the high air, then plunged at the smaller reptile like a hawk diving at a pigeon. He seized it and ripped it apart with fang and claw.

By that time, the other enemy red was fleeing north. Aoth thought it had enough of a head start to escape. But Tchazzar snarled, and Aoth felt a charge of supernatural coercion in the noise. It made his head throb even though it wasn't directed at him.

The lesser red flailed, then labored onward clumsily like it was carrying an enormous weight or its muscles were cramping. As a result, Tchazzar had no trouble overtaking it.

When the enemy red turned to fight, it regained its agility. Either Tchazzar had contemptuously restored it, or that particular curse could only afflict a fleeing victim. The Threskelan wyrm found rising air, soared, then dived as Tchazzar had hurtled down at his comrade.

The war hero spat flame. Which should have had little or no effect on a fellow red. Yet it blasted chunks of flesh from his foe's skull and burned or melted its eyes in their sockets. Aoth winced to imagine the heat and force required.

Tchazzar then flicked his wings, got out of the way of the blind, maimed wyrm, and seized it as it plunged by. He held onto it for the heartbeat it took to bite its head off, then let the bloody, burning pieces fall.

After that, he turned his murderous attention to an unfortunate company of kobolds. But he couldn't attack everyone at once, and so a fair number of the enemy would get away to regroup later.

For, the Firelord knew, Tchazzar's warriors were in no condition to pursue them. Somehow they'd averted complete destruction while waiting—and waiting—for the self-proclaimed god to make his move. But they'd taken a brutal mauling.

NINE

The Market Floor echoed with the fast, complex clatter of the victory drums, and dancers leaped and whirled to the rhythms. Khouryn reflected that dragonborn could be remarkably nimble for such a solidly built people, although in the present circumstances they weren't always nimble enough. Many dances involved simulated combat with live blades, or tossing weapons into the air and catching them, and some folk watched from the sidelines with freshly bandaged hurts to attest to a fumble.

He and Medrash tried to slip past one such celebration, convened beneath a platinum and purple banner of Bahamut. But someone recognized them, and people clustered around to shake their hands and press wooden cups of wine and apple brandy into them.

Khouryn supposed it made sense. Thanks to the mounted charge and the other tactics he'd introduced, he and Medrash had emerged from the recent battle as heroes. Unfortunately, so had the leaders and warriors of the Platinum Cadre, and people—including many of the cultists—had a tendency to see all the innovations as parts of a greater whole. Especially since Medrash and Patrin had both proclaimed themselves the exotic sort of champion called paladins and fought side by side to save the vanquisher.

Since there was drink involved, Khouryn didn't mind the attention all that much. He suspected it bothered Medrash more, but the Daardendrien's natural courtesy masked it.

Eventually they managed to make their escape. They found a twisting staircase and descended into the Catacombs.

Balasar stepped from a shadowy niche in the wall. "It took you long enough," he said.

"Your fellow maniacs are dancing all over the Market Floor," Medrash said. "It ties up traffic." He and his clan brother clasped hands.

Khouryn peered down the corridor with its dim, infrequent lights. "You're sure you weren't followed?" he asked.

Medrash smiled slightly. "He wasn't. If there's one thing he knows how to do, it's sneak. He learned it breaking curfew and the rest of our elders' rules."

"Fair enough." Khouryn raised his hand to his chin, then made himself lower it again. He'd never considered himself vain, at least not about his appearance, but since the venom had burned his beard he'd acquired the unconscious impulse to cover the sad remains. "So, why did you want to meet us?"

"Did someone look at the bag?" Balasar asked.

Medrash nodded. "The wizard couldn't tell a thing."

"I swear," Balasar said, "the talisman that interfered with the horses was in there."

"We believe you," Khouryn said. "Why else did the riders regain control as soon as you stole it? Why, if the contents weren't incriminating, did they turn to dust as soon as a hand other than Nala's untied the cord? But we can't prove anything."

"So the Platinum Cadre are marvels," said Medrash, "winning new converts by the day. They'll march with the rest of us when we head back onto Black Ash Plain to break the tribal alliance once and for all. Where, for all we know, Nala will betray us again."

Balasar grinned one of the fang-bearing grins so often unsettling to folk unaccustomed to dragonborn. "Maybe not."

Medrash's eyes narrowed. "Meaning what?"

"I haven't reported everything I've done as a spy. It's dangerous to write very much, and impossible to hide a big sheet of parchment behind a stone. So you don't know about the glassblower and her sand."

He proceeded to tell how he'd followed said glassblower and two other cultists into the Catacombs, where he'd run afoul of a flying creature and a group of reanimated corpses.

"Later," he concluded, "I made my way back to the spot where the winged thing ambushed me. There was no sign of it, so maybe I actually did kill it. But when I pressed on, I couldn't find where Raiann and the others had gone, or anyplace interesting."

"Still," Khouryn said, "I think you were close." He reached to stroke his chin, then lowered his hand again. "I've never actually run into a creature like the one you met, but I think I know what it is—a portal drake. The kind of watchdog a dragon priestess might use to guard the approach to something important."

"Which means Torm has given us one more chance to unmask Nala before the army marches," Medrash said. He always stood tall, but now seemed to draw himself up straighter still. "Lead on, kinsman."

Khouryn's nerves felt taut as they prowled along. It had nothing to do with the darkness or the stone overhead and all around. To a dwarf, such an environment was arguably more congenial than clear skies and green fields. Nor was he worried about the portal drake. Even if it was still alive, the three of them could handle it.

He was concerned because by then, Nala almost certainly knew someone had fought the reptile and survived. She didn't know it was Balasar, or she would have tried to murder the Daardendrien as, Khouryn suspected, she'd sent the devil on the balcony to dispose of him. But she'd likely emplaced something worse than a portal drake and zombies to keep her secrets safe.

"I can't believe Patrin knows," Medrash said abruptly. "It's difficult to imagine how he could *not* know, being a champion of the dragon god and Nala's lover too, but I can't believe he understands the vileness."

Khouryn grunted. "I think it's the same with most of the cultists, like the ones who wanted us to join their revels. They're just misguided. At least until Nala has enough time to really twist their heads around."

"That's true," Medrash said. "We're fighting to save them as much as anyone else."

"A noble sentiment," Balasar said. "But it won't mean a fish's toenail if we can't figure out how to win. We're coming up on the corner where the portal drake attacked me. I'll give the signal Raiann gave. If the wretched beast is still alive, that may convince it to leave us alone." He whistled three ascending notes, the sounds reverberating off the walls.

Afterward, they stalked around the right-angle bend without incident. The tunnel beyond looked no different than the dark, lonely ones they'd just traversed.

"Can one of you find the way from here?" Balasar asked.

"I can ask the Loyal Fury for a sign," Medrash said.

"And I can be a dwarf," said Khouryn. "Maybe Lady Luck will smile on one of us." He pulled off one of his leather and steel gauntlets and ran his fingertips along the right wall as they moved ahead. The granite was smooth and cool to the touch.

He wasn't as attuned to rock or as adept at stonework as the master quarrymen, miners, and builders of his people. From childhood it had been clear that the Soul Forger had created him for war, and he'd pursued his calling gladly. Yet even so, he fancied he had a fair chance at finding something that even a dragonborn as clever as Balasar had missed.

Behind him, Medrash murmured a prayer. The holy Power he was drawing down warmed the air and made Khouryn feel vibrantly healthy and alert. But it didn't produce a disembodied hand with an outstretched finger, or any other supernatural signpost to point the way.

Fortunately, it didn't need to.

Though Khouryn was currently running his hand along the right wall, he suddenly sensed something different about the left one. When he looked straight at it, he spotted the minute cracks that outlined a hidden door. Maybe he'd unconsciously noticed them before, or else some subtler instinct was at work.

"Here," he said, pointing. "A door of sorts. I think it turns on a central pivot." He pushed on the wall, but there wasn't any give at all. "Or at least it should."

"You mean it's latched or locked," Balasar said. He ran his hands over the surface. "I don't feel a catch, a keyhole, or anything like that."

"It could be magic," Khouryn said. "We might need a talisman, or to speak a password."

Balasar whistled the same three notes that had supposedly calmed the portal drake. They didn't open the wall. "I guess we could bring a mage down here."

"That may not be necessary," said Medrash. He planted his hands on the door and chanted somewhat louder than he had before. Khouryn had a sense of fierce but beneficent Power gathering. Then, grunting, Medrash pushed with all his might. And for that one moment he evidently possessed a giant's strength, because something crunched and then the section of wall scraped partway open.

If it had opened fully, the space would have been just large enough for a donkey cart to squeeze through. On the other side were stone sarcophagi like Balasar had described, though Khouryn judged that this was a larger and even more opulent tomb. Tapers burned in five-branched candelabra, the flames variously red, blue, white, green, or teardrops of shadow. The statue of a five-headed dragon reared in the gloom.

As they crept inside, Balasar murmured, "I wonder why the family thought they needed a secret way in and out of their crypt. Or do you think the builders installed the door on the sly, so they could rob the dead?"

"I don't know," Khouryn said. "But I'll tell you something I *have* figured out. Nala doesn't really worship Bahamut. This is a shrine—"

He suddenly sensed motion on his left. He pivoted just in time to see Medrash cut at his head.

* * * * *

Aoth noticed that the faces around the crackling, smoky campfire all had one thing in common. They reflected a grinding weariness. Most of them looked worried too. But, included in the council of war simply because they were mages, Oraxes and Meralaine were surreptitiously trading smiles as they sat side by side on the ground.

Aoth supposed they were too ignorant to be scared. Or maybe youthful infatuation trumped mundane concerns. He wondered with a touch of wistfulness if he'd ever suffered from that particular delirium. Maybe not. His temperament had always been phlegmatic and pragmatic. Certainly, with a hundred years behind him, he was in no danger of experiencing it now.

Although Cera had showed him he could still like a woman well enough to do something reckless to help her. He smiled and hoped she was keeping out of trouble in Soolabax.

Then Tchazzar came striding up to the fire with a crimson cloak billowing out behind him and Jhesrhi in tow. Everyone rose to bow or salute as quickly as stiff, aching limbs would allow.

The war hero sat down on the campstool reserved for his use. He flicked a hand as though brushing away a gnat. "Sit. Report. You first, Captain."

"I'll let Shala and Hasos speak to the condition of the troops, Majesty. I spent most of the day with the scouts."

"And?"

"Threskel has more companies in the field, essentially a whole other army we haven't fought yet. They're maneuvering to keep us from retreating to Soolabax and to keep reinforcements from reaching us."

"How is that possible?" Shala asked, the firelight gleaming on the bits of steel trim on her masculine garments. "Threskel is a poor country. Even if Alasklerbanbastos spent every coin in his hoard, how can he field so many troops?"

"I can speculate," said Aoth. "Ships supposedly in the service of High Imaskar have been raiding the Chessentan coast and Chessentan shipping for a while."

Tchazzar gave a brusque nod. "The ships with dragonborn for crew."

Aoth hesitated. Did Tchazzar truly not remember they had reason to doubt those particular pirates were actually Tymantherans? "That's what the survivors claimed. At any rate, there was nothing to indicate the raiders were in league with Threskel. But it's possible they've formed an alliance, and the pirate fleet landed troops to help Alasklerbanbastos fight us."

"It would have been nice," said Hasos, his head wrapped in bloody bandages, "if the great sellsword captain had noticed the existence of such an alliance before now."

Aoth glowered, partly because he too had been privately wondering if he should somehow have predicted what was coming. "My lord, I remind you that I'm not one of His Majesty's envoys or spies. I'm just a war leader. Now, if you want to cast blame because no one spotted the new troops before they reached their present positions . . . well, maybe there you have a point. But it's hard to look everywhere at once, and we were busy keeping track of the three dragons and their minions."

"Besides," Gaedynn said, "this is your country, milord—give or take—and what useful intelligence have your own scouts ever gathered about anything? Perhaps you should pry their eyes open before you criticize the way my fellows do their jobs."

Hasos sucked in a breath, no doubt for an angry retort, but Shala spoke first. "Captain, a moment ago you said, 'ships *supposedly* in the service of High Imaskar.' What did you mean by that?"

Grateful to her for interrupting the budding quarrel, Aoth said, "Ever since we learned the truth—well, part of it—about the Green Hand murders and the violence in Soolabax, we've known Chessenta has enemies who are using misdirection against us. And none of us scouts saw any Imaskari today. Even though, with that marbling in their skins and those black clothes they like, they'd be hard to miss."

"Maybe they hired mercenaries and stayed home themselves," Hasos said.

Aoth shrugged. "Maybe."

"Whoever they are," Tchazzar said, "they mean to kill us if they can. What is the state of the army?"

"One man in nine is either dead or unfit to fight," Shala said. "The rest are exhausted. Even after scavenging what we could from the battlefield, we're short on arrows. I recommend we not fight again if we can possibly avoid it. If we fall back toward the Sky Riders—"

Tchazzar's glare was enough to cut her off. "We will *not* go any closer to the Sky Riders," he growled.

Shala met his gaze for what seemed like a long time, then finally bowed her head. "As you command, Majesty."

"Exactly," said the living god, "as *I* command. Now, let's talk about why we're in this fix."

With that, silence fell, broken only by the popping and snapping of the fire and the drone of the camp as a whole. Aoth was astonished—to say nothing of wary—that Tchazzar would redirect the discussion in such a way, and he imagined everyone else was too. He wondered if any good could possibly come of giving an honest response.

He was still wondering when Gaedynn spoke up.

"Since you ask, Majesty, I would have to say—with all respect—that even with the complication of Jaxanaedegor and the ghosts, the plan could still have worked. If you'd acted when the rest of us expected it."

Tchazzar was as handsome a man as Aoth had ever seen, yet he contrived to smile a smile as ugly as the stained leer on a lich's withered skull. "So it's all my fault, is it? Do you all agree?" He rose. "Does each and every one of you agree?"

* * * * *

Khouryn jumped back, and the sword stroke fell short. He kept backpedaling as he snatched for the urgrosh strapped to his back.

As he did, he glimpsed another Medrash trading cuts with Balasar. Or at any rate one version of Balasar. A second one slashed right, left, and right again at the Medrash and Khouryn who were trying to flank him.

Obviously the guardians of Nala's shrine could adopt the appearances of those they fought. Khouryn wished that Aoth and his truesight were there.

The false Medrash's sword whirled in a backhand cut at his throat. He parried with his spiked axe, and steel clashed on steel. But at the same moment he felt something slice across his thigh.

He didn't think the attack had cut deeply. His leather breeches had spared him the worst of it. But a sudden grogginess took hold of him. His eyelids drooped, and the urgrosh felt heavy in his hands. Insane as it was in the middle of a fight for his life, he had the feeling he was in danger of pitching over fast asleep.

He attacked furiously, recklessly, and his foe gave ground. With each swing he bellowed a war cry. The frantic onslaught woke him up, but also left him vulnerable to a sudden stop thrust. He managed to jerk to a halt with the false Medrash's point a finger-length from his chest.

Another invisible attack slashed across his knee. Once again lethargy tried to smother him, and he bellowed it—or the worst of it—away. Perhaps to achieve the same end, Medrash and Balasar were shouting too, and the clamor echoed through the crypt.

Khouryn doubted he could endure too many more doses of sleep venom or too many more slices across the leg before one crippled him. But he had figured out his opponent's favorite combination—cut high with the sword to draw a parry, then immediately slash low with whatever it was that did that.

Khouryn sidestepped the next sword stroke and simultaneously chopped with the urgrosh. Though he couldn't see his target, battle sense guided his hands, and he felt his weapon bite.

The false Medrash gave a shrill hiss unlike any sound that Khouryn had ever heard emerge from the mouth of a genuine dragonborn. The mask of illusion fell away, revealing a reptilian creature skinny as a snake, its body mottled with an intricate pattern of black and purple scales. Covered in spines, the severed tip of its long tail twitched and coiled on the floor.

Then the guardian's form rippled, and illusion veiled it once more. But not the same illusion. Khouryn was facing himself.

He assumed the trick was supposed to make him hesitate, but if so the reptile had misjudged him. He advanced, struck, and his foe didn't hop back quickly enough. The axe ripped a gash in its torso.

Pain tore down Khouryn's body as if he truly had cut his own flesh. It's not real! he insisted to himself. And when the reptile hurled itself at him, he met it with another strike.

The urgrosh smashed through ribs and into its target's vitals. The shock, or the echo of it, made Khouryn black out. When he roused, he was lying on the floor. So was his foe. Looking like its natural self again, it stared at him with lifeless, slit-pupiled eyes.

He judged that he'd only been unconscious for a heartbeat or two, because everyone else was still fighting. The other guardians had adopted the same tactic the dead one had used at the last. Medrash was dueling a copy of himself, and Balasar other Balasars.

And even there, where the fact that two were fighting one should have made it obvious, Khouryn found it difficult to pick out the real Balasar from one moment to the next. It was like there was more than simple illusion at work, like the guardians' power gnawed at his mind to promote confusion and hysteria.

Refusing to succumb to them, he studied what was happening in front of him. Then he jumped up, rushed one of the Balasars, and chopped the base of its spine. Its shroud of illusion melted away as the creature crumpled. He started toward the other, and then instinct made him stop short. He felt the breeze as the reptile's tail spikes whipped by in front of his face. He lunged into striking range and hacked one of its legs out from under it.

The real Balasar pounced to finish it off, and Khouryn rounded on the nearer Medrash. Who saw him coming and cried, "No! It's me! Kill the other one!"

"Sorry," Khouryn answered. He swung at the speaker's kidney, and it collapsed in a frenzy of skinny, thrashing limbs and whipping tail. The actual Medrash dispatched it with a thrust to the heart.

Still feeling some ache from his phantom wounds as well as the genuine gashes on his leg, Khouryn looked around. He didn't see anything else advancing to attack. "Everyone all right?" he panted.

"Just scratched up a little," Balasar said. "And craving a nap. How could you tell the difference between them and us?"

"The purplespawn copied your looks," Khouryn answered. "They couldn't copy your fighting styles. And when I stared hard, I could make out the details of what was going on."

"Purplespawn," Balasar repeated. "That's what these things are?"

"I think so," Khouryn said. "They generally live underground like dwarves do. They're supposed to be related to dark elves and dragons too, disturbing as that coupling is to imagine."

"So," said Medrash, "like the portal drake, they're the kind of creature we might expect to find in Nala's service. But before they interrupted us, you were telling us you'd discovered something you didn't expect."

Khouryn grinned. "Ah yes." Since he'd decided to linger in Tymanther, he'd often regretted that he had so little aptitude for unraveling mysteries and conspiracies; Gaedynn or Aoth could surely do better. But by the Wanderer's Eye, with help from the Daardendriens, he'd still found the end of the trail. "This isn't a shrine to Bahamut but to Tiamat. Nala is actually a wyrmkeeper, a priestess of Tiamat."

The dragonborn just looked at him.

"I don't know a great deal about either Bahamut or Tiamat," Khouryn persisted. "My people worship other gods. But I do know that Bahamut is considered good, and Tiamat evil. So, by infiltrating the Platinum Cadre, Nala has taken a group of worshipers who aspired to be virtuous and tricked them into corruption."

"But for the most part," Balasar said, "dragonborn don't know anything about any of your gods." He stifled a yawn. "They certainly don't know enough to distinguish between one dragon god and another. Now that Nala's accomplished the hard task of convincing them that any kind of wyrm worship can be a good thing, I don't think this bit of news will trouble them. They simply won't understand it."

Khouryn frowned. "Surely the cultists won't like hearing they pledged themselves to a completely different god than they imagined."

"Once they go through the initiation," Balasar replied, "Nala has at least the tip of a claw in every one of their heads." He yawned again. "They're the least likely of all to see the importance."

"Curse it!" Khouryn said. "I can't believe we've come this far and still have nothing!"

"I don't believe it either," Medrash said. He looked around and then, for want of anything better, wiped the blood from his sword with the edge of his cloak. "Torm brought us here for a reason." He smiled. "And besides, you're both forgetting we still haven't discovered the reason for that wagonload of sand."

Watching for more purplespawn or other threats, they stalked deeper into the tomb. Khouryn reflected that the owners must be—or have been—an important clan to possess such a spacious vault. Then he gasped at something extraordinary enough to push all such extraneous thoughts right out of his head.

Khouryn didn't know a great deal about glassblowing, but he recognized the furnaces, blowpipes, marver, punty, and other tools required for the work. Raiann had set up in an open space where three crypts came together, and the five-headed statue of Tiamat he'd glimpsed previously loomed over everything else.

Nala's ritual circle covered the patch of floor immediately in front of the idol. Intricately rendered in several colors, the figure was in its essence a wheel with **S**-shaped spokes.

The glass globes that Raiann crafted and Nala enchanted sat on a simple wooden rack convenient to both workspaces. Pinpoints of light from the votive candles reflected in the curves.

This, or something like it, was exactly what Khouryn and his comrades had needed to find. Yet for a moment, he felt less overjoyed than stunned by the sheer audacity and enormity of Nala's scheme. She hadn't just seized on the opportunity a menace afforded to foist her noisome creed on her fellow dragonborn. She'd help create the threat by crafting weapons to make the giants more dangerous than they'd ever been before.

"I said the barbarians had never made anything as fine—as civilized—as those orbs," Balasar remarked at length. "Do you remember me saying that?"

"I remember Nala destroying every talisman we captured as soon as she could get her hands on it," Medrash answered. "To make sure no mage or diviner could possibly figure out who fashioned it."

Balasar strode to an improvised desk, a sarcophagus with parchment and writing implements on top and a stool positioned beside it. He picked up a couple of papers and, squinting in what for him was inadequate light, skimmed the text. "Who's Skuthosiin?"

"A dragon," said Khouryn, "who used to live hereabouts. He died during the Spellplague."

"Don't bet on it. We'll have to go through these notes at length, but it seems Nala's in communication with him."

"I assume," Medrash said, "that we can obtain other samples of Nala's handwriting for comparison."

Balasar laughed. "Oh yes. We have her. We absolutely have her. When Tarhun—" His eyes widened. "Watch out!"

Khouryn pivoted. Glaring, swaying slightly from side to side, Nala stood between them and the door Medrash had forced open.

Khouryn rushed her. The Daardendriens did too. She whirled and bolted for the corridor. As she dived through the door, she hissed a phrase in what he suspected was Draconic.

The door swung shut, nearly bashing Khouryn in the nose. He tried repeating the syllables Nala had spoken. Evidently he didn't have them exactly right, because the mass of stone refused to pivot.

"Let me," Medrash said. He planted his hands on the door, rattled off his prayer or mantra, and shoved. The door grated partway open as it had before.

But by the time they stepped back out into the passage, Nala was gone. They couldn't even hear her footsteps.

* * * * *

Jhesrhi stood up. "Majesty," she said, "I'm sure—"

Tchazzar whirled. His glare silenced her. "They can speak for themselves," he rapped.

Jhesrhi swallowed. "Yes, Majesty."

The dragon turned back to the other folk seated around the camp-fire. "Would anyone else like to speak words of blame?" Evidently, no one did. He fixed his eyes on Gaedynn. "Then perhaps you, sir archer, would care to expand on what you said before."

Jhesrhi gazed at Gaedynn too, and hoped he'd understand what she wanted to convey: Control your tongue. Don't antagonize him any further.

Gaedynn took a breath and let it out. Then, a tightness evident in his normally light, flippant baritone, he said, "Majesty, if it seemed I spoke words of reproach, then I ask your pardon for expressing myself poorly. I meant that I must not have understood the battle plan, because events didn't unfold as I anticipated."

Tchazzar sneered. "No, they probably didn't. Because I'm surrounded by incompetence and disloyalty. And *that's* the reason we didn't win today. Take this little bitch, for example." Quick as a striking serpent, he grabbed Meralaine and jerked her to her feet.

She yelped, and Oraxes's jaw and neck muscles bunched, betraying a desperate resolve. It was Aoth's turn to give a silent, surreptitious signal—he made a little patting motion, telling the boy to stay put. He then stood up himself, but slowly enough that Tchazzar might not interpret the action as challenging.

"I brought Meralaine north," said Aoth, his voice as mild and devoid of aggression as his movements. "That makes her a warrior of the Brotherhood, or as good as, and my responsibility. To discipline, if need be. Please tell me how she's offended."

"Isn't it obvious?" Tchazzar replied. "I ordered her not to use necromancy, and yet she stinks of the grave."

"Our foes summoned the dead," Aoth replied. "She simply used her art to dismiss and control them. We might have fared far worse if she hadn't."

"It's true, Majesty," Jhesrhi said.

"Maybe," Tchazzar said through gritted teeth. "Maybe." He let go of Meralaine. Caught by surprise, she staggered a step and almost fell on her rump. "But who will justify what this one did?" He rounded on Shala.

Shala met his glare without flinching. "How have I displeased Your Majesty?"

"Do you think me deaf? That I didn't hear *my* troops shouting *your* name? You want the throne back, don't you, traitor? You're sowing the seeds of a coup."

"Majesty, someone had to lead after Lord Hasos was incapacitated, and I didn't tell the men what to chant. They simply fell back into an old habit, and I was too busy to correct them."

"Stand up," Tchazzar said, and Shala did. "Give me your sword." She drew the weapon and handed it to him.

Firelight ran along the blade as he sighted down its length. "A fine weapon," he said. "With a proud history, I imagine."

"Yes, Majesty," Shala said. "Ishual Karanok used it to defend Chessenta during the Spellplague."

One hand gripping the leather-wrapped hilt and the other the blade, Tchazzar held the sword at eye level. He then hissed a charm of weakening, the words so charged with malignancy that they made Jhesrhi's ears ache and her stomach churn.

When he finished, he thrust the sword back at Shala pommel first. "Break it," he said.

She hesitated. "Majesty?"

"You just told me it's the blade of a war hero. Break it to show me you understand you are no longer a war hero and never will be again."

Her square, plain features betraying nothing, Shala took the sword in both hands and did as he'd commanded. He crowed when the weapon snapped like a dry stick.

"Let that be a lesson to all of you!" Tchazzar cried. "Understand that you are blessed! Of all the peoples in all Faerûn, only Chessentans have a god incarnate guiding and protecting them every day of their lives. Never doubt or question! Be grateful and rejoice!"

A part of Jhesrhi wanted to say that was exactly how everyone felt. It seemed the best way to calm him down. But the words caught in her throat, and it appeared that nobody else was moved to speak them either.

Tchazzar took in their silence and shuddered. He grew a little taller, and his nose and jaws protruded a trifle from the rest of his face. A wisp of smoke curled from one nostril, and Gaedynn's hand slipped toward the spot on the ground where he'd set his bow.

I have to stop this, Jhesrhi thought. She struggled to figure out how, and then a putrid stench filled her nose and nearly made her gag. "Look up!" Aoth shouted, and she did.

A cloud of mist spilled down from the sky. As it reached the ground, it drew in on itself, thickening and taking on a definite, bat-winged form. Slanted yellow eyes gleamed in a scaly, wedge-shaped head.

Jhesrhi felt an odd mix of fear and relief. Fear because she'd discerned how powerful Jaxanaedegor was when she and Gaedynn were his prisoners. Relief because Tchazzar had a new target for his ire, and because for some mad reason the vampiric green had intruded without any of his minions. Which ought to mean that, his prowess notwithstanding, she and her comrades could destroy him.

Everyone who wasn't already standing scrambled to his feet. Aoth leveled his spear, and blue light seethed around the point. Jhesrhi gripped her staff with both hands and felt the pseudomind inside exult when she called for fire. Tchazzar grew to colossal size in a heartbeat, and Oraxes jumped aside to keep the red wyrm's writhing, lengthening tail from knocking him down.

Jaxanaedegor snarled, "I claim my right to parley under the Twenty-Eighth Precept!"

Or at least Jhesrhi thought that was what he'd said. Like many wizards, she spoke some Draconic. But she wasn't entirely fluent, and unless she was mistaken, the green had used an obscure or archaic dialect.

With the possible exception of Aoth, none of the other humans gathered there comprehended any of it at all. They continued readying their weapons, Shala gripping her stub of sword for want of anything better. The warriors at neighboring campfires cried out. Their footsteps thumped as they scrambled for their gear.

"Halt!" Tchazzar roared, tongues of flame flaring from his jaws. The sound was prodigiously loud, and everyone faltered.

"Lord Jaxanaedegor and I will confer," Tchazzar continued in a somewhat softer voice. "Alone." And then, to Jhesrhi's astonishment, he and the green stalked into the dark together.

TEN

16 KYTHORN, THE YEAR OF THE AGELESS ONE (1479 DR)

Medrash and his companions climbed out of the Catacombs as fast as they could. But as they scrambled up the steps that connected one of the uppermost tunnels to the Market Floor, he saw that it hadn't been fast enough.

Some—the most agitated or tainted ones, no doubt—slithering vertically in place, wyrm-worshipers surrounded the top of the stairs. They glared down at those whose path they obstructed.

Balasar gave them a charming grin. "Brothers! Sisters! Wonderful news! My clan brother and the dwarf have decided to join our faith!"

"Spy!" someone spat.

"Liar!" cried somebody else.

Others called for Nala. Her name echoed off the thick stone columns and away across the market.

"Let us pass," Medrash said. "You have no right to hinder us."

In response, some cultists inhaled deeply, readying their breath weapons. Others hefted blades and maces. Probably thanks to the dancing, they had a goodly supply.

203

Medrash cloaked himself in the majesty of Torm. The cultists' eyes widened. "Let us pass," he repeated.

The dragon-worshipers flinched. Started to clear a path. Then, in a puff of displaced air, Patrin and Nala appeared out of nowhere, the latter with a small gray drake perched on her shoulder. It had a scabby gash in its flank where Balasar's knife had pierced it.

And what a shame the blade hadn't killed the portal drake. For it was no doubt the creature's power that had enabled Nala to exit the Catacombs far enough in advance of her foes to arrange the reception.

"My friends," Patrin said, looking down the stairs, "what are you doing?"

For an instant, Medrash considered lying. But Balasar's lie hadn't accomplished anything. Besides, lying had never been Medrash's way, and it certainly wasn't the path of Torm.

"You know," he said. "Or rather, you know what Nala told you—a distorted version of the truth. Down in the Catacombs, we found evidence of her crimes. Proof that she doesn't worship your Bahamut but a different Power altogether, and has tricked the Platinum Cadre into serving that goddess as well. Proof that she herself creates the summoning orbs for the giants."

A sort of collective snarl sounded from the mob.

"Growl as much as you like," Balasar said. He reached into his jerkin and brought out one of the green globes. "Here's a talisman she hadn't yet gotten around to smuggling out. We have papers she wrote as well."

Patrin scowled. "We just won a victory against the giants. I don't suppose it was difficult to loot the bodies of a few adepts. If a clan has the resources of Daardendrien, I don't imagine it's difficult to get documents forged either."

"You know us," Medrash said. "Would any of us be a party to such a thing?"

"I don't like believing it," Patrin said. "But time after time I've seen how my faith repulses you, even when you tried to hide it. And plainly you're not above deceit, or Balasar would never have joined the Cadre."

"You have us there," Balasar said. "I did trick you. But a little trickery is one thing. A false accusation of treason is another. I ask you to believe we wouldn't stoop to that."

Nala laughed an ugly laugh. "He has the gall to say that, when we intercepted them on the way to do that very thing!"

Khouryn looked up at Patrin. "If you won't trust us, then trust the vanquisher's justice. If our accusations are false, then Nala has nothing to fear."

The wyrmkeeper touched her lover and champion on the forearm. "We've come so far," she said. "But there are still many—including counselors close to Tarhun—who despise us. Don't give anyone a chance to undo what we've accomplished."

"Iron and stone," Khouryn said, still speaking to Patrin, "just think, will you? I'm no priest or mystic, but even I now understand why your gifts are nothing like those of the rest of the Cadre. You were pledged to Bahamut before you ever met Nala. Your bond with your god shields you from Tiamat's taint. But the rank and file aren't as lucky."

Patrin hesitated, and Medrash hoped the dwarf was getting through to him. Then the other paladin said, "I do have a tie to the Lord of the North Wind. So I'd know it if anyone were subverting his worship."

"No," Medrash said. "Ever since Torm drew me to the scene of one of the murders in Luthcheq, I've prayed for him to tell me everything I need to know and what I'm supposed to do about it. But I've learned that except in the rarest instances, the gods don't operate that way. Which means that even paladins can miss the truth and make mistakes."

"My dear one," said Nala to Patrin, "remember how it was for you—for all of Bahamut's worshipers—before I heard his call and came to guide you. You were a tiny circle of outcasts scorned by all. Look at us now. Can you possibly doubt that you and I have been doing his work?"

"No," Patrin. "Of course I don't."

"So what happens now?" Balasar asked. "Are you going to set this whole mob on us? You'll make murderers of them if you do."

"That doesn't matter," Nala said. "No one will ever know what became of you." But perhaps that had been the wrong tack to take, for it drew a frown from Patrin.

"If you send dozens against three," Medrash asked, "is that in accordance with Bahamut's creed?"

Patrin scowled. "It would be better if you surrendered. I'm not sure what we'll do thereafter, but I guarantee your lives."

"I have a better idea," Medrash said. "You and I will fight a fair fight, one against one. A duel of honor that won't get anyone in trouble with the law.

"If I win," he continued, "then we all go to Tarhun together. Balasar, Khouryn, and I will present our charges, and Nala will rebut them as best she can.

"If you win, then Balasar and Khouryn—and I, if I'm still breathing—will give ourselves into your hands. You can destroy our evidence, extort promises, or anything else you like."

Nala's fingers tightened on Patrin's forearm. "There's no need for this. We *have* them."

Patrin smiled at her. "You're not a warrior, so you don't understand. There is a need, because it's the honorable thing. Besides, there's nothing to worry about. Truth and right are on our side." He gently removed her grip from his arm and looked at the cultists clustered around them. "Clear a space."

Medrash took a deep breath. He'd achieved his purpose. The mob wasn't going to tear them apart. But he hated the thought of dueling a warrior whom, despite everything, he regarded as a comrade and a friend.

Especially when he was by no means certain he was going to win.

* * * * *

Aoth felt as dumbfounded as everyone else looked. Jaxanaedegor was Alasklerbanbastos's chief lieutenant and the commander who'd nearly slaughtered Tchazzar's army. And the two of them were strolling off together like old friends? What in the name of the Black Flame was the Twenty-Eighth Precept anyway?

"Well," Gaedynn said, an arrow still resting on his bow, "that was interesting." He turned to Jhesrhi and arched an eyebrow. "Can you explain it?"

"No," she said. A line of blue and yellow flame rippled down her staff, then guttered out.

"How odd," the archer said. "I thought you were privy to all his divine secrets."

"Don't start," Aoth said. "We have work to do." He gestured to Oraxes and Meralaine. "You too."

Shala started around the campfire. "Captain, if—"

"No, High Lady," said Aoth. "Thank you, but no. This is a matter for the Brotherhood." He led his fellow mages and Gaedynn into a stand of oaks.

"Actually," Oraxes said, "Meralaine and I aren't sellswords either."

"Shut up," said Aoth. "Here's the plan. I'm going to sneak after the dragons and eavesdrop."

Gaedynn smiled. "That sounds a little dangerous."

"That's why I need every enchantment anyone can cast to help me hide."

"It also sounds like work for an expert scout."

"You don't speak Draconic."

Oraxes swallowed. "I speak some. And I can veil myself even better than I can somebody else."

"Thanks," said Aoth. "But it's my stupid idea, and I'll run the risk. If I get caught, none of you knew anything about it."

"Captain . . ." Meralaine's voice trailed off, but she finished her thought by indicating Jhesrhi with a tiny jerk of her head.

"It's all right," Gaedynn said. "She's still one of us. Aren't you, Buttercup?"

"Of course!" Jhesrhi snapped. "But I don't like this."

"Neither do I," said Aoth. "Now everyone start conjuring."

* * * * *

As he climbed the last few steps, Medrash studied Patrin. Bahamut's champion wore sturdy garments incorporating a fair amount of leather. They'd provide him with a measure of protection, but not nearly so much as actual armor.

That was good as far as it went. But it just meant the two combatants were equal in one regard, because Medrash wasn't wearing armor either. When he'd found Balasar's note, he hadn't known how dangerous the night would become, and hadn't wanted to make himself conspicuous by clinking around the city in plate or mail.

He suspected there were ways in which his foe actually had the advantage. Medrash had already exerted himself and expended mystic Power. He'd been scratched by a purplespawn's tail, and though he'd used Torm's gifts to heal himself, he might still have a trace of sleep poison in his veins to slow him down. Whereas Patrin was presumably fresh.

But at least Medrash had truth and right on his side, and never mind that Patrin had just asserted exactly the same thing.

As he took his starting position opposite the other paladin, Patrin said, "I never wanted this. I still believe our gods intended us to be friends."

"Then don't fight," Medrash said. "Come with us to Tarhun and let him determine the truth."

Patrin shook his head. "I can't. Not now that I know you hate us enough to lie." He drew his sword, gave Medrash just enough time to do the same, and charged him.

Medrash spat lightning. It flickered down Patrin's torso, and he stumbled and shuddered. Medrash sprinted forward, his point extended at the other warrior's sword arm.

But Patrin recovered from the shock before his adversary could close the distance. He sidestepped and shouted Bahamut's name. His blade blazed with silvery light as he cut at Medrash's flank.

Medrash saw that his own attack was going to miss and snapped his blade across his body just in time to parry. Charged with the Platinum

Dragon's Power, Patrin's stroke almost jolted his weapon from his grip. But only almost, and then he plunged on by.

Which carried him out of striking range but put his back to his foe. Using one of Balasar's favorite moves, Medrash ducked, whirled, and slashed.

The cut didn't hit anything, because Patrin wasn't rushing in to take him from behind. Instead, Bahamut's champion chanted, swept his sword through a star-shaped figure, then thrust it out.

Once again the blade flared with white light, and for that same instant, Medrash saw the ghostly form of a pale, gleaming dragon behind his foe. Bahamut's head snapped forward, and his jaws gaped.

Medrash threw himself to the side. Still, he couldn't avoid the blast entirely, and it was as fierce and frigid as any north wind that ever blew. It staggered him and chilled him.

Patrin rushed in and cut at his opponent's flank. Still off balance and shuddering, Medrash managed to parry, but not well. His defense robbed the stroke of some of its force, but Patrin's sword jolted through it to gash his forearm.

Patrin instantly followed up by spewing flame in Medrash's face. Burned, dazzled, Medrash reeled backward and swept his blade through a defensive pattern. He prayed that one of the parries would intercept Patrin's next sword stroke even if he couldn't see it.

Steel rang on steel as he deflected a thrust at his leg. Since he still could barely see, he riposted by drawing down Torm's Power, then clenching his off hand and punching.

Light blazed at Patrin, and a gauntleted fist punched in the center of it. The blast—or the punch; they were one and the same—hurled Bahamut's champion backward. He reeled but stayed on his feet.

Medrash reached out to Torm again. The resulting surge of vitality washed the blurriness and the stinging from his eyes. His sword arm kept bleeding though, and it was starting to throb.

"That's first blood," Patrin said, "and a wound that guarantees you can't win. Please yield. There's no dishonor in it."

Medrash shook his head. "I won't fail Torm and our people," he rasped.

"Then I'll make it quick." Patrin advanced.

It actually wasn't quick. Medrash judged that although Patrin was a good swordsman, he was a notch better, and the difference protected him for the next several phases. It enabled him to parry or dodge sword stroke after sword stroke ablaze with argent Power. But with fatigue and blood loss slowing him down, he could neither go on the offensive nor score with a riposte.

He might be able to channel a little more of Torm's might, but not, he judged, enough to save him. Not unless he used it cleverly. He struggled to think of a tactic, and finally a notion came to him.

First he had to open up the distance. He punched the air, and a flash hurled Patrin back as it had before. Medrash swayed as though the magic had taken everything he had, which wasn't far short of the truth.

Patrin rushed him. Medrash waited until his opponent was almost within striking distance, then clenched his empty hand and jerked his arm back.

For an instant a huge, ghostly fist gripped Patrin and pulled him forward. If Medrash was lucky, maybe it squeezed hard enough to do some damage.

But that wasn't the reason he'd evoked the effect. It was a magic paladins used to drag reluctant foes within reach of their blades. He hoped that if an opponent wasn't reluctant, if he was already charging in, then the unexpected yank would throw him off balance.

Patrin pitched forward. Medrash lunged. His sword drove deep into Patrin's chest. Bahamut's champion crumpled to his knees, then fell forward.

For a few heartbeats, everyone was silent. Medrash could feel the shock and the welling grief of the other cultists like a great reverberation implicit in the stillness.

Then Nala screamed, "He cheated! The Daardendrien cheated! Kill them!"

Her followers surged at Medrash, and at Balasar and Khouryn at the top of the steps, like a noose snapping tight around a hanged outlaw's neck.

Patrin heaved himself up on an elbow. His form glowed with pearly light, and somehow—even fallen, struggling in a spreading pool of his own blood—he seemed indomitable and majestic.

"Stop!" he croaked, and there was power in that too. It should have been inaudible to anyone even a pace or two away, but Medrash was certain the entire crowd could hear it. "He didn't cheat. Do what I promised. Don't disgrace your god. Or me." His body slumped. He plainly couldn't hold his head up any longer.

But he didn't have to. His plea had quelled the fury Nala hoped to incite.

Medrash kneeled down beside Patrin and pressed his hands against the dragon-worshiper's back. Straining, he channeled a whisper of Torm's Power through his own body and into that of the other paladin, but nowhere near enough to mend a fatal wound.

But Nala was a healer! Medrash looked up just in time to see her vanish, whisked away by the power of the small gray drake on her shoulder.

"It's all right," Patrin wheezed.

"I didn't want to kill you," Medrash said. "But I knew I only had one chance. I had to make sure I ended the fight."

"It's all right," Patrin repeated, his voice growing even softer. "I prayed for truth and right to prevail, and they did. If Nala was what I thought . . ." He shuddered and then lay absolutely still.

For a moment, Medrash hated himself. Perhaps he even hated Torm, whose path had led him to that moment. Then that feeling crumbled into a pure and bitter regret. Clenching himself against the urge to howl out his grief, he stayed beside the corpse until Balasar came and gripped his shoulder. "Let's find somebody to stitch up that arm," the smaller Daardendrien said.

* * * * *

Aoth could see his hands and the spear he carried in the right one, but then, nothing was ever invisible to him. It was somewhat reassuring that he could also see a ghostly shimmer crawling on his limbs, a manifestation of the enchantments Jhesrhi, Oraxes, and Meralaine had cast to veil him.

He was about to find out how well they'd done their work. The wyrms hadn't gone very far from camp. They were just ahead, their long necks rising like strangely curving tree trunks with all the spiny, leafless branches on one side.

Jet spoke to him across their psychic link. *Even if they don't see you, what about their noses? What about their ears?*

Aoth sighed. *Who woke you up? Gaedynn?*

If you need a diversion, tell me and he'll provide it.

No, he won't. Neither will you.

Do you have any idea how sharp a dragon's senses are?

Yes. But if the magic worked, I have no scent, and just in case it didn't I'm downwind. And as far as noise is concerned, I do know how to sneak. I sneaked up on Malark on top of Szass Tam's mountain.

And then he spotted you. And he wasn't even a very old dragon, or undead, or a living god. Why are you doing this? Surely not just because you promised your new female.

No. Because she was right. We need a better understanding of what's going on. All our lives may depend on it. Now stop pestering me and listen through my ears. If I do get into trouble, tell Jhesrhi and Gaedynn everything you heard before . . . well, before.

He skulked up to a broad, weathered stump. Good cover against many creatures, but not those tall enough to peer right over the top of it. He crept even closer to the dragons until he found a mossy old oak with a thick trunk. As he hid behind it, he realized that Tymora had favored him in one respect, anyway. Tchazzar and Jaxanaedegor weren't conversing in the seemingly archaic Draconic dialect the vampire had used in camp. They were speaking the tongue as Aoth had learned it.

"—possibly trust you?" Tchazzar said.

"How can you not?" Jaxanaedegor replied. "Since I had some inkling of their purpose, my agents in Mourktar fought Alasklerbanbastos's to make sure Jhesrhi Coldcreek and Gaedynn Ulraes ended up as *my* prisoners. Then, after I verified my information, I gave them a chance to escape and even allowed them to carry a staff of fire away with them. Because I suspected that if they actually found you, you might need a fountain of flame to restore you to yourself."

In other circumstances, Aoth might have laughed in amazement. Whatever he'd expected to hear, it wasn't that.

Meanwhile, Tchazzar snorted and tinged the air with smoke and sulfur. " 'Gave them a chance.' "

Yellow eyes glowing like foxfire, Jaxanaedegor bared his fangs in what might have been a grin. "I couldn't just unchain them and wave good-bye. I have to assume the dracolich spies on me as he does on others."

"I assume his scrutiny is also supposed to excuse the attack you led against me."

The green flicked his wings. It sounded like the crack of empty sails when a gust of wind finally filled them. "That's exactly right, and look how I managed it. Alasklerbanbastos lost a powerful artifact and three of the dragons who were truly loyal to him. It all would have gone better still if you'd joined the battle sooner."

"Don't presume to criticize me!" Tchazzar snarled. "Not you, a leech and the spawn of the dark! Not you of all creatures!"

Aoth winced at the red's vehemence, and even Jaxanaedegor seemed slightly taken aback. "I . . . intended no offense. I'm simply trying to convince you that I'm on your side, so that together we can exploit an opportunity."

"Which is?"

"It may end up being a good thing that your army took a beating. Alasklerbanbastos is wary, and he didn't recruit all his sellswords and such because he meant to put himself in any real danger. But he also hates you with the cold, gnawing hatred of the undead. If he believes he has you at a serious disadvantage, he'll come out of his caves to deliver the death stroke."

"He does have me at a disadvantage!"

Jaxanaedegor smiled. "I can fix that. I'm directing the troops who are presently maneuvering to contain and isolate you. I can make them zig when they ought to zag, thus allowing reinforcements to reach you."

Tchazzar grunted. "That would be helpful, but not necessarily sufficient."

"Then it's good that I have more to offer. I've communicated with some of the dragon princes and convinced them their arrangements with Alasklerbanbastos are contrary to their long-term interests. As a result, the warriors they provided will prove less useful than he expects."

Aoth nodded. He'd wondered how High Imaskar, never before feared as a naval power, had conducted such a damaging series of raids on the Chessentan coast. And why he hadn't seen any Imaskari among the troops who'd debarked from the pirate fleet to fight for the Great Bone Wyrm. The answer to both riddles was the same—High Imaskar had granted Murghômi warships free access to the Alamber Sea to fight on its behalf.

Which *partly* explained why there'd seemingly been dragonborn among the raiders. Wyrmkeepers were the dastards who knew how to disguise abishais as Tymantherans, and the principalities of Murghôm, city-states ruled by dragons, were presumably crawling with them.

Unfortunately, the revelation raised new questions. In fact, it lent new levels of complexity to a situation that was already convoluted enough to make the War of the Zulkirs seem straightforward. But maybe if Aoth kept listening, he'd finally understand.

"And what of the other dragons Alasklerbanbastos commands?" Tchazzar asked. "Will they 'prove less useful than he expects'?"

"Actually," said Jaxanaedegor, "yes. I told you, we've already started the process of culling the herd. I should be able to eliminate at least one more of those who are truly loyal and blame her destruction on you. Which is to say, the majority of dragons who follow Alasklerbanbastos into battle will be just as tired of him as I am."

"How confident are you that he hasn't discerned their true sentiments? Or yours?"

"Reasonably. His hatred of you—and Skuthosiin, and Gestaniius—blinds him to other concerns. He blames you for every setback and misfortune he ever endured. In addition to which, his arrogance makes it difficult for him to imagine that any of his servants would dare rise up against him. He believes that even I must perforce content myself with fawning at his feet and begging for crumbs from his table."

"As opposed to playing the game on your own behalf."

"Yes. As opposed to that."

Aoth frowned. "Playing the game" was likely just a metaphor for striving for power. Yet something in the dragons' voices made him wonder if the phrase had some deeper meaning. If it had some connection to the Twenty-Eighth Precept.

He was still wondering when the red dragon's head whipped around in his direction. "What's that?" Tchazzar snarled.

"What?" Jaxanaedegor asked.

"The hiss of breath," Tchazzar said. "The thump of a heart." He crouched low, the better to peer along the ground.

I can reveal myself, thought Aoth. I can claim I followed to protect him if Jaxanaedegor played him false.

But instinct—or maybe just fear—persuaded him to remain motionless instead. Tchazzar took a long stride closer to his hiding place. So did Jaxanaedegor. Their yellow eyes, each bigger than a human head, glowed like terrible mockeries of the moon. Their smells washed over Aoth—sulfur and smoke from the red, stinging foulness from the green. He clenched against the urge to cough or retch.

After what felt like a long time, Jaxanaedegor said, "I don't hear anything."

"Neither do I, now." Tchazzar said. A tiny bit of the tension quivered out of Aoth's body, but he kept holding his breath.

Then Tchazzar whirled toward the other wyrm with a speed astonishing in anything so huge. The vampire leaped backward just as quickly. "But if this is a trap, I'll tear you apart!" Tchazzar said.

"If I broke the Precepts," Jaxanaedegor replied, "Brimstone would cast me out, and I wouldn't risk that any more than you would. Besides, my best assassins don't breathe, and their hearts don't beat."

"All right." Tchazzar stood up straighter; he wasn't coiled to spring anymore. "Suppose I decide I'm willing to trust you. What do you want in exchange for your help?"

"Very little. To be the supreme master of my own lands, and no one else's vassal."

"I'm fighting this war to bring Threskel under my control."

"At this point you ought to be fighting to preserve your life and keep Alasklerbanbastos from bringing all Chessenta under his control. But leave that aside. After we win you can credibly claim to rule Threskel, because you actually will govern most of it. Your humans won't care who or what is still inhabiting Mount Thulbane and its environs, because to their way of thinking, the country is a wasteland."

"To everyone's way of thinking," Tchazzar replied. "Which makes me wonder why you're willing to settle for such a meager reward."

"There are two answers to that. The first is that punishing Alasklerbanbastos for his bullying and arrogance will be satisfying for its own sake. The second is that the game has barely begun. I have a long-range strategy that starts with complete control of my own domain, however modest others may judge it to be."

"All right," Tchazzar said. "If you deliver all you've promised, then neither I nor any of my servants will interfere with Mount Thulbane or the lands around it. I swear it by our Dark Lady and my own divinity."

"We have a bargain, then. You'll hear from me by one means or another."

Jaxanaedegor turned, trotted, lashed his wings, and flew up toward the stars. Tchazzar watched the vampire's dwindling form for a time, then abruptly dwindled himself—into human guise. Smiling, one hand resting on the hilt of the sword sheathed at his side, the red dragon sauntered back toward camp. Aoth waited a while, then followed.

* * * * *

For all Nala knew, pursuit was right behind her. Mages, or Lance Defenders riding bats, could have departed Djerad Thymar almost as quickly as she had.

That meant there was no time to bury the portal drake. She could only lay its body gently on the ground.

Despite its wound, she'd pushed it hard, commanding it to shift through space again and again to carry her clear of the city. And the faithful creature obeyed until the strain stopped its heart.

Its death was a tragedy. Worse, it represented yet another crime against the Dark Lady, who'd given Nala the drake to aid her in her holy task. She looked back at Djerad Thymar, rising like a black arrowhead against the starry sky, and a spasm of hatred shook her.

All the goddess's foes were going to pay. Medrash. Balasar. The dwarf. All of them. Because they hadn't won anything. Nala knew where to go and what to do to continue her work. Denying fatigue, fear, or any feeling but rage, she ran across the fields.

ELEVEN

19–24 KYTHORN
THE YEAR OF THE AGELESS ONE (1479 DR)

Balasar rode at the wooden target Khouryn called a quintain. He grinned when the blunt tip of his practice lance thumped home, spinning the horizontal arm out of his way. He had some catching up to do if he was going to practice the strange new form of fighting when the army returned to Black Ash Plain, but he seemed to be getting the hang of it.

Behind him, some of his comrades raised a shout. He turned his horse around, then gaped in surprise.

Dozens of folk were marching toward the muddy training field from the place where Djerad Thymar rose like a broken-tipped blade against a cloudy sky. Several of them were carrying purple pennons with silvery dragon shapes coiling down their lengths.

Balasar hadn't seen such banners since the night Nala fled and her treason became common knowledge, rekindling the average dragonborn's hatred of wyrm worship. He hadn't expected to see them ever again.

By the broken chain, he thought, what's the matter with you people? Go home, lie low, and if anyone asks if you ever belonged to the Platinum Cadre, lie till your scales fall off! Don't throw your lives away!

For it was possible that that was exactly what they were doing. A lancer whooped, couched his weapon, and rode at one of the cultists carrying a banner. The dragon-worshiper made no effort to dodge or otherwise defend himself. The lance slammed him in the chest and hurled him and his pennon to the ground.

It was conceivable that the impact had seriously injured or even killed him. Or that the horse trampled him; tall grass kept Balasar from seeing. Other lancers turned their steeds toward other living targets, and those cultists too made no effort to protect themselves. One warrior dropped his blunt length of ash and drew a sword of gleaming steel.

Balasar sent his horse racing toward the slaughter in the making. "Stop!" he bellowed. "Stop!"

No one paid him any attention.

But then Medrash galloped across the field, between some of the riders and the folk on foot. Even spattered with mud from the practice, even in the midst of the spring sunshine, he seemed to glow, and when he shouted for everyone to halt, his voice boomed like thunder. The lancers reined their horses in.

Balasar sighed and shook his head. Spit and roast him if he ever groveled to Torm or any other jumped-up spook. But there was no denying that it had taught Medrash some useful tricks.

"What's wrong?" shouted one lancer. "These are the traitors! You brought them down!"

"I helped bring down their creed," Medrash answered. "That doesn't mean they deserve to be attacked on sight. Nala tricked them as she did the rest of us."

"She tricked them worse," said Balasar, riding out to take up a position beside his clan brother.

"Some of them were dragon-worshipers before Nala ever declared herself their prophet," another lancer growled.

"And if I hadn't infiltrated the cult and exposed it for what it was," Balasar said, "some of you fools would be lining up to join. So the least you can do is accede to my judgment—and Medrash's—when we tell you you don't need to hurt these people. In fact, if you give yourself over to rage and viciousness, you're embracing the same qualities that the dragon goddess tried to instill in them. So save your strength for killing ash giants!"

"And for practice," Medrash said. "You all need more before we ride south. I suggest you get on with it."

The riders stared back at him for a moment, then sullenly started turning their mounts around. An archer set his horse cantering, then loosed at a target. The arrow pierced the outer ring.

Meanwhile, Medrash rose in his stirrups and peered. Balasar looked where his kinsman was looking. Two of the cultists were helping the fellow who'd taken the blow from the lance get back on his feet. Evidently he wasn't badly injured.

Medrash then regarded the group as a whole. "Get out of here," he said. "Before your presence provokes them all over again."

A brown-scaled female named Vishva stepped from the front of the crowd. Like a number of the cultists, she had little puckered scars on her face. They were the spots where she'd worn her piercings before her clan expelled her.

"With all respect," she said, "we can't do that. We came here for a purpose."

"I don't care," Medrash replied.

She continued as though he hadn't spoken. "Those few of us who were closest to Nala, who understood what she was actually doing and helped her make the talismans, went to ground when she disappeared. The rest of us want to go on fighting the giants."

Medrash snorted. "That's out of the question."

"We need to prove our loyalty and atone for our transgressions."

"Well, you'll have to find another way to do it. Even if Tarhun would tolerate your presence in the ranks, the Lance Defenders and the rest of the army wouldn't. They'd treat you as these fellows"—he jerked his head to indicate his fellow mounted warriors—"wanted to treat you."

"Maybe not," Vishva said. "Not if Clan Daardendrien and the very warriors who unmasked Nala sponsor us."

Balasar laughed. "What a good idea! In case you haven't noticed, the fight against Nala made Medrash and me heroes. Why would we want to jump down into the mud with you?"

"If you won't vouch for us," Vishva said, "then we'll march without it, alone if need be. And if it's only to lay down our lives, so be it. At least we'll die with our honor restored, like Patrin."

Medrash scowled. "Wait here." He rode a little distance from the cultists. Balasar followed.

"What do you think?" Medrash asked.

"I think I'm surprised you'd even bother to inquire," Balasar said. "You despise the very idea of dragon worship, remember? Our elders raised us to despise it. And since these people are still flying their banners, they still are wyrm-worshipers. They're just trying to renounce Tiamat and give their devotion back to the real Bahamut. From a rational, decent perspective, what's the difference?"

"We said we were trying to save them as much as everyone else," said Medrash.

"You and Khouryn said that," Balasar said. "I was busy trying to figure out where the cart had gone and keeping an eye out for trouble."

"How have we saved them if they die on Black Ash Plain or at the hands of their own people before they even get there?" asked Medrash.

"We saved them from Nala's lies," said Balasar. "If they turn right around and commit suicide, that's their problem."

"Even if we could convince them to stay home, what sort of lives would they have?" Medrash asked. "People have always scorned them. They'll hate and persecute them now. Unless they can redeem themselves."

"Is this about you feeling guilty over Patrin?" said Balasar. "Because you're a warrior from a warlike clan. It looks stupid if you feel bad just because you killed somebody."

"I keep remembering how he said that Bahamut and Torm were friends, and we should be too," Medrash said. "I remember that it felt . . . right to fight alongside him. And in the end, even though he realized I'd given him his death, he saved us from the mob."

"I liked him too," Balasar said. "But shepherding his fellow idiots won't bring him back."

"You're the one who spent time with them. So tell me, are they deranged or depraved beyond all hope of redemption?"

Balasar sighed. "No. Nala dirtied them up a little, but essentially they're just people. They joined the Cadre because they were unhappy. It's not all that different from when you pledged yourself to Torm."

Medrash smiled a crooked smile. "I don't like the comparison, but we can save that for another time." Sunlight glinting on the white studs in his face, mail clinking, he urged his horse back toward the cultists. Balasar clucked, bumped his mount with his heels, and rode after him.

Medrash raked the dragon-worshipers with a stern gaze. "You claim you want to atone," he said. "But you still carry Nala's taint. Right now, even as you're asking for our help, some of you are swaying back and forth."

"Can you cleanse us?" Vishva replied. "Nothing would please us more."

"Are you sure?" Medrash said. "If I break your ties to Tiamat, you'll lose her gifts. You won't be able to use your breath attacks more often than any other dragonborn. You won't feel the fury that fills you with strength and burns away your fear. As far as Balasar and I are concerned, that . . . weakening is necessary. We won't sponsor warriors who fight like rabid beasts and gorge on the raw flesh of the fallen. But it means that for you, battle will be more dangerous than before."

"We want to be clean," Vishva said. Other cultists called out in agreement.

"Then you will be." Medrash slid his lance back into the sheath attached to his saddle, then raised high his hand in its steel gauntlet. He whispered something too softly for Balasar to make out the words.

Brightness pulsed from the gauntlet like the slow, steady beats of a heart at rest. Each pulse gave Balasar a kind of pleasant, invigorating jolt, like a plunge into cold water on a hot day.

But the cultists didn't look invigorated. They grimaced and cringed away from the light.

Medrash whispered faster, and the glow throbbed faster too. The distinct shocks of exhilaration Balasar had been experiencing blurred into a continual soaring elation.

The cultists fell to the ground and thrashed. Dark fumes rose from their bodies, five from each. The strands of vapor coiled and twisted around one another like serpentine necks supporting heads that wanted to peer in all directions at once.

The smoke, if that was the proper term for it, looked filthy. Poisonous. Even Balasar's euphoria didn't prevent a pang of loathing. If I'd let it in during my initiation, he thought, that stuff would be inside me too.

As they pulled free of the cultists' bodies, the lengths of vapor whipped one way and another as if they too were convulsing in pain. Some looped around and struck like serpents, seemingly trying to stab their way back inside the flesh that had hitherto sheltered them. But each glanced off like a sword skipping off a shield.

Then, all at once, they leaped at Medrash. Balasar opened his mouth to shout a warning. A final burst of brilliance flared from the paladin's gauntlet, and the vapors frayed to nothing midway to their target.

The light went out of Medrash's hand, and his arm flopped down at his side. His body slumped as if he was about to collapse onto his horse's neck.

Trying for a better look at his clan brother's face, Balasar leaned down. "Are you all right?"

Medrash swallowed. "Yes," he rasped, and then, with a visible effort, sat up straight. "It's just that that was . . . taxing."

"I don't see why," Balasar said. "All you did was the break the hold of a goddess on dozens of people at once. A hatchling could have done it."

Medrash smiled slightly. "Next time we'll find that particular hatchling and give the job to him."

The members of the Cadre started slowly and shakily drawing themselves to their feet.

"Is everyone all right?" Medrash asked.

"I . . . think so," Vishva quavered. "That hurt. It really hurt. But it's better now."

"Better than better," said a fellow with umber scales. A grin lit up his face.

"I was so sick," said a female—astonishment, revulsion, and relief all tangled together in her tone, "so *ugly*. And I didn't even know!"

In another moment, a dozen of the cultists were clamoring all at once.

"Thank you," shouted Vishva, making herself heard above the din, "and thank Torm, who lent you his glory! Thank Bahamut, who led us to you!"

Medrash looked like he didn't know to respond. In the end, he settled on gruffness, perhaps to hide whatever he was feeling.

"Now comes the hard part," he said. "Stripped of your powers, you're nothing special. We can only hope that some hard training will make you marginally useful. As spearmen." He turned to Balasar. "Khouryn doesn't have a prejudice against Bahamut worshipers. Do you think he'll teach them, and lead them into battle when the times comes?"

Balasar grinned. "Oh, I'm sure he'll be as thrilled as I am."

* * * * *

Studying the rolling scrubland beneath them, Aoth and Jet floated on the night wind. Jaxanaedegor could shift the companies under his command as he saw fit. But he couldn't neglect dispatching scouts to range across the countryside, or officers loyal to Alasklerbanbastos would realize something was amiss. Someone had to keep those scouts from reporting that reinforcements were reaching the Chessentan army.

Aoth spotted four kobolds skulking along the lee of a low rise. He kindled light in the point of his spear, swept the weapon down to point at the scouts, then extinguished the glow. He hoped that if the kobolds even noticed, they'd think they'd merely seen a shooting star.

Jet furled his wings and plunged at the kobold at the back of the line. Rising in the stirrups, Aoth braced for the jolt to come.

Jet's talons stabbed home, and his momentum smashed the kobold to the ground beneath him. The scaly little creature likely died without ever even realizing he was in danger, and the *thud* of his demise was relatively quiet.

But not quiet enough. The other three kobolds spun around.

Jet yanked his gory claws out of the dead scout's body, then pounced. He slammed another kobold down on the ground, raked with his leonine hind legs, and tore lengths of gut out of the warrior's belly.

A third kobold hissed rhyming words and jerked a length of carved bone through a zigzag pass. Hoping to blast the shaman before he finished his spell, Aoth aimed his spear at him.

Then Eider plunged down on the reptilian adept to rend and crush the life from him. Gaedynn pivoted in the saddle, drew, and released. The arrow hit the last kobold in the throat, where his hide and bone armor didn't cover. He toppled backward, thrashed, and then lay still.

Jhesrhi and Scar glided to earth. "You didn't leave any work for me," the wizard said.

"We didn't want you to get blood on your new clothes," Gaedynn answered.

Jhesrhi scowled.

Making sure they hadn't missed any kobolds, or anything else requiring their attention, Aoth took a look around. Everything was all right.

Which was to say, they'd tackled the kind of task that sellswords were supposed to perform, and done it well. Wishing that the rest of life was as simple, he said, "This is as good a place as any for a talk."

Gaedynn smiled. "I had a hunch. Why would you take both your lieutenants off on a patrol, unless it was to talk where no one could overhear?"

Aoth swung himself off Jet's back, then scratched his head. It made a rustling sound and tinged the air with the smell of feathers. "I told you about Tchazzar and Jaxanaedegor's palaver. You've had some time to mull it over. What do you think?"

Jhesrhi dismounted and removed a leather bottle from one of Scar's saddlebags. "Essentially," she said, "assuming we can trust Jaxanaedegor, it was all good news. He and his minions will betray Alasklerbanbastos, and we'll all destroy the Great Bone Wyrm together."

Gaedynn snorted. "There's a subtle analysis."

"It's a sound analysis!" Jhesrhi snapped. "And you're a jackass if you don't like it. We're going to win, collect plenty of gold for our trouble, and restore the Brotherhood's reputation. Which is exactly what we came to Chessenta to do."

"So it is," said Aoth. "And half the time, I feel like a fool for trying to look any deeper. But the other half, I worry that something bad will take us by surprise if we don't. So, what do you make of the part of the conversation that Tchazzar didn't share with us? The part that wasn't just him and the vampire conspiring to bring Alasklerbanbastos down?"

Jhesrhi frowned as though she felt rebuked, although that hadn't been Aoth's intention. Pulling the stopper from her bottle, she said, "Have it your way. If you insist on fretting, I do have one bone for you to gnaw on. Do you know the tales of the final Rage of Dragons?"

"I recall a bit of them," Aoth said, "and I lived through a nasty little piece of the Rage myself."

"Well, Brimstone was the name—or, to be precise, the nickname—of one of the wyrms who helped destroy the lich Sammaster and put an end to the madness." Jhesrhi took a drink, hesitated for an instant, then offered the bottle to Aoth.

He made sure his fingers didn't brush hers as he took it. It turned out to contain lukewarm water. Too bad. He'd hoped for something stronger.

Gaedynn shrugged. "The last Rage happened even before the Spellplague. With all respect to our hoary old captain here, I don't see how it could have anything to do with our current problems."

"Neither do I," Jhesrhi said. "Especially since in Karasendrieth's song cycle, Brimstone dies at the end. But it's all I have, so I thought I'd mention it."

Aoth wiped his mouth and passed the water to Gaedynn. "This is just a guess, but maybe Brimstone's a nickname you'd assume if you hoped to command a dragon's respect or even his obedience. And Jaxanaedegor did speak of this Brimstone like it's someone who could impose some sort of sanction against him and Tchazzar both."

Seeming to sense its dislocation by sheer instinct, Gaedynn smoothed down a stray wisp of his coppery hair. "But really, what sense does that make? Jaxanaedegor's overlord is Alasklerbanbastos, and his stated goal is to slay the Bone Wyrm and be free. And Tchazzar is even less inclined to acknowledge any sort of authority. How could he, when he believes he's not just a god, but the greatest of gods?"

Jhesrhi glared. "He never said that."

"Not in so many words," Gaedynn answered. "Not yet. But it's coming."

"Here's one thought," said Aoth, "unlikely though it may seem. More than once, Tchazzar and Jaxanaedegor spoke of playing a game. Some games need an overseer to tally points and enforce the rules."

Gaedynn's eyes narrowed. "Brimstone could be the overseer, and the Precepts could be the rules," he said.

"You're both letting your imaginations run wild," Jhesrhi said. "Aoth, you have to remember you don't speak Draconic perfectly. Even if you did, you don't understand exactly how dragons think or what sort of relationships exist among them. Surely if they referred to a game, it was just a figure of speech."

"Maybe," Aoth admitted.

"Even if they do think of the war as being, in some sense, a game," Jhesrhi said, "what does it matter? Won't we fight it and profit by it the same as ever?"

"I hope so," said Aoth.

"It may not matter to us sellswords," said Gaedynn, "who wanted to fight somebody someplace. But if it's all just an amusement, that's hard luck for the Chessentans and Threskelans, with no choice but to struggle and die for their masters' entertainment."

"It clearly isn't just an amusement," Jhesrhi said. "Tchazzar and Alasklerbanbastos have been trying to destroy one each other for centuries. There aren't two more committed enemies in all the length and breadth of Faerûn. In addition to which, Tchazzar wants to control all the lands that are rightfully his, just like any other king. And since when do you care about the Chessentans, the Threskelans, or anybody else outside the Brotherhood?"

Gaedynn smiled a crooked smile. "Fair enough. You have me there. Which doesn't change the fact that Tchazzar is keeping secrets from us—and is crazy besides. He's no more trustworthy than Nevron or Samas Kul."

"He's sick from his ordeal. You've never suffered anything similar, so you can't understand."

"You have no idea what I've suffered."

"Actually, I do. You told me. And no matter how much you secretly pity yourself because of it, you got off lightly."

Gaedynn hesitated, then said, "If we compared scars, I might concede that yours run deeper than mine. But we're talking about Tchazzar."

"Fine. Let's talk about him. Let's give him credit for getting better."

"Absolutely. He seemed much better, freezing in terror when we needed him. And afterward, when he abused Meralaine and Shala for the heinous offense of helping to keep us all from being overrun."

Aoth frowned. Gaedynn's antipathy for their employer was unprofessional and quite possibly dangerous. Which didn't change the fact that he agreed with the archer's opinion.

"He was a great ruler," Jhesrhi said. "That's why, a hundred years later, people prayed for his return. And he'll do great things again. He's already started."

Gaedynn sighed. "I understand that he's rubbed balm on the galls that have pained you your whole life through. But that doesn't make up for everything else he's done. Or everything he's going to do."

Jhesrhi sneered. "You're not a prophet. You don't know what he's going to do."

"That's true," said Aoth. "None of us does. And, through no fault of either of you, this talk hasn't shed much light on that or any other part of our situation. The only thing I'm sure of is what I already knew going in: We need to abide by our contract, fight the Threskelans, and beat them. If we don't, the Brotherhood is finished."

Gaedynn smiled. "But while we're fighting?"

"We keep our eyes open," said Aoth. "Figure out as much as we can."

"Spy," Jhesrhi said.

"Watch and think," Aoth replied. "Does that bother you?"

"I'll do it," she said. She climbed back onto Scar's back and brushed a fingertip down his neck. The griffon leaped and lashed his wings.

Gaedynn gave Aoth a sour look. "I don't like you making her uncomfortable."

Aoth sighed. "Why? Because it's your job?"

* * * * *

As Khouryn bowed, he took stock of Tarhun. Viewed in bright sunlight, patches of the vanquisher's hide were mottled and a paler green than the rest. That was particularly true around the square gold studs, which the red saurian's fire had likely heated until they themselves were burning hot. But the eyes above the piercings were intact, and the hulking dragonborn stood straight and tall. He looked ready to lead an army once again.

"The healers gave me a great deal of attention," Tarhun said. It startled Khouryn, who'd tried to make his appraisal without staring. "Too much, perhaps, considering that other warriors lay maimed and dying."

Khouryn shrugged. "You're the leader."

"True. A leader who had difficulty walking abroad until recently. So I need my officers to tell me how the preparations are going."

"Well. We're just about ready to march."

"I understand that you want to take the Platinum Cadre along."

"I don't want it. Medrash does. And Balasar too, I think, though he doesn't say it outright. But they can't turn them into cavalry. We don't have enough war-horses for warriors in disgrace to rate mounts. So I get stuck using them as spearmen."

Tarhun peered at him. "Are you implying you don't trust them?"

"I trust them to be free of Tiamat's influence. Because Medrash says he purged them, and I trust him. Do I trust them to stand their ground and follow orders when things get ugly? I don't know. But then you never really know about that, do you?"

The vanquisher smiled. "No, you don't. Not when the swords slide out of their scabbards and the arrows start flying. You're all right, Khouryn Skulldark, and Tymanther owes you a debt. There's a permanent place for you here, if you care to claim it."

Khouryn smiled. "Thank you. I appreciate the offer for the honor that it is. But the Brotherhood of the Griffon is my home." At least until the day came, if it ever did, when he could return to East Rift to stay.

"Majesty!" a voice called. "If you're ready for us, we're ready for you."

Khouryn and Tarhun turned toward the pit, a raw wound in the earth amid the grass and splashes of red and purple wildflowers. Staves, wands, or orbs in hand, an assortment of wizards stood around the edges. To Khouryn's knowledgeable eye, the majority didn't look like battle mages. They were too diffident, too vague and abstracted, or just too old and rickety, stooped and gaunt with folds of loose hide hanging. But dragonborn didn't produce an abundance of arcanists, and the vanquisher had mobilized all there were to deal with the current crisis.

"All right, Kriv. Tell me what's going to happen," Tarhun said.

The mage who'd spoken before stepped forth from his fellows. He had bronze hide with black freckles, yellow eyes, a single onyx ring in his left nostril, and a hexagonal brass medallion engraved with a triangle affixed to the center of his forehead. He carried one of Nala's green globes in his upturned hand.

"At one point," Kriv said, "some of my more . . . imaginative colleagues hypothesized that the talismans actually create the reptilian creatures from the raw stuff of primordial chaos. Even though the sheer force required would be prohibitive. And now that we've had the opportunity to conduct a proper examination of some functional orbs, it's clear that they merely transport beasts that already exist in our world from one point in space to another."

Tarhun nodded. "Go on."

"The difference," said Kriv, "is of practical significance. Because it's possible for countermagic to prevent such an effect."

"You mean, to stop the orbs from working," the vanquisher said.

"Yes."

"I like it," Khouryn said. "It doesn't necessarily mean we won't have to fight any of the brutes. If they're already alive in the world someplace, the place is probably Black Ash Plain. But if the giants don't know that they need to march them to the battlefield, we may not have to contend with many. And in any case, the shamans won't be able to make them pop out of nowhere and surprise us."

Kriv smiled. "That was our thought. So, with Your Majesty's permission, we intend to conduct an experiment in two parts. First, to make sure we truly do understand the operation of the talisman, I'll summon a saurian. Then I'll attempt to summon another, and my fellow arcanists will thwart me."

"Do it," Tarhun said.

Kriv walked to the edge of the pit, peered down at the bottom, raised the orb so its green curves caught the sunlight, and chanted words of power. The other wizards, Tarhun, and Khouryn moved up to look into the hole as well.

A feeling of pressure built up in the air. It made Khouryn's skin itch and the pulp in his teeth throb in time with the beating of his heart. In one place and another, individual blades of grass grew long, forked, and writhed in a way that reminded him of Nala.

The chant ended on a rising note, and the sense of pressure vanished abruptly. But nothing appeared at the bottom of the pit.

Tarhun whirled. Khouryn didn't know what had alarmed the monarch, but he figured he'd better spin around too, and snatch for the urgrosh on his back.

Three green kobolds crouched before them. No—not kobolds, for though they at first glance resembled them, they were inhaling in the characteristic manner of creatures readying breath weapons.

Somehow, Tarhun spat his first. The crackling, twisting spear of lightning stabbed one creature in the chest.

Khouryn charged another. It spewed, and he twisted aside. The fumes from the sizzling glob stung his eyes as it passed, but did no actual harm.

He sprang, struck, and his axe crunched into the saurian warrior's skull. He sensed a threat on his flank, wrenched his weapon free, and pivoted. But he needn't have bothered.

Like all the preeminent folk in Tymanther, Tarhun mostly fought with a greatsword. It was a symbol of his rank. It was also a weapon that was damnably hard to ready quickly when a warrior wore it sheathed across his back. Yet somehow the vanquisher had managed to draw it, and he cut into the last saurian's torso with one precise little chop.

A moment of silence followed.

Kriv said, "That was . . . regrettable. But one has to allow for a degree of error when testing new magic."

Tarhun grinned. "If one wanted to make sure one wasn't charged with attempted regicide, one might have allowed for it by digging a bigger pit." Kriv's eyes widened. "Please. I'm joking. It's all right. After my injuries, I needed to test myself, and you gave me the opportunity."

Khouryn said, "I take it you can call the saurians, but not control them."

"Correct," the wizard said. "Since we decided the best tactic is to suppress the summoning, analyzing the other aspect of the talisman's power didn't seem as crucial."

"Fair enough," Tarhun said. He gave his sword a one-handed shake and flicked gore from the blade. "So let's see you do it."

"Of course, Majesty. I'm, uh, reasonably confident I can center the effect in the pit this time around."

He raised the globe and recited as before. But after a moment, one of his fellows started chanting too. Then another joined in, and then another, their voices weaving a complex contrapuntal pattern.

A whine sounded beneath the measured insistence of the voices. Khouryn felt momentarily dizzy. Two more stunted reptilian warriors flickered in and out of view at the bottom of the hole, present one moment, gone the next.

Then Kriv cried out, dropped the orb, and reeled backward. Khouryn grabbed him and kept him from falling on his rump.

"Uh, thank you." Kriv clumsily tried to get his feet back underneath him. Khouryn held onto him until he succeeded. "I'm all right now."

Tarhun peered at him. "Are you certain, my friend? You have a nosebleed."

Kriv brushed his hand across his snout, bumping his piercing in the process, then peered at the streak of blood on his index finger. "So I see. I have a pounding headache too."

"Then I insist you see my personal healers."

Kriv smiled at the implicit honor the vanquisher had shown him. "Thank you, Majesty. I will. But after we're finished here."

Khouryn said, "You've already shown us plenty. If your countermagic will give the giant adepts a kick in the head, it's even more useful than you promised. We're going to crush the bastards."

"I hope that's so," said a female voice. "But you need to understand that our foes have other cards to play."

Khouryn looked around. The speaker had snow-white scales, a color Khouryn hadn't seen before, and several silver skewers pierced into the edges of her face. They ran into and out of little pinches of hide, with most of their gleaming lengths extending out the backs.

"Please explain," Tarhun said.

"I was one of Kriv's more imaginative colleagues," she said. Her crimson eyes shot the summoner a sardonic glance. "Perhaps because of that, once we verified that his idea was correct, he wasn't very interested in my help. And possibly that was for the best, because it gave me time to study the papers Nala left behind."

The vanquisher frowned. "I assumed you scholars had already made a thorough examination."

"We had," said Kriv.

"Within limits," the albino mage replied. "The fact of the matter is, Nala wrote in what I would describe as an esoteric, liturgical form of Draconic. Whereas we're arcanists, not clerics. In addition, she was writing for herself and felt no need to explain every aspect of the plan to herself. Thus, certain facts only emerge by implication."

"What are they?" Tarhun asked.

"Last century, when this land was Unther, Skuthosiin was a lord. He wants to be one again. To that end, he united the ash giant tribes."

Khouryn fingered his scraggly beard. "You all told me it would take someone powerful to make the barbarians set aside their feuds."

"I see how it was meant to work," Tarhun said. "If Tymanther prevailed, but only through the efforts of dragon-worshipers, that would ultimately provide an entry for a dragon to claim a place of honor among us. And if the giants won, it would make him master of the realm."

"Since the first possibility has fallen through," Khouryn said, "he'll put everything he has into the second. He'll finally come out of hiding to lead the giants into battle himself."

"And not just him," the white-scaled wizard said. "He evidently has lesser wyrms serving him, although I wasn't able to discover their names or much else about them."

Tarhun looked down at Khouryn. "What do you think?"

"It's not the best possible news. Especially considering the casualties we've already taken. But we finally won and pushed the whoresons back. We need to press the advantage. And at least we now know who we have to kill to break the giants' alliance."

Tarhun smiled. "I agree. And you'll see that nothing brings out the best in dragonborn like the chance to slay true dragons." He turned his smile on the mages. "Thank you all for the fine work you've done. And the fine work you're going to do when we face the foe on Black Ash Plain."

* * * * *

Her voluminous, bejeweled sleeves sliding down her skinny arms, Halonya raised the square little basket in both hands. "O mighty Red Dragon," she said, "lend me your wisdom."

Which seemed nonsensical to Jhesrhi. Halonya was performing the divination on Tchazzar's behalf. If it would only yield insights the war hero already possessed, what was the point?

Not that there was much point in any case. Jhesrhi had met seers who could glimpse the future. She was certain Halonya wasn't one of them.

But watching intently, Tchazzar plainly thought otherwise. He'd proclaimed Halonya his high priestess, and to his mind, that sufficed to invest her with sacred Power.

Halonya dumped the ivory tiles onto the ground, rattling and pattering from the basket. Jhesrhi suppressed a smile when the priestess peered at them, stooped, peered again, and then with obvious reluctance got down on her knees. She likely thought the position undignified for one of her elevated status and probably didn't want to risk soiling her ornate robes. But in the darkened pavilion, with only the wavering yellow glow of two hanging lanterns to see by, she couldn't make out the etched symbols unless she got up close.

Jhesrhi wished Gaedynn were there. He too would have appreciated the humor. But Tchazzar had wanted to dine with her and Halonya alone.

Halonya picked up a tile. "Here is fire. Pure and noble. Light and salvation for all who follow it. But there are some so evil that they only wish to put it out."

Tchazzar frowned. "Go on."

The priestess ran her eyes over the scattered tiles, then picked up another. "Here is the evildoer known to all—the serpent. The dead thing in the north. But the fire will fight death with death and cast it down."

Since Tchazzar had told Halonya he'd made a pact with a vampire to destroy a lich, she surely hadn't had to overtax her imagination to come up with that particular prognostication. Jhesrhi supposed she should be glad the priestess hadn't said anything to shake the war hero's confidence in the plan. Because, with Alasklerbanbastos rapidly advancing, it was too late for second thoughts.

"In the long run," Halonya continued, "the greater danger will come from enemies in hiding." She pointed to a tile. "Here's the mask. The pretense of faithfulness and friendship. And look who's hiding behind it." She jabbed her finger at a different ivory rectangle. "The sun, jealous because fire shines brighter." She pointed again. "The spear, always ready to stab anyone for coin." And again. "The leper, flinching from every touch so people won't find out she's full of poison."

In other words, Jhesrhi thought, the priests of Amaunator, Aoth, and me. Curse you, woman. Curse and rend your jealous, lying soul.

Jhesrhi didn't want to let the slander pass unchallenged. Yet at the same time she didn't want to acknowledge that she recognized to whom it referred, lest that give it a kind of credence in Tchazzar's mind. So she simply heaved a sigh.

Tchazzar turned on his campstool. "What is it?" he asked.

"I'm no diviner," Jhesrhi answered. "It's not one of my talents. But while in Thay, I read a treatise on the Four and Forty Tiles by Yaphyll herself." She gave a Halonya a smile. "You recognize the name, I'm sure. The only oracle to foresee Mystra's murder and the coming of the Blue Fire."

Halonya scowled. "What about her?"

"She says that one tile can only influence at most two others. Which means the mask can't possibly veil the sun, the spear, *and* the leper. Especially when there are other pieces—like the ox and the river—that fell as close or closer to it. Or is there some subtlety I'm missing?"

The former street preacher hesitated. "Maybe not. It was a long journey up from Luthcheq with the troops. I'm tired."

Jhesrhi felt herself relax, because her statements had been as much a bluff as Halonya's performance. She had no idea whether the late Zulkir of Divination had ever written about the Four and Forty Tiles. If so, Jhesrhi had certainly never read the results. But Halonya feared to contend with her in a contest of erudition, and Tchazzar was evidently no expert on that particular form of prophecy either.

"Maybe I can try again later," Halonya continued. She shifted her gaze to Tchazzar. "If it's just the two of us, it might help me concentrate."

"Maybe," said Tchazzar. He rose and lifted her to her feet—a tacit reassurance of his continuing favor—and she set about readjusting her layers of silk and velvet and dangling, clinking golden chains and amulets. "Or maybe you'd do better with a different style of prophecy! One that reflects my aspect as a god of fire!"

He picked up the bottle of Sembian red from its folding table and, careless in one of his sudden excitements, splashed more wine into the golden goblets his guests had set aside. "Imagine," he continued, "a man—or an orc, a kobold, or whatever—burning alive. He'll cry out. His limbs will twist and his skin will char. Smoke will rise. But the precise way it all happens will vary from case to case. And surely you, the chief priestess of a greater deity, will read meaning in the patterns."

Halonya turned white and swallowed. "I . . . I'll try if you want me to, Your Majesty."

Tchazzar laughed loud and long. Jhesrhi couldn't tell whether it was because he'd been joking about the whole idea of the immolations or simply because he found Halonya's squeamishness amusing.

Finally, blinking tears from his eyes, he said, "I do love you, daughter, and I was wise to call you to my side. Important as it is, my temple can wait. I need both my truest friends to bring my luck."

"I never want to be anywhere else," Halonya said.

After that, for a heartbeat, no one spoke. Then Tchazzar fixed his gaze on Jhesrhi. "And you?" he asked, a coolness lurking in his tone.

Caught by surprise, Jhesrhi stammered, "Majesty?"

"Surely you understand my plans for you," Tchazzar replied. "I want you to stay in the land of your birth. You'll look after your fellow wizards. Protect them and help them find their proper roles. And as you get that sorted out, you'll assume additional offices and honors. In the days to come, you and Halonya will be the two greatest ladies in all the East. Surely that will please you."

Jhesrhi supposed it would. After all, it was vindication, a lofty purpose, luxury, and power all bundled up together.

Whereas the Brotherhood was home. But Khouryn had already gone, and given the countless chances and perils attendant on the sellsword's way of life, there was no guarantee he'd ever come back. And no matter how often she and Gaedynn resolved not to, they always went back to hurting each other. They'd been doing it ever since escaping the Shadowfell.

Still . . .

Suddenly she noticed the way Tchazzar was frowning at her hesitation, and the excitement gleaming in Halonya's eyes. She didn't want to believe the dragon was mad—at least not severely and permanently so—but sane or otherwise, he was certainly prideful enough to resent a refusal. And Halonya would do everything in her power to keep the wound rubbed raw.

Was he petty and shortsighted enough to answer a rebuff by turning against the Brotherhood? Or stripping Chessenta's mages of their newly granted legal protections? Jhesrhi didn't want to believe that either. But she also didn't want to assume better of him and be wrong.

She swallowed away the dryness in her mouth. "Thank you, Majesty. Of course I'll stay if you'll have me."

Halonya scowled, then struggled to twist the expression into a smile before Tchazzar noticed. It gave Jhesrhi another moment of spiteful amusement.

But no matter how exuberant the dragon seemed at her acquiescence, and no matter how she tried to respond in kind, that was the last bit of genuine enjoyment that came her way. Nor did she feel any gladder as, unable to sleep, she prowled through the camp later on.

Could she truly acquit herself well as a courtier? She, who felt ill at ease around nearly everyone?

Even if she could, did she have the right to abandon her comrades? Especially with Khouryn already absent?

The more she weighed her choices, the more intolerable each of them seemed. But finally she saw a glimmer of hope. If she was staying, maybe the entire Brotherhood could too.

She didn't know whether Aoth would agree. But he might. Even if he didn't, if she persuaded Tchazzar to ask, then neither the war-mage nor Gaedynn could say that she'd simply turned her back on them.

It was late. Selûne and her trail of glittering tears had nearly set in the west. But Jhesrhi was too energized to care. She strode through the moist night air with the snores of sleeping men snorting and buzzing around her and the butt of her staff thumping the ground.

When she got close enough, she smiled, because spots of light still shined inside Tchazzar's spacious tent. She wouldn't even have to wake him. She started forward, and then a sentry stepped into her path. In her eagerness, she hadn't noticed him before.

He wore a scaly chasuble, part vestment and part armor, and carried a pick in his hands. One of the wyrmkeepers, then, who'd resumed wearing their customary regalia after Tchazzar proclaimed they could legitimately serve as clergy in his own church. Jhesrhi felt a twinge of distaste.

"The god," he said, "is not to be disturbed."

"He'll see me," Jhesrhi said.

"Perhaps in the morning," he replied.

"I'm one of Aoth Fezim's lieutenants, which means I'm a high-ranking officer in this army. I'm also the protector of all Chessenta's wizards. His Majesty appointed me to that office earlier tonight."

"Be that as it may, the god is not to be disturbed."

Jhesrhi clenched herself against the urge to knock the fool out of her way with magic. Then she noticed details that made impatience give way to puzzlement.

She might have expected to encounter a sentry within a few paces of his commander's tent. Instead, the wyrmkeeper had stationed himself a stone's throw away, as though to make absolutely certain that he himself couldn't intrude on Tchazzar's privacy. There were other guards too, shadows blocking every approach to the pavilion, each of them standing just as far away.

But more interesting still was the roiling of mystical power that she suddenly discerned. She half felt it as a crawling on her skin, half saw it as sickly foxfire on the fabric of the tent. Tchazzar wanted privacy because he was conducting some sort of arcane ritual.

She gave a brusque nod to the wyrmkeeper, then turned and stalked away. Stepping over pegs and rope, she stopped in the narrow, shadowy gap between two humbler tents and pondered what to do next.

Earlier, Tchazzar's offer had so flummoxed her that she'd forgotten that she had, in fact, agreed to *spy* on him if circumstances warranted. As they seemingly did now.

But since she'd agreed to serve him as her true liege lord, would it be wicked to follow through? One thing was certain—it would be dangerous. A dragon might sense magic at play around him.

Yet she found that her loyalty to Aoth, Gaedynn, and the rest of the Brotherhood outweighed all other concerns, ethical and practical alike. A day might come—indeed, seemed nearly at hand—when she'd have to tell them she was no longer one of them. But until then, she'd keep faith with them.

She whispered to the air. A cooperative breeze could carry sounds if they originated only a short distance away. And she'd been making friends with the winds thereabouts since Aoth, Tchazzar, and the other captains had selected the land for their battleground.

The cool breeze caressed her face and stirred strands of her hair, and then she heard Tchazzar like he was murmuring in her ear. He chanted sibilant, rhyming words in Draconic, meant to activate some enchanted object. The words were unfamiliar, but she recognized similarities to the charm that enabled her and Aoth to speak through a pair of fires despite whatever distance lay between them.

The incantation ended with three staccato syllables like raps from a hammer. A moment of silence followed. Then a new voice said, "Tchazzar." Jhesrhi suspected from its depth and sibilant snarl that it too belonged to a dragon, one in his natural form.

"Skuthosiin," Tchazzar answered. "Alasklerbanbastos has crawled out of his hole to attack me, and Jaxanaedegor is eager to betray him. This is our moment. Come north and help me make the kill."

"I can't," Skuthosiin said. "My agents in Djerad Thymar failed me. If I'm to rule the south, I'll have to win my crown in open battle. In fact, I came to this talk hoping you'd help me."

"Forget the south for now!" Tchazzar said. "I'm offering you your chance at the Great Bone Wyrm!"

"Even if I were willing to forgo Unther," Skuthosiin said, "the dragonborn have to change or die. Otherwise, their enmity will get in the way of every move we make. Ask Gestaniius to help you."

"He's on the other side of the Dragonsword Mountains. He wouldn't arrive in time," Tchazzar said. "Curse it, green, the three of us are allies. You owe me your help."

"What about the help I already gave?" Skuthosiin said. "If not for me, your sellswords would never have come to Chessenta. Nor would they have searched for you in the Sky Riders."

"A search you waited one hundred years to initiate!" Tchazzar said.

"A search for a false friend who killed and devoured me for my power," Skuthosiin said.

"It was the Dark Lady's will that we three fight for supremacy," Tchazzar said. "I knew she'd bring you back to life."

Skuthosiin laughed a rumbling laugh. "You neither knew nor cared, and I don't blame you. I was trying to do the same thing to you and Gestaniius. But let's not pretend there are any great bonds of fellowship between us. My proxies fetched you back because I hoped you'd prove useful."

"I'm far more than *useful*," Tchazzar said, his voice grating. "I'm the Chosen of Tiamat, and a god in my own right!"

"Then you shouldn't need help to squash the occasional dracolich."

A long pause followed. Jhesrhi imagined Tchazzar glaring and trembling with the futile urge to strike out at a creature hundreds of miles beyond his reach.

"I promise you," the red dragon said at last, "you'll have your new Unther, and the dragonborn will die. But first you have to help me."

"I already explained why that's impossible."

"Then in accordance with the Sixty-Seventh Precept, I cut you off. You won't have an inch of Alasklerbanbastos's lands or one clipped copper from his hoard."

"You can't do that. The One Hundred and Seventh Precept—"

After a moment, Jhesrhi inferred that Tchazzar had ended the spell of communication, because there was nothing to hear but thumps and clacks. Evidently the war hero was kicking his camp furniture around.

She tried to make sense of the conversation that had triggered his frustration. It was like the parley with Jaxanaedegor; much of the import was maddeningly opaque.

But she understood that Skuthosiin and possibly other wyrms meant to exterminate the dragonborn, and it didn't matter that Aoth and Cera had proved the Tymantherans innocent of crimes against Chessenta. Tchazzar wanted to kill them too.

Tchazzar, to whom she'd pledged her absolute fidelity.

TWELVE

28 Kythorn – 5 Flamerule
The Year of the Ageless One (1479 DR)

Summer had come, and, as Khouryn had observed on the march southwest, Tymanther was blooming. Trees were full of green leaves and singing birds; pastures of grass and the sheep, goats, and cattle grazing there; and fields of oats and barley. In contrast, Black Ash Plain had simply gotten nastier. The hot air was smokier, and some of the cinders adrift on it were stinging hot.

I don't blame the giants for wanting to steal somebody else's country, he thought. I wouldn't want to live here either.

He wondered how they even managed to live in the midst of such desolation, then dismissed the question as irrelevant. His concern was to make sure that a goodly number of them didn't live much longer. To that end, he took another look at the ash drifts and cracked, rocky soil to either side of the column.

Towers of ash glided in the distance, somewhat like ships under sail except that they moved independently of the wind. Then suddenly a gray-black bump bobbed up and then back down out of sight behind one of the true cinder dunes, if that was the right term for them.

They were drifts big as hills, and a fellow could climb them like hills until he set his foot wrong. Then the ash would swallow him like quicksand.

Despite the haze in the air, and the smarting blur in his eyes, Khouryn knew he'd just seen a giant skirmisher. He drew breath to shout an alert, but one of the dragonborn marching under the banners of the Platinum Cadre did it first.

So instead Khouryn shouted, "Form up! Protect yourselves!" He was sure there were only a few giants lurking on their flank, or somebody would have spotted one before then. Since they were too few to pose a serious threat, their purpose was to slow the advance, giving the bulk of Skuthosiin's army more time to prepare. By halting and covering up with their shields, the Tymantherans were essentially giving them what they wanted. But they had to do something to keep the barbarians from picking them off one and two at a time.

Five giants popped up, and their long arms whipped. They didn't throw spears or any other sort of crafted weapon. They must have been hoarding those for the true battle to come. But they were an offshoot of the race called stone giants and, like others of their kind, could fling rocks with deadly force and accuracy.

The impacts cracked and banged. One dragonborn fell down. But no stones streaked past shields to hammer the bodies behind them.

The barbarians ducked back down. Several crossbows clacked, an instant too late to have any hope of hitting their targets.

A female voice chanted words that sent a pang of chill stabbing through the hot air.

Khouryn turned. Several paces to his left, Kanjentellequor Biri, the albino wizard who'd unraveled the deeper secrets of Nala's papers, had somehow prevailed on two spearmen to open a gap in the shield wall. Where she stood, inviting another stone as she rattled off her incantation and flicked a rod of roughly hewn and polished quartz through small, repetitive downstrokes.

Just as Khouryn reached her side, hailstones pounded down to batter the far slope of the dune. A giant howled.

Khouryn gripped Biri's wrist and hauled her back behind the warriors. "I didn't tell you to do that," he said.

She grinned. "But it worked. They had cover, but not in relation to something that dropped straight down from overhead."

"You didn't have any cover either. It's only by the Luckmaiden's grace that you didn't end up with your brains splashed across the ground. As it is, you showed the giants where you are."

Tarhun had scattered the mages throughout the army, partly so the giants couldn't target all of them at once. He'd also instructed them to refrain from casting spells till he said otherwise.

Biri's smile melted away. Despite his time among them, Khouryn wasn't good at guessing how old a dragonborn was. But he got a feeling the wizard was younger than he'd first supposed. "I just wanted to help," she said.

"You already have," Khouryn said, "and trust me, you will again. But for now, let the soldiers do the work. They can handle it."

As if to illustrate his point, a squadron of outriders charged the giants. Khouryn couldn't see everything that happened next. His hulking spearmen with their overlapping shields were in the way, and so was the ash dune. But he made out Medrash's heater, painted with the steel gauntlet of Torm, and Balasar's targe, emblazoned with the six white circles of Clan Daardendrien. He also saw giants toppling with lances embedded in their guts, or blood streaming from sword cuts on their necks and chests.

The infantry raised a cheer. Except that there was something wrong with it. Khouryn strained to make out the one voice that wasn't jubilant, all but lost amid the clamor.

"Turn around!" someone bellowed. "Turn around!"

Khouryn did, and suffered a shock of amazement and dread. A brown dragon was heaving itself out of the ground. Huge as the burrowing creature was, it defied common sense that so few of the dragonborn had noticed its relatively blunt head with its mass of short, thick horns looming high above their own. But there hadn't been anything there just a moment before, and almost everyone was watching the fight between the outriders and the giants.

The dragon glanced around, then oriented on Khouryn. Or maybe on the wizard standing beside him.

"Crouch down behind me!" he shouted. He wanted to tell her to close her eyes and turn her head too, but the brown didn't give him time. Its neck whipped forward. Its jaws opened and spewed its breath weapon.

Khouryn covered up with his shield and squinched his own eyes shut, which was possibly the only thing that saved them from the hot grit that rasped across his skin. When he opened them again, sand and ash hung so thick in the air as to make the smoky haze he'd despised before seem clear by comparison.

Dragonborn cried out, because the brown's breath had scraped them, or simply in fear and confusion. Khouryn could see some of the nearer ones, milling around or sprawled on the ground, but he couldn't see the wyrm. A moment before, the sudden appearance of such a behemoth had seemed a nightmarish impossibility. Its vanishing felt like another, even though he assumed the cloud was actually responsible.

He only knew when it charged because its strides jolted the ground, and because dragonborn yelled as it trampled them or brushed them out of the way. "Run!" he rasped, his mouth foul with sand, and then his huge foe pounced out of the murk. The scalloped, winglike frills that extended down the sides of its body were undulating. Maybe that was how it kept the air agitated and full of grit even when it wasn't spitting the stuff out of its gullet.

It struck at Khouryn, and he met its head with a thrust of his spear. The weapon drove straight into a nostril. The brown screeched and recoiled, jerking the spear out of his hand. It whipped its head back and forth until the foreign object tumbled out.

That gave Khouryn just enough time to discard his shield and snatch the urgrosh off his back.

The brown dragon clawed at him. He spun aside and chopped at its foot. The axe glanced off its scales.

At almost the same instant, the head at the end of the long neck arced over him, too high for him to attack. The brown was reaching for Biri. But she conjured a blast of frost that spattered the wyrm's jaws and eyes and made it falter.

"You get away from it!" Khouryn bellowed. "Spears, follow my voice! It's here!"

The dragon lifted a forefoot high. He only just spotted the action in the brown, swirling gloom. It stamped down at him. He sidestepped, cut, and that time hacked a gash in its hide.

Thunder boomed and light flared as Biri burned the wyrm with lightning. From a safer distance, Khouryn hoped. They were holding their own, but it couldn't last—not unless they had help. Where were the damn spearmen?

There! Shadows swarmed out of the murk on either side of the dragon. Spears jabbed.

The brown struck left, then right, biting a dragonborn to pieces with each snap. Some spearmen cried out and retreated madly. But others were less frantic. They fell back just far enough to protect themselves, then attacked again as soon as the wyrm pivoted away.

Not that such maneuvering was easy. The dragon was faster and less predictable than the Beast. Its rippling alar membranes could swat a warrior, or its sweeping tail could shatter his legs, whether it was facing him or not.

Still, most of the warriors managed to stay alive for a few moments. Long enough for Khouryn to charge the wyrm and, taking advantage of his shorter stature, dash on underneath it.

He reversed his grip on the urgrosh and stabbed repeatedly upward with the spearhead. At first the dragon didn't seem to notice. But then when he yanked the spike free, arterial blood spurted after it, spattering his arms, and the reptile jerked.

The brown wheeled, stamping, trying to claw and crush him or, failing that, at least get him out from underneath it. He scurried to avoid its feet, keep its ventral surface above him, and go on stabbing.

That worked long enough for him to draw a second huge spray of gore. Then the wyrm lashed its winglike frills and pounced far enough that he had no hope of keeping up with it. The same leap carried it back in striking distance of Biri.

Its head hurtled at her. But, galloping, Balasar reached her first. Leaning out of the saddle, he scooped her up, and the brown dragon's fangs clashed shut on empty air.

Meanwhile, Medrash charged the wyrm, and his lance plunged into its flank. The brown jerked and roared. It was still roaring when a second lancer speared it a couple of heartbeats later.

Like the brown, hunched, long-armed saurians Khouryn and his comrades had met before, the dragon dissolved into a flying swirl of sand. The grit streamed through the air and hissed down the hole from which the reptile had first emerged.

Where, Khouryn hoped, it would return to dragon form and bleed out. Although he wasn't certain of it. Dragons were notoriously hard to kill.

But as he could see since the cloud of sand was subsiding, at least they'd driven it off before it could kill or injure very many of them. The spearmen who'd surrounded it deserved much of the credit, and half of them wore purple and silver tunics or tokens.

Khouryn caught Medrash's eye, then jerked his head toward the group. The paladin nodded in acknowledgment.

Balasar set Biri back on her own two feet. Then he grinned, bowed from the saddle, and said, "A thousand thank-yous for the dance, milady." To say the least, his gallantry seemed incongruous amid the warriors noisily spitting out sand and ash on every side, but it made the mage smile in return.

But her smile withered as soon as she turned and took a good look at the corpses, and at the wounded clenching their teeth against the urge to cry out as the healers set to work on them. Khouryn realized that what looked like minimal harm to a hardened sellsword might seem like ghastly carnage to even a dragonborn, if she'd never been to war before.

She asked, "Is this my fault?"

"No," Khouryn said. "The dragon was going to hit us at some point, and some of us were going to die when it did. But follow orders from now on."

* * * * *

The unnatural power of his condition compensating for the lack of hide stretched across the bony framework of his wings, Alasklerbanbastos floated on the night wind and studied the enemy camp. Gliding at his master's side, Jaxanaedegor surreptitiously studied him.

Tchazzar and his servants weren't relying on invisibility to mask their true strength. It was difficult to keep such a glamour in place for days on end, and a wizard as accomplished as a dracolich was apt to see through it anyway. Instead they were using other tricks. A paucity of campfires, tents, and noise. Men and beasts tucked away wherever there was cover to obscure their numbers. Freshly turned earth to give the appearance of a mass grave. Lamplight and motion inside the healers' pavilions. The absence of any whisper or tingle of mystical power at work.

Finally the Great Bone Wyrm wheeled. Jaxanaedegor did the same, and they beat their way back toward the north and the massed might of Threskel's army.

But they didn't go all the way back to their own camp. Alasklerbanbastos evidently didn't want to wait that long to talk. Blue sparks jumping and cracking on his naked bones, he spiraled down to the crest of a low hill. From there, he'd be able to spot anyone or anything suicidal enough to approach him.

You're always so wary, Jaxanaedegor thought. But not wary enough of me. I could strike at you right now, while you're on the ground and I'm still on the wing.

But it was just a pleasant fantasy. Neither the high air nor the element of surprise would suffice to defeat a creature so endowed with every other advantage. Jaxanaedegor set down on coarse grass and weeds that had already started to wither simply because the dracolich was near.

Pale light gleamed in Alasklerbanbastos's eye sockets, and the air around him smelled like a rising storm. "There are more soldiers," he growled, "than you led me to believe."

Jaxanaedegor felt a pang of uneasiness. He made sure it didn't reflect in his tone or expression. "Truly, my lord? I estimated their numbers as accurately as I could."

"Yes, *truly*," the skeletal dragon replied, with the sneering mimicry his vassal had come to hate. "Are you sure Tchazzar hasn't received reinforcements?"

"I can't imagine how. They would have had to swing far to the east. Even if they'd had time, our watchers in the Sky Riders would have spotted them."

Alasklerbanbastos grunted.

Jaxanaedegor had hoped he wouldn't need to encourage the undead blue to attack. It seemed better—safer—if Alasklerbanbastos arrived at the decision on his own. But if he was having second thoughts, Jaxanaedegor supposed he'd have to give him a nudge.

"If I did underestimate," the vampire said, "I apologize. But even so, there are more of us than there are of them, and you can feel the pall of demoralization hanging over their camp. The battle we already fought cost us, but we won. We crippled them."

"They supposedly had necromancers. And sunlords." Alasklerbanbastos was particularly cautious of those who wielded special power against the undead.

"We killed them," Jaxanaedegor said. "Or most of them, anyway."

Using the tip of a claw, Alasklerbanbastos scratched a rune in the dirt. A different symbol inscribed itself beside it, and then another after that, until there were seven in a line. Despite his own considerable knowledge of arcana, Jaxanaedegor didn't recognize any of the characters, nor did he have any idea what the magic was meant to accomplish. Not knowing twisted his nerves a little tighter.

"But you didn't kill Tchazzar," the Bone Wyrm said.

"No," Jaxanaedegor replied. "But our spies say he's behaving erratically, and I myself told you how long it took him to join the battle. He's not the same dragon you remember, and surely not Tiamat's Chosen anymore."

"He was dragon enough to kill three others when he finally did take flight."

"My lord," Jaxanaedegor said, "if you think it prudent, return to the safety of Dragonback Mountain. That's a king's prerogative. Your knights and captains will stay to fight for you and die for you if need be. That's a vassal's duty. But I ask you to consider whether you truly wish to forgo the joy of destroying Tchazzar with your own breath and claws. I ask you also to consider the effect on your reputation."

Sparks crawled on Alasklerbanbastos's fangs, and the light in his orbits grew brighter. "Meaning what, exactly? Choose your words carefully."

"Great one, you know *I* fear you. How could I not? How many times have I felt the pressure of your foot on my spine or the top of my head? How many years have I lost to true death, my ghost wandering Banehold until it suited your whim to pull your stake from my heart? But *xorvintaal* . . . changes things. Every dragon is studying every other for signs of weakness. And, while one wins points for achievement and guile, a player can also score for daring and renown—if he makes the right move."

At first Alasklerbanbastos didn't reply. The moment stretched until it seemed that something—Jaxanaedegor's composure, perhaps—must surely snap.

Then the dracolich snorted. "You may be right about the game. You're certainly right that it's past time for Tchazzar to die, and that I want to be the one who dowses the flame. Come!" He lashed his rattling, fleshless wings and climbed.

Jaxanaedegor followed with a certain feeling of joyful incredulity. He possessed considerable faith in his own cunning. Still, perhaps there was a buried part of him that hadn't believed he could bring the scheme to fruition.

Yet he had. After centuries of preliminary maneuvering, the two most powerful wyrms in Chessenta were going to meet in final battle.

During the early phases of the combat, Jaxanaedegor would perform as Alasklerbanbastos expected, and if the army of Threskel gained the upper hand, he'd simply continue to do so. But if, as he hoped, Tchazzar seized the advantage, then Jaxanaedegor and his followers would switch sides just as he'd promised the red. And whichever elder dragon ultimately won, he'd reward Jaxanaedegor for playing a key role in his victory.

There was even a chance that Alasklerbanbastos and Tchazzar would destroy each other, making Jaxanaedegor the most powerful creature in Chessenta. He reminded himself it was such a remote possibility that he didn't dare base his strategy on it. But if it happened, it would be the sweetest outcome of all.

* * * * *

From on high, the Threskelan army looked rather like a mass of ants creeping across the ground. Aoth supposed he should be glad the ground was where most of them were. He and his comrades had apparently wiped out most of the Great Bone Wyrm's flying minions in the previous battle.

Of course, there were dragons in the air, as well as bats with suspiciously phosphorescent eyes. Aoth reminded himself that if he could trust Jaxanaedegor—a significant if—then most of the flyers were actually on his side.

Whether they were or not, he was ready to fight. Partly, he supposed, because an honest battle would provide a respite from mysteries and pandering to Tchazzar's eccentricities. But mostly because a decisive victory that night would restore the Brotherhood's reputation. Afterward would be time enough to fret over the meaning of the dragons' Precepts and to decide how much longer to remain in the war hero's service.

Time enough as well to sort out Jhesrhi. She'd told him that Tchazzar had expressed sympathy with Skuthosiin's desire to slaughter the dragonborn—not that he knew what to make of that either—but he sensed there was something else, something more personal, that she was keeping back.

You can guess what it is, said Jet. *Tchazzar wants to make her a princess, and she's decided to let him.*

Aoth sighed. *You may be right. What sellsword doesn't want to retire to a life of luxury? And this is the country of her birth.*

So you'd leave her to the whims of a mad king?

Not happily, but it's her choice. Anyway, if the Great Bone Wyrm slaughters us all before morning, it won't much matter, will it? Why don't we focus on winning the war for now?

Jet gave an irritated rasp and then, responding to his rider's unspoken will, wheeled and flew back toward Tchazzar's army. A first star glimmered in the charcoal-colored eastern sky.

Below Aoth, warriors scurried, preparing for battle. His eyes instinctively sought out his own men, griffons, and horses. It looked like the sergeants were doing a good job of putting everything in order.

Jet furled his wings and swooped toward the patch of open ground in front of Tchazzar's pavilion. The war hero stood with his legs apart and his arms away from his torso as a squire buckled gilt plate armor onto him a piece at a time. Why, only the Firelord knew. He was supposed to fight in dragon form.

Other folk were hovering around him, either because they were awaiting final orders or simply because he wanted them there. Jhesrhi, Gaedynn, Shala, and Hasos were all armed in their various fashions and looked like the seasoned combatants they were. Halonya's top-heavy, bulbous miter and garnet-dotted robe with its long dragging train made her look like a parody of a priestess costumed for a farce.

But although she was the one person manifestly out of place, it was to her that Tchazzar looked as Aoth swung himself out of the saddle. "What do you think, wise lady?" the red dragon asked. "What do the omens say?"

Halonya blinked. "Uh . . . your soldiers are strong in their faith. But the dark is rising."

Gaedynn grinned. "That often happens at sunset."

"Respect!" Tchazzar snapped.

The archer offered a courtly little half bow. It was a silent apology if one cared to take it that way.

"The dark *is* rising," the dragon said. He peered about as though a demon lurked in every deepening shadow. "We should have attacked by day."

"Majesty," said Aoth, striding toward him and the folk clustered around him, "if you recall, we wanted to give the appearance of weakness to lure Alasklerbanbastos to the battlefield. Which meant we couldn't attack at all. We had to let him advance on us, and we assumed from the start that he'd come by night."

"Actually," Shala said, "we need him to. Jaxanaedegor couldn't help us if we fought in the sunlight."

"Jaxanaedegor," Tchazzar sneered, as though it were she and not himself who'd made a pact with the vampire. "Yes, by all means, let's hang our hopes on him."

Shala's square jaw tightened. "Does Your Majesty have a shrewder strategy?"

"Perhaps," Tchazzar said. "We could withdraw. Fight at a time of our choosing."

"Majesty," said Aoth, "this *is* the time of our choosing. Of *your* choosing. And it's too late to withdraw. You can fly away, but most of your army can't."

Tchazzar turned back toward Halonya. Who, Aoth was certain, meant to go on saying exactly the wrong thing.

He whispered words of power, then pointed his finger at the gangly, towheaded youth who was trying to strap Tchazzar's armor on, having a difficult time of it as his liege lord fidgeted and pivoted back and forth. The cantrip sent a chill stabbing through the squire. He stumbled, and his hands jerked, jamming the war hero's gorget into the soft flesh under his jaw.

"Idiot!" Tchazzar snarled. He spun, grabbed the boy, and dumped him on the ground. Then he started kicking him.

Aoth winced. But he hoped that with a battle and an archenemy awaiting his attention, Tchazzar could be persuaded to stop short of doing the lad permanent harm. And in any case, the chastisement gave Aoth the chance to shift close to Jhesrhi and whisper, "Distract him."

She immediately headed for the war hero. "Majesty, please!" she said. "I understand that you're upset. But I have something I need to say."

"What?" Tchazzar said.

"I think . . . I think that walking among us mortals in a form of flesh and blood, you sometimes half forget what you truly are—a god. Above all signs and auguries except the ones you find in your own heart, and your own nature."

Tchazzar frowned. "I suppose . . ."

"If you want to know how the battle will go, then I promise, just peer into flame, and your own divinity will show you." Jhesrhi waved him toward a fire crackling and smoking several paces away.

Halonya scowled and started to follow.

Aoth grabbed her by the forearm and clamped down hard enough to hurt her. "Lady," he whispered, "a word."

She sucked in a breath.

"Scream," he said, still just as softly, "and I swear by the Black Flame, I'll kill you. I can do it with one thrust of this spear. Even Tchazzar won't be able to act fast enough to save you."

"This is sacrilege," she said through clenched teeth. But her voice was as hushed as his own.

"What do I care? I'm a mage and a Thayan, remember? Now, this is how it's going to be. Right now, Jhesrhi is doing her best to nurse Tchazzar through his case of nerves. When they turn around again, you'll help her. You'll convince him to follow through and fight."

"You can't bully me."

"Maybe not. But I truly will kill you if you don't do what I say, and I won't have to be this close to do it. I know spells—"

"Let her go," Hasos said. From the sound of it, he was standing right behind Aoth.

"No," said Aoth.

"I have my dagger in my hand. You told the priestess that even Tchazzar couldn't act quickly enough to save her. Well, neither your griffon nor Ulraes can save you."

"Listen to me," said Aoth, wondering how many more heartbeats he had left before Tchazzar turned back around. "You and I have had our differences. But I've learned that you're an able warrior when you need to be. So you know Tchazzar *has* to fight tonight. He'll lose Chessenta if he doesn't. Halonya will lose her holy office. You'll lose your barony, and the men-at-arms who followed you to this place will lose their lives. As a worshiper of Amaunator and Torm, you also know the difference between a true cleric revealing insights and a charlatan improvising blather."

Hasos stood silent for what felt like a long while. Then he said, "My lady, please forgive me for intruding on a private conversation." Aoth sighed in relief.

"Come back!" Halonya said. "You cowardly, blaspheming son of a—"

"Shut up," said Aoth. "You know what to do. You know what will happen if you don't. Make your choice." He stepped away from her.

Gaedynn gave him an inquiring look, and Shala helped the scraped and bloodied squire to his feet. Then Tchazzar whirled around. For the moment at least, his uneasiness had given way to a grin.

"I saw victory!" he said. Aoth wondered if Jhesrhi had surreptitiously supplied the images, or if the red dragon's imagination had done all the work.

"I'm glad to hear it," Shala said.

Tchazzar looked to Halonya. "Still," he said, a hint of hesitation returning to his voice, "you had . . . concerns."

The high priestess took a deep breath. "No longer, Majesty. I too saw triumph in the fire, even from over here."

"Then why are we standing around?" Tchazzar cried. "To your stations! Boy, why is my collar lying on the ground? And what happened to your face?"

* * * * *

As it turned out, riding a giant bat wasn't much like riding a griffon. Both the voice and the touch commands were different. The animal moved differently, perhaps even more nimbly, in the air, and Khouryn was still learning how and when to lean to aid its maneuvering.

It also seemed incapable of making anything comparable to the diversity of rasps and screeches a griffon could emit. Which might be the only reason it wasn't subjecting him to an ongoing critique of his technique.

But his clumsiness notwithstanding, it felt good to fly again. And the loan of the winged steed was a mark of Tarhun's trust, even though it was also a practical necessity if he was to scout the giant stronghold from the air.

Biri's arms shifted their grip around his waist. "Have you ever flown before?" he asked.

"No," she said. "I always wanted to. It was why I meant—well, mean, I guess—to join the Lance Defenders when I'm older."

So she was young. "Well, ordinarily this isn't the first flight I'd pick for you. Or the first time aloft on a bat that I'd choose for myself. But our companions know their business. We'll be all right."

"I know," she said. "The Daardendriens are very brave." Her front brushed his back as she twisted to look left.

She could have said that the Lance Defenders were very brave, for it was active members of the corps who made up most of the scouting party. She could also have looked right, toward Medrash and his borrowed bat, instead of to the left and Balasar.

But she hadn't done either of those things. So Khouryn sighed and said, "Balasar's a fine warrior and my good friend. But not a suitable match for you."

"I don't know what you mean," she replied.

Did the love-struck young ever listen to sound advice? Probably not. The Shining Dancer knew, Khouryn hadn't. Nor did he regret it, despite all the horror and heartbreak that followed.

The smell of smoke that tainted the entire wasteland grew stronger. Black masses rose from the ground, and veins of glowing, flickering red threaded their way among them.

The dragonborn called the place Ashhold. In one sense that was a misnomer, because the dark shapes were mostly extrusions of basalt, not the ashen spires encountered elsewhere on the plain. But it was a sacred site to the giants, where the fires that burned beneath their country found their way to the surface and, by ancient custom, the tribes set even the bitterest feuds aside. It was also the redoubt to which the survivors of Skuthosiin's horde had retreated after Tarhun's warriors pushed them out of Tymanther.

Khouryn could see why. The hillocks of rock shouldn't be as tough to crack as a castle with continuous walls, battlements, and other civilized defenses—thanks be to the Lord of the Twin Axes that the giants lacked the knowledge to erect such a structure. Still, they provided the advantages of high ground, partial cover, and a maze of obstructions to confuse an attacking force and break it up into smaller, less-effective units. The patches of flame and hot coals would further complicate the assault.

So far, no giant was bellowing the alarm. The bats were evidently hard to see in the smoky, benighted sky. With the tap of a finger against the surprisingly soft fur on its shoulder, Khouryn made his steed swoop a little lower. Then he studied Ashhold and imagined the various ways in which it might be attacked with the troops at the vanquisher's disposal, and how the giants might respond in each instance. The possibilities danced before his inner eye like pawns and pieces moving on a sava board.

"Go farther in," Biri said, "and lower."

"Why?"

"Magic. I feel a lot of force stirring. I see it too, like a spot in the air after you glance straight at the sun. It's there." She stretched her arm past his head to point the way.

He was reluctant to take greater risks than they had already. But he'd brought her along to provide a wizard's insight, so he supposed he'd better give her a look at what she needed to see.

He nudged his bat with his knee, but it ignored the command. Apparently the beast too sensed mystical energy rising and was leery of it. He kneed it again, harder, and then it wheeled and beat its way in the right direction.

Ashhold opened up at the center, rather like a real castle with a courtyard. In the middle of the space burned the greatest of its fires, leaping up from a forked crack in the baked and barren ground. Crouching on a low, flat protrusion of basalt, the glow of the flames glinting on his dark green scales, a gigantic green dragon stared into the blaze and hissed words of power. A dozen giant adepts chanted contrapuntal responses.

Since he was so close, even Khouryn could feel magic accumulating, as a queasiness in his guts and an ache in his joints. He ignored the discomfort to peer at the huge green, who surely had to be Skuthosiin.

His first impression was that the wyrm was deformed, even though he couldn't pick out anything that was specifically wrong with him. The dragons he'd seen hitherto were terrifying but beautiful. Even the burrowing brown had been magnificent in its way. In contrast, Skuthosiin made him want to wince and avert his gaze, like a sick person covered in weeping sores.

He remembered the stories he'd heard. At one time, Skuthosiin had been a Chosen of Tiamat. He'd died, and his goddess had restored him to life. Maybe he'd come back tainted.

A giant standing atop one of the masses of rock abruptly shouted. Evidently he'd spotted one of the bat riders gliding and wheeling overhead.

Skuthosiin didn't even deign to raise his head, nor did any of the other mages involved in the ritual. But as Khouryn turned his bat, and his comrades likewise prepared to flee, shadows the size of hounds—but with the serpentine shapes of dragons—darted up the sides of various stones. They silently lashed their scalloped wings and leaped into the air.

As soon as they soared very high above the fire, they became difficult for even dwarf eyes to see. Agitated, Khouryn's steed veered one way, then the other, while the Lance Defenders' bats did the same. Evidently they too were having trouble perceiving the shadow things.

A dragonborn cried out. His bat tumbled with one of the ghostly dragons ripping at each leathery wing.

Medrash called out to Torm and shook his fist. White light flared from his steel gauntlet. It revealed the locations of the shadows, seared them, and dashed them toward the ground. The two clinging to the wounded bat lost their holds, and the steed spread its torn wings and leveled out of its fall.

Unfortunately, the blaze of holy Power dimmed immediately, and the dark things winged their way upward again. Khouryn took a frantic look around and decided the creatures were fewest in the northeast.

He pointed. "I want a blast of fire right above that rock with the two lumps on top."

Biri chanted and thrust out her wand of quartz. A red spark flew from the tip and exploded into a roaring mass of flame.

The fire washed over shadow things and burned them to nothingness, breaking the circle they'd formed around the scouts. "This way!" Khouryn shouted, urging his mount toward the gap. His comrades streaked after him.

Medrash hurled another flash of Torm's Power to slow pursuit. Khouryn glanced back—with a dragonborn seated behind him, he had to lean sideways to do it—and met the gaze of Skuthosiin's lambent yellow eyes.

To his relief, the green was still perched on his makeshift dais, still performing his ritual, and showed no signs of joining the chase. But his stare was chilling.

Khouryn spat the chill away.

As the scouts raced on, leaving the shadow things behind, giants hurled javelins and rocks. But as far as Khouryn could tell, none of the missiles found its mark, and after a few more heartbeats he and his comrades were clear of Ashhold entirely.

But they didn't slow until they reached their own camp, an orderly sprawl with a scarcity of campfires. The foragers couldn't find fuel, and even had it been otherwise, Black Ash Plain in summer could blunt anyone's enthusiasm for heat and smoke.

It seemed to Khouryn that his bat landed with an awkward bump. Unlike a griffon, the beast wasn't built to prowl around on the ground. But it had its own virtues, and he gave it a pat before allowing a black-scaled Lance Defender-in-training to take charge of it.

"That's the kind of young fellow you should be ogling," he murmured.

Like Skuthosiin—well, not really—Biri declined to respond to the provocation.

Medrash and Balasar gave up their borrowed steeds, and the four of them strode onward to the center of the army. Where Tarhun awaited them along with a motley assortment of senior Lance Defenders, clan war leaders, and mages.

Smiling, the vanquisher rose from his campstool as they approached. "Did everyone get back safely?" he asked.

"Yes, Majesty," Medrash said, saluting. "They spotted us, but we managed to break away."

"And that's not the only piece of good news," said Balasar with a grin. "We didn't see all that many of the giants' pets. Apparently the adepts haven't figured out that we can keep them from calling the beasts from afar. Which means they really won't be much of a factor in the fight."

"True," said Medrash. "That much is good news."

Belatedly registering his clan brother's somber demeanor, Balasar said, "All right, what did I miss?"

"Since you aren't versed in a mystical discipline," Biri said, "I understand why you didn't sense it. But Medrash is right. The ceremony Skuthosiin is performing is something powerful and bad."

"You saw Skuthosiin?" Tarhun asked.

"Yes," Khouryn said, "and, if anything, he looks even nastier than his reputation. So I can believe he's about to dump something hellish on our heads. The only question is, what form will it take?"

Biri hesitated. "I'm sorry. I wasn't able to tell that."

Balasar gave her a smile. "It's all right, sweetling. You did fine. We might not have gotten out of there without you."

A clan leader scratched her chin with the claw on her thumb. She had a row of little ivory moon piercings—waxing from new to full, then waning again—running across her brow. "If we don't know exactly what Skuthosiin's doing," she said, "do we know how much longer it will take?"

"No," Biri said.

"So if we want to interrupt the proceedings," Khouryn said, "we should attack now."

Tarhun frowned. "At night. After rushing our preparations."

"I admit it would have its drawbacks," Khouryn said.

"Which is why the giants won't expect it," Balasar said.

"I'm no longer a member of the Lance Defenders," Medrash said, "but I still remember what I learned when I was. The bats will spot what we can't. They'll let us know what's lurking in the dark."

Khouryn had no difficulty believing that was true. A griffon didn't need to be able to talk to alert its rider to the presence of danger, and a bat probably didn't either.

Fenkenkabradon Dokaan, commander of the Lance Defenders, was a bronze-colored warrior almost as big as Tarhun. He carried a sheathed greatsword tucked under one arm, and branching steel piercings like miniature antlers jutted from his temples. He grunted and said, "One of your escort told me you just now ran into shadow creatures the bats had trouble seeing."

"With respect, High Lord," Medrash replied, "magic and unnatural creatures always pose special problems. My observation is still sound."

Dokaan gave a brusque nod. "Fair enough. It is." He turned toward Tarhun. "Majesty, I think Sir Khouryn's plan has merit."

Several other officers and clan leaders tried to speak at once. Somewhat to Khouryn's surprise, they all seemed to be expressing support. But maybe it shouldn't have surprised him. They were the warrior elite of a valorous people, and they were heartily sick of the giants.

"So be it," said Tarhun. "Ready the troops."

* * * * *

Jet flew a zigzag course to throw off the aims of archers and cross-bowmen. Aoth chanted words of power and repeatedly jabbed his spear at the Threskelan company below. Hailstones the size of his fist dropped out of thin air to pummel the foe.

Aoth wanted to conserve his power. But that particular war band had soldiers riding bounding drakes, as well as a pair of shambling, long-nosed war trolls. It made sense to soften them up a little.

Once Jet carried him beyond the reach of their arrows and quarrels, he twisted in the saddle and looked for some sign that Tchazzar had entered the battle. The Firelord knew, it shouldn't be hard to spot.

But you're afraid he'll balk, the griffon said.

Jhesrhi stayed behind to encourage him, Aoth replied. *Unfortunately, Halonya's there too, without me to intimidate her. We just have to hope—*

A roar thundered across the scrubland, drowning out the rest of the muddled cacophony of battle. Wings lashing, golden eyes burning, blue and yellow flames leaping from his mouth, the red dragon rose from the center of the Chessentan formation.

In the night, few of the advancing enemy could see Tchazzar as clearly as Aoth could. Yet even so, every one of them faltered. Lurching, stumbling hesitation rippled across the battlefield.

Congratulations, said Jet. *One of your schemes finally worked.*

Not yet, said Aoth, *but it's off to a reasonable start.*

Tchazzar was supposed to fight hard during the opening movements of the battle, wreaking havoc on Alasklerbanbastos's army and creating the appearance that he was squandering his strength. Assuming he conducted himself as he had in past conflicts, the Great Bone Wyrm would let his archenemy wear himself down, then attack when he judged he had the advantage. At which point Jaxanaedegor and his fellow traitors would turn on their overlord, and they and Tchazzar would take him down together.

It would be a neat trick if it came together. Aoth could think of a dozen ways it could go wrong. But then, that was the case with most such plans.

Tchazzar hurtled toward a blue dragon on the wing. The blue had an unusually long beard of bladelike scales dangling beneath her chin, and the massive horn on her snout lacked a secondary point. By those details, Aoth identified her as Venzentilax, one of the wyrms genuinely loyal to Alasklerbanbastos.

She spat a bright, twisting flare of lightning. Tchazzar didn't even try to dodge. Nor did he jerk, falter, or reveal any other sign of distress when the attack hit him, although it blackened a spot at the base of his neck.

"Watch out!" a griffon rider shouted. His mount gave a piercing screech, and others took up the cry, spreading the alarm across the sky.

Aoth turned to behold a flight of undead hawks the size of horses, with green phosphorescence shimmering in their sunken eyes and bone showing through holes in their rotting feathers and skins. The raptors had come up on his flank while the dragons' duel distracted him.

He pointed his spear and started to hurl fire at the hawks. Then Jet lashed his wings and flung himself sideways.

Even so, a stab of cold chilled both the griffon and Aoth to the bone—he could feel the familiar's distress through their psychic link. Both undead, another mount with another master plunged down at them. They'd flown in higher than the hawks, and that had kept Aoth from noticing them before. Even fire-kissed eyes couldn't spot trouble if he was looking in the wrong direction.

The steed was the reanimated corpse of a chimera. It had the pallid wings, hind legs, and serpentine tail of a white dragon, while the rest of the body was leonine. Three heads sprouted from the shoulders—the wyrm's, the lion's, and the odd one out, a ram's complete with curving horns.

The rider had three heads too, although they all looked the same—naked human skulls perched atop a single skeleton. It clutched a staff in its bony hands.

Beating his wings, Jet flew out from under the chimera. Aoth tried to aim his spear and recite an incantation, but the aftereffects of the jolt of cold made his hand shake and his mouth stammer. He botched the spell, and as his attackers dived past, the skull lord—as such things were called—glared at him. Pale light seethed in the orbits of the fleshless head on the left, and cold burned through him once again.

But that was even worse than the dragon head's frigid breath, because it also sent terror howling through his mind. Suddenly, all he wanted to do was flee.

He looked around, but horribly could find no clear path to safety. His sellswords and the undead hawks were fighting on all sides. Apparently the griffon riders had discovered that their bows were of little use, for they were relying on their mounts to fight the raptors, beak to beak and claw to claw, with the losers falling to earth in pieces.

Get hold of yourself! snapped Jet. *You aren't really afraid! The skull lord put it in your mind!*

Aoth realized it was true. He struggled to focus past the fear and activate the countermagic bound in one of his tattoos. A bracing sting of power restored him to himself.

But why let the skull lord know it? He mimed panic while the undead chimera wheeled and climbed for another pass. Jet floundered in flight like a mount infected with his rider's distress or confused by nonsensical commands.

The chimera swooped at them. Aoth let it get close, then leveled his spear and spoke the single word necessary to release one of the spells bound inside the weapon.

The fiery blast sent the ram's head tumbling in one direction and the dragon's in the other. The wings tore away to drift like burning kites on the night wind, while the remains of the body dropped away beneath them. The skull lord's six orbits stared upward in impotent astonishment or rage.

Are you all right? asked Aoth.

Just a little frostbitten around the edges, said Jet. *That was like being back in Thay.*

What it was, said Aoth, *was a reminder that we have other things besides dragons to worry about.* Twisting in the saddle, he looked to see which of his fellow griffon riders needed help.

* * * * *

Nala cradled the green orb in both hands and focused her will on it. If she established a psychic bond, she'd be able to summon dragonspawn a shade more quickly in a little while, when the defenders of Ashhold needed them.

As they would. Created from actual wyrm eggs with rituals imparted by Tiamat herself, dragonspawn had proved insufficient to win the last big battle in Tymanther. But surely this time would be different. The giants were fighting on their home ground, where the towering masses of rock and the channels of fire running through the ground would make a mass charge of lancers impossible. What was more, Skuthosiin himself would take the field.

And after he won, the green would surely recognize just how valuable a weapon her talismans had been.

Nala needed that because the failure of her schemes in Djerad Thymar had cost her his favor. He'd granted her asylum among the giants, but hadn't seen fit to include her in his great magical ritual or even explain what it was meant to accomplish. That had to change if she was ever to assume her rightful role as a high priestess of the Nemesis of the Gods. Indeed, if she was even to be certain of avoiding the grim fate he intended for every other Tymantheran.

Her mind reached into the globe in somewhat the same way that she might have stuck her hand through a hole. Then her companion, a giant shaman who was doing the same thing with a gray talisman, cried out.

Nala glanced around in time to see the adept flounder back against a basalt wall. Blood streaming from his mouth and his left eye, he heaved the globe away from him. It smashed against the rock face on the other side of the relatively narrow alley in which they'd taken shelter.

Nala felt a stab of outrage. She and her true acolytes had worked long and hard to make the globes. Then, perhaps because the giant's distress alerted her, she sensed resistance in her own orb. A heartbeat earlier it had been a doorway. Now it was a trap snapping shut. She snatched her psychic presence clear before it could catch her.

"Betrayer," the shaman mumbled. He pushed off the wall, swayed, and stumbled toward her, enormous gray hands outstretched.

"Don't be stupid," she said. "I didn't ruin the talismans. The vanquisher's wizards found a way to do it. If you're hurt, let me help you." She grabbed hold of one of the giant's fingers and rattled off a healing prayer. Tiamat's Power manifested as a glow of warmth at her core, which then streamed through the point of contact.

The giant grunted.

"Better?" she asked.

"Yes," he said, no longer sounding dazed. Although he seemed nonplussed that his menacing advance hadn't frightened her.

"Then go find the other shamans. Warn them not to use the orbs. Or if they already did, heal them so they can fight."

He studied her for another moment, and she in turn could see just how reluctant he still was to trust or obey any dragonborn. But at last he said, "All right." He swiped blood from his face, turned, and loped away.

Nala headed for the other end of the passage and the shouting, crashing cacophony of battle. It was maddening that the talismans had failed—had, indeed, become a means for the enemy to cripple the adepts—but since they had, she needed to find a new way to make herself not just useful but indispensable to the defense.

The passage narrowed down to an opening narrow enough that no adult giant could squeeze through. It seemed like a good place to crouch and study the combat without being noticed.

Giants perched on the ledges and tops of the stony eminences, hurling javelins and rocks at foes who remained, for the moment, out of Nala's view. Then motion flickered above one such elevated position, there and gone too quickly for her to see it clearly. A shaft of wood sticking straight up from the top of his bald, knobby head, a barbarian toppled and crashed to the ground. She realized a Lance Defender had swooped down and speared him.

A volley of crossbow bolts pierced several of the slain giants' fellows and made the rest dive for cover. Then her countrymen came streaming through one of the broader passages dividing the towering stones.

By the Five Breaths, how she hated them! She'd brought them gifts that would have made them a great people, and they'd spurned them. Driven her into exile to live among savages. And now come to deprive her of even that miserable refuge.

In her heart, she begged the Dark Lady for revenge.

A long shape burst from the earth right in front of a company of Tymantheran spearmen. For an instant in the darkness, it looked like a new basalt spire suddenly rising to claim a place among the old ones. Then it swayed, opened its jaws, and roared.

The brown dragon bore ugly, half-healed wounds, yet it had come to fight the intruders anyway. Nala loved it for its courage.

It spewed hot sand, and dragonborn reeled, scorched and scraped bloody. The grit stayed in the air too, in a blinding, choking swirl. It afflicted Nala as much as anyone else, but she laughed anyway. Because she could just make out how helpless the soldiers were as the brown repeatedly struck and lifted its head, dispatching a foe with every bite.

Then white light flashed in the front rank of the foot soldiers. In the darkness, churning dust, and general confusion, Nala found it difficult to be sure, but it seemed to her that one of the soldiers vanished, and another dragonborn appeared in his place.

The newcomer was on horseback, and the horse was galloping. It only took it an instant to close the distance to the startled dragon, and then the rider's lance plunged into the creature's chest.

The brown jerked, then snarled and raised a clawed foot to retaliate. But at the same instant, a second lancer drove in on its flank and speared it in the base of its neck.

The wyrm thrashed, then tried to dissolve into sand. Nala could just make out its outlines softening and streaming. She surmised that it wanted to pour itself down the burrow to safety.

The first rider pulled his lance free, then stabbed repeatedly. Each attack flared with mystic power. The force, or the agony it brought, evidently hindered the brown's ability to transform, for the process slowed, then stopped. Leaving the sacred creature sprawled lifeless on the ground.

The cloud of sand subsided, and then Nala could see Medrash and Balasar clearly. Their comrades saw them too and raised a raw-throated cheer.

Though Nala had imagined herself full of hatred before, it had been a feeble thing compared to the loathing that gripped her now. Her breath weapon burned in her throat, and she shivered with the urge to hurl herself forward and attack. But that would just be throwing her life away. Which was the last thing she truly wanted to do, considering that Tiamat had just answered all her prayers.

Instinct—or perhaps the Dark Lady's whisper—told her that the paladin of Torm and his clan brother would prove to be pivotal figures that night, just as they and Khouryn Skulldark had been in Tym'anther. And if she stalked them and waited for the right moment to strike, then she too would play a crucial role.

But how could she be sure of keeping them always in sight amid the frenzy of the battle? By the looks of it, they were already preparing to press on. For a moment, the problem perplexed her, and then she smiled at her own foolishness.

For of course she too was dragonborn, and how likely was it that anyone would notice her telltale swaying or recognize her in some other fashion, in the dark, with far more obvious dangers looming on every side? As long as she didn't get too close to Medrash, Balasar, or any members of the Platinum Cadre, she should be fine. She discarded her robe of shimmering scales, then slipped from the notch between the stones to join the vanquisher's troops.

* * * * *

As Scar carried Jhesrhi up into the sky, she watched Tchazzar blast Venzentilax with his fiery breath. The quasi mind in her staff exhorted her to find a target and conjure a blaze of her own. Soon, she told it, soon.

Tchazzar had invited her to ride him into battle, as she had when he'd rescued Gaedynn and avenged himself on the shadar-kai. But she had a hunch it would be imprudent for a fragile human to sit on his back while other dragons tried to kill him. She also wanted to fight astride her griffon in concert with the rest of the Brotherhood. Impossible as it seemed, she might not get another chance.

It was a pity the red dragon hadn't insisted that Halonya ride him, to use her alleged clerical powers in the fray. But alas, Tymora hadn't smiled so widely as that. Halonya was still back in camp, safe as any of them were that night and likely nursing her many grudges.

The reanimated carcass of a huge bird of prey flew toward Jhesrhi's flank. She spoke to the wind, and the air thinned beneath the zombie's pinions. It floundered and tumbled, and, deciding not to waste any more magic on it, she had Scar swoop down on top of it and rip it apart with talon and claw. Which meant she had to endure its putrid stink, but fortunately only for a moment.

Up ahead, other griffon riders were fighting similar products of necromancy. Points of green light streaked across the dark as Aoth cast darts of force. She was about to urge Scar onward to the heart of that particular fight when something else snagged her attention.

A huge draconic skeleton lumbered out of the night. For a heartbeat Jhesrhi thought it was Alasklerbanbastos himself. But it didn't have a glow in its eye sockets, or small flares of lightning leaping and arcing from bone to bone. In fact, the bones looked like they didn't even all come from the same body, giving the thing a lopsided appearance and a limp.

It was a necromantic construct then, not unlike the undead hawks. But it was plainly a far greater threat, and one that Jaxanaedegor hadn't warned his new confederates about. Maybe his overlord had never told him of its existence.

The siegewyrm, as such colossal automata were called, was advancing on a formation of archers. With every lurching, uneven stride, jagged spurs of bone sprouted from the ground around it like fast-growing saplings. The bowmen drew and released with commendable coolness, but most of their shafts simply glanced off their target. Even Gaedynn, standing in the forefront, seemed unable to score a hit that mattered.

Jhesrhi felt a twinge of guilt that she hadn't enchanted any more arrows for him since their escape from the Shadowfell. But she'd simply never found the time.

Well, she'd help him now. She spoke a word of command and pointed her staff. An explosion of flame bloomed at the point where the siegewyrm's wings connected to its spine.

The detonation jolted and blackened bones, but it didn't shatter any of the big ones or break the linkages between them. She drew breath to try again, and then, vertebrae scraping and rattling together, the siegewyrm twisted its neck and raised its head to stare at her.

Pain ripped through her. Scar screeched as the same agonizing shock apparently jolted him. Together, they fell.

Struggling against the paralyzing pain, she told the wind to support the griffon or, failing that, to cushion his landing. No doubt fighting the same fight, Scar managed to half spread his wings. They thumped down hard, but not hard enough to kill them.

Although it seemed likely they'd only prolonged their lives by a few heartbeats. The siegewyrm heaved itself around in their direction. Spurs of bone as long as her staff and as sharp as Scar's talons stabbed up from the ground as it advanced.

Hands shaking, she lifted her staff and tried to focus her will. She felt Scar shuddering too. He was trying to find the strength to take to the air again. Then the construct lumbered into striking distance, and she and her mount were out of time.

A second griffon swooped onto the siegewyrm's back. Clinging, Eider tore and bit. Gaedynn leaned out of the saddle and smashed with a long-handled maul. Bone chips flew.

The skeletal dragon twisted its neck to retaliate. Eider lashed her wings and flew beyond its reach.

Meanwhile, veering to avoid the jagged bones sprouting from the earth, archers charged the undead wyrm. Jhesrhi saw that most of the ones who dared were sellswords of the Brotherhood. They battered their huge foe's legs with mace and axe.

Oraxes and Meralaine attacked the thing as well. Jhesrhi hadn't spotted them, but, sensitive to magic, she could half hear them chanting incantations even amid the clamor of battle. She could also see it when their wizardry produced its effects. Oraxes created a flying blade of yellow light to hack at the siegewyrm's neck. The necromancer's power pulled darkness boiling out from between its ribs and through the cavities in its skull and, judging from the way it jerked, hurt it worse than anything else so far.

But not enough to stop it. Its lashing tail knocked men flying through the air. One archer plunged down on a spike of bone and, impaled through the midsection, writhed there screaming. The siegewyrm struck and bit another man to pieces. It stared, and three more mercenaries crumpled in agony just like Scar and Jhesrhi had.

Gaedynn and the others had saved them. She had to return the favor, or the siegewyrm might kill them all.

Weak and shaky with pain as she was, she might in other circumstances have found it impossible even to make the attempt. But fortunately she had a cure for her debility, since her comrades had bought her the chance to use it.

She fumbled with the buckle securing the pouch on her belt. Something flickered at the edge of her vision. She turned her head.

Another length of bone was leaping up from the ground, at an angle. She jerked herself sideways. The spur stopped growing when the jagged point was a finger joint short of her face.

She sat frozen for an instant, then finished extracting the pewter vial from the bag. The potion inside was tasteless but warm, and the glow spread out from her stomach to melt away her pain.

She drank half, then dismounted. She showed the bottle to Scar, and the griffon raised his head and opened his beak. She poured the remaining liquid in, and his feathered throat worked as he swallowed.

The elixir worked as quickly on him as it had on her. He gave a rasping cry, then whirled around to face the siegewyrm.

"Yes," she said. "Let's kill the wretched thing." She swung herself back into the saddle and, begrudging the time it would have taken to refasten the safety harness, urged Scar into motion. He trotted, leaped, beat his wings, and carried her skyward.

Where she could see that while her allies had inflicted a degree of damage on the automaton, it showed no signs of breaking down anytime soon. Meanwhile, with nearly every bite and sweep of its tail, it was doing grievous harm to the men scrambling around it.

Jhesrhi didn't have the natural affinity with lightning that she did with earth, fire, wind, and water. But she hurled a bright, roaring thunderbolt anyway, in the hope that the siegewyrm would prove more susceptible to it than it had to flame.

It didn't.

How should she attack it, then? It must have some weakness. She peered down, searching for a clue to what that might be.

Another mage—Oraxes or Meralaine, she assumed—assailed it with a conjured burst of flame. The flash produced a metallic glint at certain of its joints, particularly the points where bones from different dragons fit together.

Evidently artificers had cobbled the construct together with wires and hinges. Smiling, Jhesrhi whispered sibilant words to the powers of rust and corrosion.

Tendrils of vapor swirled around the siegewyrm, and the metal in its joints sizzled like bacon in a frying pan. It lurched as its left hind leg started to separate from the rest of it.

Oraxes and Meralaine chanted, using their magic to heighten the effect of Jhesrhi's spell. The fumes thickened, and the sizzling noise grew louder. The hind leg finished falling off, and the right wing broke into several pieces. Slumping, the entire construct looked on the verge of collapsing into a heap.

But it wasn't finished yet. Somehow it managed a final lunge that sent sellswords reeling and put it in striking distance of the two adolescent mages from Luthcheq. Oraxes jumped in front of Meralaine.

Then Eider slammed down on top of the siegewyrm's skull, which broke away from the neck bones behind it. At last, the entire automaton disintegrated into clattering pieces. Eider flapped her wings and returned to the air before the skull finished its tumble to the ground.

The sellswords raised a cheer. Oraxes and Meralaine hugged. Gaedynn flashed Jhesrhi a grin, as he had on many other occasions when they'd accomplished some notable feat or desperate endeavor together.

But then something, joy or authenticity, went out of the smile like he'd remembered something unpleasant. She realized he somehow knew she'd promised to stay in Chessenta.

She wanted to tell him it had been a difficult choice. That she'd made it partly to help the Brotherhood, and that she still wasn't sure it was the right one.

But even if there were time for it, and even if they were close enough to converse without shouting, what difference would it make? The two of them had never been like those children embracing below, and they never could be.

Feeling old and bleak inside, she pointed to signal her intention to join up with Aoth and his squad of griffon riders. Gaedynn gave her a casual wave of acknowledgment and sent Eider swooping toward the ground.

THIRTEEN

Medrash assumed it would be immediately apparent when Skuthosiin joined the fight. The fact that the dragon had yet to do so meant that he was still trying to finish his ritual.

Accordingly, Medrash, Balasar, and others who rode with them pushed toward the heart of Ashhold. Unfortunately, with almost every step of the way contested, their progress seemed excruciatingly slow. Medrash fought the urge to spend his Power freely and clear the path as expeditiously as possible. He was certain he was going to need it later.

One of the hound-sized shadow dragons swooped down out of the black, smoky sky. Had he been forced to rely on his eyes alone, he might not have seen it until its fangs were already in his throat. But he felt it too, as a sickening, plunging locus of vileness. That gave him time to swing his sword. His lance had shattered early on, on a giant's crudely fashioned granite shield.

His blade split the murky creature's skull, and it dissolved into black, rotten-smelling smoke. At the same instant, Balasar grabbed one of the crossbows hanging from his saddle and shot it one-handed. The quarrel hit the giant, who'd been about to heave a boulder, right between the eyes. The missile slipped from the barbarian's hands to tumble banging down the side of the basalt eminence on which he stood. He toppled after it a heartbeat later.

The riders pushed on to yet another point where the way diverged. Pulling on the reins, Balasar swung his chestnut steed to the right.

"No," Medrash said. "It's the other way."

"Are you sure?" Gritting his teeth, Balasar worked the pull lever of the weapon he'd just discharged. "It's a maze in here."

"I'm sure," Medrash replied. Now that they were close, he could feel the unnatural power of the ceremony—or perhaps of Skuthosiin himself—just as he had the foulness of the shadow thing.

He led his fellow riders, and the foot soldiers trailing along behind, around two more turns and through two more bands of giants trying to bar the way. Then he gasped.

Because while simply feeling the vileness had been unpleasant, seeing it was worse. He'd already noted that Skuthosiin seemed hideous, even if he couldn't say why. Now that he was closer, that ugliness seemed to stab into his eyes.

And, repulsive as the dragon was, the fire leaping out of the fissure was worse. When Medrash had seen it before, it had simply burned yellow like most flames. Now it changed color from one moment to the next. It was red, then blue, then green, then bone white, then shadow black.

Medrash could just discern that something was inside the fire—or, to be more accurate, coming through it. Using it as a passage from somewhere else. Whatever it was, its several parts swayed in a way that reminded him of Nala, and, even barely glimpsed, it radiated a terrifying feeling of might, malice, and contempt.

He realized he absolutely had to stop it from emerging into the mortal world. And do it now, before the mere threat of such a disaster panicked his companions. Which meant there was no time to look for the vanquisher's wizards and ask them to help.

He reached out to Torm. Cold and bracing as a mountain spring, Power surged through him and collected in his hand.

He didn't know a specific prayer to disrupt such a ceremony. But, guided by instinct, he focused his thoughts on the idea of forbiddance, tucked his sword under his shield arm, lifted his empty hand high, and swung it down at the ground.

Made of steely shimmer, a huge, ghostly gauntlet appeared in midair, swept down, and covered the source of the fire with its palm. Startled, the giant adepts cried out and recoiled.

Pain seared Medrash's actual hand, as if it were bare and he were really using it to smother a fire. He had a muddled impression that his flesh didn't burn constantly. Perhaps it charred one instant, froze the next, and suffered some other sort of injury the moment after that.

But he couldn't really sort out the differences in sensation. It took all the will and focus he could muster to hold his hand in place despite the agony, and to keep the Loyal Fury's Power pouring into it.

Until—after what was likely only a matter of heartbeats, even though it seemed like forever—the phantasmal gauntlet vanished, and Medrash saw that the fire beneath was gone.

That was the only way he could tell. His hand was still ablaze with pain. Yet even so, he felt a surge of satisfaction, and when Skuthosiin's head whipped around to goggle at him, that only made the moment sweeter.

"Sorry," Balasar called. "Were you using that fire?"

Skuthosiin's eyes flicked to the giant shamans. "Kill them," he snapped.

The adepts produced some of Nala's globes, held them at eye level, then gasped and staggered.

"Oops," Balasar said.

Medrash drew a bit more of Torm's Power to quell the throbbing in his hand. It didn't end it altogether, but it muted it. When he tried to grip the wire-wrapped hilt of his sword, he found that he could.

"You see how it is," he said. "We know how to counter all your tricks. Surrender, and perhaps Tarhun will show you mercy."

"Surrender?" Skuthosiin repeated. "Are you insane? Do you think I really need tricks, or any sort of help, to slaughter mites like you? This is the end of you and all your people." He sprang forward.

Medrash rode to meet him. Balasar and the other riders pounded after him.

The fight was going to be terrible. In all probability, many dragonborn would die. But Medrash was satisfied because his comrades hadn't quailed, and, in his furious eagerness to engage, Skuthosiin had opted to stay on the ground where lance and sword could reach him. And as more and more Tymantherans, including the mages, arrived in the heart of Ashhold—

Something seared Medrash's back. His steed pitched forward and fell. On either side of him other horses dropped as well, and yellow flame glinted on the riders' armor.

He hit his head hard, and something cracked. Suddenly everything seemed dim and far away. Unimportant. Some instinct insisted that he try to get up anyway, but he discovered he couldn't move.

* * * * *

Her mouth still warm and tingling, Nala rejoiced to see that Medrash wasn't standing up, or stirring at all.

Despite her best efforts, the paladin and the other riders had gotten ahead of her and interrupted the ritual before she could reach the center of the giants' refuge. But even though that disruption was sacrilege, from a practical standpoint it might actually have been for the best. Because her miracles would play a greater role in Skuthosiin's victory and show him how valuable she truly was.

She'd drawn down Tiamat's glory to augment the power of her breath weapon, then spat it at the horsemen. The burst of fire dropped half a dozen riders. Her only regret was that Medrash and Balasar weren't close enough together for her to burn both of them. But the paladin was the more important target, and if the Dark Lady smiled on her, she still might be the one to kill his clan brother.

She glimpsed a glint from the corner of her eye and turned toward the spear points swinging in her direction. For of course the foot soldiers among whom she'd advanced had seen her blast their mounted comrades. They'd stood stupefied for a heartbeat, but they meant to strike her down for her treachery.

She had no time for another prayer, whispered or otherwise, but her own innate vitality was sufficient for a second blaze of fiery breath. She spat it, and the two warriors who were threatening her reeled backward.

She darted out of the massed infantrymen, racing closer to Skuthosiin and the riders assailing him. Some of the foot soldiers hesitated to follow, but others scrambled after her.

She judged she had just enough time and distance for an incantation. She hissed Draconic words of power, touched the end of her thumb to the tip of her middle finger to make her hand resemble a saurian head, then, quick as a striking serpent, jabbed it at four different spots on the ground.

Each as big as a dragonborn, four rearing, snarling wyrms appeared where she'd pointed. Her pursuers quailed until they realized the apparitions were incapable of doing actual harm. By then she was close enough to Skuthosiin for the green to lash out at anyone who dared to keep following, and no one did.

* * * * *

Clouds shrouded Selûne and the stars. To Aoth, the air smelled like a storm was coming.

It is, said Jet, *and its name is Alasklerbanbastos.*

I know, answered Aoth. Because the deepening darkness seemed blacker and felt somehow dirtier than just the clouds could explain, while the breeze carried a hint of old rot as well as the imminence of lightning. It was like the worst of his experiences in Thay, with something unimaginably strong and vile rising to poison all the natural world. *I just wish he'd get on with it.*

Back on the ground for the moment, Tchazzar incinerated a formation of kobolds with a blast of flame. Either he was trying hard to convince the Great Bone Wyrm that he was squandering his power—or else, in his excitement, he really was.

Whether he was thinking, the result was the same. At the northern edge of the battlefield, pieces of darkness seemed to thicken and arrange themselves into a structure, like ghostly hands were building it. And even wyrmkeepers and vampires instinctively shrank away.

In a moment, a murky skull with a spiked snout sat atop the stacked vertebrae of the neck, and fleshless wings arched to either side. Then, inside the core of the thing's body, lightning flared repeatedly from rib to rib, and its eye sockets lit with a spectral glow. The structure changed from dark to leprous white as lengths and curves of shadow turned into bone.

Alasklerbanbastos strode forward. Chessentans who were nowhere near him screamed. So did some of the Threskelans.

Go ahead, said Jet, *if it will make you feel better.*

Aoth snorted. If he'd ever done any screaming, it had been a long, long time ago. But even to a man who'd survived the nastiest parts of the War of the Zulkirs, the Great Bone Wyrm was an appalling spectacle. Now that the two of them were in the same place, he could tell that the dracolich was even bigger than Tchazzar. And as they advanced on each other, and warriors left off struggling to scurry out of the way, it was difficult to resist the idea that here were the only combatants and the only fight that really mattered.

Aoth spat away that notion as well. Whatever their pretensions, neither wyrm could stand up to a proper army all by himself. That was why they bothered to command armies. Besides, what was about to happen would be very little like the duel of titans his imagination was suggesting.

Or so he hoped. Jaxanaedegor and his followers were taking their time about striking at their master. Aoth hoped they were simply making sure they'd take the dracolich completely by surprise when he'd have nowhere to run.

The battlefield was strangely quiet as the undead colossus and the self-proclaimed deity approached each other. That was because a good many warriors were simply standing and watching, and it enabled Aoth to make out the words when the wyrms spoke in the same esoteric form of Draconic that Jaxanaedegor had used when he first appeared to Tchazzar. Or maybe it was their innate magic, roused by their utter mutual hatred, that made their words audible even high in the sky.

"I invoke the Five Hundred and Fifty-Fifth Precept," Alasklerbanbastos said. "To the death, and winner take all."

"That's exactly how it will be," Tchazzar replied. "For I promise I'll find your phylactery."

"Take it if you can." Without cocking his neck back or doing anything else that might have warned of a live dragon's intent, Alasklerbanbastos simply opened his fleshless jaws and spat lightning.

The flare dazzled Aoth, and the thunderclap spiked pain into his ears. The attack pierced Tchazzar and made him thrash.

But as soon as it ended, the red dragon spewed a blast of flame. It cracked some of Alasklerbanbastos's naked bones, sent chips of them flying, and jolted the dracolich backward.

Tchazzar instantly sprang high and lashed his wings. He plainly meant to pounce on top of his foe before the Great Bone Wyrm recovered.

Unfortunately, Alasklerbanbastos was more resilient than expected. He lifted his head, stared at Tchazzar, and the glow in his eye sockets flared.

Aoth remembered how the dracolich's gaze had paralyzed him. Tchazzar merely seemed to twitch in midleap. But perhaps that was enough to impair his agility, for Alasklerbanbastos dodged out from under his adversary's claws. And when the war hero came down, the dracolich met him with a clattering sweep of his bony tail.

The blow caught Tchazzar across the side of the head and bashed him stumbling to the side. Alasklerbanbastos backed away, opening up the distance, and hissed words of power.

A web of shadows seethed into being. It covered Tchazzar like a net, and wherever it touched him, scales sloughed away and the flesh beneath them withered.

With all his might, he should have been able to break free. But as he gathered himself to try, Alasklerbanbastos snarled another spell.

Tchazzar roared, then thrashed wildly, as a beast would struggle against a net without truly comprehending what it was. Without intellect to guide it, raw strength wasn't enough to snap the strands, and they rotted their way deeper into his body.

Like the paralysis, the red dragon's frenzied confusion only lasted a heartbeat. Then he stopped his useless flailing. But at the same moment, Alasklerbanbastos spat another bolt of lightning.

Tchazzar went rigid, then slumped when the flare blinked out of existence. He kept on fighting the web, but seemed dazed and too weakened to have any hope of escaping.

Alasklerbanbastos started another spell.

Aoth looked around. Jaxanaedegor and his minions were nowhere near the Great Bone Wyrm. Maybe they hadn't expected the dracolich to gain the upper hand so quickly and completely. Aoth hadn't expected it either, even though every soldier knew combat was often like that. A duel between even the greatest warriors could start and end with a single cut.

Anyway, one thing was clear. If Jaxanaedegor hadn't already started maneuvering to attack, he certainly wasn't going to do it now.

Aoth supposed he should order the Brotherhood to retreat. Try to get them off the battlefield and out of Chessenta without taking any more casualties.

But then they'd have lost again and further tarnished their reputation. He might never see Cera again. And he could guess what fate awaited a priestess of the sun in a land newly conquered by an undead monstrosity.

To the Abyss with it. It was as reckless as anything Aoth had ever done in Thay, madder than anything he'd ever wanted to do again. But he aimed his spear and sent Jet swooping at the dracolich.

* * * * *

Skuthosiin spewed vapor. Balasar held his breath and squinched his eyes shut. His exposed skin stung even so, but his precautions—or the protective amulet Biri, the pretty young white-scaled mage, had for some reason given him—kept the vapor from rotting his lungs or blinding him.

His poor horse wasn't as lucky. He felt the animal toppling beneath him. He opened his eyes, dropped his lance, dived out of the saddle, and rolled to his feet. At once he had to jump to keep his mount's spasmodic legs from kicking him. To either side, other horses lay or rolled convulsing. As did some of their riders. Other dragonborn coughed and retched or swiped tears from their streaming eyes.

Balasar realized he needed to keep Skuthosiin's attention fixed on him until his fellow survivors recovered the capacity to defend themselves. "I'm still here!" he called to the hideous creature. "You just can't do anything right, can you?"

Skuthosiin snarled and clawed. Balasar dodged left and then, as the dragon's foot smashed down and jolted the earth, glimpsed motion at the edge of his vision. He pivoted to find Skuthosiin's tail whipping at him. By avoiding what amounted to a feint, he'd stepped right into the true attack.

He leaped and folded his legs underneath him. He felt the breeze as the tail whipped by. The blow slammed into his still-thrashing horse, smashing it into shapelessness and smearing parts of it across the ground.

As the tail completed its arc, Khouryn was there to intercept it. Bellowing, he jammed his spear straight down through the tip, nailing it to the ground.

Skuthosiin jerked his extremity free, snapping the point off the weapon in the process. The shaft remained in the wound and wobbled as the tail swirled around.

Many wearing the badges and colors of the Platinum Cadre, other spearmen scrambled after the dwarf. They formed up to attack and fall back as he and the Beast had taught them.

Balasar felt a surge of pride. Skuthosiin was deadly, slaughtering an opponent with almost every moment that passed, but his comrades kept attacking anyway. They came from a race of dragon-killers and were proving themselves worthy descendants of their forebears.

Unfortunately, valor alone didn't guarantee a victory. Their chances would have been better if Medrash were still in the fight, but something—Balasar hadn't seen what—had struck his clan brother down an instant after they charged.

Hoping Medrash was still alive, Balasar drew his sword, lifted his battered targe into a high guard, and advanced on Skuthosiin.

* * * * *

Aoth rattled off words of power. A shaft of sunlight that would have done Cera proud shot from the head of his spear. It slashed across Alasklerbanbastos's skull and stabbed into his eye sockets.

It was powerful magic. Yet the dracolich didn't even look up, any more than Aoth would have reacted to a buzzing fly when intent on fighting a foe. Still staring at Tchazzar, the Great Bone Wyrm kept on hissing and growling his own incantation.

Aoth's neck muscles tightened in anger. He cursed, then unlocked the most powerful spell currently stored inside the spear, poured extra force into it, and sent the results streaking from the point in a stream of sparks.

The sparks detonated in rapid succession as they hit the Bone Wyrm's wings and spine. Each booming, fiery blast jolted him downward like a gigantic boot stamping on his back. A couple of small bones and pieces of bone fell away from his body. He stumbled over the words of his incantation, and Aoth felt the accumulating power dissipate in a useless sizzle.

Let's see you ignore that, he thought. Then Alasklerbanbastos raised his head and spread his jaws.

Jet lashed his wings, and then the world turned into glare and a pounding bang. It took Aoth an instant to understand that in fact the thunderbolt hadn't hit them. The griffon had dodged it.

Alasklerbanbastos spread his own wings, gave them a clattering flap, and climbed into the air.

Keep away from him! said Aoth.

Obviously! Jet snapped. He veered, and darts of blue-white light crackled past them.

As they dodged back and forth across the sky, Aoth hurled fire, acid, and every other force that seemed like it might be capable of hurting an undead blue dragon. More often than not, the attacks hit their target. But none of them made Alasklerbanbastos falter for even a heartbeat.

Whereas he only has to hit me once, said Jet.

I know. Aoth looked for Jaxanaedegor and found him hovering far from the action. He peered down at Tchazzar. The red dragon was still writhing under the web of shadows.

A boom jolted him and tumbled Jet end over end, like the griffon was somersaulting. Only his buckled harness held Aoth in the saddle. For a moment, the mind meshed with his own was dull and oblivious, and then, with a screech, the familiar snapped back to full wakefulness. He beat his wings and somehow regained control of his trajectory.

But by the time Jet pulled out of his fall, Alasklerbanbastos was plunging down at him, enormous claws poised to catch and rend.

Jet swooped one way and another, trying to get out from under the dracolich. Alasklerbanbastos matched him move for move. Aoth hurled flame from his spear. It splashed across the Bone Wyrm's legs and ribs and must have been doing *some* harm. But the undead blue kept closing in.

Until an arrow plunged into his right eye socket.

Aoth suspected that the shaft hadn't actually injured Alasklerbanbastos. But judging from the way he jerked, it must have at least startled him. And perhaps it was a maddening distraction to have it bouncing around inside his hollow skull. Because the next time Jet veered, the dracolich failed to compensate. The familiar streaked into the clear, and Alasklerbanbastos plunged on by.

Aoth glanced around and wasn't surprised to spot Gaedynn grinning at him from Eider's back. Though he'd been leading griffon riders for almost a hundred years, he'd met few archers who could have made that shot.

He *was* surprised at how many other griffon riders were coming on behind the redheaded scout, ready to aid their captain in his suicidal folly.

Their shafts fell on Alasklerbanbastos like rain and seemed to do as little harm. The dracolich shook his head, opened his jaws, and spat out Gaedynn's arrow. Then he lashed his wings and climbed. The light in his eye sockets glowed brighter. Lightning crawled on him and leaped from one bone to another.

Aoth pointed his spear and rattled off words of command. A blade of emerald light leaped from the point of the weapon and streaked at the ascending dracolich. Guiding it with little shifts of his hand, trying to match Gaedynn's accuracy, he made it hack repeatedly at the spot where Alasklerbanbastos's left wing connected to the shoulder bone.

Alasklerbanbastos twisted his head to regard the sword of light. No doubt to get rid of it before it accomplished its purpose. But then Meralaine recited an incantation. Her voice was a girl's voice, high and breathy, yet the charge of dark magic it carried made it seem somehow cold and leaden, as well as enabling a fellow mage to catch the sound even across the sky. Though Aoth didn't take his eyes off Alasklerbanbastos to look for her, he surmised that the necromancer had persuaded some griffon rider to carry her aloft.

Her spell made the dracolich hesitate. Only for a heartbeat, but in that instant, the flying blade accomplished its task. The wing broke away from the body. The Bone Wyrm started to fall—

—and then stopped.

Because, Aoth realized, while wings helped Alasklerbanbastos maneuver across the sky, it was ultimately magic that held him up. As it was still supporting him, while the wing also stopped tumbling and floated upward again.

But the wretched creature had to fall! In desperation, Aoth shouted an incantation intended to shred enchantments to nothing. He didn't know if it had any chance of working, but it was the only idea he had. Meralaine joined in on the first refrain, reinforcing his power with her own.

Alasklerbanbastos plummeted again, and this time fell all the way down to the ground.

Aoth prayed to Kossuth that the dracolich would smash apart, but the Lord of Flame apparently didn't hear. Although Alasklerbanbastos hit hard enough to snap some bones and jolt others loose from their couplings, the damage looked relatively superficial. Worse, either because of some innate capacity or because he used enchantment, he instantly started to mend. Pieces of bone, the severed wing included, flew through the air to reunite with his body.

Curse it! thought Aoth. The thing seemed as unstoppable as Szass Tam himself.

Alasklerbanbastos flexed his legs and spread his wings. Then his head whipped around as a flash snagged his attention.

Jhesrhi was on the ground near Tchazzar, casting flame from her staff to burn away the web of darkness. Maybe to restore his strength as well, as she had in the Shadowfell.

Alasklerbanbastos took a first stride in her direction. Jet furled his wings and dived at the dracolich. Aoth hurled darts of scarlet light that stabbed into the undead dragon's spine but failed to divert him from his purpose.

Springing from the ground, Scar flung himself at Alasklerbanbastos. Who snapped him out of the air and gnashed him into pieces.

Eider plunged down on top of the dracolich and began to tear with her talons. Alasklerbanbastos shook himself like a wet dog and sent the griffon and her rider tumbling.

Oraxes hurled his own darts of light. Lances leveled, Shala and Hasos galloped at the undead blue. Soldiers rushed in, swinging axes and jabbing with spears.

Still intent on Tchazzar and Jhesrhi, Alasklerbanbastos didn't so much fight the other opponents seeking to bar the way as simply wade through them. Unfortunately, he seemed to do it almost as easily as Aoth could have walked through a puddle. Meanwhile, Jhesrhi stood her ground and threw fire from the staff. She plainly meant to free Tchazzar or die trying.

Put me on top of him, said Aoth. *Right where Eider landed.*

All right, said Jet, *but I don't promise that I'll be able to hold on either.*

You don't have to. Just set me there. Aoth willed the straps that held him in the saddle to unbuckle, and they did. He released the magic bound in every protective tattoo on his body.

Then Jet thumped down. Aoth swung himself off the familiar's back, grabbed a knob of bone, and shouted, "Go!" With a reluctance that throbbed across their psychic link, the familiar lashed his wings and took off again. Aoth charged his spear with raw force and stabbed at sections of rib that—he hoped—Gaedynn's mount had already weakened.

Pieces of two adjacent ribs snapped loose and fell away. Aoth jammed himself feet first into the breach he'd created. It was a tight squeeze, and a jagged tip of broken bone scratched his cheek. But then, releasing the charm bound in another tattoo to soften the fall, he dropped inside.

Where he found it all but impossible to stand. The dracolich's motion bounced him around, and the bottom of the rib cage was like a floor with planks missing. Small lightning bolts crackled across the space he occupied, stinging and jolting him. They'd do worse than that once they wore away his protective enchantments.

He grabbed a rib to find and keep his balance, released the remaining energy in the spear, and jabbed at the curves of bone around him. If Tymora smiled, maybe Alasklerbanbastos would find the assault from the inside as difficult to ignore as Gaedynn's arrow rattling around in his head.

For two or three heartbeats, that didn't appear to be the case. But then the dracolich whirled around like a hound chasing its tail. Head bent backward at the end of his long neck, he glared at the pest infesting his core.

"Not this time," said Aoth. He made sure he didn't meet the Bone Wyrm's gaze. And wished the creature didn't have a hundred other ways of attacking him.

Alasklerbanbastos's fleshless jaws opened. Aoth shouted a word of defense, and the world blazed white.

* * * * *

Medrash's vision had cleared, and to a degree so had his thoughts. He could see and understand what was happening before him, and that was hellish. Because his friends and comrades needed him.

Chopping with his urgrosh, or jabbing with the spike on the butt, Khouryn was fighting as brilliantly as any warrior Medrash had ever seen. Grinning, shouting taunts, waiting until the last possible instant to dance out of the way of an attack in order to land a counterstroke, Balasar was equally superb. And they had help. Dragonborn kept streaming into the heart of Ashhold. Bat riders wheeled and swooped overhead, hurling javelins or thrusting with lances and polearms. Some of the mages had arrived as well. Cloaked in a protective blur, Biri hurled bursts of frost from her rose quartz wand.

Yet Medrash's instincts told him it wasn't going to be enough. Skuthosiin had gashes and punctures all over his prodigious body, but they weren't slowing him down. He seemed to fell an adversary with every snap of his fangs, snatch of his talons, or swing of his tail, and when he managed another burst of poison breath, he was apt to kill several at once. To make the situation even more dire, a couple of the ash giant shamans had shaken off their debility, some of the hulking barbarian warriors had retreated into the heart of Ashhold, and they were all making a stand with their dragon chieftain.

Medrash reached out to Torm. As on his previous attempts, he failed to make contact. Even though he felt like his thoughts had cleared, his injury seemed to hinder his spiritual gifts just as it had paralyzed his body.

It occurred to him that he was likely dying. In other circumstances, that might not have dismayed him. But now it felt like failure. Like he'd be abandoning Balasar and the others.

He groped uselessly in the void. Then a familiar figure crouched over him. "Patrin?" he croaked.

The newcomer's eyes widened in surprise, and Medrash realized he'd been mistaken. The fellow was younger and thinner than Bahamut's knight had been, and his hide was brown-freckled ochre, not crimson.

Medrash decided that it was the youth's purple and platinum tunic, and the dark, that had confused him.

"I'm . . . I'm not him," the newcomer said.

"I see that now," said Medrash. "Go. Fight. Don't worry about me."

"I'm not him," the youth repeated, "but the wind whispered to me. It said that now the god needs *me* to be his champion in this place. It told me to heal you. But I don't know how!"

Even with his body broken and useless, Medrash felt a twinge of repugnance at the thought of accepting any boon from a dragon god. But he was far too desperate to pay it any heed.

"Put your hands on my shoulders," he said. "Now reach out to Bahamut with your mind. You just have to concentrate and believe the Power will come. And be ready when it does. Sometimes—"

The newly anointed paladin cried out. A cold, stinging Power burst out of his hands and surged through Medrash, sharpening his thoughts and washing the deadness out of his limbs. Which brought a certain amount of pain, because the magic didn't entirely heal his burns and bruises. But he so rejoiced in the return of sensation that even discomfort was a kind of joy.

The dragon-worshiper's eyes rolled up into his head. He toppled sideways.

Medrash sat up and caught the unconscious youth, then laid him gently on the ground. He wished he could put him somewhere safer, but with Skuthosiin slaughtering dragonborn every moment, there wasn't time. Besides, nowhere in Ashhold was truly safe, nor would be until the fight was won.

He stood up and found his fallen sword, then tried to assess how much mystical Power remained to him. To his surprise, he had plenty. Bahamut had left him some blisters and scrapes, but had evidently refreshed his paladin gifts.

A Daardendrien warrior with a broken leg lay in front of Skuthosiin. Jaws open wide, the green dragon's head arced down at him.

Medrash shouted, "Torm!" The world blurred for an instant as he switched places with his injured kinsman.

Sidestepping, he slashed at the side of the dragon's head as it plunged by. He missed the slit-pupiled yellow eye, but his blade split the scaly hide beneath.

Skuthosiin whipped his head up high, almost snatching the sword from Medrash's grip. But he held on tight, and, slinging drops of gore, the blade pulled out of the wound instead.

Skuthosiin glared down at him, and the spiritual deformity that made him profoundly if indefinably hideous seemed to concentrate in his gaze. Perhaps it was supposed to make Medrash avert his eyes, or to churn his guts with nausea, but it did neither. It only made him even more determined to destroy the threat to his people once and for all.

"I don't care how many little gods you have propping you up!" the dragon snarled. "My lady is the only one that matters!"

"Prove it," Medrash said. He raised his sword, and white light blazed from the blade. Skuthosiin recoiled. Medrash dashed forward to strike while the wyrm was still dazzled. Other warriors did the same.

* * * * *

Aoth had tattoos to blunt pain and avert shock. To keep him awake and active even when wounded. Sprawled inside Alasklerbanbastos's rib cage, he released their power.

And that was all he did. He didn't know how badly he was hurt—badly, he suspected—but he was sure he couldn't withstand another blast of the dracolich's breath. His only hope was to lie motionless and convince Alasklerbanbastos he was dead already.

Just look away, he thought, watching the Great Bone Wyrm through slitted eyes. There are dozens of people beating on you and trying to kill you. Look around at them.

Alasklerbanbastos's head whipped away. Then Tchazzar crashed down on him like an avalanche.

* * * * *

Nala tried to avoid conflict as she skulked around the edges of the battle. It wasn't too difficult. With Skuthosiin and various giants to fight, her fellow dragonborn tended to overlook her. Which was fortunate, because she needed to make haste.

Impossible though it seemed, she could tell that the tide had turned against her master. Probably realizing it, he had at one point spread his wings to take to the air. But, chanting in unison, three of the vanquisher's wizards had created a web of blue light that covered the center of Ashhold like a lid on a jar.

The barrier at least kept the Lance Defenders on their bats from harrying Skuthosiin any further. But in Nala's judgment, they weren't really the problem. Nor, for all their power, were the mages. Nor the common warriors, jabbing and hacking with dogged determination. It was Medrash. The paladin was exalted, fighting like one of the dragon-killing rebels in the tales of treason and blasphemy that made up the history of their people.

Nala had to strike him down and make it stick. Then Skuthosiin could still prevail, and would unquestionably know whom to reward for his victory.

She could smite Medrash with the Five Breaths as she had the redspawn devastator. He wouldn't get back up from that. She just needed a clear path between them, but with combatants scrambling and pushing one another back and forth, that wasn't easy to come by.

Yet finally she found it. Wishing she still had the wyrmkeeper regalia she'd discarded—she didn't actually need it, but it would have made the magic easier—she raised her shadow-wood staff, focused her thoughts, and took a deep breath.

Then a jolt stabbed through her torso from back to front. She looked down and saw a finger-length of bloody blade protruding from her chest.

The pointed steel jerked backward and disappeared. She crumpled to her knees. Balasar stepped into view and grinned down at her.

"My feelings are hurt," he said. "Why would you think you ought to kill Medrash ahead of me? I'm the clever one. I tricked you into letting me into your filthy cult, didn't I? And I spotted you slinking around tonight and did a little sneaking of my own."

She struggled to wheeze out a curse, but couldn't manage it.

"Ah well," he continued, "I forgive you the injury to my pride. And now, much as I'd like to stay and chat with such a lovely lady, I have a dragon to butcher."

Yes, she thought, go. She'd find the strength to heal herself. She'd rise up like Medrash did. And how he, his clan brother, and all Tymanther would regret it when she did!

Then Balasar aimed his point at her heart, and she realized he had no intention of leaving her alive.

* * * * *

Aoth had been in many bizarre and dangerous places in his hundred years of life, but few stranger or more perilous than inside the body of one dragon when it was fighting another.

Grappling, snapping with their fangs, slashing with their claws, lashing with their tails, the two wyrms rolled over and over together. Their snarls, grunts, and the thuds, crashes, and tearing sounds as their attacks landed were deafening.

Aoth had found it difficult to keep his feet before. It was impossible now. He bounced around like a pea in a barrel tumbling down a hill.

The noise and punishing bumps made it almost impossible to think. Still, he realized that at the moment, the greatest danger to him was Tchazzar. Already damaged by Eider, Jet, and Aoth's own efforts, sections of Alasklerbanbastos's ribs were snapping and crumbling by the moment. If the red dragon smashed completely through, the blow could easily pulverize Aoth as well. And if Tchazzar spat another blast of fire, it would roast him in his cage.

He had to get out. He cast around and saw that one of Tchazzar's strikes had broken away more bone and slightly widened the breach through which he'd entered. That was one tiny particle of luck, anyway.

He'd need both hands to reach the hole. With a pang of regret, he let go of his spear, gripped sections of rib, and alternately climbed or crawled, depending on the attitude of Alasklerbanbastos's body at that instant. Lightning crackled from bone to bone, piercing his shoulder in its transit. His teeth gritted and his muscles knotted until the flare ended.

When he reached the hole, he had to judge the speed and direction of the entangled dragons' movement and pray it didn't change. Because if he emerged at the wrong moment, their weight would come smashing and grinding down on top of him.

He made his best guess, swarmed out, and jumped. He landed hard. Wings—some bare bone, some sheathed in crimson hide—flailed against the ground, and tails whipped through the air. The storm of motion was all around him, and he was sure *something* had to hit him. But nothing did, and then the dragons rolled farther away.

He ran to put even more distance between them and him, just like everyone else was doing. Jet plunged down in front of him. "Get on!" the griffon rasped. "I'll take you to the healers."

Suddenly feeling weak and dizzy, Aoth clambered into the saddle. The straps buckled themselves. "Not yet. I need to see what happens."

"You need—"

"I said, I'm going to watch."

Jet screeched in annoyance, lashed his wings, and carried his master aloft.

As he did, Tchazzar broke Alasklerbanbastos's various holds on him, got his feet planted, and struck, all in a single blur of motion. The red dragon's fangs closed on the dracolich's neck, right beside the head.

Aoth grinned, because it was a shrewd tactic. The grip would keep Alasklerbanbastos from using his own teeth or his breath.

Flames leaping between his fangs, Tchazzar bit down hard. Aoth saw the effort manifest in every bunched muscle down the length of the war hero's body. Surely in another moment his teeth would clash together, and Alasklerbanbastos's head would fall away from his body.

But the dracolich roared words of command. Several tendrils of power leaped from the empty air above Tchazzar and stabbed into his body. The magic was shadow dark, not bright, but it crackled, twisted, and smelled like lightning.

Tchazzar leaped out from under the evidently excruciating effect, but he had to let go of Alasklerbanbastos to do it. The dracolich's skull dangled from his neck like a half-broken twig at the end of a dead branch. But it was still attached—and, with a succession of little jerks, it started to hitch back into its proper position, even as chips of bone floated up from the ground to patch the cracked, gnawed vertebrae behind it.

Then, at last, Jaxanaedegor plunged down on top of his master. Another green wyrm followed, and then a red. Tchazzar lunged to join them.

The four dragons ripped into the dracolich like a pack of starving wolves assulting a deer. Alasklerbanbastos spat all the lightning he had left—then, roaring, struck and clawed with all his might. It wasn't enough. Gradually his foes bit, smashed, and wrenched him into such a scatter of broken bone that not even magic could go on putting him back together.

Aoth relished every moment of it.

* * * * *

Skuthosiin told himself he wasn't tiring, nor weakening from blood loss. In his former life he'd been a Chosen of Tiamat, and he was still an ancient wyrm. No horde of scurrying little dragonborn could bring him down.

Although admittedly, it wasn't just dragonborn. Acting through his champion, Torm himself was striving to kill Skuthosiin. But that didn't matter either. Because, his paladin gifts notwithstanding, Daardendrien Medrash was as tiny and fragile as the rest of his kind. Skuthosiin only had to score once with his fangs or claws to tear the wretch to pieces.

To that end, he slashed with his forefoot. Medrash jumped back. But perhaps he too was tiring, because he didn't recoil quite far enough. Skuthosiin didn't connect with his body, but the tip of one talon snagged the top of the swordsman's battered heater. As it jerked free, splitting the top half of the shield in the process, it yanked Medrash off balance.

Skuthosiin struck like a serpent.

Scrambling faster than should have been possible for such a squat, short-legged creature, Khouryn Skulldark knocked his comrade aside. Now he was under Skuthosiin's jaws. Well, that was all right too.

Except that at the last possible instant, the dwarf hopped to the side, and Skuthosiin's teeth clashed shut on empty air. Then something slammed into the side of his head.

Or at least it felt like a simple impact. But as Skuthosiin reflexively heaved his head high, he realized Skulldark had actually chopped him with his axe. The weapon was still buried deep in his flesh, perhaps even in the bone beneath, and the wound gave a first excruciating throb. Skuthosiin snarled.

Something else snarled back, close to his ear. Or perhaps it was a breathless but savage laugh. Dangling, Skulldark still clung to the haft of the axe. Either he'd been too surprised to let go of his weapon when Skuthosiin lifted his head, or else he'd chosen not to.

Clinging to the axe with one hand, Skulldark drew a dirk with the other and stretched his arm to the limit, trying for Skuthosiin's eye. Unable to reach it, he plunged the knife through hide and into the flesh beneath.

Enraged, Skuthosiin lifted his claws to swipe both the dwarf and his weapon away. Then white light blazed before him as, seeing his distraction, Medrash charged his sword with divine Power, rushed in, and cut at the base of his neck.

Balasar darted in beside his clan brother and slashed with his own blade. So did Tarhun—Skuthosiin hadn't even noticed his arrival on the scene—swinging a greatsword bloody from point to guard. Spearmen jabbed, and mages hurled bright, crackling thunderbolts and fire.

Skuthosiin toppled sideways. It was impossible, but it was happening anyway.

He struggled to get back up again, but merely thrashed and writhed. As his vision dimmed and his body went numb, even those useless convulsions subsided.

He hoped that when his head smashed against the ground, it had smashed Skulldark as well. Or that he'd pulped the dwarf during his death throes. But then he saw Skulldark sitting a few yards away, bruised and bloodied but alive. And watching him, no doubt to make sure he was really finished.

After a futile attempt to spit poison in the sellsword's direction, Skuthosiin decided that he truly was. He watched worthless giants flee into the night, heard dragonborn start cheering, and then knew nothing more.

FOURTEEN

7–14 FLAMERULE
THE YEAR OF THE AGELESS ONE (1479 DR)

Kassur Jedea was a skinny, graying fellow in his middle years. But he looked older. Aoth, leaning on his spear—which rather to his amazement he'd recovered intact from the midst of Alasklerbanbastos's scattered, shattered bones—his burns, scrapes, and bruises aching despite the healers' prayers, ointments, and elixirs, wondered if the nominal monarch of Threskel had looked so elderly a tenday earlier, or if he'd aged all at once in anticipation of what was about to happen.

Kassur kneeled stiffly before Tchazzar, removed the simple gold circlet that served as a crown in the field, and laid it at the red dragon's feet. "I surrender my kingship," he said in a tight baritone voice. "I surrender myself to Your Majesty's judgment."

Tchazzar let him kneel there in silence for another moment. Then he bent over, picked up the circlet, and offered it back to Kassur. "Keep it," he said.

Kassur blinked. "Majesty?"

Grinning his broad white grin, Tchazzar stood up from his folding camp chair and hoisted the Threskelan back onto his feet. He pressed the circlet back into Kassur's hand.

"Keep it," he repeated. "I don't need to proclaim myself king of Threskel so long as the man who holds the title acknowledges himself my vassal. Because I'm the war hero and a living god, and that sets me higher any king, wouldn't you agree?"

"Of course, Majesty!" Kassur jabbered.

"Some would say," Tchazzar continued, "that because you took up arms against your rightful liege lord, you're unworthy of your title and estates. But I know Alasklerbanbastos left you no choice, as he left none to any Threskelan. So I won't punish any of you. Keep your lives and your freedom, your coin and your lands. Simply heed my command that from this day forward, all Chessentans, whether born in the north or the south, will live together peacefully as one people."

Sunlight gleaming on their helmets and mail, people started cheering. Aoth judged that as was only natural, the defeated Threskelan troops were the most enthusiastic. But by and large, even the victorious Chessentans seemed to support the red dragon's decision to show mercy. And it was probably a shrewd one if the war hero wanted to rule a united realm hereafter.

Gaedynn leaned sideways and murmured behind his upraised hand, "I guess we won't be sacking Mordulkin and Mourktar."

"Then Tchazzar will just have to dig deeper into his own treasury to pay us," Aoth replied. For Kossuth knew they'd earned it.

The red dragon let the assembled warriors cheer and pound their weapons on their shields for a while, then raised his hands. Gradually the throng fell silent.

"We'll need both unity and courage in the days to come," Tchazzar said. "Because while Chessenta is no longer at war with itself, it still has neighbors scheming to destroy it. Those of you who hail from the south know to whom I refer—the dragonborn of Tymanther, who raid our ships and our coasts and commit murder in Luthcheq."

What in the Hells? thought Aoth. What in the names of all the Hells? Wondering if he could possibly have misheard, he turned to Gaedynn. Who, for once, looked as taken aback as Aoth felt.

"I know," Tchazzar continued, "that we lost many fine warriors fighting among ourselves. But the dragonborn have committed outrages against Akanûl as they have against us. I have the word of a spokesman for Queen Arathane—"

"Zan-akar Zeraez," Gaedynn whispered.

"—that the genasi will aid us in our quest. We'll crush this threat and plunder Tymanther to punish her for her treachery. After which you have my promise to divide the loot fairly. By summer's end, no one will call Threskel a country of paupers anymore!"

Cheering erupted again, even louder.

* * * * *

Medrash and Balasar hurtled at the open space in the center of Djerad Thymar. Trying to overtake them on his own bat, Khouryn felt a pang of incredulity that they were really going to do this.

But they were. They were racing as Lance Defenders traditionally raced, and the course ran through the gaps in the outermost row of columns and on across the Market Floor. Where Khouryn discovered that Balasar's airy reassurances were true. If a rider maneuvered properly—veering, swooping, and climbing—he could find enough clearance, vertically and horizontally, to avoid smashing into any of the massive pillars, permanent structures, temporary kiosks, or dragonborn who happened to cross his path.

Some of those folk reflexively ducked, or cursed and shook their fists. But more of them simply grinned their fanged grins and turned to watch, cheered Khouryn on, or shouted good-natured jeers because he was in last place.

He was too intent on guiding his mount to answer. Too tense as well. But he was also grinning.

He burst out into Selûne's silvery light. He cast around, then cursed. Because Medrash and Balasar had already turned their bats and climbed halfway up the truncated pyramid that was the City-Bastion.

By the time Khouryn flew his bat through the rectangular opening to the Lance Roost, his friends had already landed on one of the platforms. As Khouryn set his own animal down, Balasar said, "Did you see? I won. As usual."

"And I came in third," Khouryn said. "Also as usual."

"But you're riding well now," Medrash said. "And your mount has learned to trust you." He swung himself out of the saddle and scratched his own bat's throat. It tilted its snub-nosed head back to facilitate the process.

Khouryn took a breath. "In that case, I suppose it's time for me to leave."

He'd do it flying. Tarhun had made him a gift of his bat. From what he understood, no one not a dragonborn had ever before received such an honor.

"I wish you wouldn't," Medrash said. "We defeated the ash giants, but we took heavy losses doing it. We could use help putting the army back together."

"Otherwise," said Balasar, tossing the reins of his bat to the cadet waiting to take charge of it, "they're liable to make me do it. The vanquisher is threatening to order *us* back into service with the Lance Defenders. What kind of reward is that for all my valor?"

Khouryn chuckled. "The world is full of injustice."

"If you won't stay," Medrash said, "where will you go? East Rift?"

Khouryn sighed. "No. Our business here took too much time. I don't regret a moment of it, but I can't take any more. Not when I have no idea how the Brotherhood is faring in the campaign against Threskel." In an effort to avert the melancholy suddenly threatening to take possession of him, he forced a grin. "Besides, I can't go home to a kingdom of dwarves with my beard in this condition."

"Give Aoth, Jhesrhi, and Gaedynn our regards," Medrash said, "and travel with Torm's blessing." He raised his hand, and his steel gauntlet shimmered.

Khouryn felt a tingling surge of well-being. "Thanks," he said, then shifted his gaze to Balasar. "Be careful of Biri's feelings. She's young, and she wants more than a dalliance."

"Indeed she does," Medrash said. "But she'd make a good wife for a notable warrior from a prominent clan. And I've heard the elders say it's past time for Balasar to settle down."

Balasar gaped at him, for once at a loss for words.

Khouryn laughed, tugged on the reins to turn his bat, and tapped it with his heels. The animal hopped off the edge of the balcony, plunged for an instant, then spread its wings. It fluttered back out into the balmy summer night.

* * * * *

Her bare body pressed against Aoth's, Cera looked at her lover's tattooed face, noted the pensive frown, and sighed.

Amaunator had answered her prayers by bringing him back from the war alive and well, give or take a few mostly healed burns and scrapes. They'd celebrated by having Jet fly them to one of her favorite places, a cool, clear pond where willows and purple and yellow wildflowers grew on the surrounding slopes. The griffon had then gone hunting while the two humans swam, started their lovemaking in the water, and finished on the soft, thick moss carpeting the shore.

It should have been a perfect moment. Except that Aoth was plainly brooding. Again.

Well, she supposed that except for the flawless order manifest in Amaunator, nothing was ever truly, completely perfect. But that was no reason not to chastise him. Glad that he didn't shave all his hair, she twined her fingers in the most abundant growth he had left and tugged hard.

"Ouch!" he said. "What was that for?"

"The same as usual," she said. "I just shared my womanly treasures with you. You're supposed to be deliriously happy."

He sighed. "I know I am. I mean, I am! Being with you makes me very happy! But I also mean, I know I'm supposed to be."

"You're babbling," she said.

He smiled. "I am, aren't I? I'll try to speak more clearly. I shouldn't care that Tchazzar is lying to provide an excuse for an unjust war. The Brotherhood would starve if we only fought for noble causes. I also shouldn't care that I like Medrash and Balasar. Every sellsword knows that from time to time he'll look across the battlefield and see friends standing on the other side. All that should matter is that our employer has another campaign in the offing, he stands an excellent chance of winning it, and we'll earn a lot of gold helping him."

"But you do care," Cera said.

"As do you," said Aoth. "Because we still don't know how the puzzle fits together, do we? Wyrmkeepers disguising abishais as dragonborn. Games and Precepts. What does it all truly mean? By the Black Flame, spying on Tchazzar and Jaxanaedegor just made me feel even more confused than I was before."

"Have you thought of any way to sort it out?"

Aoth grunted. "Maybe. If I'm willing to commit still more treason, and my friends are too. I know Gaedynn would be. He hates Tchazzar. But Jhesrhi's the really important one. And up to now, she's done everything I've asked of her. But this—"

"She'll help you," Cera said.

"You sound pretty sure, considering you hardly know her."

"A priestess learns to read people and recognize how they connect to one another. You're Jhesrhi's father, whether you and she realize it or not. Gaedynn is the man she'd choose if she could ever have one. The Brotherhood is her family and her home. I admit Tchazzar did a fair job of tempting her away with balm for hurts she's carried since she was a child. But by now she knows him for the cruel, mad thing he truly is."

"I hope so. If you're mistaken, I suppose I'll find out when I confide in her, she tattles to him, and he orders my arrest."

"That won't happen. Now, since the Keeper actually assigned the task of solving this mystery to me, and then I merely goaded you into helping, you'd better have a task for me as well."

He scowled. "Yes. A hard one. And the fact that Tchazzar would view it as treason may not even be the bad part."

"I'll do it."

"Don't promise till I tell you what it is."

* * * * *

Tchazzar pivoted before the full-length mirror, checking the lines of his scarlet, gold-trimmed doublet. He supposed that if any of his fellow gods were watching, they were amused. For how could a deity appear less than magnificent to mortal eyes? And even if he could, it was beneath his dignity to care.

But Tchazzar had discovered his fate was linked to Jhesrhi Coldcreek's, and he wanted to tie her to him with bonds of affection and gratitude as well. Yet despite all the favor he'd shown her, she often seemed morose and aloof.

But perhaps the ice was starting to melt, because, for a change, he hadn't been the one to suggest they spend time together. She'd diffidently proposed it, and he intended to be as charming a supper companion as any lady could desire.

Someone knocked on the door.

"Yes," Tchazzar said.

"Lady Jhesrhi is here," the servant answered.

So she was, waiting in a portion of the royal apartments that afforded a panoramic view of the rooftops of Luthcheq and the crimson sunset beyond. She looked endearingly uncomfortable wearing a trailing formal gown the color of honey, with her blonde hair arranged in elaborate braids.

They exchanged greetings, and then he did her the honor of pouring her a goblet of tart white wine. Careful not to let their fingers touch, he placed in her hand. She sipped, and smiled a wan little smile.

"Come say good night to my little brother Amaunator." He waved her to one of the two leather chairs positioned before the row of open casements. "And as we see him off for the evening, you can tell me about your day."

Jhesrhi hesitated. "It was pleasant."

Tchazzar gave her a look of mock severity. "It's foolish to lie to a god."

"It was, truly. It's just that I keep thinking of Scar."

"He was a brave and faithful creature. He gave his life to keep Alasklerbanbastos away from you."

"I know."

"But fine as he was, I'll find you a flying steed that's even better."

"That's . . . generous, Majesty. But you needn't bother. Much as Scar's death saddened me, I've also been thinking that it was a . . . passage. A sign that my time with the Brotherhood is over, and I truly am meant to stay and serve you when they move on."

Tchazzar smiled. "That's what I've been telling you."

The wizard stared straight ahead. Tchazzar had the feeling that it wasn't just to drink in the spectacle of the sunset. She was hesitant to meet his gaze. After a time she said, "I've also been thinking that I could find a . . . particular relief by staying here."

"My lady, you're welcome to whatever I can give you."

"You've given me so much already. You probably see how unhappy I am and think me a terrible ingrate. But . . . by the stars, I hate talking about this! . . . but you know how I hate to be touched. But do you know I hate myself for hating it? That I'd give anything not to be so freakish? To share in the same simple comforts and pleasures that everyone else enjoys?"

"Yes," said Tchazzar, "I do." Since he had the insight of a deity, he must have realized it, mustn't he?

"Well, it occurred to me . . . I mean, you're different. You're a god, not a man. And I have no trouble touching you when you're in dragon form. So I thought . . ."

"That I could help you overcome your aversion?"

She still wouldn't look at him. "Maybe. Or that even if I never learn to bear the touch of ordinary people, from time to time perhaps you would condescend . . ."

He had to hold in a grin that might otherwise have spooked her. For that was the way to bind her to him, as he'd captured the hearts of so many women in the past. And now that he understood it was possible, her severe, tawny beauty leaped out at him and made his mouth grow warm.

He just had to proceed gently and patiently. And, for the time being, not acknowledge in any way the consumation toward which they would travel together.

"My lady," he said, "*condescend* is the wrong word. It will give me joy to help you." He extended his hand. "Shall we begin?"

Jhesrhi flinched. "Right now?"

"Why not? The first course won't arrive for a while. Just rest your hand on mine, as lightly as you like. I won't even close my fingers around yours."

She took a deep breath, then slowly did as he'd bidden her. Her fingertips were rough and calloused.

After a moment, her hand started to shake.

"You can stop whenever you like," he said.

"No," she said, her voice tight. "But talk to me. Give me something else to occupy my mind."

"Of course, my lady. What shall we talk about?"

"Anything! Tell me why we had to fight in the north. Tell me about Alasklerbanbastos."

* * * * *

By the time Jhesrhi reached her apartments, her guts were churning. But she couldn't let it show quite yet. Life at court was still strange to her, but she had learned that everyone lived for gossip, and servants were prime conveyors of that commodity.

So she snarled for her maids to get out. And, knowing how their fussing, chatter, and mere presence often irritated her, they scurried away without questioning her command.

Just in time. Jhesrhi stumbled on into the lavatory and dropped to her knees in front of the commode. The fine supper Tchazzar had given her came up in a series of racking heaves.

It left a nasty acidic taste burning in her mouth. She spat some of it away, but for the time being would have to tolerate the rest. Because she had another vile sensation to deal with—or maybe just the memory of one. But whatever it was, it was even more repugnant.

She poured water from the pitcher into the basin, then focused her will on it. It steamed as it grew hot. Then she rubbed soap onto a brush meant for cleaning fingernails and scrubbed her hand till it was raw.

When it was finally enough, and her feeling of violation subsided, she took a bottle of wine from the cabinet and rattled off a cantrip. Magic popped the cork out of the neck. She used the first mouthful of something red and sweet to rinse her mouth, spat it in the spattered and stinking commode, then flopped down in a chair and took a long pull.

She wanted to drink until her memories of the evening grew dim and meaningless. It had disgusted her to play the weak, helpless, pleading damsel, especially since the lie was built around a core of truth. She *was* freakish and broken, even if it was beyond Tchazzar's power to mend her.

He'd keep trying though, since she'd opened the door. He'd paw her whenever he could, and how was she supposed to bear it?

She couldn't imagine. But the ploy had been the only one she could think of to lower the red dragon's defenses and cozen him into telling her what she needed to hear.

As she'd promised she would when Aoth had asked her in his apartments the night before. Even though he'd asked in a diffident manner quite unlike the man she knew.

"I don't know if it's right," he'd said. "I've always believed that 'right' is honoring your contracts. I don't know if it's prudent. I've always thought that prudence is not sticking your nose into things that are none of your business. I definitely don't know if it's right and prudent *for you*. You're on your way to a splendid life in the country of your birth. All I can offer is more of the same mud, blood—"

Perhaps it was his guilt, and the affection that underlay it, that abruptly made all other loyalties seem inconsequential. At any rate, she'd lifted her hand to silence him. "Stop. Please stop. I'll do it whatever it is, if only to stop you blathering."

And since she had, and since it had worked, she supposed she mustn't drink herself into a stupor after all. She needed to work on what Tchazzar had given her. She set the bottle on the floor and snapped her fingers. Her staff leaped from the corner into her hand.

* * * * *

Though Gaedynn had never admitted it, he occasionally found Aoth's augmented vision annoying. Like now, for example. Gaedynn was supposed to be the master scout, but it was the war-mage—with plump, pretty Cera riding behind him—who sent his griffon swooping toward a particular barren crag. Presumably because he'd spotted the cave mouth they were seeking.

Eider followed Jet down, and then Gaedynn saw it too, not that there was much to see. Just a crack in the sloping granite. But at least it had a ledge in front of it big enough for griffons to set down on.

The riders dismounted, and Cera somewhat awkwardly adjusted the round shield on her arm. She was game and sharp, but no trained soldier, and Gaedynn wondered if Aoth had been wise to bring her.

Maybe not, but then again if any of them were truly wise, no one would have embarked on this secret expedition.

"Are you sure this is the place?" Gaedynn asked. He squatted to examine the ledge more closely. "I don't see any claw marks or other signs that a dragon's been here recently."

"No," Aoth admitted. "But Jhesrhi got Tchazzar talking, and he told her he hid Alasklerbanbastos's phylactery where no one would ever find it. He also told her stories involving an old secret refuge he had in the Smoking Mountains. Afterward, she skimmed some of the histories archived in the War College and performed a divination, all in an effort to figure out where the place was. And this is the location, give or take."

Gaedynn straightened up. "Well, we might as well go in and look around. And if we don't find anything, we can probably count ourselves lucky."

Cera peered at him. "But you won't feel that way."

He smiled. "No, sunlady, I confess I won't."

Aoth looked at Jet. "I don't think you and Eider can squeeze through that narrow gap."

"No," the black griffon rasped.

The Thayan turned to Cera. "That makes it even more important that you stick close to me and do anything I tell you to."

She grinned. "So you want a repeat of last night." Aoth scowled. "All right, I understand!"

Gaedynn laid an arrow on his bow. "Perhaps you could kindle a light to help us on our way. And then, with this sour old codger's permission, I'll go first."

Cera recited a prayer and swung her gilt mace through an arc that mimicked Amaunator's daily transit across the sky. Gaedynn couldn't see the results until they entered the cave. But then it became apparent that she'd cloaked herself in a warm golden glow that pushed back the dark for a stone's throw in every direction.

Gradually the way widened until several people could walk abreast. The ceiling lifted away from their heads until Gaedynn would have needed to rise on tiptoe to touch it. He watched for movement at the point where Cera's light failed, and for sign on the floor. He listened and sniffed the air. And detected nothing but stone and darkness.

Then Aoth rapped, "Stop!"

His nerves jangling, Gaedynn froze. "What is it?"

"If you take another step, the ceiling will fall on you. I can see the cracks running through the granite, along with a flicker of magical force."

Gaedynn took a breath. "In its way, that's helpful. It tells us this really is Tchazzar's secret hiding place, and at least suggests he's hiding something here now. Still, it would have been nice if those miraculous eyes of your had noticed the cracks a little sooner."

"Sorry. They're very tiny cracks, and it's a very faint flicker. If it makes you feel any better, there's a chance that if the ceiling comes down, it will crush Cera and me too."

"That is comforting. But on the whole, I think I prefer that we all remain unsquashed. What should I do, back up?"

"No. It's like you're at the center of a spiderweb that sprang into being around you. You'll break a strand whichever way you step."

"That's . . . inconvenient."

"I can try to dissolve the enchantment," Cera said, with only the slightest quaver in her voice.

"I know," said Aoth. "But do you think you can channel enough power to outmatch Tchazzar?"

Cera frowned. "Perhaps not."

"Then maybe we should try another way. When he set this trap, Tchazzar wrote runes on the ceiling with a wand or his fingertip. I can see those too, and I think they contain the phrase that allows safe passage."

"You 'think,' " Gaedynn said.

"Yes," said Aoth, "and I *think* I can pronounce them correctly too, even though Aragrakh isn't my best language."

"Then take your shot," Gaedynn said.

Aoth raised his spear over his head and held it parallel to the floor. The point glowed red, like it had just come from the forge. He hissed sibilant words that filled the air with a dry reptilian smell, as though a wyrm were lurking just a pace or two away.

The cracks in the ceiling became visible as they too flared with crimson light. Despite himself, Gaedynn tensed. But then the glow simply faded away.

"It's safe now," said Aoth.

Gaedynn grinned. "Of course it is. I never doubted you for an instant."

They prowled onward. Until Aoth called for another halt.

"What is it this time?" Gaedynn asked. "Am I about to burst into flame?"

"No," said Aoth. "Or at least I don't think it's another snare. But there's *something* just ahead of you. Tchazzar dug into the floor, then fused the broken stone back together."

Cera smiled. "And you can see that too."

"I have to admit," Gaedynn said, "the bastard's clever. To those of us without truesight, there's nothing to distinguish this bit of passage from the rest of the cave. No trap or guardian in the immediate vicinity. No widening out into a vault or anything like that. Even if a searcher knew something was in here somewhere, he'd likely walk right on by."

"But we won't." Aoth stepped past Gaedynn, and then the head of his spear glowed blue as he charged it with force. He gripped the weapon in both hands and plunged it repeatedly into the floor. The resulting cracks and crunches echoed away down the tunnel.

Something scuttled into the light.

Big as a man, it looked like a scorpion carved from black rock and possessed of a pair of luminous crimson eyes. But it was charging faster than anything made of stone should have been able to move—and, intent on his digging, Aoth plainly didn't see it rushing forward to seize him in its serrated pincers.

"Watch out!" Gaedynn said. He drew, released, nocked, drew, and released.

Both shafts pierced the creature's body but failed to stop it or even slow it down. Nor was there time for a third shot. Gaedynn dropped his bow, snatched out his short swords, and lunged past Aoth, interposing himself between the war-mage and the beast.

When Gaedynn got close to the thing, he discovered its body was blistering hot—standing near it was like standing too close to a fire. It snatched for him, and he sidestepped and thrust. His primary sword chipped a dent in the scorpion's claw, then popped out of the wound and skated along, leaving a scratch behind.

The scorpion reached for him with its other set of pincers. He stabbed again. The claws snapped shut on his blade and yanked it from his grasp.

At the same moment, the pincerlike parts on either side of its mouth spread apart. A glowing red drop of some viscous liquid oozed out, and Gaedynn's instincts warned him the beast was about to spit. He poised himself to dodge.

Then, behind him, Aoth growled a word of command. A flare of silvery frost shot past Gaedynn and burst into steam when it splashed against his foe. Cera called out to Amaunator, and the light with which she'd surrounded them burned brighter.

The scorpion fell down thrashing. Its pincers clattered, and Gaedynn's bent and twisted sword clanked on the floor. He lunged and drove his remaining blade into the creature's left eye. It heaved in a final convulsion, then lay still.

It was still hot though. Stepping back from it, he panted, "Let me just point out that I said, 'No guardian in the *immediate vicinity.*' I never said there wasn't one lurking around somewhere, listening for the sound of digging."

Aoth grinned, lifted his spear, plunged it down, and broke away another chunk of floor. And that was sufficient to reveal what lay beneath.

It was a gem the size and shape of an egg. Or at least Gaedynn thought it was. At certain moments, it looked less like a solid object than a mere oval of shadow with tiny blue lightning bolts flickering inside it.

"Is that it?" he asked.

"That's it," Aoth answered. "Alasklerbanbastos's spirit. His life."

"I still say that if Tchazzar weren't as crazy as a three-tailed dog, he would have destroyed the thing."

Aoth shrugged, and his mail clinked. "Maybe he thought that would be letting his old enemy off easy. I mean, it would be hellish to be stuck inside a stone, alone and bodiless, for eternity, wouldn't it? Or maybe he plans to haul out the Bone Wyrm by and by, and torture him for his amusement."

"Except that we're going to haul him out first," Cera said. She drew a deep breath, opened the leather pouch on her belt, produced a gold box large enough to hold the phylactery, and dropped to one knee beside the hole. His pulse ticking in his neck, Gaedynn did his best to believe that the spellcasters knew what they were doing.

EPILOGUE

Blind and deaf, aware of nothing but the alternating mumble and yammer of his own thoughts, Alasklerbanbastos floated in the void. Deliverance came as a sudden feeling of soaring.

For an instant, the mere fact of sensation filled him with such ecstasy that he could think of nothing else. Then he remembered that Tchazzar, Jaxanaedegor, and the rest of the traitors had destroyed his body and sent his ghost into his phylactery. So it was almost certainly the red dragon calling him forth, and not because the lunatic had decided to show him any mercy.

Well, so be it. Tchazzar would no doubt thrust him into some weak and possibly crippled form, but Alasklerbanbastos still had his spells. And with magic, many things were possible.

For a heartbeat, he felt heavy as lead, and then merely corporeal once more. But that didn't entirely relieve him of the feeling of burdensome weight. Someone had buried the body he now occupied, a frame of rotting flesh as well as bone.

Which was strange. Tchazzar couldn't possibly expect a mere grave to hold him.

Puzzled, Alasklerbanbastos snarled an incantation and noticed how odd it felt to have an actual tongue curling and flapping in his mouth again. Then the earth above him rumbled and split, revealing a glimpse of the stars. He heaved himself up into the open air, and dirt streamed from his wings.

When he noticed the crooked talon on his right forefoot, he realized he'd entered the corpse of Calabastasingavor, a relatively young blue Tchazzar had killed at the start of his campaign. That explained all the charred, flaking patches on his hide, not that they or the provenance of his new body mattered at the moment.

What did was that much to his amazement, neither Tchazzar nor Jaxanaedegor was anywhere to be seen. Instead, it appeared that Aoth Fezim, Gaedynn Ulraes, and a woman with a mace and shield had taken it upon themselves to call Alasklerbanbastos back into the world.

The idiots apparently thought themselves safe because they had his phylactery. They had no idea how fast and to what lethal effect he could strike, even locked in a youthful dragon's body. He drew breath to roar a word of power, and then conjured sunlight blazed around the woman.

Agony ripped through Alasklerbanbastos's frame. Magic was suddenly impossible. So was moving, or even standing upright. His legs buckled beneath him, dumping him back down into the pit.

Fezim came to the edge and peered down at him. "I know liches aren't as susceptible to sunlight as, say, vampires," the Thayan said. "But none of you undead like it, do you?"

"How are you doing this?" Alasklerbanbastos growled.

"We tampered with your phylactery," said Fezim. "You could say we poked a hole in it to let the light in. And my friend the sunlady can make a very bright light when it suits her. She's going to hold on to the stone for now, to guarantee your cooperation."

"What is it you want?"

"Answers. She and I were the disembodied souls who spied on you dragons palavering atop your mountain. What was the point of that council? Why are so many of your servants trying to turn everyone against Tymanther? When wyrms talk about Precepts, what does it mean?"

Alasklerbanbastos hesitated. "I can't tell you."

"No, I think you probably can."

The light spilling over the edge of the grave blazed brighter. Alasklerbanbastos screamed, and parts of his hide burst into flame. He convulsed, and his thrashing brought earth pouring down, half burying him again.

Finally the light dimmed, and the searing flames went out. "Well?" said Fezim.

Alasklerbanbastos surprised himself by laughing a grinding laugh, and he found it gratifying when the impudent mites before him flinched. "All right, human. I'll tell you what you want to know. But I warn you. You won't like it very much."

* * * * *

On the trip north, Khouryn had named his bat Iron, for the gray-black color of its fur and its manifest endurance. The animal was demonstrating the latter quality now. It had already flown for hours, but showed no signs of fatigue as it wheeled and swooped over the rooftops of Luthcheq.

Unfortunately, despite Iron's willingness to carry him wherever he wanted to go, Khouryn could see no sign that the Brotherhood of the Griffon was currently in the city or anywhere near it. Not that he was surprised. He'd assumed his comrades would be somewhere in the north fighting Threskel. But it meant he'd have to ask somebody to point him in precisely the right direction.

He could inquire of Nicos Corynian, but the nobleman might not be privy to all the latest news and every detail of the war hero's plans. Whereas someone in the War College surely would be. So Khouryn sent Iron winging toward the citadel.

Even a giant bat wasn't a griffon, and as far as Khouryn knew, Iron and its kind had no special yen for horsemeat. Still, it might be asking a lot of human grooms to take charge of such an exotic and intimidating animal. So he set down on top of the great mass of sandstone, where the Chessentans had carved battlements and emplaced catapults and ballistae. A sentry noticed his sudden, plunging arrival and yelped.

"It's all right!" Khouryn called. "I'm the dwarf sellsword. Remember me? I want to see Shala Karanok. Or whoever's in charge, if she's gone north."

"Wait here," said the guard, then scurried away. Khouryn frowned. So much had happened since his departure that he'd half forgotten that the average Chessentan didn't like dwarves—until the sentry's curtness reminded him. But maybe the fellow was just rattled.

Whatever he was, he eventually returned with two others like him, as well as an officer with a jutting plume on his helmet and a baton tucked under his arm. Khouryn greeted them and repeated his request.

"It's been arranged," the officer said. "But what about your . . . animal?"

"He'll be all right here for a while," Khouryn said, "as long as no one bothers him."

"Then come with us."

The soldiers took Khouryn down several stairways into the heart of the cliff, then through a series of passages. The corridors became more ornate, more palatial, as they progressed toward the east and the rest of the city. Finally they arrived at cast bronze double doors decorated with a relief of warships fighting. A guard stood on either side of the entry.

"You have to surrender your axe and dirk," said the warrior on the left.

Khouryn frowned, but he knew better than to argue. "It's actually called an urgrosh," he said, pulling the weapon off his back.

Once they'd disarmed him, the doorkeepers opened the valves. When he saw who waited on the other side, he stopped short.

The hall was predominantly green, with jade tile on the floor and ships on the tapestries battling amid emerald seas. At the back rose a dais surmounted by a thronelike chair.

The skinny woman who appeared to be in charge hadn't presumed to occupy it. But she'd had someone carry in an almost equally fancy seat of her own and place it right in front of the platform. Glowering, she perched there, a splash of red amid all the green, her ruby- and topaz-bedizened robe hanging on her like a tent.

"Go on!" the officer said. "And bow!"

Khouryn obeyed. To the best of his recollection, he'd never seen the woman in red before. But she was evidently somebody important.

"Good evening, milady," he said. "I apologize for disturbing you so late in the evening. But I'm Khour—"

"I know who you are!" she snapped.

"Oh. Well, then you probably realize why I'm here. I want to rejoin Captain Fezim's company as quickly as possible."

She smirked. "I'm sure you do, dwarf. I'm sure you do."

He hesitated. "Excuse me?"

"You must think I'm a fool. You dare to come here on the back of one of the dragonborn's special steeds. Yet you imagine I'll simply smile and send you on your way."

"I realize there was a . . . problem between Chessenta and Tymanther. That's why my men and I had to take Ambassador Perra home. But—"

"There's more than a *problem*, dwarf. There's war! And since His Majesty is away raising fresh troops, it's my responsibility to watch for spies and enemies."

His Majesty? The more the madwoman talked, the less Khouryn understood. "Milady, please believe I mean no offense. But I think I really need to speak to Lord Corynian. Or Shala Karanok." Or anyone but you.

"The Red Dragon put me in charge in his absence! Shala Karanok is only a minor functionary now, and will be lucky to cling to even that. And you're my prisoner. You'll pay for every threat and insult your master and his witch . . . I mean, you're going to tell us everything you know about Tarhun the Vanquisher's schemes! Arrest him!"

Hands fell on Khouryn's shoulders. He spun, breaking their grips, and drove a punch into a guard's gut. The human doubled over. Khouryn backpedaled, looking for a way out.

The madwoman in the gaudy finery might be it. If he could get his hands on her, he could threaten to break her neck if the guards didn't let him go. He charged her, and then a man in a chasuble of shimmering scales stepped out of the shadows. He hissed words of power and whirled a hand with rings on all five fingers through a serpentine pass.

Khouryn's muscles locked, and he pitched forward onto his face. He was still lying that way when something hard slammed down on the back of his head.

This ends *Whisper of Venom*,
Book II of Brotherhood of the Griffon.
Find out what happens next in
The Spectral Blaze (June 2011).

About the Author

Richard Lee Byers is the author of over thirty fantasy and horror novels, including ten set in the FORGOTTEN REALMS®. His short fiction has appeared in numerous magazines and anthologies. A resident of the Tampa Bay area, he is a frequent guest at Florida science fiction conventions and spends much of his free time fencing and playing poker. Visit his website at www.richardleebyers.com.

DUNGEONS & DRAGONS

JAMES WYATT

THE GATES OF
MADNESS

PART
FOUR

An exclusive five-part prequel to the worlds-spanning
DUNGEONS & DRAGONS event

THE ABYSSAL PLAGUE

PANDEMONIUM

Joy and fury warred together within the shadowy substance of the Chained God. The key to his prison was on its way to his former domain, the isle of madness in the Astral Sea, where it would open the doorway and welcome him home. Freedom had never been so close; not in countless thousands of years, stretching back almost to the dawn of time. He could taste it, feel it in the minds of his servants who were planning the ritual. He was so close to them that he could almost feel the dirt beneath his knees as he spoke through his servant: *"My name is Tharizdun!"*

As close as his servants were, the other gods had servants of their own, who seemed determined to interfere. Pelor and Ioun, gods of the Bright City, were maneuvering their pawns into position. Ioun and Pelor knew the secret of the Living Gate, a secret that only he shared, of all living beings. Only the three of them had peered through the gate while its guardian slept, so long ago—back at the beginning of all things. Were they afraid that he would destroy the universe, as he had almost done before? Or did they fear the secret they kept?

It didn't matter. The Chained God roared, and the void of his prison echoed with the sound, sending ripples across the liquid surface of the Progenitor. When he was free, the streets of the Bright City would run with the blood of its gods.

* * * * *

Nowhere entered the portal mere seconds after Brendis, but after he'd stepped through he found himself a hundred yards behind the paladin, racing along a crowded street in an unfamiliar city. Although the gentle rise of the street gave him a good view at least another hundred yards in front of Brendis, he couldn't see the cultists they'd been chasing, No one was even running in the same direction, which probably meant they had left the main road and disappeared into an alley or side street.

"Brendis!" he shouted as he slowed to a jog.

The paladin shot a glance over his shoulder, but he didn't seem to notice Nowhere in the crowd. He turned back and scanned the street ahead of him, and began to slow his pace. Nowhere turned to the street behind him, looking for any sign of Sherinna or the newcomers. No luck.

He scratched his jaw and scowled. Sherinna could take care of herself—she'd be all right. So why was he so distressed not to see her behind him?

Nowhere couldn't tell whether Brendis, who had come to a stop and was now gaping around at the city, was actually looking for the cultists or just admiring the sights. There was a lot to see. The architecture was eclectic, and people of every race thronged the street. Nowhere jogged until he caught up with the paladin.

"What now, fearless leader?" he asked Brendis.

Brendis creased his brow and looked up into the hazy gray sky. "Am I crazy?" he said. "Or is there more city up there?"

Nowhere followed his gaze. He couldn't make anything out through the haze, but as he let his eyes drift back down, he noticed that the street they were on rose gently and kept rising—there was no crest to its hill. Eventually it disappeared into the smoky haze, but Nowhere had the distinct sense that it continued up and around. Perhaps Brendis was right, and the city actually formed an enormous ring.

A few of the people who passed them on the street glanced upward to see what Brendis and Nowhere were looking at, but most continued on without breaking stride. But as Nowhere tilted his head back to stare into the haze again, he heard a chuckle from a well-dressed dwarf woman.

"Welcome to Sigil, boys," she said. With a wink, she continued on her way, leaving Brendis gaping after her.

"Sigil?" he said. "Where in the world is Sigil?"

"The City of Doors, it's sometimes called," Nowhere said. "They say it's not in the world at all, but it's not in any other plane, either."

"So you should feel right at home," Brendis said with a wry grin. "We're nowhere."

Nowhere paid no heed. How many times had he heard similar jokes? Still, there was some truth to it. Sigil was a city unlike anything Nowhere had ever seen—bustling, alive, and evidently quite prosperous. It was supposed to be riddled with portals, connections to anyplace one could imagine in all the worlds of creation. If that was true, it offered unlimited access to anywhere Nowhere might want to go.

More important, no one had given him and his horns a second glance since he arrived in the city. He'd seen more tieflings in five minutes of scanning the crowd than he'd ever seen in one place in his life. This was a city he thought he could learn to call home.

"So what's the plan?" he asked.

Brendis drew a slow breath and let it out deliberately. "I think we need to assume that the others didn't make it through the portal in time, and it's up to us to stop those cultists."

"So we just abandon Sherinna and the others?"

"I don't see an alternative. Sherinna can take care of herself. For all I know of her magical talents, she could be opening another portal right now. Maybe she did make it through, and got lost in the crowd the way you almost did."

"I didn't get lost. I came out in a different place than you did."

Brendis shrugged. "Whatever. She can handle herself. And if the Sword of the Gods is with her, then maybe he can lead them right to us."

"So we need to find those cultists."

"Right," Brendis said. "We know they're heading for Pandemonium."

"So we need to find a way from here to there. Do you think such a way exists in a place they call the City of Doors?"

"I have to imagine that's why the cultists came here."

Nowhere grinned. "Follow me, Brendis. This is my specialty."

* * * * *

Albric closed his eyes, quieting his thoughts so he could hear the voice of the Elder Elemental Eye. The voice of Tharizdun, he reminded himself, and a renewed thrill of excitement coursed through him. Each time he remembered how his god had spoken through Jaeran, the one-eyed leader of Sigil's little cult of thieves, he shuddered with a joyful terror.

Jaeran stood at his side now, holding Albric's arm so he didn't fall when the vision came. "Even in the City of Doors," Jaeran said, "finding a way to Pandemonium is no easy task."

"The Eye will lead us true," Albric said without opening his eyes. He still didn't dare to speak the name of his god aloud. He spoke it in his mind, though, imploring the Chained God to lead him.

Tharizdun! he called in his thoughts, and fire surged through his body. *Tharizdun, lead me!*

Though his eyes remained closed, a landscape suddenly appeared to his senses. It was a realm of madness, where pulsating globules of liquid flesh floated in air, wreathed in blue and purple flames. Lightning flashed among them, forming fleeting connections from one to another as eyes and mouths bobbed to the surface and submerged. Shadows of geometric shapes drifted among the blobs, as if a weak and distant sun careened behind impossible structures erected somewhere beyond vision. A translucent tube stretched out before him, undulating slowly as lightning coursed past it, and Albric realized that its mouth opened right beside him. It was a path, the way he was meant to tread. Though it wasn't revealed to his senses, he knew that the tube—which reminded him suddenly of a gullet, constricting in pulses that added to its waving motion—opened onto a doorway to Pandemonium.

He shook off Jaeran's hand and walked into the mouth of the tube, which sprouted teeth like slabs of granite as he passed, ready to close down on any acolyte who proved unworthy.

He felt Jaeran close at his heels, but the others were beyond his awareness—they might have been among the floating orbs of flesh, for all he knew or cared. They were on their own. They would follow or they wouldn't. Tharizdun would ensure that he had acolytes enough for the rite.

The tube carried him along without any conscious effort on his part. He had no idea what was happening to his body in the streets of Sigil, nor did he care. Perhaps he was walking along the path laid out for him by Tharizdun, or maybe he was traveling outside of space and time. Once or twice, globules of flesh drifted near the path, and lightning danced around him, but the tube seemed to insulate him, and the flesh-blobs couldn't hinder his progress along the path. Then the tube came to an end, squeezing him out in front of a blazing ring of green flame. Albric opened his eyes.

The wretched tenements of the Hive were nowhere to be seen. He was in a back alley somewhere, but the surrounding buildings were large, clean, and in good repair. A short stairway up the side of a building led to a door, but the ring of fire corresponded not to the door, but to a decorative arch beside it, at the edge of the landing.

"The arch," he said, pointing.

"How do we open the door?" Jaeran asked.

Albric frowned. "What?"

"Most of the portals in the City of Doors require a gate key, an object you need that will turn a mundane door or archway into a portal. Without a key, you step through that arch and you're just falling six feet off the end of the landing."

An armored woman opened the door at the top of the stairs and stepped out onto the landing. She held a halberd and took up a stance that clearly signaled her intent to block access to the arch. An instant later, another woman strode out onto a stone bridge that spanned the alley above them. This woman wore flowing robes and carried a slender staff, but her dark hair and eyes were twin to those of the first woman.

Albric climbed one stair, and the woman with the halberd shifted her stance ever so slightly. "We mean to make use of the portal behind you," he told her.

The woman frowned. "I don't know how you learned of it, but our sacred duty is to ward that portal."

"Who appointed you to that duty?"

"I am sworn to Pelor's service, my sister to Ioun's."

Albric couldn't explain the rage that welled in his gut, nor was the howl that tore from his throat entirely his. Jaeran joined him an instant later, and Albric saw both women cover their ears, their faces wrenched in agony. Wailing cries that came from no mortal voice echoed in the alley around them, unearthly and haunting. For a moment, Albric saw the two women and his acolytes as more floating globules, and he saw lightning and fire sundering their minds.

Tharizdun's howl of fury burned in his throat, sucking every last breath of air from his lungs until darkness began to swallow his vision. He fell to his knees, but the two women were already sprawled on the ground, utterly broken. The cry died in his throat and he drew a shuddering breath as Jaeran's voice trailed off.

Slowly Albric got to his feet and climbed the rest of the stairs to the landing. The woman lay insensible, her wide eyes staring at nothing. He bent over her and spoke, his voice raw from screaming.

"Who is your god?"

A trail of spittle dribbled from the woman's mouth as she answered. "The only god, the Chained God, the unknowable and invincible."

"Rise and follow me," Albric said. He turned to his acolytes and pointed up to the bridge. "Gharik, get the other one down from there. She will complete our circle."

The woman on the landing managed to find her feet, and she stared at the golden symbol of the Elemental Eye that hung around Albric's neck.

"What is the gate key that will open this portal?" he asked her.

"You wear it already," she said. "The talisman of the Chained God is the key to his former home."

Albric smiled. "The Eye has led us true." He stepped closer to the arch, and darkness began to swirl in the opening.

He waited until Gharik had returned with the second sister, and then he stepped through the arch, off the edge of the landing, and into blackness.

* * * * *

Miri wiped her eyes with the back of her hand and cursed herself as she started walking down the bustling street. People washed around her like a river flowing both directions at once, sometimes bumping into her but mostly just passing too close.

How did I get so dependent on him? she wondered.

She knew the answer, though. She'd depended on Demascus since he first appeared at the dairy where she earned her living churning cream into butter, lifted her to her feet, and took her away. And before that, she had depended on the dairy's owner, dear, harsh Carina, who cared for her after her mother was killed. It was no wonder Demas, as she'd grown to call him, thought of her as a child—she had never really grown up.

She let the flow of people carry her along the street, searching the crowd in the desperate hope of finding a familiar face. Each time she saw a tiefling—how was it possible that so many tieflings lived in this city?—she started, thinking it might be the man she had just met in the ruins of Bael Turath, the one who called himself Nowhere.

Miri chuckled to herself. Where has Nowhere gone? she thought. It's an odd name. Where do you go when you're looking for Nowhere?

Suddenly it struck her as less an amusing play on words than a hint of something profound. Searching for Nowhere seemed like a metaphor for a worthwhile spiritual pursuit. She wondered what Demas would say about it.

Another person in the crowd jostled her, and she realized she had stopped paying attention to her surroundings. The crowd had thinned a little. On her right was a shop displaying bolts of cloth in vibrant colors and exotic patterns, beautifully and carefully woven. Just past that was a tailor's shop, its window sporting gowns and robes made from the same fabrics. She glanced across the street, to her left, and stopped in her tracks.

A small temple stood there, set back from the street and partially hidden by tables and awnings that extended from the sides of the shops that flanked it. Seven wide stairs led up to a narrow doorway between two graceful columns, and the entablature above the columns featured the stylized eye of Ioun.

It almost seemed impossible, but after all the time she had spent following Demas wherever his god led him, she had to believe that Ioun had guided her footsteps to the threshold of this temple. She hurried across the street, up the stairs, and between the columns into the chamber within.

The noise of the street faded when she entered, and she felt herself start to relax. A statue of Ioun dominated the small chamber, depicting her with one hand up in blessing, the other holding an open book. Garlands of wilting flowers were draped over the statue's neck and arms, and Miri wondered if she should go find a fresh sacrifice to offer. She hesitated, realizing she had no idea what she was supposed to do, and turned to leave.

Two smaller statues stood in the corners near the doorway—twin angels, majestic beings of fire and lightning, lifting their hands in adoration of Ioun, ready to receive the blessing of knowledge she dispensed. Was she supposed to adopt the same pose? She stepped closer to examine one of the angels more closely.

Its face was blank, just eyes and the suggestion of a nose. But the shape of it—the structure of the cheekbones, the chin, even the ill-defined nose—made her think of Demas. She fell to her knees beside the storm of fire that formed the angel's lower body, her gaze fixed on the angel's blank face.

"Demas," she said. Tears welled in her eyes. "Demas, please hear me. I don't know how to do what you do. Ioun won't lead me the way she leads you. I don't know how to find you in this city, and I don't know what else to do."

Sobbing, she leaned forward to rest her head on the statue's cool stone. "Demas, please, just come find me. Let Ioun lead you—surely she can lead you to this, her house. I'll be right here. Just come find me."

Unsure of what else to say, Miri curled up on the floor before the angelic statue. With one last look up at the face she imagined to be Demas's, she drifted to sleep.

A hand on her shoulder brought her gently awake. She opened her eyes to see the angel—a living angel, not the statue, wreathed in divine light—crouched beside her, his hand on her shoulder and compassion in his pale blue eyes.

"Miri, get up."

As she stood, Miri saw the face of Ioun herself behind the angel, serene and severe. An excitement coursed through her like nothing she had ever known, a thrill that ran down her spine and brought tears to her sleepy eyes. *Is this how Demas feels when he speaks with Ioun?*

"Come, child, we need to hurry," the angel said. "We still have to find Brendis and the tiefling."

The divine light dimmed as Miri blinked and rubbed her eyes. The angel was smiling, though Ioun's face remained impassive. Miri frowned.

Angels can't smile, she thought.

"Demas?"

The glow faded completely, and she saw Demas as he was. It was Sherinna who stood behind him, not Ioun. Miri threw her arms around him, her joy and relief at seeing him tempered by a vague disappointment.

"Of course, child," Demas said. He slowly, hesitantly, put his hands on her back. "Who did you think had found you?"

I thought you were an angel. "I thought . . ."

She clutched him tighter and closed her eyes so she couldn't see Sherinna's frown.

I thought Ioun might speak to me too.

* * * * *

The wind that howled around Albric was so fierce that for a moment he thought he was falling. He braced himself for impact, then one of the acolytes bumped into him in the darkness, he stumbled forward, and realized that his feet were planted on solid rock. He willed a shred of power into his holy symbol and made it glow with a sickly purplish light.

The light glittered on flecks of mica scattered over the walls, ceiling, and floor of a tunnel. As he turned in a full circle, the rest of the acolytes appeared in the tunnel, with Jaeran bringing up the rear.

Each one seemed to step through the solid rock wall, and once Jaeran was through there was no sign of the portal behind him.

"How will we get back?" Niala, the elf woman from Jaeran's band of thieves, asked. She had to shout to make herself heard over the wind.

"I would kill you where you stand," Albric growled, "but the ritual requires eight. When the Chained God walks free, will you ask him to carry you back to the slum you left behind? Remember why we are here, worm, and what sacred task lies before us."

Niala fell to her knees at Albric's feet. "Forgive me," she said. "I spoke without thinking."

The twin sisters cackled with a single voice, the sound mingling with the howl of the wind in the tunnel until Albric thought he heard a cacophony of voices. The maddening chorus reminded him of the unearthly voice he'd heard issuing from Jaeran's mouth, as well as the howl of fury both men had unleashed to break the sisters' minds. Tharizdun was calling him onward. He put his face to the wind and started down the tunnel.

The tunnel coiled to the left, descended steeply, and then opened into a huge circular vault that could not have been natural in origin. The wind howled less insistently, and eight pedestals stood arrayed in a circle at the center of the room. Atop each pedestal sat a crystal orb the size of Albric's clenched fist, glowing with purple light.

Albric walked to the circle and stood behind one of the pedestals, facing the center. He watched with satisfaction as Jaeran and the others filed in, taking their positions without a word or a questioning glance. They knew what they were to do. Tharizdun was speaking to them all now.

His head swam with the realization. They were in the heart of Tharizdun's long-abandoned dominion, the home he had constructed for himself before the Dawn War, before he planted the shard of utter evil in the depths of the Elemental Chaos that gave birth to the Abyss. Had this vault with its eight pedestals been standing prepared for this moment since that most ancient time? Had Tharizdun foreseen his imprisonment and the need for eight acolytes to set him free?

They stood like the points of a compass, with Jaeran facing him across the circle. Gharik and Haver stood on either side of Albric, while Jaeran's thieves, Niala and Braghad, flanked their leader. That left the two sisters, the former guardians of the portal, facing each other. They all stood still and silent as the wind whipped around them.

Albric drew the shard of the Living Gate out of the folds of his robe and stepped to the middle of the circle. He set it carefully in a slight depression that marked the circle's center, then returned to his position. He raised his hands, and the others mirrored the gesture in perfect unison. Their will was gone, replaced by the will of the Chained God.

He opened his mouth, and eight voices chanted as one: "Tharizdun! God of Eternal Night, the Black Sun, behold us gathered in your darkness." The wind seized their voices and scattered them throughout the vaulted cavern, turning eight voices into eight thousand.

"Tharizdun! Ender and Anathema, Eater of Worlds and Undoer, come and wreak destruction."

The shard of the Living Gate rose slowly from the floor as if lifted by the wind, and it began to spin, first slowly, then wildly, wobbling and shaking as it whirled.

"Tharizdun! Patient One, He Who Waits, Chained God, your waiting is over and your freedom is at hand!"

The shard's wobbling spin widened until it circled a point in space, about ten feet above the indentation in the floor. Its orbit grew slowly wider, and as it did, something took shape at the center, a pinprick of utter blackness in the dark chamber. The shard circled still wider and the pinprick grew to a marble's size, then a child's ball, and soon a king's orb of perfect nothingness. The larger the blackness grew, the darker the room became, as if it were a void that drew all light into its emptiness.

The void doubled in size once more, and the shard of the Living Gate clattered to the chamber floor, skittering a few feet toward Gharik. Albric fell to his knees as a sensation of power, of presence, of malign majesty and terrible, terrible fury broke over him.

The rite worked! Albric was certain the void he had created led directly to the prison of the Chained God. He was in the presence of the divine.

Some of the acolytes cowered on the floor, covering their faces, not daring to lift their eyes to the face of their god. But Albric knew their work was not yet finished. The void was too small a passage for Tharizdun to use. But as Albric stared in awe, something came through.

At first, Albric thought it was the blood of his god. It seemed to form on the surface of the black sphere before dripping down in viscous blobs, then pooling together in and around the depression in the floor. It was not blood, Albric realized, but rather some kind of liquid crystal, bending and reflecting the feeble light of the orbs. Streaks of silver writhed among flecks of gold inside the substance, and it pulsed and surged as it gathered together in a thick pool on the floor.

Albric's eyes found the shard of the Living Gate as the Chained God made his will known. Infused with the substance Tharizdun called the Progenitor, the shard would form a new Living Gate, a portal large and strong enough to shatter the walls of his prison and break his chains forever. Albric began to crawl toward the shard.

But there was another voice in the chamber. "Touch the Voidharrow," it whispered, and its voice was the voice of the howling wind, the voice that echoed from every surface of the vaulted hall. "Take it into you and let it transform you. It will grant you power beyond your imagining."

Albric hesitated. Was the whisper another expression of Tharizdun's will?

While he paused, he saw Haver, Niala, and both sisters scramble to the edge of the viscous pool, reaching hesitant fingers toward the liquid.

"Wait!" he shouted, but the wind stole his voice.

When flesh came close to the liquid, the substance rose to meet it, coiling around fingers, then engulfing hands. Serpents of liquid crystal wound up their arms, and found ears, nostrils, and screaming mouths as entrances to his acolytes' bodies. The rest of the acolytes looked on, at first in horror, as the bodies of the first four began to change.

Albric snatched the shard of the Living Gate from the floor, then looked up to meet Gharik's gaze. "Gharik, help me!" he ordered.

Gharik nodded, then crawled over to Albric. "What is the will of the Eye?" he asked.

"He wants us to fuse that substance—the Progenitor—with this shard to make a new Living Gate."

"Are you sure?"

"Yes. But what the Eye desires and what the Progenitor wants do not seem to be the same thing. Come with me."

Albric cradled the shard of the Living Gate under one arm as he crawled awkwardly toward the Progenitor. Gharik followed, but Albric wasn't sure whether he did so out of obedience or because he'd started listening to the liquid whispers.

Haver—or a creature that had once been Haver—stepped between Albric and the pool. Red crystals jutted from its hulking shoulders, and its arms were as thick as tree trunks. Its face was still mostly Haver's, contorted in agony as it transformed, becoming something alien and terrible. Just as Albric tensed to fight the creature, it staggered away, racked with the pain of its transformation.

"Gharik, hurry!" Albric shouted. "Take the shard, and touch it to the substance."

Gharik's eyes grew wide with fear, but he knew better than to disobey or even question Albric. The shard trembled in his grip as he slowly stretched it toward the Progenitor liquid.

The substance recoiled from the shard, and the whispers in the chamber grew louder, more insistent. "Touch the Voidharrow! Let it change you! Witness the power it grants!"

Jaeran's dragonborn acolyte, Braghad, was the next to succumb to the whispers. He tried to push Gharik away from the pool, but the big man held his ground and thrust the shard of the Living Gate into the liquid. The shard erupted in brilliant light that cast stark shadows all across the vault. At the same time, a snaky tendril of the substance wound its way up Gharik's arm and into his mouth. Albric seized the shard from Gharik's hand and pushed the screaming man away.

Jaeran stood before him then, madness in his eyes. "Let me help you," he shouted over the echoing whispers.

Albric eyed him, unsure of his intent. "Help me do what?"

"Open the gate! Free the Chained God!"

Albric held out the glowing shard and Jaeran gripped it. The Progenitor substance was crystallizing around it, expanding it, fusing with it. Albric couldn't tell where the original shard stopped and the hardened Progenitor began, or if they were really just one substance.

Jaeran and Albric gently shaped it as it exploded in size. When it grew large enough, they set it down on the stone floor, and it began to form an arched gateway.

The acolytes—still in the throes of transformation—were scattered throughout the chamber, writhing in pain. Haver, though, seemed to be reaching the final stages of metamorphosis—he stood still, hunched forward with massive claws resting on the ground in front of his feet. His face was no longer recognizable as human, let alone as Haver. As Albric's eyes rested on him, he writhed in pain and grew visibly larger.

The gate was finished. With one voice, Jaeran and Albric chanted another invocation to Tharizdun, the words forming in Albric's mind without any conscious effort. The gate opened, and Albric saw an ever-changing landscape on the other side. It was a maddening procession of worlds, the far end of the gate flitting through them so quickly he could barely make out the details of any one: verdant forest to bare desert, rocky coast to mountain peaks, with no sense of reason or pattern.

"We have to focus it," Jaeran said.

Albric bent his will to the gate, and the flickering landscape slowed ever so slightly. He saw a forbidding city towering over a desolate wasteland, then a city full of graceful towers with a fire-ringed galleon drifting through the sky above it. Faerie lights danced along a wooded seashore.

As he watched, something wrapped around his ankle. It was warm and firm, more like flowing sand than an ooze. Its touch sent tiny pinpricks of pain across his skin as it coiled its way up his leg. He looked down and saw that the Progenitor pool had split into two long tendrils, one of which was writhing up his leg as the other did the same to Jaeran.

Peering around the edge of the gate, he met Jaeran's gaze and nodded. First things first—they must free the Chained God.

THE GATES OF
MADNESS

Continues in

EBERRON

TIM WAGGONER

Lady RUIN

DECEMBER 2010

DUNGEONS &DRAGONS®

FROM THE RUINS OF FALLEN EMPIRES, A NEW AGE OF HEROES ARISES

It is a time of magic and monsters, a time when the world struggles against a rising tide of shadow. Only a few scattered points of light glow with stubborn determination in the deepening darkness.

It is a time where everything is new in an ancient and mysterious world.

BE THERE AS THE FIRST ADVENTURES UNFOLD.

THE MARK OF NERATH
Bill Slavicsek
August 2010

THE SEAL OF KARGA KUL
Alex Irvine
December 2010

The first two novels in a new line set in the evolving world of the DUNGEONS & DRAGONS® game setting. If you haven't played . . . or read D&D® in a while, your reintroduction starts in August!

ALSO AVAILABLE AS E-BOOKS!
Follow us on Twitter @WotC_Novels

WELCOME TO THE DESERT WORLD
OF ATHAS, A LAND RULED BY A HARSH
AND UNFORGIVING CLIMATE, A LAND
GOVERNED BY THE ANCIENT AND
TYRANNICAL SORCERER KINGS.
THIS IS THE LAND OF

CITY UNDER THE SAND
Jeff Mariotte
OCTOBER 2010

*Sometimes lost knowledge is
knowledge best left unknown.*

FIND OUT WHAT YOU'RE MISSING IN THIS
BRAND NEW DARK SUN® ADVENTURE BY
THE AUTHOR OF *COLD BLACK HEARTS*.

ALSO AVAILABLE AS AN E-BOOK!
THE PRISM PENTAD
Troy Denning's classic DARK SUN
series revisited! Check out the great new editions of
The Verdant Passage, *The Crimson Legion*,
The Amber Enchantress, *The Obsidian Oracle*,
and *The Cerulean Storm*.

Follow us on Twitter @WotC_Novels

RETURN TO A WORLD OF PERIL, DECEIT, AND INTRIGUE, A WORLD REBORN IN THE WAKE OF A GLOBAL WAR.

TIM WAGGONER'S
LADY RUIN

She dedicated her life to the nation of Karrnath.
With the war ended, and the army asleep—
waiting—in their crypts, Karrnath assigned her
to a new project: find a way to harness
the dark powers of the Plane of Madness.

REVEL IN THE RUIN
DECEMBER 2010

ALSO AVAILABLE AS AN E-BOOK!